Pieces of My Sister's Life

Pieces of My Sister's Life

Elizabeth Joy Arnold

BANTAM BOOKS

PIECES OF MY SISTER'S LIFE
A Bantam Book / August 2007

Published by Bantam Dell
A Division of Random House, Inc.
New York, New York

Cover photo © John Lund & Sam Diephuis/Getty Images
Cover design by Marietta Anastassatos

ISBN 978-0-7394-8729-7

Printed in the United States of America

In loving memory of Marie Alice Tull

As the winter solstice approaches, the Beast of the Atlantic Nor' Easter awakens, like the Vampire rising from dormancy, to menace our Island. It revives itself, siphoning the last dregs of heat energy from the ocean surface and alchemizing it with the briny spray, to make prodigious sheets of rain and winds of frightful power. Aye, it is physically manifest; like a monstrous Steam Engine, But this Devil's spawn also has an immanent cunning, its capacity to addle the great ocean, the exercise of its winds to set the Sea churning upon herself. The Beast's foul breath goads her skin into dips and swirls, eddies and vortices, which agitate the reposeful depths, and they rise up in protest. Unaccustomed to the surface, and buffeted by the Beast's winds, the depths rapidly lose their equilibrium. As back falls upon forth, to lashes at fro, the roiling becomes a full-scale riot; and the Sea loses all providence of her own natural ebb and flow.

With the Sea in its claw, the Beast unleashes the Tides onto our humbled shores. Screaming gales pour through our very souls, as the Beast prepares to devour the Island wholly, like Jonah was swallowed by the Great Fish. Aye, but the Beast is an evil and diabolical one. At the brink of our Armageddon, the Beast relents suddenly, as if relishing the promise of another violation of its wretched victim.

Whence the Beast continues towards the Mainland, it does not yet glance aback at the destruction it hath wrought. But the Sea, our life's blood and earthly salvation, she will return to us as she has for perpetuity, and we shall forgive her with no conditions.

Thomas Rathburn
Southeast Lighthouse Log
Block Island
December 1798

Pieces of My Sister's Life

Prologue

THERE'S A PHOTOGRAPH I keep in my bottom drawer, buried beneath the strips of wrapping paper that haven't yet found a gift that fits them. In the picture two girls stand arm in arm on the Rhode Island shore, dressed in new pink bathing suits. They face away from the water so their dark hair blows against their sunburned cheeks. They're laughing because they think they know each other.

In those years we weren't speaking I'd pull the picture from my drawer at least once a week. I'd study it like it was a microscopic specimen, a DNA spiral or an amoeba. I'd look into those little girls' eyes, searching for a soul. But no matter how closely I scrutinized, still I couldn't tell which was me.

I don't take out that picture anymore. The only pictures I let myself see were taken over the past year, pictures in which we look so different even I can't recognize our likeness. Much more disturbing in their own way, but for me less painful than those two girls who believed all of life would be an arm-in-arm, pink-bathing-suited affair. I don't want to remember how alike we were. Seven years old and we had one face, one body and one future. Only a decade later and I wanted Eve dead.

* * *

We lived in our own world, Eve and I. I can imagine us floating together in our mother's womb, not caring if anyone else existed. And that's pretty much how it was for the first years of our life, the comfort of us watching them.

Our world had its own language, which we spoke before we learned the words outsiders could understand. Daddy said he used to stop by our door and listen, two babies barely old enough to walk, jabbering away like foreigners. It wasn't a language with grammar or syntax so much as an understanding arising from shared experience, maybe also a twinnish telepathy inherent in our shared genes. I wish I could remember what it was like and what we were saying, but the language is like those two girls at the beach, a piece of another life.

I try to pinpoint a defining moment when things changed. Maybe it's that a world can only stretch so far before it finally breaks, that a two-person world strains under the weight of three.

The third was Justin, and I met him at the age before girls stop playing with boys. It was soon after our mother left, the day after we'd moved to Block Island, a two-hour ferry ride from New London with the few belongings our mother hadn't taken with her. And that day, dizzy from the loss of everything we'd known, I found him.

He was at the end of our shared drive, straddling the branch of an apple tree that seemed to be made for climbing, carrying a cardboard sword and wearing a football helmet. I liked him at once.

I walked up to the tree without speaking, wondering if he'd mind if I climbed up there beside him. He peered down at me and lifted his sword. "You're on my property," he said. "Who are you?"

I stepped back, opened my mouth and closed it again, smiled.

"You can't remember?"

I shook my head, finally managed to speak. "I'm Kerry."

He jumped down with a roar and lunged forward with his sword. I grabbed onto my stomach, choked, teetered and finally fell. From then on we were friends.

Justin was three years older at an age when three years may as well be three decades. But he played with us, maybe drawn in by the allure of leadership and protection, maybe because Eve and I were the only other kids on a street lined with old couples and divorcées. We idolized him. He was our hero, gave us the guidance our father didn't have the time or the sense to provide. And if in the beginning I sometimes felt a vague sense of loss without knowing why, soon I learned to ignore it, forgot the language Eve and I once shared, lived in a bigger and only slightly colder space.

We taught Justin how to skip rope and fold origami swans, how to press fall leaves in cellophane to make their color last forever. He taught us how to dig quahogs from the sand with our bare toes, how to cut an earthworm quick and clean so both halves could squirm away. We ran six-legged races, my right laces tied to Justin's left, Eve's left tied to his right, and we showed off to his mom and felt like things would never change.

But the times I remember most are those rich rainy afternoons on our covered front porch, when Justin told his stories. I have no idea how a child just starting in life could be filled with a lifetime of imaginings. But already at the age of nine Justin had conjured the first hints of the magic that would later make him famous. Already he'd been to Canardia, a world with butterflies as big as birds, oceans that reflected rainbow colors, and waves that washed up on the shore with the sound of an angel choir. There were fairies and bandits and child heroes just our age who at the last minute always managed to prevail.

This magic world took over where our old world had left off. I'd hold Eve's hand and close my eyes, fight bandits and fly with the fairies. I'd come time and again to the edge of death, huddle close and feel the damp chill of Eve's skin against my arm. I would laugh when I was afraid. I'd feel part of something bigger.

I remember one night Eve and I in bed lying head to toe, feet pushed up into the legs of each other's pajama bottoms. Eve, tracing her finger along the stitching in our quilt, said, "I'm gonna marry Justin Caine someday."

And I wanted to fight back, wanted to tell her how it was. To tell her that he was mine and she was mine, so to take him would break me in two. But I couldn't think of the right way to say it. I smiled and shrugged and pulled my feet out from her pajama legs. I let her think that we could both live in this straining world of two that became three. Although even back then we both, in a way, knew the truth.

I was questioned thoroughly after Eve's death, four hours of interrogation by a man with eyes too kind to be questioning a murderer. The police had analyzed her blood and found the morphine, and then they'd turned to me. The police had asked questions before, in the middle of that horrific year we turned seventeen. And this round of questioning might've turned out different if the man had known what to ask, given any hint of knowing what had happened long before Eve's death. But his questions had no real meaning, so I answered calmly and rationally, with the right degree of indignation. Maybe that means my conscience is finally clear. Maybe the grip of the past has loosed its hold.

This is part of what I've learned, that we weren't wrong for going after what we wanted. It was the events that were evil, but us, we were kids. We were stupid; we didn't understand the power of our own choices. I learned so damned much those last few months of her life. So much she gave to me, so much her dying taught me. That's what it is to be a twin; you become wiser than you could ever be on your own, wiser even than two people together. Seeing life from two sides, two souls, you learn the true meaning and measure of everything that comes your way. It's the only way that I know to see the world through God's eyes.

ONE

Pull of the Ocean

March 2007

I

I GLANCED DISCREETLY at the wall clock above the ballet barre. Estella Baker had been holding me imprisoned in the YMCA dance studio for the past half hour, talking about everything from her grand-nephew to her gout. Every week after class she'd thank me for the lesson, and then reminisce about some scene from her youth that the taped music had brought to mind. I let her because I assumed she had no one else to talk to, and I knew what sort of poison loneliness could be.

Five-thirty. Shit. By the time I got home it would already be dark out, and I hated walking in the dark. Walking alone at night was like lying in bed waiting for sleep: there was nothing to distract you from yourself.

"Hessie's always been narsistic," Estella said. "Narsistic, is that the word? I seem to be losing my vocabulary lately. You know she's had her breasts done." She pulled a tissue from the arm of her leotard, dabbed at her nose and then tucked it back inside.

I gave her a polite smile. When I'd come up with the idea of teaching dance, I'd pictured a class full of women who looked like belly dancers, with long dark hair and perfect waists, women who, like me, had once imagined they'd grow up to be dancers but had never managed to get past the imagining stage. Instead what I got was a class of ladies in their sixties, wearing leotards that bulged in odd places, who had about as much grace as overstuffed sofas. It was okay, though. They were very appreciative.

"Well, they sure don't look done," I said, since she was obviously expecting disdain. "Maybe they're a work in progress."

"I know!" Estella said. "They're so tiny. You know she had her arms done, too? Her arms!"

When she'd gone I threw a dress on over my leotard, pulled on a pair of sneakers and jogged the twelve blocks home. The streets were crowded with tourists deciding where to eat, mostly young couples alone or burdened with strollers and diaper bags. Cities were made for couples. Go to a restaurant or movie and I'd be stared at, whereas on the island single people were embraced, befriended, invited to join. Here I didn't even like calling for pizza; I was sure the delivery boy pictured me scarfing down the whole pie, wallowing in grease.

I climbed the stairs and locked the inside of my apartment: doorknob, deadbolt, chain. After thirteen years, I still hadn't gotten used to the idea of such surplus safeguards. On the island we'd leave home with our windows and door open wide to vent the dead inside air. In this city you weren't safe unless you fastened a trip wire to the entrance and connected the other end to a hydrogen bomb.

The message light was blinking on the answering machine. I was pretty sure I knew who was calling. Seth Powell lived downstairs. We'd met in the elevator last month and he'd latched onto me immediately, and since he was a single man in a city without any single men, I'd let him latch. He was funny, and cute enough, and we kissed on the first date because sometimes you just want to be kissed by a funny, cute enough guy. But he was also the type of man who called me "babe" and wore red and blue makeup to Patriots games. A prototype of too much testosterone, who in cave days would've pounded his chest at cave women and fathered hundreds of cave children. I sighed and poured a glass of wine.

I wanted to be alone. I'd been out all week attending a training seminar for my "real job" at U.S. Trust Investments, basically just videos and exercises teaching us how to scam strangers. We'd tell them we were born in their town, had graduated from their alma mater. We'd hear a baby in the background and use this to direct our next line of attack: A boy or a girl? How old is he or she? You know I have a son or daughter just exactly that age? And how wonderful it is for me knowing I've already invested in his or her future.

I was real good at casual lying. I'd had skillful teachers in my past. "So sorry," I'd tell Seth, "but I'm seeing someone else." And the truth was I did have plans with this Chianti: full-bodied, Italian and dependable. All you could ask for in a date.

I turned on the CD player to Norah Jones, who, regardless of reality, always managed to make me feel better about myself. *We're alone*, the music seemed to say, *and we're all we have, but also we're kind of cool....* So armed, I started the answering machine. I listened to silence for nearly a minute as I studied the buttons, sure I'd done something wrong. But then came the voice.

"Kerry?"

The glass slipped from my hand and shattered, leaving a full-bodied, Italian, dependable stain on the rug.

"It's your number, isn't it? I mean, of course it's you." He cleared his throat, spoke slower, deeper. "This is Justin…Caine. I need to speak with you about something important, something I can't leave in a message."

I backed away, staring at the machine.

"Look, this isn't easy for me. You have to understand how hard it was even looking up your number. I know it's been so long, but there's things happening, something you need to know."

Deep down part of me had been waiting to get this call. Part of me knew he'd figure out the truth about Eve, see what she really was. I'd played it over in my mind so many times, even practiced how I'd react, how I'd steel my shoulders. *I'm sorry,* I'd say, *but you're ten years too late. Go back to your wife.* In my mind the words sounded strong and indifferent and slightly accented, like a British aristocrat. But hearing Justin's voice, older maybe, with a new edge but so much the same, everything loosened inside me. My legs felt like putty. There was no strength, no indifference, only the loss.

"Listen, I need you to call me back. I can't tell you through a recording, this is way too important."

I shook my head, looking through the bars on my front window. The window had been barricaded by the last tenants, who'd owned a cat and a small child. I'd never taken the time to remove the bars, even though they made me feel like I was living in the type of place where people drank from unbreakable glasses and made license plates. But even without the bars I'd still feel it, looking down at the lights that flickered day and night:

neon pizza, laundromat, the sign that flashed red letters, *C-R-E-D-I-T,* each in turn, bright enough to stain the walls I'd painted sage green into a sickly brown.

"She's dying, Kerry," he said suddenly. "That's why I'm calling. It's just a matter of time now. She's dying."

I stopped the machine and blinked, blinked again. Nuh-unh. No way. I knew the truth. All these years I'd been able to close my eyes and see it, see her with Justin, with their child, living my life. And always, always happy. I would've felt it if there was anything wrong. I would've known.

I swallowed hard, rewound the machine, listened again.

She's dying. The words smacked me in the chest with the pain of a broken rib. "What?" I asked the machine. "What? What?"

"You need to come down here, really as soon as you can make it. She needs you here." His voice hitched and there was a beat of silence before he continued. "The number's the same. I'll talk to you soon, right? I'll talk to you."

I stopped the machine, my hand trembling so much that it took two tries, then stood with my eyes closed, palm flat against the telephone. "Dying," I whispered, then pressed my lips between my teeth. I turned off Norah Jones and replayed the message, hearing the tone rather than the words. "Justin," I said. "Justin?" I had to see his face. If he was lying, I'd see it in his face. I went to the bookshelf and pulled out one of the thin novels I'd read so many times I knew the words by heart. I stared at his face on the back cover, noises rising from deep in my throat like a hurt kitten or a pleading dog. Justin wouldn't lie about this. Even Justin wouldn't.

Justin Caine, the blurb read, *is one of America's best-loved children's writers. His magical Canardia series, named for himself and his wife, Eve Barnard-Caine, have become bestsellers in three countries. He and his wife and daughter live in their childhood home in Rhode Island.*

The photograph on the back cover was of Justin with Gillian. She had his sandy blond hair, my square chin, his cocky smile and my gray-green eyes. She was the child we would have had, and she was Eve's.

She's sick, Kerry, she's dying.

I stared down at the faint scars on my wrist, two lines intersecting, jagged and angry. LoraLee had said long ago that sheer wanting could make things happen. I'd thought once that I wanted this. I'd tried to make it happen. And up till now I'd thought it would be a release.

August
1993

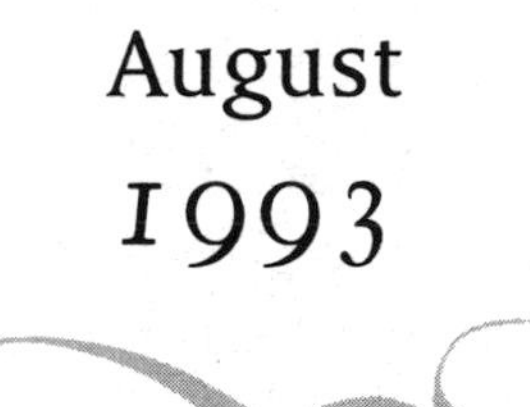

2

OUR DADDY ALWAYS LIVED on the edge of two worlds, between the present and the past we never talked about. It was what made life so hard for him, and in the end it was why death came so easily. I think we understood this all along, but on this day, his dying day, it was the last thing on our minds.

It was one of those late summer days that always come way too soon, slapping you in the face with all your June plans (Let's learn how to drive! Let's get dreadlocks!) that never got past the planning stage. Last night the temperature had managed to touch fifty before changing its mind, and this morning had been cold enough for sweatshirts and wool socks. Sun and moon shared the sky, twin gray spheres behind the haze of clouds. It was the summer of our sixteenth year.

We slapped down Water Street in our flip-flops, hand in hand, past the swanky hotels with their mansard roofs and attitudes, the not-so-swanky shops below them with their doors flung open to plead for end-of-season business. It was always a little weird in summer not knowing the faces we passed, all versions of the same stereotype with their sunglasses and pasty legs. The tourists made me and Eve feel lucky as we watched them cooing over flowering bushes and ocean views. They made us remember that not everyone lived this way.

We ran down to the jetty with its week-too-old-fish smell and sat with our legs dangling above the water, listening to the boats clock against their moorings and waiting for Daddy to come back from his last charter. Sunday afternoons were our time; at four o'clock when the day-trippers were drying off and changing to hop on the five o'clock ferry, Daddy would fold his sign down early and take us for a run. It had been that way every summer for as long as I could remember.

After a minute of sitting, Eve crossed one leg over mine and began combing her fingers through my hair. "What kind of mood're you in?" she said.

I shook my head. "Hunh?"

"It's just if you're in the wrong mood you overreact to things."

"I'm not in a mood. I mean, you're annoying me a little, but other than that I'm fine."

She was quiet a minute, and then she said, "Okay, I think today's Mom's birthday."

I felt an aching stretch, like my lungs had grown too big for my ribs. "How do you know?"

"His calendar. *D B-day,* it said. Diana's Birthday, it has to be."

I watched a wave lick against an algae-stained hull, dimly felt Eve pulling my hair back into a braid. "It could be anything, an appointment with Dr. Bradley or... a day to Drink Beer."

"Right, Kerry. He needs a reminder to drink." She peered into the distance at a departing ferry, the people waving like they were setting off on a journey that mattered. "You know I can't even remember her face? I remember her hair was dark and real long, past the waist. I remember she was tall and she could blow smoke rings with her cigarette, but that's it."

I fingered the birthday bracelet at my wrist. Our mother had given us the bracelets soon after we were born, and we wore them always, had added links to them when they started to pinch, and gave each other tiny charms to dangle from them, a new one for each birthday. Other than our thick brown hair and ability to tan without burning, they were the only things she'd ever given us that were worth having. "I think she was a dancer," I said.

Of course I had no idea if she was a dancer or a plumber, but I'd always imagined her in ballet shoes and swirly skirts. Since Daddy danced like a spastic turkey, I thought that must be where I'd gotten the genes for my one talent. In my heart I was a dancer, even though we couldn't afford real lessons. When I was eight the instructor of my Modern Movements class had told my father I was destined for greatness if he wanted to ship me to ballet school. Which of course he didn't, so the only type of dance I knew was Modern Movements, which tended to make one look like a flat-footed hippopotamus. But I was painfully sure that dancing stardom was one of those things I would've had, if only.

"If she dances, it's in a strip club," Eve said.

I didn't react to this, so she added, "On men's laps."

"You're so full of it," I said, but the image of our mother (still in ballet shoes) doing a lap dance was now lodged firmly in my mind. "I have this dream sometimes," I said to shake it, "Mom out on a boat somewhere, and she's writing in a journal about everything that's going on, and she's thinking about when she'll come back and show us."

Eve pulled my hair so tight I felt strands popping from my scalp. "Don't be an ass, Kerry."

I bit the inside of my cheek. It was dumb, sure. Obviously. But part of me still believed it, since it upheld the two basic tenets of childhood, that mommies don't leave, and daddies don't lie. Daddy told us when she first left that she was sailing round the world and would be back before we knew it. And for years we'd believed him, had stood for hours at the New Harbor dock waiting for her to emerge from a ferry with a book's worth of stories and piles of exotic gifts (castanets! berets! jalapeño condiments!). We'd speculated on what she was seeing: African tribes with bongo drums, beautiful geisha girls wearing red kimonos and chopstick-fastened buns.

But even though we never talked about it, inside we knew something darker. We remembered fractured images of spat words, a thrown vase, and darkest of all, bloody sheets washed in a sink, red water spiraling down a drain. We didn't know what they meant. We had chosen not to know.

I squinted out over the horizon, focusing on the wake of a returning speedboat, the folding and unfolding of water. "There's a reason she hasn't come yet. Even if we don't know what it is, there's some kind of reason." In my mind I'd come up with a dozen maybe-plausible excuses, from abduction by aliens to an intricate story involving her association with satellite spy technology, leading to her kidnapping by the KGB. The Book Nook carried a magazine I bought every month called *Untold Truths,* full of stories about conspiracies and UFOs and the mysteries of Atlantis. It gave clear evidence that essentially anything was possible.

Eve stopped braiding and followed my gaze out to the ocean. When I glanced at her she pulled away and my hair fell in my face. "If she gave a damn, how hard do you think it would be to find us? You want to know what I dream? I see her on Times Square, and she's wearing a glossy orange miniskirt and fake eyelashes, asking men if they want a good time."

I gripped the edge of the jetty, stone grating against my palms, and said nothing. Eve gestured with her head as Daddy's boat approached the dock, then turned to me. "And when she thinks of us she cries."

I watched her a moment, then rested my head against the bony ridge of her shoulder.

"C'mon," she said, pulling herself to her feet. She held out her arms to help me up, and we walked down to the dock where Daddy was helping two giggling middle-aged ladies from the boat. They were the good kind, the kind with flowery cotton pantsuits, so charged up on adrenaline that they always pressed bills into my father's hand when they shook good-bye. (*I got so excited I almost peed!* I'd once heard one of these ladies say.) Sometimes I felt a little bad looking down on grownups, but really sometimes there was no helping it.

Daddy grinned when he saw us, and the two ladies widened their eyes. "These are your twins?" one said. "Aren't they beautiful." The other gave a closed-mouthed Betty Rubble giggle and reached to touch Eve's hair. "Two peas in a pod," she said. "Bet you're having to chase the boys away." Something about our identical faces made tourists treat us the way they'd treat pregnant women, as prized rarities, a symbol of miraculous possibilities. Still we smiled because smiling was expected, and they rewarded my father with five-dollar tips.

After they left, Daddy pressed us briefly against him, the bristles of his beard scratching against my forehead, his chest smelling of scotch, of sea and sweat. We jumped onto the boat as Daddy folded his cardboard sign. *See the island as only birds can see,* it said.

Eve was first, as always—first born, first to walk, even first to wear a bra. She strapped the parasail harness between her legs as Daddy took the helm and rumbled through the obstacle course of anchored boats. As we reached the open sea, Eve gave a thumbs-up and Daddy gunned the motor, floating her into the air. I leaned over the bow and let the cold water spit into my face.

When I turned back I saw that Daddy's eyes were red. I felt a pinch of fear and I walked quickly to the stern, peering up like I was suddenly totally fascinated by the sky. Above me Eve swung her legs scissor-like to make herself dip and sway.

Minutes later Daddy walked towards me, also watching the sky. "School starts next week," he said. "You girls just won't stop growing up, hunh? Getting closer and closer to leaving me."

I shrugged and fixed my mind on trying to divide ten by three so my expression would look suitably distracted. Was today Mom's birthday? Would that be enough to make him cry? Mom leaving, walking away like a tourist boarding the ferry, with that same resignation and superficial regret. I couldn't ask because we didn't mention our mother to him, that was the unspoken rule. Instead I raised my eyebrows. "Actually, what we decided is after high school we're doing like Justin, staying here to work. We'll open a shop, a gift shop, maybe, with those lamps made out of conch shells. And we'll take care of you when you get old."

Daddy smiled and pulled a metal flask from his pocket. He took a swig and began to reel Eve back to the boat. "Hell, I wouldn't wish that on anybody. No, sweetheart, you're too smart for that. You'll study fish, what's it called? A marine biologist. And Eve, she'll study law. She could argue the hair off a dog. And then you'll fall in love with millionaires, live in some fancy high-rise on the mainland and buy pocketbooks to match your shoes. You'll forget all about me."

"That's stupid," I said, but I didn't tell him how really wrong he was, since I knew my plans would be more of a disappointment than a comfort. I couldn't see the point in wasting four years on college, and the man I knew I'd marry was right here.

It was my turn with the parasail, the boat dropping from beneath my feet, the heart-plunging freedom, wind tearing my eyes and biting my nose. I looked out over our island, the green hills, the interweaving stone fences and the waves battering the cliffs. The land was so narrow between Great Salt Pond and the ocean, like all it would take was a good-sized wave to snap the island in two.

Below, Eve stood at the bow, laughing, arms flung and head thrown back. I looked out over the horizon at a sailboat topping its reflection, a tiny white, impervious diamond. I pictured my mother at that safe distance, watching for land and wondering if we were watching her. There was a sudden fisting of my stomach and I saw it then, that loss was easier when you convinced yourself the loss was not worth mourning. This was something Eve must have already understood.

"Blue," Eve said. It was later that afternoon and we were sitting in the bedroom with our elbows on my desk, eyes closed, palm against palm.

"Good," I said. "And . . . ?"

"And something swimming, I don't know. All I see is spots. Is it fish?"

This was a game we played weekly, practicing. We were pretty good at it usually, had about a fifty percent success rate. Twins share an aura, we were sure of it. I pictured it as a sort of minty mist, like toothpaste breath. Cells might split but the aura cloud stretched between us, no matter how far apart we might be. Lots of nights we'd woken screaming at the same nightmares, would cry at each other's twisted ankles and scraped knees. One time my hair got hopelessly stuck in a zipper on the very same day Eve's got hopelessly stuck with gum, and we both walked around with our hair cut lopsided for a month.

When we were little this silent bond was something private, something not to reveal. But now we knew it was a gift that could be marketed. Our plan was to go on *Ripley's Believe It or Not.* Before we did, though, we'd have to pull off better than fifty percent success.

"Kind of like fish," I said, "but not really."

"Sky, clouds... Forget it. I can't concentrate." Eve began to play with my fingers, running her thumbs over the rough edges of my nails. She raised one eyebrow, a trick she'd mastered recently that I'd tried unsuccessfully for hours to replicate. "I think Justin's in love with me," she said.

I felt a sudden sinking, like ice puddling into my gut. "Right."

"I'm serious, I can tell. When we pass on the street he looks real fast into my eyes, not my face. Believe me, that's not a friendly kind of look. Or maybe it's not love, just sex."

I pulled my hands away. "You're full of it."

"He's always had a crush on me. Remember back ages ago when we were all in the bubble bath?"

The bubble bath was actually one of my favorite memories, the kind you replay so many times you're not sure if it was even real. Eve and I were in the tub, the bathroom door open for anyone to see. Justin walked by, calling our names, looking to show us some school project he'd put together with baking soda, vinegar and a toilet paper roll. Eve had glanced at me, then grinned and called back. He stopped short and stood outside the door, red-faced and frozen until Eve said, "C'mon in."

He'd stripped, facing away from us, then slid into the tub. We splashed him and he splashed back until the bubbles were nearly gone, and then he lay on my side of the tub, Eve angled between faucet and wall, knees against knees, washcloths over our groins, and we talked.

"Someday I'll have my own telescope," Justin had said, peering through one end of the carboard toilet paper roll. "Look in one end and you see the atoms, the other end and you see the universe."

"Gimme that," Eve said, taking it from him. She held it to one eye and scanned up his legs. "I'll have these X-ray glasses," she said, "where you see through clothes down into your guts."

He gave her a sideways smile. "Think about it though, it's like there's three worlds. There's the tiny one, and to them we're like the universe. And then there's the infinity telescope world, and to them we're little as atoms."

"Like what God would see," I'd said.

And Justin had nodded seriously. "To God we're like atoms and to the atoms we're like their God."

"Every time he looks at me?" Eve said now. "I get the feeling that's what he's thinking about. How my legs looked, and my boobs."

I swatted her. "You didn't have boobs."

"The stuff he said back then, it was pretty deep for a kid, you know? Pretty damn intense."

"So," I said, glancing at her. "So, you in love with him too?"

"No! Jeez, no." Eve held her up her fingers and inspected her peeling nail polish. "I'm planning never to fall in love with anybody except maybe Antonio Banderas."

"Good luck with that," I said, and then I smiled. "Eve Banderas. It sounds like a drag queen."

"Whatever, he's probably a pig anyway. I'm not falling in love with anybody; I'll just have affairs."

I managed, with much self-restraint, not to roll my eyes. The truth was, Eve had fallen in love with basically every boy in our school at one time or another, except Mattie Burns, who had pink freckles and seemed to be prematurely balding. She'd flirt with them until they started to get interested, and then she'd decide they were losers and fall right out of love again. "Much healthier," I said. "All men are pigs except for Daddy."

"Especially Daddy, talk about pigs. I can't believe Mom even stayed with him as long as she did."

"Eve!"

"I'm serious. I bet she was so fed up having a husband like that, waking up in bed next to that sweaty, hairy drunk every morning, that she just up and left."

"My guess is she got sick of you," I said, knowing even as it came out of my mouth how stupid this would sound.

Eve's face tightened and she gave me a look so disparaging it didn't need words, like I'd done something kindergarten-ish, stuck out my tongue and waggled my fingers. I spun away, annoyed.

I walked into the kitchen and opened a cabinet, needing something I couldn't name, staring blindly at cans of tomato soup and bottles of Heinz 57 Sauce. And then I went outside and stood on the porch and watched a pickup rumble past, carrying lumber for one of the new houses on the south end.

After we'd come back from our parasail I'd seen Daddy at his desk, head in his hands, surrounded by a monthly accumulation of mail, arranged into three precise rows. He'd been looking down at the floor, fingers kneading his temples, shoulders hunched. Even from the hallway I could smell the bite of cheap wine shimmering from his pores.

First I thought it might be the bills that got him hunched like that, but then I realized it must be something more. I'd watched the top of his head, the graying strands in his curly hair, and I'd wanted to say something but had no idea what that something should be. So I'd stood a minute longer, feeling helpless, then turned and left the room.

He'd gone out on the boat after dinner, which he only did on the nights he was sad, when two teenage daughters and a never-ending supply of drinking buddies just wasn't enough. He'd stand there on the deck and look out at the dark water, thinking about everything he'd lost. The ocean was like that at night; it could pull you down with it so the only things you saw were the things you couldn't have.

Now I watched a yellowed leaf dance towards the porch, the first I'd seen that year. When it hit, I crunched my sneaker against it, ground it against the cement into yellowed-leaf dust. And then, without letting myself think, I started towards Justin's house.

For the past year Justin had worked in his dad's repair shop, fixing cars and renting out the bone-rattling mopeds that the tourists loved but everyone else despised. I hadn't seen him much that summer. Along with his new job, Justin had gotten a driver's license and bought a used car that clanked when he started the engine. He'd also gotten a new girlfriend named Leslie. She was a senior, blonde and giggly and sweet. Eve and I hated her.

Passing the tree between our houses, I knocked four times on the trunk, discreetly in case anyone was looking. Four was my lucky number, seeing as I was born on the fourth day of the fourth month, and I used it whenever I needed to get ahold of myself. I had these quirks somewhere on the normal side of the continuum of obsessive compulsion, things like knocking on trees, avoiding numbers divisible by three, and leaving the bathroom before the toilet stopped flushing. Not big quirks, nothing that got in the way of my life, but they were close enough to crazy that I hid them even from Eve.

I knocked four times on the Caines' front door and Mrs. Caine answered, thick waist wrapped in one of her loose sarongs, blonde hair mussed into tufts around her face like a dandelion cloud. "Well, Kerry," she said. "We hardly see you anymore now you're all grown up, but suddenly both of you one right after the other! We've missed you."

I blinked. "Eve was here?"

"I keep meaning to invite the three of you to dinner. I'm so terrible about these things. Writing letters, phoning friends, I always mean to but I never get up enough momentum to actually do it."

"She was here to see Justin?"

"Yesterday afternoon, but he was working late. Work long hours now while you're young and have the strength, his father says. But me, I think work wastes the best years of your life, don't you?" She shrugged. "He's out in his office if you want him."

"Thanks." I turned back outside. My heart was pounding and I felt like I was racing. First one to the finish wins the prize.

I walked out to the shed between the Caines' house and ours. Justin was on the floor, leaning against two bed pillows, scribbling on a notepad, his sandy hair messy and falling in his eyes. His office, which had once been a potting shed, was littered with papers covering the floor and taped to walls. Years ago he'd painted the inside walls hunter green and set rows of ocean-tumbled stones on each of the potting shelves and window ledges, along with things in shapes he'd found interesting: gnarled sticks and batiked scarves, a honeycomb and a half-burned candle. The yellowish light against the dark walls made the room seem like a cave, silent and intimate and maybe or maybe not hiding something dangerous.

Justin smiled distractedly as I entered, then turned back to mutter at his paper. "Morwyn sat at the mirror pool and lit her lantern, and in the light reflected from the flame she saw him. Or in the light reflected from the moon? If she sees the moon, she can think about what time it is."

"Hi," I said.

"Because she has this sense she's going to meet him at dawn," he said.

I sat beside him, my fists tucked under my thighs. I thought I could feel the warmth from his body. "She'll meet him?"

"Mmmm." He leaned back on his hands. "Sorry. Leslie hates it when I do that, how it takes so long for me to leave that world and get back to this one. Come back to *earth,* she says."

"I like it." I felt my face flush. "I mean, it's a great world in your head. I'd rather hang out with you there than here." Our eyes met for a brief second, and in that second I felt a lifetime flow between us. Justin's eyes always drew me in, full of unexplored paths and hiding places. Ever since we first met they'd been this way, the dusty blue of a man who'd traveled far and seen worlds beyond worlds. Sitting there with him, I could feel our whole past, all those days when we'd shared everything, had known our place in the way little kids do and been joined by that knowing.

I bent to look at his notebook, and with my face beneath his I could taste his breath, vaguely peppery like he'd just bitten into a taco. I closed my eyes and drank it in.

And then I felt him touch my hair, a brief glancing whisper of a touch. He flinched back immediately, like he could feel the tingles radiating from my scalp and down my spine, prickling out to the tips of my toes. Eyes still closed, I leaned towards him, fingers and chest and lips aching.

"Ick," he said. "Don't get freaked out, but it's a baby bug."

I pulled back and made myself breathe, looking down at his hand where a tiny red spider was scuttling across his palm.

"Probably fell into your hair from the ceiling, this place is full of them. It's actually kind of cute, though, hunh?"

We bent our heads and watched the spider scurry up his arm, trying to hide in a fold of his shirtsleeve. And suddenly the picture came back to me, our bodies side by side in the bathtub, his naked ten-year-old chest. "Do you like Eve?" I said it before I knew what I was about to say, and instantly wished I could swallow the words back from the air.

Justin shook his head. "Do I what? Course I like her."

"No, I mean..." I inhaled deeply. "I mean do you *like* her like her."

Justin flashed a sideways smile. "Are you asking what I think you're asking? I have a girlfriend, remember?"

"It's just she was telling me today she thinks maybe you have a crush on her. She said something about the way you look at her, I don't know."

"You serious? Guess I'll have to stop looking at her then."

I grinned. "Or maybe just act grossed out next time you see her. Tell her she has a booger on her nose and she could use a shower."

Justin studied my face. "She's been coming by the garage every day for the past couple weeks. And last night she showed up there pretty late and found me with Leslie. Don't know how long she was watching before we saw her."

I watched the little red spider emerge from his shirt-sleeve, scurry down his arm and drop to the floor. "Were you guys kissing?" I said.

Justin raised his eyebrows and I shook my head. "I can't believe Eve would sneak around like that."

"You think she's jealous?" He started to laugh, then suddenly cut short and looked into my face. He watched me a long while and when he spoke his voice was deep and gentle. "You remember when we were kids and I used to tell my stories? Eve, she'd be laughing when she wasn't supposed to laugh, sitting there munching on snacks and slurping pop like she was sitting at some movie."

I rolled my eyes. "One time she compared your stories to *Lost in Space*."

He kept his eyes on my face like he was searching for something. "But you, you'd close your eyes and everything about you would get so perfectly still." He smiled quickly and turned away. "Which was actually one of the reasons I thought I had to write these stories down someday."

"Well I'm glad," I said, because I couldn't think what else to say.

"When I get published I'll write you in my acknowledgments: To Kerry, who was my inspiration."

His inspiration. My face was hot. I looked down into my lap, then back up.

Justin grinned. "Even though when she talks to me her face turns so red I get scared of explosions."

I felt a stabbing mortification and erupted into a fit of uncontrollable giggles. I grabbed a pillow from under his arm and aimed it at his head. He hooted, wrenched the pillow from my hands and pressed it over my face.

I fell back against the floor, hands grasping at him, fingers brushing at hair and cotton shirt, at the same time pulling him closer and pushing away. Words streamed through my head like an insane mantra, *Now, now, now.* He pulled back the pillow and looked into my eyes; the words stopped, time stopped, he leaned close. I could feel his breath on my face.

The door opened. "Kerry?" Mrs. Caine called.

Justin pulled away. I lay there in the burning glow, stunned.

"Kerry, honey, you have to go home now. Justin, why don't you bring her home."

Justin jumped to his feet, sounding winded. "You okay, Ma?"

She shook her head. "There's people waiting for you, Kerry. There's people who can explain."

Was she crying? I sat up and stared at her, sure I'd had this dream before. A fantasy turned nightmare at the last second before I woke.

But her clutch felt real as she pulled me into her arms, the crush of her hands against my head. "It'll be okay," she said. "I promise everything'll be okay."

These same words have, I'm sure, been said many, many times in many different situations. But I can tell you that always, they are a lie.

3

IT WOULD'VE BEEN EASIER, I think, if we'd had an older sister to lean on, or a younger one to take care of. But as it was, there was only Eve and me, and we were no more comfort to each other than we were to our own selves. We held each other wordlessly, slept in one bed like we had years ago. Each morning before I opened my eyes I expected to hear Daddy clattering in the kitchen, hear him whistle "Sweet Molly Malone," fuzzy through his beard. I lay in bed disoriented, like you feel when you wake in an unexpected place. And my head would swirl and slowly rearrange.

People came and went around us. All of them came, from Ginger Dean's six-week-old daughter to Emmeline Sugar, locally believed to be the oldest woman on earth. I imagined them standing in a line that stretched from our door down the street, all dressed in black and carrying umbrellas like the nannies in *Mary Poppins.*

Justin came and sat with us, not asking questions or offering meaningless platitudes. He just sat with his arms around our shoulders, and we stared at the wall and thought of nothing, diluting the pain between three.

Letters came, first sympathy cards and then money left

by our doormat in mystifying, unmarked brown envelopes. Twenty dollars here, ten dollars there; we pictured a neighbor, one of the older women with watery-pale eyes, scuttling up our front steps, full of pity and self-pride.

Our grandparents came from West Virginia, our grandparents who hadn't approved of Daddy's marriage or later of his divorce, who hadn't seen us for nearly ten years, who wanted us to call them Bert and Georgia. Without asking our consent they'd determined we'd return with them to West Virginia, once the shock wore off and things settled down. Perhaps as much as anything, this kept us clinging to each other, as if it could hold us in place.

We heard them talking, Bert and Georgia, heard their whispers and this was how we learned the truth about Daddy's death. The words they used were *reckless* and *carousing*. He'd been in his boat. He'd been drinking. And they blamed it all on us, we knew they did, saw it in their appraising eyes and heard it in their voice.

They also told us they'd hired a PI, that they were searching for our mother. And for weeks, until time erased illusion, Eve and I clung to the certainty that now, when we really needed her, she'd come back.

The day after the funeral, the First Warden came with a manila envelope holding Daddy's belongings. Eve stared at it, eyes wide with fear; these things had touched our father after he was dead! But I opened the envelope and pulled out Daddy's Timex, held it against my cheek and slipped it loosely over my wrist. Then his wallet, leather bleached by ocean water, holding two crumpled bills (one printed mysteriously in a child's handwriting with the words *Wheat Noodle*) and his boating license. At the bottom of the envelope was a thick silver chain strung with a small key, cylindrical with carved notches. I fingered the grooves, rough against my skin. This was Daddy's but I'd never seen it before.

I slipped the chain over my head and felt it slide cold between my breasts. From that time on I wore the necklace day and night, tried it on every keyhole from the front door to the rolltop desk. Every step I took, it swung heavy on my chest, like a question. I knew there was something, a locked journal or jewel box that held some kind of answer to Daddy's sadness and maybe his death. All the time I wore it, until the day we discovered what it meant, I never told Eve.

Eve and I didn't talk much about Daddy. I guess we thought that by not talking about it we could keep from blaming him or blaming ourselves. But of course his death and the accountability were always there behind it all, like the coppery smell of winter or damp in the air.

One day I came home to find Eve on the front step, her smile still and unnatural as a wound. I stood watching her, uncertain. "You know what happened?" I said. "I'm walking downtown and there's Ellen Harte, she sees me and she gets all teary, and just like that she wraps her arms around me. So I'm standing there with my head in her boobs and what am I supposed to do?"

Without speaking, Eve reached into her back pocket and handed me an envelope. It was made out to our mother with an address in New York, which had been crossed out and labeled *Address Unknown.* It was postmarked three days before Daddy's death.

"It was in his desk," Eve said. "He couldn't find her. He died because of her."

Something shivered in my chest. I dropped the letter.

"Open it."

I shook my head.

"Open it!" She snatched the envelope from the step, pulled out a card and threw it at me, its corner smarting against my cheek.

I caught the card against my neck, examined it. It was sketched with a cake and poetry: a birthday card. Inside, it was lettered in Daddy's flat script.

Diana,

Well I guess I don't have much new to say to you this year. Except the girls are fine and growing up to be women so fast you wouldn't hardly believe it. They'll go off in a couple years, I'm sure of it, and it'll be just me again. Hasn't been just me for so long, I can't hardly imagine what it'll be like. You know how it feels, how they're part of you under separate skin and then where does it all go? Out in the world with them maybe, even if that's not something I can see. I know they've turned out good, and that's what matters. But it doesn't mean we still don't wish you were here all this time.

As always,
Thomas

I reread the card without wanting to, and then again until the words blurred in my head.

"'This year,'" Eve said. "Nothing new to say to her 'this year.'"

"He was writing to her the whole time. The whole time?"

"Fucking liar." Eve's voice was dark, hollow, coming from somewhere deep inside her. "She's sailing around the world, he says. She'd be here if she could, he says. And yeah, we knew that was bullshit."

"But she knew where we were."

"The whole time we were waiting she knew. We're like these imbecilic pet dogs or something, thinking any day now she'll come home and walk us."

"We could find her, Eve. I'm sure we could get a forwarding address."

"Are you kidding? How pathetic would that be, having to chase after our own mother?"

"Maybe if she knew about Daddy..."

"She'd what, decide she really does give a damn? To tell you the truth I'd rather stay with Bert and Georgia. At least they're pretending to be grandparents. At least they came."

I watched Eve for a minute, then sat on the step beside her. I looked out over the gravel drive, spinning inside like a child who's stared too long at the sun, hurting, burning from it but still not willing to let go. I took Eve's hand and made the hope flicker out again. "You're right," I said without turning to face her. "Okay."

I knelt in LoraLee's front yard, helping her pull the pansies that had been bitten by last night's frost. LoraLee had been my confidante since a time before I'd needed a confidante. She lived near the junkyard in a two-room cabin with no plumbing, decorated with odd findings from the trash heap. The islanders said she was a witch.

I remember watching before we'd ever met as she sat in her garden, brown skin and thick black braid beneath her wide straw hat, hands resting over unopened flower buds. I'd stood there listening to the clink of wind chimes made out of soup can lids, bent forks and green sea glass that hung from the roof and tree branches. LoraLee's eyes were closed, lips moving in a silent chant, and I thought I could see the buds brighten and swell. I was six at the time and in love with fairy tales, and standing there I'd remembered how Seth Morgan said he saw her sitting on a broomstick one night looking up at the full moon. Janie Cross told me that LoraLee gave her dog the evil eye for peeing on the lawn, and the next week her dog came down with liver disease and died. I remembered, and I watched her flowers grow, and I knew for sure I was witnessing true magic.

One day I hid behind LoraLee's stone fence, watching her spray cabbage with an antique perfume bottle. Straightening, she'd looked my way as if she could see (witchlike!) through brambles and stone. She didn't seem at all surprised, just smiled and waved me over. I'd peered back at her, thinking about Hansel and Gretel, but then I'd steeled my shoulders and let her invite me inside for tea.

Her cabin was a warm kind of dark, the color of cedar wood. One wall was hung with an orange blanket she told me was woven in Kenya; the tiny figurines she carved and sold watched from broken tables and ladder-back chairs missing their ladders. She whittled a new figurine that day, a little girl wearing a daisy chain who I thought was too brown and wood-veined to look like me but was maybe more like the girl I wished I could be, strong and rough-edged, perhaps of African descent. LoraLee explained to me about flowers, about roots and buds and blooms, growth and destiny, and seeds planted in my soul. They were concepts a little beyond me at the time, but I liked the sound of them all the same.

From that time on she was the one I turned to when I had nowhere else to turn. I'd come to her door and she'd be waiting with spice cookies and tea. She'd sit in her rocker with her whittling and listen, and then she'd tell me the truth about the world, her voice smooth as molasses. I usually left with answers. I always left feeling better.

That day, three weeks after Daddy's death, I knelt in her garden and eyed the fading flowers. It hurt my heart to kneel there among the endings, and so after a while I brushed off my hands and sat on the front step. LoraLee nodded without looking up, and after a minute came to sit beside me.

I lifted the stained hem of her skirt and held it as if it could give me comfort. "If my father could see us, he'd die all over again," I said. "He'd want to come down and make things right."

"Well I'm sure he wish he could," LoraLee said.

"Do you think he can? See us, I mean."

"Why yes, I do. I think he see you in his heart jus' like you sees him."

"Daddy didn't believe in heaven. He believed in God, but he didn't believe in heaven."

"That right?" LoraLee looked out across the yard, didn't speak for such a long time that I dropped her skirt, embarrassed. Immediately she took my hand and squeezed. "Your daddy were a very smart man," she said.

"What?" This was worrisome. Of course she couldn't really know for sure one way or another if there was a heaven, but when LoraLee said something it was usually true.

"If you believes in that sort of heaven, you gots to also believe in hell, and I think there ain't nothin' so bad a body could do to deserve an eternity shovelin' and burnin'."

I stared down at the chipped concrete of the front step. LoraLee looked at me a long while, then squeezed my shoulder and lifted the pail of dead flowers we'd pulled. She led me to the back of the house, where she emptied the pail on the compost heap and stirred the rich soil over it.

"See this?" she said. "Everything go back to the earth in time. All this here were alive and now it dead, and now it goes back to the earth. And comes spring I takes that earth which is full up with goodness, and out of the goodness come new life. That's how it works."

Looking into the pile of weeds and rotting vegetables, it molded, changed, became my father's face. I suddenly remembered the dull shiver of earth I'd sifted onto his casket. I flinched away.

LoraLee made a hushing sound and pulled me against her bosom. "Oh, chile, don't you unnerstan'? S'like when you lays on your back on a summer's eve, and the stars so bright they reach down to you and you reaches up to them. They pulls you inside till you is them and they is you. That's what happen, Kerry, what I thinks. You don't go to heaven, you becomes it."

I pulled away and looked down at her hands, that strange wooden ring she always wore. The pads of her fingers were wrinkled, like they'd been soaking in water for hours. LoraLee touched the tear snaking down my cheek and shook her head.

"The troubles is bad, Kerry, but it's the sadness what take away your life. You needs to put your heart at rest and feel the hope of what come to be."

"I know," I said, but what I really knew was that there was no hope. There was the darkness of a West Virginia cabin that smelled like old age. There was the bleakness of no ocean and no tourists and a winter that lasted well into spring. And there was the loneliness of grandparents we hardly knew, who didn't have the faintest idea how to love us.

Back home I could tell immediately that something was wrong. Tension hung over the house like a yellow oil, seeping through walls and bones.

I could hear their mumbling in the kitchen, the spitting *S*'s of anger. Hurrying past on my way upstairs, I saw my grandmother at the table, face red, and my grandfather appeasing her with a nod that seemed more fear than agreement.

I ran up to the bedroom. It looked empty but I knew Eve was under the bed.

She liked it down there. I understood this, and I'd tried it a few times, but even though it did feel safe lying there in the dark, it also felt too dusty and claustrophobic for my taste.

I lifted the bed skirt and crawled in beside her. She

was pulling the threads edging a mouth-sized tear in her jeans, and she barely turned to acknowledge my presence. "I'm leaving," she said.

I turned onto my side so I could see her.

"I'm packed and everything. I was waiting till you got home." She examined a tuft of thread in her palm, squeezed it into a fist. "I can't take this anymore, Kerry. Did you know Georgia chews her ice cream? That's what kind of people they are."

I shook my head. "You're not making sense."

"She was eating Daddy's pistachio. Just took it out from the fridge without even asking, like it belonged to her. So I said it would maybe do her some good to go on a diet."

"Eve!"

"And she turns real pale, and says what was wrong with Daddy that he never taught me any respect. So I'm leaving."

"You can't really leave, not for good." But I knew what she meant. Eating Daddy's ice cream was like shrugging at the fact it wouldn't ever be eaten otherwise. "But maybe you could stay with LoraLee, at least for a little while. I'm sure she wouldn't mind."

Eve glanced at me. "See, I was over at Justin's yesterday, and Mrs. Caine was acting all sorry and sweet, and she said if there was ever anything she could do and how I'd always be welcome."

My legs felt suddenly like the insides of a jelly donut. "You can't."

"It won't be a big deal, Kerry. I'll be right next door. We'll have you over for dinner and you'll see me in school."

The pictures seared through my head: Eve and Justin sharing breakfasts, sharing a bathroom, sharing a bed. "Fuck that. I'm coming too."

Eve smiled at me like I was a not-completely-funny joke, but I didn't care. "You really think I'd stay here alone? They'd drive me bonkers." I stared at the heels of my hands, then pressed them against my eyes.

Eve stroked my arm, then slid out from under the bed. "I'll help you pack."

I could feel my pulse quickening with excitement or fear. I crawled out and looked up at her, then saw the suitcase on the end of the bed, filled and zipped like finality. "They'll send us back. Bert and Georgia, they'll make us come back."

Eve raised her eyebrows, smiled with half her mouth. "They won't," she said. "I've got plans. You just wait and you'll see."

We were lucky that only Justin was home. I'm sure that greeted with adult faces of questioning discomfort we would have realized the insanity and turned back. But Justin only glanced at our bags and nodded like he'd known it was only a matter of time.

He set us up in his office with sleeping bags and hot cocoa and talked to us about the sorts of things (sports, the love lives of the stars) that kids tend to talk about in abnormal situations, precisely because they are so mundane and unrelated to their lives. It was exactly what we needed, enough to give us composure and confidence so that by the time Justin's parents came home, we knew just what to say.

"They're always telling us how they're too old to be watching over two teenage girls," Eve said.

I nodded. "Seems like they're always either out in the shops or sleeping, and Bert, he always smells like whiskey."

Mrs. Caine raised her eyebrows. "He drinks?"

"It's hard for us 'cause it's so much like Daddy was on his bad days," Eve said. "The things he says, how he smells, it just brings it back." Her eyes were suddenly misty with tears. I wondered if they were real. "It just makes us remember all the things we've been trying to forget."

Mr. Caine's face flushed red, and Mrs. Caine's eyes softened with pity. I felt a twinge of guilt. "It's not like they're not trying," I said. "I know they're doing good as they know how to do. It's just they haven't had to take care of a kid for years and years, so I guess they just don't realize."

Justin's parents watched each other in silence. I tapped four times on the underside of the table, and then again on the chair.

Finally, Mr. Caine squeezed Eve's hand. "I guess you could stay here tonight," he said. "I can let your grandparents know. And tomorrow we'll have a talk with them."

Mrs. Caine bent to hug me, then Eve. "Don't worry," she said. "I know it's hard now, but I promise you'll always be taken care of."

Later, Eve and I lay in the dark, whispering. "Did you see their faces?" Eve said. "They looked like they wanted to pull us onto their laps and feed us chicken soup. I know they'll keep us."

I buried my head in the sleeping bag. Had Justin slept here? Was this the scent of his sleeping body? "Would Bert and Georgia ever let us?"

Eve made a soft snorting sound. "I can't think of anything that'd make them happier."

I tried to smile. "Remember when the Potters' grandkids came up for the summer? How ever since Christmas the Potters were talking about it? And they put up a tire swing and bought a rocking horse and those lawn statues of geese and elves."

"Yeah, well." Eve was silent for a minute. When she spoke again her voice was soft. "It's impossible to love teenagers unless you loved them when they were kids. And maybe it's the same thing, impossible to love old people unless you loved them from the beginning. If we were six instead of sixteen, things would be different for sure."

"I guess," I said. But I remembered when they'd first arrived for Daddy's funeral, how Georgia had gathered me in her arms, whispered hushing noises in my ear. Maybe it would have been better if they'd never seen us grown and we could love each other in the abstract. Maybe they'd have held the picture from years ago when we'd first met, of Eve and me singing "White Coral Bells" in duet, finishing each other's sentences to make them laugh. "But what if they actually do want us?"

Eve was silent for a moment, then took my hand. Her fingers were cold and dry. "It won't matter what they want," she said. "I told you I've got a plan."

* * *

I sat with my arms folded on my desk, chin resting on my wrist, and watched Leslie at the desk in front of me, her too-tight sweater over her too-tight jeans. She looked, I thought, like the kind of girl who wouldn't wear underpants under a skirt.

"'Instantly afterward,'" Mr. Suter read, pacing back and forth across the front of the classroom, "'the company were seized with unspeakable consternation, owing to his springing to his feet, turning round several times in an appalling spasmodic, whooping-cough dance, and rushing out the door.'" He raised his head and grinned widely at us, as if expecting something. The class stared back, waiting for the clock to click towards three.

Mr. Suter was heavy. Not just heavy, he was massive, his belly leading the rest of him by a good two feet. I used to think it was cute how he was always so excited over the stupidest things. Now it just seemed sad to me, like he was acting out some stereotype. Even sadder because on this day I could hardly pay attention, let alone laugh back.

"Don't you get it?" he said. "Dickens was like the sitcom of the nineteenth century! Folks would buy their Sunday papers and turn straight to the story, maybe first because it made them laugh, but then because they got involved with the characters!"

Leslie was scribbling furiously. I peered over at her paper. *Dickens... 19teenth cenchery... Sunday papers... first laugh then charicters.* God, she was writing down everything. *Ditz,* I wrote in my notebook, circled the word and crossed it out.

Three-two-one, the bell. The class shuffled their books into their bags, not caring that Mr. Suter was mid-sentence. Only Eve and I stayed at our desks. We turned to each other, and then I nodded. "Let's go."

"You think they're home?"

"Mrs. Caine's always home, just about. This better have worked, or else we'll have gotten Bert and Georgia pissed for nothing."

Eve shrugged. "Look, the question is who they like better, us or Bert and Georgia, which is a no-brainer, and who they believe more. And we were good last night. I even felt sorry for myself. No competition."

I tried to smile. "You were good. I felt sorry for you too."

We walked home without speaking and stood outside the Caines' front door, unsure if it would be right to assume this was where we belonged.

Suddenly Eve pulled at my arm and pointed at the picture window. Bert and Georgia sat with their backs to us. On the sofa across the room, Mrs. Caine poured tea and Mr. Caine reached for a cookie. As we watched, Mrs. Caine laughed and Georgia threw back her head, tittering, "Oh, no!"

Eve watched, unblinking, then turned to me. "I'll be right back. You stay here."

I nodded, watching as Bert rose to accept a cup of tea. "Must've changed five times," he said. "I'd go to check on her, and there she'd be by the mirror, new dress, new hat, new gloves."

Eve ran across the lawn and I sat on the front step, knocked softly on the porch rail, then lined four fallen leaves neatly against the step. This done, I reached for the comfort of Daddy's key necklace and squeezed my eyes tight-shut. Of course they were getting along; the

Caines liked everybody. Bert and Georgia would tell their little stories, the Caines would laugh about the overdramatism of teenagers, and when we came inside they'd hug us and send us home.

More laughter. Georgia's voice. "Well, it could've been the most important day of my life. Wouldn't you say it's better to be prepared than look like you don't care?"

"Sure it is," Mrs. Caine replied. "I'd have done the same, I bet."

The stuttering hope of the last hours vaporized, and my body flooded with a hot red frustration. How stupid were we? How stupid to think the Caines cared how our lives would be.

"Scream."

I looked up. Eve stood in the driveway, hands behind her back. A loud whisper, "Kerry, scream." She brought one arm forward, lifted it to her head, and I gasped. Daddy's handgun.

Time stood still. I could see the image before me and struggled to put the pieces together: A finger on a trigger, Eve's eyes bright with expectation, the black barrel in wild tufts of brown hair. I screamed.

Then everything happened at once. I jumped up and ran down the drive. The front door opened, Mrs. Caine's voice, "God, no!" A cry from Georgia, Eve's eyes sparkling with a wild, neuron-firing look, the thump of someone's body hitting the porch floor as I dove for the gun. The trigger squeezed beneath Eve's finger, and for a second I imagined the ear-shattering explosion of skull and brain and warm blood on my face, and I shrieked as the gun went off, an empty click.

Eve shouted at me, animal, hysterical, "I won't! I can't!" Mr. Caine wrapped us in a bear hug, wrenched the gun from Eve's hand and hurled it into the bushes. I sank to the ground and grabbed hold of Eve's leg until she sat beside me, clutched me.

On the porch, Mrs. Caine bent over slapping at Bert's cheek, while Georgia clasped her hands, knees bending, straightening, bobbing up and down like she was preparing to jump. "Is he breathing? His heart, his heart..."

Eve smiled at me, and there was a moan, guttural, Bert's moan. "That's it," she whispered, and I didn't know whether to shake her or grab onto her and never let her go.

4

HOW COULD YOU?" Georgia said. "How could you do it?"

We were sitting in the living room. Bert was against the far wall in the recliner, arms crossed over his belly, eyes closed. I couldn't tell if he'd been drinking. Probably he had.

"You knew it had no bullets," Georgia said. "You just had to cause a scene."

"I didn't know." Eve spoke through clenched teeth.

"He was our only son," Georgia said, "our baby. And now we're doing the best we can by you, the best we can do."

I was shocked to see her tears, and I wanted to go to her, apologize, tell her that it hadn't really been her fault. But beside me Eve was trembling, and I knew my allegiances. I squeezed Eve's hand and said nothing.

"You don't get it," Eve said. "I wanted to die. I'd rather die than live with you!"

Georgia gasped. Bert opened his eyes, then quickly closed them again.

There was a hesitant knock at the front door. We all stared at it. The knock came again, and the door opened.

Mrs. Caine poked her head into the hall. "I'm sorry," she said. "Are you okay? Is everything okay?"

"Everything's fine," Georgia said. "Thank you."

"I'm here because my husband thought... I wasn't sure it was such a good idea, but he thought maybe it might help if you all talked this through with me here as a sort of mediator."

Across the room Bert gave a grunt and stumbled to his feet. His feet seemed to be giving him trouble, catching in the thick rug. "I'm too old," he slurred. "Old..."

"We worked hard all our lives," Georgia said, "just saving for our retirement."

Bert nodded. "Retirement..."

"He was our only son, and we want to do right by his children. They just don't realize the sacrifices we're making."

Bert shook his head as if in pain. "That's true."

Mrs. Caine hesitated, then said, "Well, I've maybe got an alternative."

My heart skipped a beat. I glanced at Eve.

"What we were thinking, my husband and me," she said, "is it might make sense for the girls to stay here."

Bert stumbled over the leg of an end table, sat down upon it with a thump.

"We're only right next door, so we can watch out for them, make their dinners, handle any crises."

Georgia stared at Mrs. Caine. "But you're not family."

"I know it sounds unconventional. But the girls only have two more years of school. Really, they've been through so much change already, we thought they should at least have a chance to finish out school at home."

Eve clasped her hands beneath her chin as if in prayer.

"They could help us out in the garage if they need extra money for rent. We could use someone to watch the register."

There was a loud crack from beneath Bert, and the end table toppled onto the floor. Somehow he managed to stay on his feet. "Yes," he said.

Georgia gaped at him. "Bert!"

"I'm too old for girls, Georgia. We're both of us too old." He stared at the table mournfully. "If you think it's best, I do suppose they should."

I felt Eve's hand slipping into mine. When I turned to her, she bent to whisper in my ear. "Ta-da!"

Just like that, life turned around. Bert and Georgia packed up and left, and Eve and I began our life without family. We got a quick lesson in grownup headaches, rent and groceries and electricity bills paid for with a thousand-dollar check, signed by Bert, which we found on the hall table after they'd left. I had to pinch myself daily to make sure this was real; the first few weeks I felt blanketed in a kind of haze.

We began to work at the Caines' garage, supposedly keeping the books, but mostly just sitting at the front desk searching for good radio stations, pretending we didn't know that the Caines didn't need bookkeepers.

I did a lot of remembering in those first days, spent hours poring through old photographs I'd long ago hidden in a shoebox under my bed. We were always smiling in those pictures, and looking at them I could almost forget we'd ever been anything but happy.

I was sorting through them one day, trying to place them in chronological order, when Eve walked into the bedroom. She stood without speaking for a minute, then came to sit beside me. She lifted each of the pictures in turn: Daddy riding one of our tricycles, his knees up at his ears; Daddy in his Santa Claus suit, white beard crooked to expose the brown beard underneath. These few pictures were all we had left of him, and she studied each of them so carefully, like she wanted to pull the life from them.

"I hardly even remember most of these," she said finally. "It's like they happened to someone else."

I nodded. "Like a dream. Sometimes I think, God, what if it's always like that? If when we get to be thirty we'll try and look back on now, and this'll feel like we're watching it from the outside?"

"I am watching from outside." Eve glanced at me, then turned away. "Aren't you?"

"Sometimes. I guess."

Eve's face hardened. "It'd be fine with me anyway if everything up to now just disappeared. I don't need to remember how it really was. It wasn't like this." She brushed away the pictures. "Maybe that's why I don't remember. It was all a lie."

I lifted the most recent picture of the three of us, sixth-grade Halloween. Daddy was dressed as a great big banana, a peaked yellow cap on his head. I was a cantaloupe, in a burlap sack, and Eve was a bunch of purple grapes. "Not all of it," I said. "Some of it was real."

"It's a waste of time to look through these and wish

for something you never really had." Her eyes were clouded and cold, maybe from anger, or maybe because she was fighting off tears. "I don't miss him."

"What?"

"I thought I did, but now I realize I don't. And when you think about it, we never really had him in the first place. When you face that fact it makes the rest of it not so bad."

Eve reached for the picture in my hand. She studied it for a minute, and a flush slipped over her face like a pink mask. "Remember how I had to pee so bad? And Justin had to pop my grape balloons so I could get out of that damned costume? I barely made it."

I smiled. "You were totally bawling and running in place, and balloons were exploding all over."

"I think we still have the costumes somewhere." Eve stood to rifle through the closet, reached into the back and then started to laugh. "Man, this thing's hideous." She pulled out a beige cap and a burlap sack painted with green stripes. "How come we didn't want to be fairy princesses like normal people? Try it on, Ker. See if it still fits."

"Only if you put on that purple tube dress that made you look like an eggplant."

Eve smirked and reached for the dress, stared at it. "And then we'll take pictures we can use to blackmail each other when we're rich and famous."

I stripped and pulled the sack over my head. It had been loose when I'd last worn it, but now it strained over my breasts and under my arms, its thick middle, empty of stuffing, hanging in a deflated paunch at my knees. I giggled and bobbed a plié, up and down, then flung my arms out at my sides. "Am I beautiful or what? I look like one of those mold mushrooms you find on the bottoms of logs."

"My, how we've grown," Eve said.

I turned and almost gasped out loud. The purple dress hugged her waist and hips and breasts, so smooth you could see the indentation of her navel. Her hair was pulled back with a purple sequined headband, emphasizing the cords of her neck. "Holy shit," I said. "You look like a stripper."

Eve swayed her hips and tossed back her head, singing, her voice deep and throaty. "Oooh, I heard it through the grapevine..."

I watched her sway, hands caressing her body, then turned to the mirror, my own stretched burlap image. I felt the tears of laughter drying tight on my cheeks, and I suddenly remembered years ago when we were eight or nine, Eve had stolen a pack of cigarettes from the Caines. Daddy found it and we both got spanked till our butts were blue, but even before that, when I first saw the pack in our top dresser drawer, I'd felt this same muted tremble in my stomach, like a warning.

5

ISLAND WEATHER IS FICKLE. Especially in the fall, the wind can come from nowhere, taking air that feels like summer and turning it into winter. The ferries stopped on days like this, banked on the protected mainland, isolating us completely from the outside world. The island's only twelve miles from the coast of Rhode Island, but on a stormy night it might as well be a thousand.

Eve and I sat together on the living room couch, watching the windows rattle and sheet with water. The fury of it was both frightening and fascinating, like something huge and shrieking with pain.

I remembered suddenly a long-ago winter with this same howling wind, Eve and I waking with simultaneous screams, Daddy's face a white moon appearing at our door. He'd taken us down here and we'd huddled in the warmth of cocoa and cuddles, listening to the ice pelting against the windows and wondering if the glass might crack.

"Remember Daddy reading out loud," I said now, "us sitting here like this? He used to say, 'I have two girls because I have two knees,' remember that?"

Outside there was a crash of thunder. The lights

flickered. “Amelia Bedelia,” Eve said. “You loved those books.”

“How come he stopped reading to us?”

Eve raised her eyebrows. “We stopped fitting on his knees?”

A fierce blast of wind gusted through the window seals to flutter at the curtains. There was a sudden pop and the lights flickered out. “Damn,” Eve said.

I slid away from her. After a minute I stood and walked to the window, pulled the drapes and stood there a long while without turning. “How come I never thought about how hard it was for him till after it was too late? I keep thinking about that, if I had one more day with him.”

“You’d do what, tell him you’re sorry? You understood? It wasn’t our job to take care of him.”

There was a knock on the front door, and it opened before we could answer. “You guys here? Jesus, I feel like I just went swimming.” Justin bent to rub the wet from his hair, leaving it rumpled and spiky. “I didn’t know if you’d have candles.”

He set a bag down on the floor and took out three pillar candles and a book of matches, all dripping wet. He stared at the matches, then shrugged. “Oops.”

“I’ll find some.” I went to the kitchen and searched through drawers, finally found the lighter Daddy had used for his pipe. When I got back to the living room Eve was laughing.

“Well, at least the buckets work,” Justin said, sitting on the sofa next to her. “But all I can tell you is I’ll be totally useless as a husband. I mean if you want your bike fixed, fine. If you want to hear a bedtime story, I can probably do that too, but you need someone to look at your roof, forget it."

"There's more important things than fixing leaks," Eve said. "We were just talking about bedtime stories, how Daddy used to read out loud. I was saying it's one of the best things he did for us."

I raised my eyebrows at her, but she didn't notice.

"You wouldn't think it was so important if he let the rain drench your bed," Justin said.

"I still would've thought it. Like you were saying, buckets work well enough."

"Yeah, long as I have an understanding wife."

"I got a lighter," I said, setting the candles on the coffee table. I lit them and sat on the other side of Justin.

Justin sighed and slid an arm around my back. I stiffened.

"This picture just popped into my head," he said. "Maybe fifty years from now and here we are, old bags, there's a fire going and the three of us are in the living room listening to the rain, with you guys doing knitting and me doing a crossword."

"Knitting?" Eve said. "Are you kidding?"

"Sorry, Eve. Okay, you're planning some exotic trip, or plotting to rule the world." He squeezed my shoulder. "But Kerry's knitting."

Eve snickered but I didn't care. All that mattered right then was his arm around me, a honey-thickness sinking from my shoulders down through my chest. I blurred my eyes and watched the candles dance in unison right and left. "What'll we be thinking?" I said.

"Guess it depends what we've done with our lives so far. By then if we haven't done all the important stuff, we'll probably just be waiting for life to end. But if we've done everything we wanted, we'll be reminiscing."

"That's the problem," Eve said. "These days that's how I feel, like the important stuff's never going to happen."

Justin pulled his arm away from me, leaned back to look at Eve. "You don't mean that."

"I just keep waiting for something to start," she said. "Even though I know it won't start on its own, all I can do is wait. Like everything'll be a blur until it happens, whatever it is, graduating, moving to the mainland, falling in love."

"I've been in love," Justin said. "Or at least I've thought I was in love. And it's great in its own way, but it's not everything. Not enough by itself to make you feel like you've lived."

"For me it will be," I said.

Justin slid his arm back around me, rested his damp head against my shoulder. "Yeah, you're a romantic," he said. "For you it probably will be."

I bit back a smile. There was something primal in it, the sound of the rain, the tickle of his hair against my neck. This stillness, this is how I imagined it would be if Justin and I had just made love.

But then he spoke. "I think there's two kinds of people," he said, "contented souls and restless souls. That's us, Eve, the restless souls, always looking."

Eve smiled. "And Kerry'll do her knitting, and she'll be happy with her sitting-knitting life."

"But at least she'll be happy. Whereas us, I'll be waiting to finish my story and you'll be trying to conquer the world. And either it won't happen or it will and we'll find out it's not enough. How many people live their lives just waiting?"

Eve touched her finger to a candle drip, lifted it to study the wax-covered print. "If you look more, you find more," she said. "So maybe we'll never be complacent. But at least you and me, when we look back on it all, we'll know we really lived. I'd rather have passion than peace any day."

Justin was quiet a minute, then said, "Passion's riskier, but I guess I'm with you. I'd rather have passion than peace."

I sat in the kitchen, helping Mrs. Caine with dinner. She was the kind of woman who was always smiling faintly, even when she was doing things that did not warrant a smile, like inspecting bread for mold or unclogging the toilet. I watched now how she hummed as she sponged the counters, her hands stubby in their worn rubber gloves, and my heart swelled with longing for what I'd never have.

"I'm pretty much done here," she said, then swiped her wet rubber finger across my nose. "You don't have to come over to help every night, you know. I'm pretty much self-sufficient."

"I like it here," I said. "Remember when you used to babysit? You did these cool crafty things with us, made us Fluffernutter sandwiches, let us try on your shoes. It reminds me of that."

And it was more than that. Not only did I love Mr. and Mrs. Caine, I loved their parent-ness, their husband-and wife-ness. They were more of a family than my own family had ever been, and I thought it might be useful for the future, seeing how it was all supposed to work. Most importantly I felt Justin's presence here like a fog. Oh, I knew it was totally sappy; if I'd seen anybody else acting this way, I would've laughed out loud, but I didn't care. That Justin fog was the only thing that made life bearable. I imagined his hair on my fingers when my hand brushed against a wall, smelled the warmth of his breath in steam when I washed his dinner plate. *I'd rather have passion than peace,* Justin had said, but I knew we could have both. Being in this house was both to me, haloes of the peace cast by the Caines' happy marriage, sharpened by Justin's glances across the table, a brush of fingers as we passed the salt. I could sense in those evenings how it would feel to be a wife. "It kind of feels like home," I said.

Mrs. Caine watched me, her face flushed, maybe with pleasure or maybe with sadness, or maybe just with counter-washing exertion. "Well, it *is* home," she said softly, "and we love having you here. You know you're like family." She looked down like she was embarrassed, then smiled. "Anyway, speaking of family, let's see if we can gather up the rest of them. Why don't you go tell your sister we're almost ready?"

"Will do." I smiled back and pulled her into a quick hug, then walked outside and started across the lawn. But passing Justin's office, I stopped to peer in the window. After a minute I opened the door.

At first I just wanted to sit in the center of the room and absorb the aura of it. But once I was there I had a losing battle with my brain, one side of which was trying to preach morality, while the desperate and ultimately stronger side decided that, since they just happened to be in reach, I might as well read through the papers on his floor. What I was looking for was a secret, some kind of clue about how I might tunnel my way into his soul. But what I found instead was pure magic.

The stories were short, some only one page, but together they shaped a world I hadn't seen for years, the world we'd traveled, me and Justin, hand in hand. I was Morwyn, the orphaned girl who (despite her blue face and occasional crabbiness) was irresistibly alluring. And Justin was the boy, Gaelin, who spent his time saving their world and other nearby planets, and who was fated to be Morwyn's one true love. As I read, the stories sloughed off the weight of the real world, leaving behind the simplicity of those days on the front porch, a time when the three of us were the only thing that mattered.

I was so entranced by the stories that I didn't hear Eve until her feet were right in front of my face. "Everybody's been looking for you," she said. Her voice sounded stilted and strange.

I dropped the page I was reading and jumped to my feet.

"Don't worry, I won't tell." Her gaze was level and appraising. "He's planning to marry Leslie, you know."

I bent to scatter the papers in some semblance of the disarray they'd been in before. "I doubt it."

"He's getting a ring and everything."

I looked up. "A what?"

"An engagement ring. He asked my opinion on styles. He's taking the ferry out next week. I told him I like oval marquise."

I tried to decipher her expression, but it was smooth,

completely unreadable, like she was reciting the periodic table or Latin verbs.

She tucked a strand of my hair behind my ear and smiled sympathetically. "He's planning to ask her when she graduates next spring, to keep her from going off to college. Don't let him know I told you, because I swore I wouldn't. It's just you've been so swoony lately, and I didn't want you getting your hopes up or anything."

"I don't have hopes," I said quickly. "I mean hell, if he'd marry Leslie, then I'm too good for him." How could he marry Leslie? Was she his passion? Had he even thought about me? "Do you think she'll say yes?"

Eve swirled her hair into a twist, tied it in a graceful knot. "All I can tell you is I've seen the way they look in each other's eyes. It's like magic. My guess is by this time next year she'll wear a ring on her finger and be knocked up." Eve waggled her eyebrows and grinned. "Bet you anything they've already done it."

I could see a change in her expression then, an expectation that pissed me off. She wanted something from me, although I wasn't sure what. "Well, they're awful young," I said, my voice tight. "I'd give them three years, tops."

At this, something like satisfaction flickered in Eve's eyes, but I smiled and pretended I didn't see it. Because there were times, in dealing with Eve, that you were happier if you didn't look too far.

I walked to LoraLee's that night. The air was cold, but thick with the aroma of wood-burning stoves sharpened by the ocean salt, a layering known only to people who stayed on the island year-round. I stood by her fence and watched through her window as she lit a candle and gazed into the flame. I'd seen her pray before, how the calm would wash over her face, smoothing off the lines and curves so she looked kind of unfinished, like one of the raw carvings to which she'd given a profile but no character.

LoraLee was never angry, never afraid. She owned less than anyone I'd ever known, but still she never seemed to long for the things she couldn't have. Even after time smoothed the edges, when Justin was long married and long gone, it was a kind of peace I doubted I'd ever have.

LoraLee stood to blow out the candle, then saw me. She opened her window, beaming. "Kerry, chile!"

I walked to her entryway, not wanting to talk, just to stand there in the doorway breathing in the honey scent of beeswax and candle smoke.

"Been days now since I seen you," she said.

I shrugged. "There's been school and all."

LoraLee looked at me for a long while, then finally raised her thick eyebrows. "You needs some tea."

"I'm okay."

She nodded and went to her bookshelf, reached for a thick book with stiff pages. I tried to peer over her shoulder, but she harrumphed and waved me away. She ran her finger down a page, mouthing words, then closed the book and slipped it back onto the shelf. "I got jus' the ress-pee. You bes' wait here."

It was The Book. I'd always known she must have one, couldn't hold the answers all in her head. And she'd left it there for me: serendipity. I stepped closer, listening to her kitchen sounds: cupboard doors, the swish snap of scissors. At the grind of the pestle she used for tea, I reached for it. The yellowed pages were filled with recipes, lists of strange herbs in sweeping calligraphic script. LoraLee went outside to pump water, and I flipped through the pages, delighting in their rich scent of dust and time. The crackle of the binding and scroll-work round the edges spoke of ancient truths, and I imagined the book was watching me read and conveying silent wisdom, filling me with a root of strength that reached down my back and through the floor.

The pages held mysterious titles like "Binding," "Polarity," and "Protection." Then a section on poisonous herbs that I flipped through quickly, like the paper itself might be leaching death. And then the section I wanted. I hugged myself and scanned the raised script.

In the kitchen the teapot started to whistle, and I jammed the book back onto the shelf. LoraLee shuffled into the room with a steaming mug that smelled of raspberry. She watched as I drank, nodding slowly as I sipped at the tea, bitter on the back of my tongue. My mind swam with the heat of the steam and with the tangle of learned ingredients chanting through my head.

"LoraLee," I said, "do you know magic?" It sounded stupid when I said it, so I ducked my head and faked a laugh. "That's not what I mean."

LoraLee smiled. "In town they says I's a witch."

I widened my eyes. "No they don't."

"S'okay, honey, I knows what they's sayin', people likes to talk. But there ain't no such thing as magic."

"I know that."

LoraLee shook her head. "But there is maybe such a

thing as shapin'. You can shape how you wants your life to be, and say spells to make it happen. That's what I do. That's what they calls witchcraf'. And sometime God listen, sometime He got better things to do."

I made my voice nonchalant. "What do you mean spells? What kind of spells?"

"Jus' spells what change the things aroun' you. Some peoples knows spells for power, for money. Some knows spells that makes sick people well. What I thinks is that it ain't so much the spells do the shapin'. What I thinks is that it's the wantin' make things happen."

I nodded but I felt a sudden sinking disappointment. I saw LoraLee sitting in her two-room shack decorated with things people threw away. I saw how her dress was torn at the hem and the cushion on her rocker dangled with loose threads. And I knew that if spells could work, LoraLee wouldn't choose to live this way.

Still, the rest of that afternoon I thought about it. I remembered the days I'd gone to her with a sick stomach or sick head. She'd stroked my forehead with peppermint water, fed me ginger tea. She'd pressed her fingers to my temples and told me stories about Africa and Atlanta until I fell asleep. LoraLee knew how to heal the sick and maybe that meant she knew more. Maybe it meant she knew how to make Justin love me, but just didn't want to say.

I cried all that night, silent, closed-mouthed tears. My insides felt close to bursting, like an overdone potato. Eve lay in the bed beside me, but she didn't seem to hear my clogged breaths. Or if she did, she chose to pretend that she didn't, perhaps allowing me my dignity. Close as we were, we both knew that there were times when closeness was beside the point.

As I lay in the dark, I imagined Leslie in her veil, dumb as a dead clam but still victorious. I imagined Justin holding her ringed hand and whispering his stories. I pictured him sharing the world where I'd fallen in love, everything that had once been sacred between us, and I cried.

Late the next morning, I woke after a fitful sleep to the sound of footsteps on the stairs. There was a knock on the bedroom door and Justin's voice, "Kerry?"

I bit my lips between my teeth and stumbled out into the hall. His eyes searched mine, and then his jaw stiffened and he lifted a thermos. "Eve said you were sick. Mom sent me over with soup. Jesus Murphy, you look like you've had your face stomped by a soccer shoe."

I felt my eyes sting and ran into the bathroom, slammed the door behind me.

Justin knocked on the door. "Kerry? You okay?"

I looked into the mirror. My nose was red, eyes swollen and dark, like a horrid caricature of myself.

"Kerry? What is it? You gonna be okay?"

I buried my face in my hands. "I look like crap!" Behind the wall of my hands I saw Leslie, her sparkling blue eyes which had probably never cried, her perfect little fingernails painted silvery seashell pink. No wonder he loved her.

"You're crying because of how you look?" He sounded lost. "Okay, either you're totally overreacting to my comment or you're way too vain."

"I'm not crying."

He didn't respond, probably pondering the absurdity of this statement.

I wiped my eyes and pulled my hair over my face, then pushed at the door.

Justin took one look at me and his face seemed to fold in on itself. He wrapped me in his arms, and I gulped a breath, tears freezing in my eyes. He stroked at my hair, his hands sending prickles down my back, through arms and legs. I couldn't move, I couldn't breathe, my heart slowed, beats drawn like they were pulsing through molasses.

"Oh Kerry, hush," he whispered. "It's okay. I know it's hard, you have to just let it out."

His words whispered at my hair. I clutched at his soft flannel shirt, then slowly reached out my tongue and licked it over the stitching on his pocket.

"I never see you cry, you or Eve. It's not healthy, Kerry, it'll never feel better unless you do." He pulled away, studied my face. "There's something else though, isn't there? Something happened."

I shook my head.

"I know you pretty well, and something's going on. I can see it in your eyes, you look like you're being torn apart."

"No. Nunh-unh," I said, but the funny thing was, this is what I'd been thinking all the night before, about one of his stories where a girl had literally been torn into two pieces when the boy she loved had left. Justin hadn't described the blood that must've been involved, the spilling out of guts, but I'd pictured how that kind of death would look, more revolting than romantic. Lying there, I'd felt that bleeding and spilling, and I'd known it was the worst way in the world for a person to die. Maybe his words were not just coincidence but some kind of sign, divine intervention, a way I could make him remember our world. I wiped at my face. "Hey, y'know what, Justin? You know what would help? Maybe you could read me some of your stories."

Justin stared at me like I'd gone off my rocker, and I thought I could read his mind. *Leslie never goes off her rocker,* is what he was thinking. I steeled my shoulders. "Like you did when we were kids. It used to make me forget everything, become somebody else."

Justin nodded slowly, considering. He finally smiled. "Didn't especially want to go into work anyway. If that's really what you want, really think it might help. But you have to promise not to laugh, or I'll sew your lips together. My feelings get hurt easily."

I wanted to jump, twirl Modern Movement pirouettes. Instead I rolled my eyes. "What a wimp," I said.

I dressed quickly and followed Justin to his office, my heart skipping with jumping-bean beats. I pictured how Eve might react when I told her, how she'd have to shrug and pretend she didn't care. And I'd tell her everything, the way he smiled at me, the expectation in his face, working on her until she was caught up in the thrill of it too.

In the office Justin knelt on the floor and began gathering loose pages, looking suddenly excited. "It's a real mess, not really shaped into any kind of story, just a bunch of stories that don't have any kind of chronology."

He stacked a pile of papers and rolled his sleeves to the elbows. I studied the veining on his arms as he sorted through the sheets of paper, the vulnerable hollow at the nape of his neck where the ends of his hair were sun-bleached to the color of beer. He finally threw the pile up into the air so that the stories fluttered around us. "Pick a page, any page."

I ran my finger over the scrawled script on the paper that had landed on my lap, then handed it to Justin. He glanced at it. "Okay, good choice."

He leaned beside me, resting on his elbow, and I closed my eyes and listened. His voice was smooth and deep and I fell into it, saw the marshes where fairies lived, saw little blue-faced Morwyn left stranded among the reeds.

"'For eight years Morwyn had lived there with the fairy folk,'" he read, "'so much time that her blue hair had grown long past her knees, enough time for her to wonder if there was more to learn from life. Each night she would gaze into the vast, star-stung sky, waiting for the future that felt like rushing, crushing waves against her chest. And watching her, the fairies saw what that future would bring, and they were afraid.'"

Justin stopped talking and I opened my eyes, found him watching my face intently. He blushed and glanced away. "You want to hear another one?"

And so we spent our day sorting through the pages, him leaning on one elbow, me on my back beside him with my vision blurred, listening and dreaming. I waited for the moments our eyes would meet, because each time he looked my way something passed between us, something silvery and thin as gauze. The afternoon light began to fade, but instead of switching on the lamp, Justin reached for a flashlight and read on, the two of us surrounded and held together by the dark.

When he'd finished, Justin sat up and gathered the papers into a pile. "This was amazing," he said. "Completely amazing. I've been writing this all down for months, but for some reason this is the first time I've actually sat to read the whole thing together." He smiled hesitantly. "So, you think it's any good?"

"It's totally incredible."

He traced his finger over the dim oval cast by the flashlight. "Know what I was thinking sitting here reading? Maybe I could make this about us, the two of us, a boy telling a girl the stories he's made up in his head. And they both get so caught up in the stories that they actually enter the world while he's talking, as Morwyn and Gaelin. Dream the same dream."

"About us?"

"We could name the world after us." He grinned. "Call it Ker-tin."

"Juserry," I said, playing along.

"Or last names? Barnacaine? Cainard? Canardia, how's that?"

I tried to bite back my smile. It was wonderful, not just a joining of names but a joining of souls, like a marriage. Justin pulled me into a quick hug and I thought how here it was, destiny coming together just in time. It was just like LoraLee always said, that destiny usually came to you disguised as a bang-up coincidence. "We have to celebrate," I said.

"Celebrate?"

"I'll cook you dinner. Over at my house tomorrow night."

"You can cook?"

"I'm an amazingly great cook, you'll see." I squeezed

my hands into fists. "I've got these special recipes I've really been wanting to try."

Justin smiled at me and brushed his knuckles against my cheek. Just the briefest touch, but it echoed through me and I had to bite my lip to keep from sighing. And maybe I was wrong but I thought Justin's eyes momentarily flickered a lighter blue. It almost seemed as if he'd felt something too.

6

I PLEADED A BELLYACHE. It was more or less true after all; my stomach felt like a washing machine on spin cycle, and I had way too much to do to waste the day in school. Half of my brain laughed at me, the other half steeled its shoulders and began to go down its list.

I bought frozen chicken and strawberries. Strawberry soup, the book had said, and the chicken should be cooked with apricots. I had never in my life tasted an apricot, and all I could find in the fridge was a jar of toast-crumb-littered marmalade, but it was orange and fruity; close enough.

Lettuce for salad. Dressing made of mayonnaise, brown sugar and vinegar, with poppy seeds I brushed off sandwich rolls. Apparently poppy seeds were supposed to engender lust. The dressing also called for dandelion leaves. Where the heck would I find dandelions this time of year? I remembered last spring spraying LoraLee's dandelions and pulling the withered stems. How long did it take for compost to decompose?

On the way to LoraLee's I knocked on the trunk of every tree I passed, which of course made the walk take significantly longer than was justifiable. Sometimes I wished my lucky number was two.

I jumped over the fence to her back garden, feeling utterly depraved. But honestly, nobody could consider stealing dead dandelions to be real stealing, and besides, I had no choice. I would rather have Justin fall in love with me naturally, but that just wasn't going to happen in time.

I dug through to the middle of the compost heap, where things seemed the least decomposed, the smell of green mixed with the smell of rot, like broccoli left in the refrigerator too long. Dandelions had been everywhere in LoraLee's garden (since her weed-control practices mostly consisted of hot pepper spray and lots of pulling) and I found them easily. Brown, yes, and covered with Lord knew what, but still pretty recognizable. I tucked them into my pocket, then went to LoraLee's door.

She was wearing an orange flowered dress with a pale blue apron, probably the only person in the country who could make those colors work. "Why Kerry, 'magine this," she said. "Don't you mos' often has school on a Tuesday?"

I waved my hand dismissively. "Teacher's conferences. LoraLee, could I ask you a question? Just for curiosity's sake." I gave her a quick, innocent smile and said, "I was just wondering if you ever heard of lovage root."

"Lovage root? Where you heard of that?"

I shrugged, thought fast. "In school. We're studying..." I flashed another smile. "Studying roots."

LoraLee eyed me carefully, then walked into the kitchen. She opened a cupboard door and gestured at rows of labeled peanut butter jars and margarine tubs filled with powders that were all minor variants of the same shade of brownish-gray. *Snake Moss* I saw, and *Betel Nuts.*

"You sees these here," she said. "These is the spices what I uses for my tea. Mix 'em right, and they makes goodness in your belly." She gave me a pointed glance. "Mix 'em wrong and you be sorry. This here the lovage root. It's for your heart, jus' like it sound."

She handed me a plastic bag of tan powder. I sniffed at it and detected the sweet earthiness I'd often tasted in her tea.

"I brew this for you when your heart were broke for missin' your daddy, and with a touch of raspberry oil besides."

She turned again to the cupboard. Pulse racing, I opened the bag of powder and stuffed a handful into my pocket with the decayed dandelion petals. I closed the bag as LoraLee lifted a jar of pink liquid. "Good for soothin' the soul," she finished.

I rubbed my hand against my jeans. "Do you think it really works?"

LoraLee inspected the bag I returned to her, then looked into my eyes. "It's difficult, matters of the heart."

I went to the window, rested my elbows on the chipped wooden sill. Even in the midday light, the sun seemed distant. I could blot it out with my thumb. "You ever been in love?" I said.

LoraLee made an odd grunting sound, then lowered herself into a chair by the table. "Oh, Kerry."

I sat beside her, suddenly wary. In a way, I'd never considered LoraLee a real person with real dreams and desires. I guess I'd thought she was above it.

"His name Hector," she said after a minute. "He live

with me in Atlanta some forty year ago, work hisself near to death jus' cos he haves a dream to travel up north and study for the ministry."

"Did he leave you?"

"Yep, he lef', but 'fore he go, he carve me this ring I wears." She slipped the thick wooden ring from her finger. "And he say, 'This ring my heart I gives to you, whilst I goes to find the Lord. Onest He tell me what best to do,' Hector say, 'onest I fix on my greater love, then I come back to reclaim my heart from you or to pledge eternity, one or the other.' "

I watched LoraLee's fingers caress the edge of the wooden circle. When I couldn't stand it anymore I asked, "So then what? What happened when he came back?"

LoraLee shrugged. "I's still waitin'."

I stared at her. "But it's been forty years."

"Forty year and I still has his heart." She slipped the ring back on her finger. "And he still haves mine, and I's still waiting."

I studied her face, not sure what to say, whether to console or commiserate. In the brightness of her eyes I saw dreams once so real they'd been played in two minds, now vaporous as birthday wishes. And I suddenly saw myself in forty years, saw the creases at my eyes as I watched Justin, gray haired, with Leslie by his side. They'd raised children and grandchildren and still held hands. They talked about the past and were glad for all of it. And I saw myself watching Justin with his greater love and still waiting to win back his heart.

* * *

I glanced at my watch. Two hours left. It was time to get dressed. I rooted through the closet I shared with Eve. I tried on and discarded an Indian skirt, a jeans skirt and peasant blouse, my tartan kilt. All wrong.

I began to panic. My striped pantsuit? God no, I looked like a mix between a clown and a convict. The pink bridesmaid's dress? It made me look like a Marshmallow Peep. My blue jumper? Way too conservative. Everything either made me look like I was trying too hard, or trying hard and failing miserably.

I glanced towards the door, then pulled out the grape costume Eve had tried on the other day, remembering how it hugged her hips and breasts like a second skin. It might look too sexy for this particular occasion, but then again wasn't sexy just what I wanted? I pulled it on carefully, looked in the mirror—

—and nearly cried out loud.

It was awful. My hair was frizzed with static, my face was red, eyes frantic. I looked like I was playing dress-up, like a little girl pretending to be a hooker.

I pulled off the dress and threw it onto the floor. But still I could see the horror of my monstrous purple reflection. Next to Leslie's pretty, perky perfection, I was like something that had been dragged up from the mud and left to rot.

I reached for the jumper I'd discarded and slipped it on, then pulled my hair behind my ears. Now, even if I looked like a preschooler, at least I didn't look like I was pretending to be anything else.

I smoothed careful makeup over cheekbones, lips, eyelashes, then began to play with hairstyles. When I heard the front door open, I hurriedly pulled the purple dress back onto its hanger.

Eve stamped up the stairs, calling down the hall. "Men are so freaking gullible." Her voice trilled with laughter. "You'd think a cop would be beyond it, like when they put on the uniform they should get a little more sane, but he was like a walking hard-on." She turned into the room and blinked. "Hey, what's going on?"

I slid a bobby pin into my hair. "Who's gullible?"

"Never mind. I thought you were sick."

"I was." I shrugged. "I'm better now. You think this looks better with tendrils in my face or without?"

Eve looked down at the pile of clothes on the floor. "With," she said quietly. "What're you doing?"

I smiled. "Getting dressed for dinner."

"Dressed up?"

"I'm having dinner with Justin." At the sound of his name I felt my heart doing little flips. "Just the two of us. I've been cooking."

"For Justin? You've got to be kidding. Does he know about this?"

"Of course he knows."

Eve made a face. "Really, Kerry, he's obviously not thinking of it the same way. Besides the fact that he's marrying Leslie, you have to realize he thinks of you like his little sister. If he dated you, it'd be like incest."

I didn't answer her, but inside I was seething. Mostly because I knew what she said was probably true. I knew he didn't sniff at my bottles of shampoo, pull my jeans from the clothes hamper just to touch where my legs had been. But I would change that. I would.

"Stop being bitchy," I said, and turned away before Eve could say any more.

But as I walked from the bedroom she said, "I'm sorry. Look, you want some help with dinner?"

I stopped, looking out at the hall.

"Not like I know much about cooking, but there's gotta be something I could do. Chop things up maybe."

"Okay," I said. "Okay, that'd be nice."

"Yeah, I *am* nice, aren't I? Why don't you go on down and I'll be there in a sec."

"Sounds good."

"By the way, you look real cute."

I smiled and gave her a quick hug. "Thanks."

She hugged me back, then smiled widely. "Yeah, Kerry, you look real... sweet."

Sweet. I studied her face. There was a kind of wildness in her eyes, and obviously she'd used the word on purpose. So I shrugged. "Well, good, because he goes for sweet. I mean hell, look at Leslie, she's like a pink gummy bear."

But the word echoed in my head as I ran downstairs. *Sweet.* Sweet as sugar, sweet as a baby. Sweet as a little girl in a baby jumper dreaming the impossible, tearing moldy dandelions into salad dressing like love was a chemistry equation.

I mashed the strawberries, added the lovage root and a sprinkling of dandelion leaves and dumped the mixture into a pot on the stove. I pulled the chicken from the fridge. It still looked frozen; that couldn't be good. I tried to warm it with my fingers, then spread it with orange marmalade and stuck it in the oven. I frowned at the temperature dial, then set it to five hundred degrees.

"Petit escargot flambé," Eve said from the doorway. She'd wrapped a white towel around her head. "Chef's hat," she said, grinning.

"God, Eve, only you could look glamorous in a turban."

"*C'est vrai, mademoiselle.* So what's left to do? Where's your first course?"

"I have soup," I said, nodding at the pot.

Eve raised her eyebrows. "It's pink."

"Yeah well. Listen, could you maybe do the salad? Lettuce is over there."

Eve nodded and began tearing the lettuce into a bowl. "So you and Justin, hunh? Guess you might as well go for it. It's not like stealing him away is a sin until they're actually married."

"I'm not stealing him away, Eve. It'll be his decision. If it's meant to happen, it'll happen."

She shrugged. "Right. So has he given you any sign that it might happen? Like flirted with you or touched you when he didn't have to?"

I wiped my hands on my jumper. "I don't know. Not exactly."

"Ah," Eve said.

I waited for her to continue, but she just reached for a knife and began to hum tunelessly.

"Stop acting like you're the expert on men. I just have to show him how right it would be. Leslie doesn't know him like I do. There's something between us that nobody on the outside would understand."

Eve watched me for a minute, then nodded. There was a strange flatness in her eyes, like they'd been covered by eye stickers.

I glared at her, daring her to say whatever it was she was dying to say, but she stayed silent, concentrating on the lettuce. I left her there and went out to start the fire. I stared into the flames and imagined Justin watching the orange glow on my face, stoking the fire to the croon of Johnny Mathis from the radio and realizing it was me he really loved. This would work. It would have to.

What next? What next? I lit the tapered white candles on the dining table and stepped back. LoraLee's book had mentioned using a pink or green tablecloth, and after a frantic search I'd finally ended up dressing the table with the ribbon-woven, pink-flowered sheets that had covered our beds in early girlhood, when we'd still been entranced with ribbons and pink flowers. With the candles, the effect was actually pretty romantic.

I strode back to the kitchen. Eve was stirring the soup. "Strawberry? That's pretty weird."

I checked my reflection in the oven door. "It's exotic."

"If you say so. It was Brad Carrera by the way, the gullible cop. He's just walking by and I give him this half smile, the kind that doesn't show your teeth, and he winks at me and says, 'Hey, beautiful.' And then, get this, he spins around to watch me walk. I look over my shoulder and there his eyes are, on my butt."

"Officer Carrera? Jeez! I'd've thought he'd have better taste."

She smirked, but then her smile suddenly faded. "So you really think he'll go for all this?"

I tasted the soup, then glanced at her. "You think there's such a thing as destiny?"

"Destiny?" She looked at me funny. "Like Mom leaving and Daddy dying? Is that destiny?"

"You know what I mean."

Eve shrugged. "Whatever. Maybe everybody has a destiny. But what I think is it's usually the opposite of what you thought it would be. I mean look at us. Look at most people around here. They work their butts off half the year and freeze them off the other half. And most of the time they're completely miserable."

I watched her silently, then pulled the steaming pot of soup from the stove. "Thanks for the vote of confidence."

"Look, forget it. I'm sorry, okay?"

"Bitch," I said.

She smiled. "Asshole."

"Obviously you're jealous."

"Yeah, because I'm sure it's fun to be delusional."

There was a thumping on the front door and I jumped. Too soon! Too soon! Eve squeezed my shoulder. "I'll go out the back."

I nodded and ran to the dining room. I set the soup pot on the table, smoothed back my hair, squeezed Daddy's key necklace for luck and ran into the hall. "Come in!" I called in a voice too singsong.

Justin pulled open the door. His hair was disheveled and his eyes seemed almost mournful with fatigue. He looked from my jumper to the woodstove to the lit candles, and then to his stained blue jeans. "Oh," he said. "I should change."

My cheeks grew hot. "Oh no, don't change. I was just dressed up because I went to church." Where had that come from? I made my voice somber. "I wanted to pray for Daddy, to visit him."

Justin's face softened. "Oh, that's good. Sure."

"So come on in. Take off your coat and everything, I have dinner in the oven. You want a Coke?"

Justin slid off his coat. "You look nice," he said.

I shrugged. "Don't know why I dressed up to visit Daddy. Guess I just figured on the off chance he's up there watching, I'd want him to see I'm doing okay."

"If he's up there watching, I'm sure he's glad to see it," Justin said, following me into the dining room.

"So sit," I said. When I stirred it, the soup looked better, thicker, pink juice with flecks of black, no sign of the dead dandelions. I poured it into two bowls.

Justin sat and stared at the soup, then smiled at me and reached for his spoon. "Strawberry?"

"Strawberry soup. Got the recipe from a book."

I studied Justin's face as he lifted his spoon. He held the soup in his mouth for a long while, then finally swallowed it down and nodded. "Really good," he said.

I grinned. "Thanks." My heart thudded so loudly I was sure he must be able to hear it. I watched him make his way through the bowl, watched the gentle bulk of his forearms and shoulders, the swell of chest muscles under his shirt. I was nourishing him. From my hands into his body.

I looked down at my lap and wracked my brains for conversation. "Beautiful day out, hunh? I love this time of year." And then I grimaced. How banal could you get? To distract myself from my banality, I dug into the soup.

And nearly gagged.

Now that it was hot, the soup tasted horrible, like regurgitated cough syrup. But Justin was somehow finishing his bowl, so maybe his tastes were different. Maybe he liked strawberry puke.

I whisked his bowl away. "Well, there's salad next, and I'll check on the chicken."

I strode into the kitchen, rested my cheek against the oven door, then suddenly smelled the smoke. I yelped and flung the oven open. The top of the chicken was black, its sides still pink, and I scowled at it like it had betrayed me. Maybe I could scrape it, add more marmalade. With all the time I'd spent watching Mrs. Caine cook, why hadn't I ever looked at oven temperatures?

But next was salad. Salad would be safe. Salad with dressing, then burnt chicken, then tea. And then, maybe a kiss. Maybe.

"Doin' good, Ker."

I whirled around. Eve was sitting at the kitchen table, chin in hands, watching me.

"What're you doing here?" I hissed.

"Just making sure you're getting along okay. Besides, this is the best entertainment I've had all year."

"Well, get out. I can't talk to him if I know you're out here."

"Fine, fine, I'm going." She stood. At the door she stopped and turned. "But you want my honest opinion, Justin doesn't feel the same as you. Just my opinion, but don't make a fool of yourself or anything."

I glared at her. "Well, gee, thanks for the advice." I watched until she slipped out the back door, then turned the oven down to two hundred, put the tea on to boil and walked back to the dining room. I sat at the table and gripped the seat of my chair, trying to shake back a deep, pounding nausea.

Justin eyed me. "So you said there's salad?"

I jumped up. "I forgot!"

"It's okay. Listen, can I ask you something personal? It's really personal, actually."

He was going to ask if I liked him. I'd have to give a fake you're-full-of-it laugh. "Okay," I said weakly.

"I was just wondering, and you don't have to answer if you don't want, but I was wondering, when you pray to your dad, what kind of things do you say?"

I shrugged. "I just tell him about what's happening in my life, things I'm feeling. Kind of like writing in a diary."

Justin touched my hand, a light brush of skin on skin. "Do you tell him that you're doing okay? You're happy?"

I looked at the tingling spot where his fingers had been, almost expecting it to be a different color, pink or gold. "I'm okay," I said. "I mean, happiness is relative, but yeah, I'm not unhappy."

"Because when I saw you yesterday morning, I just got scared. You always seem fine on the outside, you and Eve are both so good at covering your feelings. But I know how much it must hurt."

"I guess. But we're getting used to it." I smiled quickly. "So let's have salad."

The kitchen was empty, Eve's turban in a pile on the floor. I'd almost expected her to be there at the table, I'd almost hoped for it. But as I walked to the door to peer out into the night, I saw a scrap of paper wedged between window and frame. SORRY, it said, in Eve's block print. I lifted it, studied it as if that one word could tell me something. I wasn't sure if it made me feel better or worse. Finally I folded the note and slipped it into my pocket, because if anything happened that night with

Justin, I wanted some part of her, some sign of her contrition to be there.

When I got back with the lettuce and tea, Justin was standing, looking into the warmth of the woodstove.

He glanced at me. "I want to show you something, Kerry. I do this a lot, imagine different places for my stories, and I think I've felt where your dad is. I think I could show you." He reached for my hand.

I felt myself smiling and I tried to stop, but my lips felt too distant to control. "I try and picture it sometimes," I said, "the place he'd be watching from. But all I can come up with is stupid and fake, angels walking on clouds and playing harps. He'd be so bored he'd take the next train back to earth."

Justin sandwiched my hand between both of his. "I'll show you, okay? Close your eyes."

I stared at him, my heart galloping like it was trying to get out from my ribs, then slowly closed my eyes.

"It's not really something you can see, not a place. Just feel yourself sliding away, losing your body so you're nothing and everything both."

I peeked through my lashes. Justin's eyes were closed, a twitching behind his lids. I studied the tiny mole on his cheek, imagining how it might feel to kiss it.

"You feel it? How your head starts swirling away? That's where I find my stories, way back in that nothingness. That's Canardia."

"Yes," I said. I wanted to curl my whole body into his palm, lie between his two hands and be enfolded. And suddenly I knew I had to say it. I pulled my hand away. "I heard you're getting engaged."

Justin's eyes snapped open and his face sharpened, as if he were awakening from a dream. "You heard what?"

"To Leslie. I heard you're proposing to Leslie next spring." I shook my head. "It's okay, you don't have to pretend. Eve told me."

"If I'm getting engaged, I wish somebody would tell *me*. Eve said—"

"You're getting a ring." The words flooded from me like tears. "Eve told me all of it, how you're proposing to Leslie before graduation to make sure she doesn't go off to school."

Justin's face was red. "So, Kerry, you guys have my life all planned out?"

I stared at him, and he shook his head. "I'm nineteen years old, you know? The thought's never even crossed my mind. And Leslie, I mean don't get me wrong, I like her a lot, but I'm not ready to spend the rest of my life with her."

"You're not getting married?" He wasn't getting married? He wasn't? Wasn't? "I love you," I said.

Justin made an odd choking sound; his face went pale. Not a good sign at all.

But maybe he hadn't heard. Please God, don't let him have heard! I grabbed the teapot from the table, steam sweating my face. "So let me give you some tea."

"I know you do."

I jumped away, dropped the teapot, lovage root tea scalding the front of my jumper. My face was frozen, mouth open, couldn't think, couldn't breathe, so I choked back a sob and started to run. I ran from the room and out the front door. I would run to the wharf, run off the dock, into the ocean, to Daddy, disappear.

But as I reached the drive, Justin's hand wrenched at the straps of my jumper, pulled me backwards so I fell against his chest. His kisses rained onto my head, down my temple, past my ear, down my cheek to my lips. I grabbed him, pressed against him and he made a choking sound and froze.

We stood there, faces barely an inch apart, breathing each other's breath and then he pulled away. Time stood still, fractions of seconds that lasted an eternity as he looked into my eyes, his face unreadable, open and closed at once. "I'm sorry," he whispered. "I'm sorry." And then he stumbled backwards, turned and ran. And I sank to my knees and watched him, watching even after he'd vanished into the night.

TWO

Separation

March
2007

7

THE FERRY FROM POINT JUDITH was more empty than not, carrying more supplies than people. The choppy waves roiled my stomach, rhythmic lurches that tried to throw me onto my butt as I tapped my foot in beats of four. The wind was biting, the drizzle gnawing against my face, but I stood there outside because I somehow needed to. Maybe to make this return real in a way that called for all the senses: piercing echoes of the foghorn, ocean smell, spray and taste, and the first possible glimpse of land.

I'd packed only three days' worth of clothes, not because I planned on leaving but because I couldn't imagine staying. I'd packed those clothes and my reminders: an empty bottle that had once held poisoned liquor and the torn letters Eve and I had written to Justin the night before I'd left. I'd never read Eve's letter, had never been able to summon the fortitude to piece it together. But even in pieces the letters were a reminder of the dark sides of Eve, just as the empty liquor bottle was a reminder of myself.

I hadn't told Justin I was coming, and now I wished to God that I had. Because what if I showed up and Justin said, *Oops, sorry, big mistake! Turns out she'd rather eat her arm than see you!*

Somehow I'd found myself on this boat, but it wasn't in my nature to be impulsive. It wouldn't have surprised me just then if my body jumped ship and tried to swim on home. Or at least swam to a phone and called. If I'd called, then he'd have been prepared, which meant I might have been too, by proxy. And when I saw him I could've said, *Hey, I made it,* maybe shaken his hand like we were just old friends. Now I had no idea what I'd say, if I'd be able to speak, or if I'd just stand there with my mouth open like an idiot.

Then, out of the expanse of gray ocean, the North Lighthouse rose into view, followed by the sharp pitch of red clay bluffs that guarded the land from the Atlantic. Coming closer so fast, all so misleadingly tranquil, hardly a sign of human presence and no sign of the nightmare I'd lived. I was here. I was here, and I suddenly wanted to lunge for it, swallow it whole like I had some kind of teenage crush. I'd almost forgotten the feeling. It had been years since I'd loved anything.

From the deck, the view was strikingly the same: moored boats and returning fishermen, the harborside with its postcard-like rows of Victorian hotels and saltbox houses, marred only by the conveniences of parked cars and the Old Harbor takeout, its umbrella-topped outdoor tables folded in concession to the rain. Except for paint colors and the addition of electric lighting, the street had remained more or less unchanged since the Civil War.

I climbed from the ferry, trying to see it like a tourist

would, the sleepy gray town no more than a disappointment in the drizzly cold. And here was Daddy's dock. How could it have changed so little when I'd changed so much? Other men used it now, I could see that, had set up their own kitschy billboards and promises, but regardless it would always belong to Daddy.

I knelt on the damp wood by the second support beam, ran my fingers along the splintered plank. The initials Justin had gouged into the dark cedar with a screwdriver, JC+KB, were still there just above the water line. *Ten years from now,* he'd said, *we'll come back and show our kids how we used to carve up public property. Won't they be proud?*

I wandered the winding streets on foot, past the fences built from ocean-smoothed stones that swirled in sighs and wisps over the rolling hills; past the rocker-graced front porches with chimes that gonged and hummed like ancient cowbells; past the fields upon fields sweeping with wheat grass, flattened by the rain.

Walking down Ocean Avenue, I saw that even the shops were the same: Eisner's boutique where Eve and I stole a leather skirt after the badness started escalating, one of the last days I let myself trust her; the old printing press with its greasy windows and weed-choked steps, where once a group of tourists had stopped me, had handed me their camera and posed as if the dilapidation was something picture-worthy. Now I hurried past, scared to look in windows, scared it would somehow tunnel me back to a time when my mind was so dark, my thoughts so sour I could literally feel them burn inside me.

Up towards the center of the island were the smaller

homes with peeling shingles, the lower-priced inns further from the ocean, a cattle farm, a horse farm and the Island Cemetery. Daddy's cemetery. You could see pretty much everything up here: New Harbor to the left, Old Harbor to the right, the gentle dip and sway of hills that slid into the sea, the faded flags at the graves of veterans hanging limp as laundry.

Daddy's grave was tucked beside a low stone wall, overgrown and neglected. I knelt before it and leaned my cheek against the stone, its edges cold and soft as a dead hand. "I'm sorry it's been so long," I whispered. "I never forgot."

It was one of those unfortunate quirks of memory, though, that what I remembered most of all was not so much Daddy in life as the time I spent here with him like this, holding his carved stone like a surrogate, telling him everything and feeling his empathy. I told him about Justin, about Eve's drinking and her men, about the night I'd steered his boat with another man's blood under my nails. I told him everything until the guilt was my own and I grew too ashamed to tell.

The last time I'd spoken to Daddy, I'd lain here prostrate on this ground, wishing he'd pull me down to join him so we could lie there side by side. And then as now I'd risen, mud on my knees, realizing it was too late to ask for his help; my decisions, the consequences, were all my own.

I walked down the sharply sloped hill, feet slogging through waterlogged canvas. I strode up our street, a narrow dirt road that had no name. Past the huge oak with the knothole Justin had widened so he could practice his pitching, and then, too fast, there was home.

I stood by the wide dirt drive we'd shared with the Caines, almost expecting to hear a call for dinner, see Justin returning from work, shirt stained and cuticles ridged with oil. I searched for the words of greeting I'd use, even knowing there could be no words. And then I stopped short.

She was on the porch.

She shouldn't be sitting there, it was all wrong. I'd pictured this again and again, and each time was the same. I'd knock and she'd open the door and step back, startled. Her eyes would fill with tears. "I'm so sorry, Kerry," she'd say. It had to be that way, repentance behind a door, because I knew if I saw her face before she saw mine, I'd have to turn and run.

I pulled at the iron key strung about my neck and felt its familiar tug against my skin. One step closer. She was on the porch swing beneath an army blanket I thought I recognized. She wore something on her head, a black hat or a kerchief.

One step closer. Her eyes were closed and I could see, oh God, it wasn't her, it was me in forty years, translucent skin draping sharp angles of cheek and nose and chin, mossy sprinkles of brown dotting her temples and sideburns beneath the creased black scarf. Her face was bare, no eyebrows or lashes, making her look naked and startled.

It wasn't Eve and so my knees unlocked; I ran forward and dropped to the ground by her feet. She opened her eyes and looked into my face, no surprise in her expression, no joy or pain, only questioning, like she couldn't think who I was or why I'd be there. So I held her, rain-soaked hair clinging to my cheeks, wet blouse heavy on my breasts, my head against her lap, the smell of ginger from her mug. And for that second the years disappeared. For that first second before I really saw her face, my arms reaching around her unimaginably narrow waist, for that first second I felt like I'd come home.

8

I DON'T KNOW how long I knelt there on the porch, my head in Eve's lap, waiting for her to speak. But she didn't. She didn't cry or move to touch me. Only her legs shifted under my weight as she exhaled a long and level breath. I pulled away.

I've heard that eyes are a distinguishing characteristic, that from babyhood on they never change. But it turns out that isn't true. I didn't know the eyes that watched me, dry and guarded. It was like Eve had cried enough to last a lifetime, and now she was already dead.

"I knew you'd come."

I let her die. "I should've come sooner."

"It's good that you didn't. You missed the worst of it, and now all that's left is the waiting."

"I would've come."

Eve smiled then, but it wasn't her smile. It showed her teeth and pressed wrinkles in her hollowed cheeks. "For yourself, or for me?" she said.

I shook my head and she stood and patted my shoulder, a quick dismissive touch. "Justin called you, I guess. I knew he wouldn't be able to stop himself. I'm sure he'll be thrilled you're here. Come on in."

I saw without wanting to see the strange flatness of

the deflated breasts under her sweater and the seat of her jeans hanging loose against her body. Shake her and her bones would probably rattle like a maraca.

"Sorry 'bout the mess," she said as I opened the door. "We hardly ever have guests anymore, and cleaning's not exactly one of my priorities."

How bizarre, the casualness of this, as if I were just a visiting friend. There was a heaviness in my chest, like my heart and stomach were all one solid mass, and I wanted so much just to say *Fuck it all* and hold her, pull her so close I'd be able to feel her again. It was obvious, though, that if I did she'd pull away.

This was like a twisted dream, this hallway to someone else's home, the bottom step where I'd learned to tie my shoes, Eve standing above me, instructing where to tuck the laces. But now the hall was dressed in Victoriana and even smelled different, like old food, like a motel restaurant. It was distorted to something else entirely, and I suddenly lost all sense of direction. Which way to the kitchen? Where do these stairs go?

We walked into the den, now crowded by a white hospital bed. Eve sat on the bed and I stood beside it, trying not to stare at the bony wheelchair set where a rocker used to be. As I turned from it she reached for my wrist, held it for a brief second, then let her hand drop to her side. "Gillian's over at Mom and Dad's," she said.

For a second I was afraid she might be speaking from a cancer-induced brain funk, then realized with a slightly sick feeling that by *Mom and Dad* she must mean the Caines. "How are they?"

"Same old, same old, Dad saving the bikes and Mom saving the earth. They take care of Gillian every day after school. What with me on my last legs and Justin locked upstairs with his books, they've been totally indispensable. That's where he is now, in case you're wondering, which of course you are. Upstairs writing or staring out the window. He seems to think they're both equally productive."

Justin was upstairs. I reached for the blanket at the end of the bed and wrapped it over my shivering shoulders.

"Look at your face. You're thinking I look like shit, right? Sometimes I catch a glimpse of myself in the mirror and think some crackhead broke into the house." She shrugged. "I feel better than I look, though. This is remnants from the chemo, but now I've stopped I'll beef up, probably just in time to kick the bucket."

"You don't look bad," I said, knowing how it would sound, an empty platitude, like trying to convince a kid that her hooked nose and buckteeth were actually cute.

"Watch this," Eve said, her eyes glinting with merriment, becoming for a brief second the eyes I'd known. She reached for a button by the side of her bed. A chiming doorbell sounded from upstairs. "This thing comes with all the gizmos. Not that I need them yet, but it'll be useful in a few weeks when I don't have the breath to call them downstairs to watch me die."

"Eve..."

"Can't wait a few weeks? Well, it might be a few days or it might be months, nobody knows for sure. Makes it kind of exciting, doesn't it? Like playing the lottery, will it be today? Justin went and bought this damn bed and chair instead of renting, like he thought it would make me live longer. Guess he couldn't deal with the prospect of having to estimate a duration of rental." She flashed a grin, more a stretching of lips than a smile.

I shook my head. "Please, don't."

"It's okay, I don't want to talk about it either, there's no point. It's why Justin called you, I guess. He thinks there's something I can learn or some peace I should reach, but really I'm way beyond peace. There's no time and I don't have the energy, and besides, once I'm dead, who cares?" She nodded over my shoulder. "Speak of the devil."

"Honey?"

I looked up and there he was, and all of it hit me at once. Hundreds of remembrances flashed instantaneously through my head, of the storytelling afternoons, of secrets whispered and silent, of the night I'd first told him I loved him, and then the last night when I'd learned the pointlessness of love.

Justin's cheeks flushed and his eyes seemed to cloud. Everything I'd needed to see on Eve's face was in his, the pain, the joy, the bitter remorse. His palms opened to face the ceiling and he looked from me to Eve and back, then strode forward to pull me into his arms.

I inhaled his smell—wood, moss and pine—as if it could press out the blackness that had numbed me. I wanted to take from him what I'd needed from Eve, but I could feel her eyes at my back. I pulled away.

Eve's face was tight, watching us, eyes red with the tears she hadn't shed in greeting. And I suddenly understood she was afraid.

* * *

Eve sat in bed, hunched against the wall, her face gone slack and her eyes glazed over like the black marbles in the heads of stuffed animals. "Just a minute," Justin said. He kissed Eve's temple, then lifted her, easily as one would lift a child, settling her down to the pillow.

"She gets like this sometimes," he said, "like she's too tired even to close her eyes. It's the morphine that does it. She takes more than she needs because it's easier just to sleep."

"Jesus, Justin." How would I stand this, stand being here unless I just turned off, forgot who I was and who she'd been?

"It's why I put the bed down here. She gets dizzy climbing stairs, and a month ago she fell. I hate it taking up our den, though, it's like this constant reminder. Not like we need a reminder, I mean look at her."

I watched as he tucked her under the stark white sheets, fighting the dark heaviness that seemed dead set on becoming tears.

With his face turned in profile, I could study him closely for the first time. At first I'd thought there was no change; he had the same full lips, the heavy-lidded eyes. But there were little things that disoriented me because they didn't fit: the dimples lengthened to deeper grooves by his mouth, the slight graying at his temples and a kind of muting of intensity in his eyes, a distance. It drained something in me to see it, made me want to reach for him, but also to turn away. He brushed his hand over Eve's eyes to close them, and I saw his face flush with pain and love. I focused on the ugly steel rails framing Eve's bed so I wouldn't have to interpret the clutch in my chest.

"Come on," Justin said. "We'll get some tea."

I sat at the kitchen table as Justin filled mugs, gazing over at the wall. Still hung with crayoned drawings, but now printed with someone else's name. I examined the signatures as if they could tell me something about the girl behind them. A kindergarten scrawl, a wide-looping script, *Gillian,* the first *i* dotted with a heart. I felt Justin's eyes on me but didn't want to look up, because exchanging glances didn't seem like a good idea. I shivered and cupped my hands around the warm mug.

"It's good you decided to come," he said finally. "She needs you here."

And then the tears came after all, stinging hot. I looked away, trying to steady my breath. "Doesn't seem like she needs anybody," I said.

He raised his eyebrows at me, reproaching.

I inhaled the steam from my mug, let it condense on my nose and eyelids. "I don't know what to do for her. I don't know her anymore."

"The fact you came is enough, at least for a start. She needs to know everything she's done is forgivable before she can forgive herself."

"It's not forgivable, Justin. I can be here in spite of it, but I guess I'm not a big enough person to go beyond that."

Justin's face seemed to sag. "She's been a good wife, Kerry, a great mother. You need to let it go as much as she does. She's your sister, for God's sake."

"We'll put that on her tombstone: Eve Barnard-Caine, good wife, great mother, and also she was a sister."

The front door rattled open. There was the sound of stamping boots.

Justin glanced at me, then called, "In here, Gillie."

Footsteps slapped down the hall, stopping at the door to the den. I imagined Gillian standing there, watching her mother, maybe reaching to touch her hand.

The footsteps continued to the kitchen. "Hey, Daddy? I was gonna—" She froze and for a second I could see her as she was, this beautiful eleven-year-old girl with wise eyes. But as she looked at me her expression changed, melted, became more like the younger child I'd seen on the jackets of Justin's novels, the picture I'd held in my mind.

Her nose reddened and she began to tremble, her hands opening, closing, opening, closing, and then with a sob she ran to me, buried herself against my chest. I looked up at Justin, shocked, then wrapped my arms around her, cradled her head. I could scarcely breathe, was dizzy with love for this girl I'd never met, and so I clutched at her like she would save me, this fusing of Eve and Justin, and also of me.

I looked over her shoulder, into Justin's face. He watched us with his fist against his mouth, eyes clouded.

Suddenly, Gillian pulled away and stumbled backwards. She looked from me to Justin and back, face fragmented with confusion. She opened her mouth as if to speak, then spun away and ran.

"Gillie?" Justin strode after her. "Sweetie?"

I followed them to the den, stunned, numb like I was muffled by a thick coat of fur, and I watched as Gillian crawled into the bed beside her mother and curled, baby-like, head resting on Eve's chest. Justin watched them, face flushed, then edged forward to smooth the blanket over them both.

I stood there for as long as I could stand it, then backed away to the kitchen. *Not anymore;* I made it echo through my head, a chant, a warning. *Not mine. None of it. Not anymore.*

A shuffling woke me sometime in the dead hours before dawn. I lay there a minute, disoriented, then turned my head towards the noise. In the shadows I made out a hunched form on the floor next to the bed. "Justin?"

He didn't answer, didn't move. I heard a gulping wet intake of breath. "Justin?" I whispered again.

"I'm glad you're here," he said. "I really am."

I watched him for a minute, then reached out my hand.

He took it, held it to his cheek. "When you're asleep, in this lighting you could be sixteen again."

"How long were you sitting there?"

He didn't answer, so I combed his sweat-damp hair back from his temple, not knowing what to feel, not knowing what was right to feel. But when he climbed into bed beside me I let him; the two of us curled against each other, minutes, then hours drifting in and out of sleep, waking with the weight of his head against my chest, the whisper of his hair at my neck. It didn't feel wrong; it was like comfort, a fullness that I'd almost forgotten how to feel. And when the room finally began to fringe with the shadows of dawn, he touched my cheek and pulled away, closing the door behind him.

* * *

The sun filtered through my eyelids, a late morning sun, more cold white in it than yellow. How late had I slept? I lay awhile with my eyes closed, in the bed that had been Daddy's. I lay there thinking of the weight of Justin's head on me, still smelling the scent his hair had left on my pajama top, the homemade honey shampoo Mrs. Caine must still brew. I thought of the parts of this house that were irrefutable evidence of our childhood: the laundry chute in the front hall that Daddy boarded up after Eve slid down it, the memory of Eve's hooting war cry and the presence of the nailed boards, both precious. The lines in the closet that marked our growth: no names, only years to denote them because our heights, mine and Eve's, were always the same.

And then I thought of Eve and I didn't want to open my eyes. Wanted to stay here shut behind my own eyelids, my own space where, if things never exactly felt right, they were at least familiar.

It was the sound of Gillian's voice from downstairs that finally got me up. I dressed quickly and walked downstairs, following the sounds to the kitchen, where Eve, facing away from me, was spreading peanut butter on bread. I stood outside the doorway, listening.

"What's it look like?" Gillian said.

"It's beautiful, Gillian, big stone buildings and quiet like in a church. All these people walking around with armloads of books, or sitting in the courtyard discussing physics."

"You mean *gym*? How come?"

Eve smiled. "Physics, not phys ed. It's a kind of science. I don't know anything about it either, except that you'd have to be smart to discuss it."

"How come you didn't go there?"

"'Cause I'm not one of those smart people. I just didn't ever care enough about school to even think about college. But you, you're much smarter than me. Someday they'll have a quote in their catalogues. They'll say something like 'The University has graduated such notables as the eminent Gillian Caine.'"

"Ha-ha," Gillian said, and then her eyes flicked my way. Her face hardened and she stepped away from the door. "We should go soon."

"Think Miss Jasper'll mind if I miss the Conservancy meeting this afternoon? I think I'm quitting it anyway. I don't really care about birds and flowers anymore, least not as much as they do. Hell, I don't think I ever did. I mean, who gives a damn if we lose more scrub grass? Your dad just made me join to keep me busy. It was that or the quilting circle, and those old ladies cutting up fabric and sewing it back together would drive me absolutely nuts."

Gillian's eyes were still on me. I tried to smile, the wide, fake smile you give young babies to make sure they understand you're being friendly. Her mouth twitched and she looked up at Eve. Eve turned and raised her eyebrows like she was surprised I was still in her home. "So you're up," she said.

"You going somewhere?"

"Taking the ferry out to Connecticut. Justin and I went to see Yale a few years back when we were traveling for a book tour. I've been telling Gillian I'd take her when I felt better, and this seemed like as good a time as any."

I waited for her to ask me along. Maybe this was what she was thinking, that it might be good to spend time with me away from the pressing memory of these walls. But she only packed her sandwiches into paper bags and turned to Gillian. "We better take off. Next ferry's not till noon."

I searched her face. Still Eve, I could see that now where I hadn't seen it yesterday; same crooked smile, same brusque but graceful swing of her hips as she walked. But somehow different, something missing, like varnish sanded off a table. She passed me, Gillian in tow, pulling coats from the hall closet.

"When do you think you'll be back?" I said.

"Not sure. But don't wait on dinner, I never eat much anyway and I'll buy Gillian some McDonald's. Justin went downtown for the paper, but he'll take care of you when he gets home."

Gillian turned to look at me, her face still and hard, then took her mother's hand and walked out the door.

I stood there a minute unmoving, dizzy with the sudden strange sense of the room expanding, emptying, too much space around me. *Hey!* I wanted to call. *Wait for me!* I watched their blurred figures through the frosted glass of the front door, listened to the crackle-crunch of gravel as they drove away. I sank onto the bottom step, trying not to think what this meant, her leaving me the day after I'd arrived.

It was then I noticed the new runner that led from the hallway up the stairs. I fingered it, the beige shag now a beige oriental. And clean. All bloodstains gone.

I stared at it, the memories mounting like stacked dominoes, tipping one on another on another. Set so long ago and perfectly placed and stored beneath layers of dust. But now laid flat beneath this new rug and that closed door, my sister on the other side.

I touched the places where his blood had been, a drop on the landing, a smudge on the second stair. In the years I'd been away I'd wondered how they could stand to live in this house, with everything that had happened here. But now I realized this was the biggest difference between us. That where the past would always haunt me until I died, all Eve and Justin had to do was change a rug, and they were able to forget.

October 1993

9

BACK THEN I believed in magic. Maybe part of me still does. Part of me thinks the night of our first kiss was magic, and that the sickness after was recrimination for venturing into the forbidden, like the Little Mermaid's bleeding feet. A small price to pay.

I didn't sleep at all that night. In the beginning I was sure it was my racing thoughts that made me feel so weird, but when I had to run to the bathroom, doubled over in pain, it was obvious that there must be something more.

Later, lying with my cheek against the toilet seat, I remembered the kiss (THE KISS!), and between waves of nausea, the brightness of it was enough to make me dizzy. I replayed it over and over, a million times over. What was Justin thinking now? And why did he run away? Was he feeling fear? Mortification? Pity? I staggered back to bed and collapsed on the covers. Eve rolled over and stared, her mouth freezing mid-yawn.

The nausea reeled back through my belly and I brought my knees up to my chest. Eve came to kneel by my bed. "Oh God, Kerry, you... what happened?"

I squeezed my eyes shut and rolled against the wall.

Eve ran to the bureau, brought back a hand mirror. I

opened my eyes, and in a wave of dizziness I saw myself, unrecognizable, lips swollen Betty Boop–like over my protruding tongue. I pressed my hands against my face.

Eve sat by me and began to stroke lightly at my hair. I imagined her hand was Daddy's hand and then my mother's, the same long fingernails and faint scent left over from the morning's spray of perfume. I heard her hushing voice and looked into her eyes, and then like a sudden plummeting over an edge, I remembered her words the day before, *He's planning to marry Leslie, you know.* I remembered the tilt of her head when she spoke and a sort of complacency, and focusing on a tiny hard core inside the haze of my nausea, I glared into Eve's eyes and pushed her hand away.

The next day Mrs. Caine brought me to the medical center. Dr. Bradley said I'd had an allergic reaction and set me up on one of the center's five beds. He dripped electrolytes into my body and gave me a shot of antihistamine which fogged my brain and shrank my tongue and lips back to size. Justin was brought in hours later.

When the doctor asked what we'd eaten, I couldn't think what to say. Tell him we ate rotted flowers and root powder? They'd lock me up and throw away the key. I finally said we'd eaten "maybe not all the way cooked" chicken, which seemed to satisfy them well enough.

Back home I slept, nursed tea and toast and slept some more. My dreams were cocaine-wild, ten-dimensional, infused with colors and textures I'd never seen before. I dreamed of Justin at different ages, in different forms. I saw him grow from baby to child to man, and then still growing, arms to branches, hair sprouting shoots and leaves. "Kerry..." he called, voice echoing off tunnels of rock. I wondered if it hurt, becoming a tree.

"Kerry?"

I opened my eyes. Justin sat on the end of my bed, face pale, eyes dark and hollowed.

I reached forward and he stared at my hand for a minute, then took it. "How you feeling?"

"Had a dream." My voice was dry and broken. I tried to swallow.

"I wanted to talk to you."

Don't ruin it, please oh please. Who's it hurt to just not ruin it? "You were a baby and then you were growing, and then, how wild is this, you were a tree!"

"About the other night."

I shook my head. *Please.*

"I don't know what's happening, Kerry, what I was doing."

I reached for a cup of now-cold tea by the bed. I couldn't look at him, couldn't stand to see any kind of pity, regret. "I'm sorry if I poisoned us."

"I saw Leslie last night."

I hunched beneath the covers, focusing on the pinkness of his lips so I wouldn't have to hear his words.

"And I told her what happened, I had to. Maybe it was because I was sick, delirious, but it just came out. All of it. I never hurt anyone like that before."

All of it. Leslie would hate me. She'd flash me dirty looks in school. I wouldn't be invited to their wedding. "I'm sorry," I whispered.

Justin touched my hand. "I'm not," he said, then stood and left the room.

* * *

"Kerry?"

I wrestled back from the depths of dreamless sleep. "Justin?"

But it was Eve at the end of the bed, wearing a narrow, closed-mouthed smile. "Hey, dollface, welcome to the land of the living."

Where am I? Where's Daddy? Oh. "Hi."

"Listen, Kerry, snap out of it. We got problems."

My eyes blurred. I looked up at the ceiling. "I have to tell you something, Eve. I need to tell you so you can tell me if it's real."

"Mr. Hodges called, the sonofabitch, and he says, 'Miss Barnard, you know you're two weeks late on the rent?' I want to tell him, you just try being in high school with no parents, no money, and worrying about some fucking SOB coming to take away the roof over your head just so's he can afford another Renoir to hang over his toilet."

I nodded, picturing Justin's eyes before (THE KISS!), how they'd melted, all the hard edges gone. What did it mean?

"But thing is, our bank account's at practically zip. And what with the bill from the medical center and next month's rent, we're wiped clean. The garage only nets us two hundred a week, which means we still have to cough up at least another three hundred bucks."

"Oh," I said. "Okay."

Eve's forehead creased. "And we got another brown envelope on the porch, ten bucks, which is starting to piss me off. Don't they realize we're in such deep shit that ten dollars is just insulting?" She rolled her eyes to the ceiling. "And get this. Talk about being on my very last nerve, Bert and Georgia called last night, right after Mr. Hodges. See what you miss when you're asleep? You'll never guess."

Sudden certainty punched at my stomach. "They found Mom."

"What?" She gave a sharp laugh. "No, no, they just called to say they wanted us to come for Christmas. 'You girls should be with your family,' Georgia said. Christmas is for families, just like a Hallmark card. I wanted to ask Bert to blow into her ear, see if he could feel a breeze out the other side."

I nodded. "Do you know if Justin's home?"

"You don't get it. I heard Georgia's voice, Kerry, they're serious."

"We could ask them for money."

"Are you kidding? That'll be just the proof they need to show we're failures, that we can't make it on our own. They'll say, *Why, how much do you need, dearie?* and then, *You know, don't you, that living with us would be absolutely free?*"

"Justin kissed me."

Eve froze, staring at me. I burst out laughing, couldn't help it. "We had dinner and I told him... God, I told him I loved him. And then I ran and he grabbed me and he kissed me. He kissed me!" I pulled Eve into my arms and spoke into her hair. "And now I don't know if it's true."

"What's true?" Eve's voice was a whisper.

I pulled away. "What he said to me was more or less that he was glad it happened. At least I think that's what he said. I was so sick yesterday, maybe I dreamed the whole thing."

Eve was trembling. I could see the quiver in her fingers, the pinched creases in her face. "How come you told me he was getting engaged?" I said.

Eve smiled stiffly. "He's not? I guess I thought—" She shook her head. "I don't know, Ker, I just didn't want you to get hurt is all. I know how caught up you get in things, how you lose yourself, when Justin's just an if-it-feels-good-do-it kind of guy. I didn't want you to waste your time hoping for something totally impossible."

"He'd never hurt me."

Eve shrugged and turned to the window. "So did he say he loves you?"

"No, not really. I don't know. He might have implied it, I'm not sure."

"Implied it?" Eve was scraping at the cuticle of her thumb, a habit we'd both had and both overcome years ago. But when I took her hand to stop her, she pulled away and smiled. "What was it like? The kiss?"

I bit back a smile. "I don't know if I can really explain it. It's like, imagine the best movie we ever saw, not the sappy romance-novel kind but the kind where a couple's reunited after twenty years. It was like that except better; he grabbed me and then he kissed real soft all down my face." I traced my finger from Eve's temple to her lips. She flinched. "I thought I was going to pass out."

Eve closed her eyes. "Oh, Kerry." We sat in silence for a minute, and then Eve opened her eyes and grinned. "Remember how we used to do hickeys on our arms?"

"I know! And pretend to make out with pillows?"

Eve hooted with laughter. I grabbed my pillow, buried my face against it. "Oh, daahling, your lips are so soft and sweet. How I adoore you."

Eve grabbed her own pillow. "Take me now!"

I watched her for a minute, her wet, smacking kisses, until she pulled back the pillow, her face red. I smiled, feeling suddenly older. "But really it turns out it wasn't like that at all. I mean no comparison. It was like a million tiny nerves that spark from your lips all through your body, even outside your body. I can't explain it, Eve, there's no way to explain it in words. You won't understand till you do it yourself."

Eve stood suddenly. "Good, Ker. That's good." She started towards the door, then turned. "I'm glad for you, Kerry, really I am. He was bound to choose one of us, I guess."

I watched her leave, my smile slowly fading. I curled under the blankets, trying not to listen to her retreating footsteps, trying not to think. Because deep down I understood. Deep down I knew this was exactly how I would have reacted if the situation were reversed, as if Eve had stolen Justin away.

Nothing much changed over the next week. Justin and I didn't talk to each other beyond saying "Hey." I avoided his eyes and he avoided mine. He stayed home on the nights he'd usually spent with Leslie, even though he didn't say anything to indicate he wasn't seeing her anymore.

I returned to school, although I might as well not have for all the attention I gave it. I drew hearts in the corners of isosceles triangles and traced his name with my finger round the edges of my desk. Leslie pointedly ignored me, and I started to feel bad. I thought I should do something nice for her, maybe buy her flowers. Or a sympathy card. But I didn't want to look like I was gloating, and besides, Leslie was the type who'd never have to look for a boyfriend; once word got out that she was free, they'd look for her. So what I'd done was wrong, but not that wrong. Not really.

The next Saturday it snowed, the first snowfall of the season. I was watching out the bedroom window when Eve came upstairs to find me. She laid her head on my shoulder and we stood there looking out, our thoughts the same. "You think we should?" she said finally.

It was Daddy's ritual at the first snowfall to take us outside so we could catch the snowflakes on our tongues. And I knew it would feel wrong to do it without him, but it would also feel much worse not to do it at all. "He'd want us to."

"I hate when people say that, how he'd want us to go on the same. That's total crap. If I died, I wouldn't want you going on the same."

I took her hand and smiled. "We have to. We'll probably still be doing this when we're sixty."

"I really hope not," Eve said, "or they'll be locking us away in a nursing home and teaching us how many crafty things you can make out of Popsicle sticks."

Out on the lawn, I watched as Eve tilted back her head. After a minute I closed my eyes and threw out my arms, mouth open wide, and I felt him. I really did. I knew if I could just reach a little farther, I'd feel his hand. He'd grab for me, hold tight, he'd laugh like a kid, dance me in a jig that would make Eve roll her eyes. And at the heavy thud of footsteps on the walk, I almost called his name. But of course it wasn't Daddy at all. It was Justin.

He stood, watching, hands fisted at his sides, his eyes liquid and unfocused. But when our eyes met, the look hardened instantly. He glanced at Eve. "Expecting two inches," he said.

Eve looked from me to Justin and back. "It's freezing out here. Let's go in."

I nodded, but my feet wouldn't move.

"Actually," Justin said, "I was wondering, Kerry, if you could help me down at the garage. We've got these discrepancies with the bills, and I know you're good with numbers."

Eve's laugh was dry. "Numbers? Kerry? Nice try. That's really lame."

I couldn't look at her. "Okay," I said. "Sure." I raised my hand good-bye, but still couldn't look. Only after Justin and I pulled out from the drive did I look into the side mirror to see her standing in the same spot on the lawn. Her arms were limp by her sides, snow freckling her hair. It made me feel like crying, but it also gave me an awful feeling of victory.

We drove in silence for a while, my insides stuttering with an unbearable thrill. Suddenly Justin pulled to the side of the deserted road. Both of us stared at the dashboard. "Look," he said finally, "I don't know what to do."

I didn't answer, didn't know what to answer. Outside all was so hushed under the blanket of snow, it almost seemed like the whole world was waiting with me.

"I've been thinking," he said, "nonstop I've been thinking, and going over it and over it and I still don't know what to do."

His fingers on the steering wheel were white from

gripping so hard. I felt like pushing, pushing, but could only sit and listen and wait.

"It felt right," he said softly. "I mean more right than I've ever felt, like something I've been waiting for, but the thing is, I know you too well." He shook his head briskly, then leaned back to stare at the car roof. "That didn't come out right. I swear I don't know what the hell I'm trying to say."

Without letting myself think what I was doing, I slid to kneel on the seat beside him, put my hands on his cheeks and guided him to my lips. Justin stiffened and inhaled sharply, then like a rubber band stretched tight and suddenly released, he loosened, enfolded me, his hands on my neck, up in my hair. His lips pressed at my teeth, the breath heavy through his nose. He made a choked, pleading sound and then sliced his face away. "I can't!"

I tried to catch my breath. "Justin, please, you... You can't why?"

"I can't tell you why, it's too complicated. Because you're sixteen, because... I don't know."

"Because I'm like your little sister," I whispered.

Justin turned to look out the fogged window. I slid back to my seat, huddled against the door. "That night—" He pressed his fist against the window, making a knuckle-shaped smudge in the steam. "That night I kissed you I don't know what happened. It was like my head started spinning around in circles and circles and I couldn't see straight, I couldn't walk straight or think straight and I don't know what that means." He shook his head. "Because you should feel like my little sister, and you don't."

I began to shake then, maybe from cold, from fear or want or all three. I trembled in waves that shivered up and down my spine, but somehow I managed to take his hand. We sat like that for I don't know how long—minutes, hours, days, years—and the snow enveloped the car and folded us in, so all we could see was the white and our joined hands.

10

FOR DAYS I was disoriented, didn't know where I was, didn't care. Even when I was finally able to look around at where I'd landed, still I felt like I had no feet, like I was a pair of bodiless eyes staring out at the world, trying to figure out how they'd gotten this way and what to do with themselves. It was too much.

It's funny when a dream you've had forever finally comes true. You'd think it should feel like coming home, but instead it's unsettling, kind of the same way it would be if you went for a walk and suddenly realized you'd ended up at the Emerald City or on Sunnybrook Farm. You no longer know if it's safe to trust your own eyes.

Daytimes we kept our distance, even when we were alone, as if a glance, a secret touch would brand us and give us away. Afternoons when I sat at the front desk at the Caines' shop, I'd try (mostly unsuccessfully) to calculate hours and parts, try (always unsuccessfully) to ignore the fact that Justin was there in the workroom behind me, like a hot wave of water pushing at my back.

But then after dinner, I'd join him in the potting shed and we'd devour each other, starving, like we'd been apart for weeks rather than just hours. And when it got so

I could hardly breathe, when I would have done anything, anything he asked, he'd pull away with soft butterfly kisses, we'd lie side by side, hands interlaced, eyes closed, until I could breathe again.

"I think my parents are starting to suspect," he said one night, his cheeks still flushed. "They're trying to coax it out of me. 'You look *happy* these days,' my dad keeps saying. He's pretty much the least subtle person I ever met."

"Are you happy?" I said.

"You're fishing, aren't you." He grinned and lifted our interlocked hands to kiss my fingers. "Of course I'm happy."

"Me too. I mean, obviously."

He laughed. "Obviously, yes."

I told Eve everything, of course. She was Eve, after all. I'd never kept a secret from her. And sometimes I almost felt like she was there while Justin and I talked, while we kissed. Which sounds a little perverted, but it wasn't like that, it was comforting. Justin would ask a question and I'd think what Eve might say. He'd touch me, and half my pleasure came from knowing I'd tell her later. I know it sounds so naive, but it was like by sharing these intimacies I could keep myself from choosing one over the other. I could fill this empty part of me without giving up the other parts that made me whole. This was how I lived with the shadow I saw in Eve's eyes when I came home. By pretending I could balance it out with my own joy.

* * *

And in the end, it was really Eve who left me first.

We lay on my bed, our feet against the wall. We were in one of our trippy moods, rocking back and forth together, humming Billie Holiday. We got in these weird moods sometimes, where we'd fall into giggles and not be able to stop, or spin until we collapsed, dizzy and nauseous on the floor. It was a way of decompressing our heads.

Suddenly she stopped and played her foot over the loose rubber of my sneaker tread. "Hey, listen, I got an idea." She raised an eyebrow. "I've been thinking for a while how our hair's a mess. Let's change it, something radical."

I pulled away from the wall and swept the hair over my forehead. "How 'bout bangs?"

Eve watched me for a long while, then nodded. "Bangs it is. Justin'll love it." And she flashed me a grin, crooked, like she was holding something large and unpleasant on her tongue.

Our straight, dark hair had always been cut exactly the same, all one length well past our shoulders. Usually we got our hair cut by Gary the barber, who took the ferry in weekly to pay house calls. But Gary's idea of the word *radical* was more along the lines of using a scrunchy to hold your ponytail, so we decided to splurge and go to Aztec, the salon where cuts were thirty dollars a pop even without blow-drying or shampoo. *Hair Design,* the sign said, as if they could take a paintbrush, scissors and glue and *presto,* design you into someone else.

We started down the hill on High Street, the pitch so steep our walk quickly became a run. As we rounded the hill to the harbor, we almost ran head-on into Ryan

Maclean, who was carrying a steaming styrofoam cup to his car. We knew Congressman Maclean only through the stories we'd read in the local papers about the first islander voted into higher office. He was one of those semi-residents who lived in the large houses on the north side of the island and moved to the mainland in the winter when the island was not such a pleasant place.

He sidestepped away from us and gave a wide grin, his teeth so toothpaste-commercial white they seemed fluorescent. "You almost got a coffee bath!"

I smiled, then noticed his eyes were on Eve. Luminous eyes he had, the kind of eyes you saw on actors. Were you born with those eyes, like a genetic marker, before you realized what you'd grow up to be? Or did the eyes come out of a career in public speaking and lies?

Eve gave him a slim smile. "I can just see it in the papers, 'Congressman Accused of Scalding Two Teenage Girls.' Might hurt your chances of reelection."

"Or I could make myself into a hero, rush you off to the medical center and stay by your side even when I'm s'posed to be campaigning. That's good press." He rolled his eyes in a weird, giddy circle. "So you're both voting next week, right? Being good citizens, all that?"

Eve threw back her head and laughed for no apparent reason, maybe just to show him the line of her neck.

"I guess we'd vote for you if we were old enough to vote," I said.

Eve kicked my ankle. "Sure we'll vote for you. You're a shoo-in anyway."

"From your lips to God's ears," he said. "And with lips like yours, God's bound to listen."

She laughed again and kissed her fingers, touched them to his arm. "Seeya in the news."

"Eve!" I whispered loudly as his car disappeared around the corner.

"Oh, he loves it," she said. "You saw how he looked at me. All men are the same, even married ones. Maybe especially married ones, because they know their days of fun are over. Just wait'll we get bangs, we'll be invincible."

The hairdressers smiled when we entered, sat us on high pink swivel chairs. We sat on opposite sides of the salon, looking in the globe-lit mirrors at the backs of each other's heads. My stylist was a man named Jean-Paul who spoke with a faint accent that made him seem trustworthy. I squeezed my eyes shut as he sprayed water with his spritzer and held his fingers against my forehead. I tensed at the cold of metal against my skin, heard the snip of scissors and felt the plop of wet hair at my feet. I held my breath and opened my eyes.

It was an improvement, I decided, made my eyes look wider and defined my cheekbones. I thought we should probably go all the way, pay a little extra for them to curl our bangs with a round brush and spray. But when I turned to tell Eve, I saw the sharp scissors angled perilously close to her ears. I cried out to warn her but it was too late. The six-inch-long section of hair that looked just like my hair fell to the floor. Oh God, poor Eve.

I went to her, stood by her side and watched, feeling empty and afraid. Like me she was keeping her eyes closed until the end. Couldn't she feel the scissors and the falling hair, hear the razor cleaning the fuzz at the nape of her neck? I wanted to shake her, cry for her, but instead I just stood mutely, cringing as she opened her eyes.

She studied herself in the mirror, then smiled. "Oh, Ker, d'you like it?"

I hated it. It looked good, kind of tousled and sexy, and I wanted to pull it long again or cut mine just the same. But it was too late. To copy would be to admit that she was better. "I thought we were just getting bangs," I said.

"I know, I guess I just decided I needed a change." She held up a page torn from a magazine, a lanky model with the same short tousled cut.

Something in my chest dropped, shifted my center of balance so I felt floaty, weightless. Eve had brought a picture. She'd known what she was going to do even before she'd left the house. She'd known and she hadn't told me, which meant that Eve not only wanted a change, she wanted a separation.

I looked at us standing side by side in the large salon mirror. I blurred my eyes until all I could see were two like patches of peach haze. Eve touched the ends of her hair and her voice was hazy, vaporous with awe. "We hardly even look like twins anymore," she said.

The next day I went to LoraLee, hardly sure what I was looking for. She sat by the window rocking, whittling a gnarled stick with her pocketknife. Sunlight flecked shadows through tree branches onto her face, making her seem wrinkled and wise.

I sat on the floor across from her. "I feel funny," I said.

LoraLee raised her eyebrows, still focused on her whittling, wood curls floating to her feet.

I shook my head. "It's like when we were little, Daddy would get a card for our birthday, just one, that said *Happy Birthday Twins.* And it would piss Eve off every time. It's like we're one person, she'd say, like he thinks we don't deserve our own." I pulled my knees up to my chest, rested my head on them. "But me, I'd love it how we shared one birthday. I loved how when kids sang at our party, half of them would sing 'Happy Birthday Eve and Kerry' and the other half sang 'Happy Birthday Kerry and Eve,' so it all blurred together into one name." I looked out the window at the bare branches. "How come I'm always the one pulling at her?"

"You don't need to pull so hard. You stop pullin' and she miss that, see she gotta try harder."

"Sometimes I think she wishes I was ugly."

LoraLee smiled. "If you was ugly, then she'd be ugly too. You's identical."

"That's not what I mean. Not that she wants me to be ugly, but that she wants me to be less than her somehow. Because there's things happening for me lately, really good things, and I think she maybe wishes they were happening to her instead. And then yesterday, yesterday she got her hair cut short." I swallowed sharply. "The older we get, the less she's like me."

LoraLee raised her eyebrows. "I ever tell you the story 'bout my grandaddy's babies?"

I shook my head and she smiled. "See, my grandaddy, his name were Mr. Mason Mays, he have four girl and he name them after the season, first Summer, then Autumn—that's my momma—then Winter and then

Spring. And then he have another girl and he don't know what to name her so he go back and start with Summer again. Now Summer Number One, she a beautiful chile. She haves skin like cocoa and a high proud nose. But Summer Number Two, she nothin' to look at, ashy and thick and born with a split lip they never quite puts back together right. So one day my grandaddy, he sittin' with them at the dinner table and he say, 'So you sees what happen when you gives one name to two chile unner one roof?' He say, 'Summer One gone and took all the beauty and nothin' lef' for Summer Two 'cept the parts nobody wants, and them parts don't fits together right besides.'"

LoraLee looked up from her carving, dark eyes flashing with humor. "And that night when Summer One asleep, Summer Two sneak up behind her, grab a handful of braids and cut them with a pair of prunin' shear. Next mornin' Summer One see the hole in her hair, see the braids peekin' out from unner Summer Two pillow. So that night while Summer Two asleep, Summer One sneak up and scissor all the hair from her head. Now not only she ugly, she ugly and bald. Look like she put a finger in a plug socket."

I waited for more, but LoraLee just raised her eyebrows and smiled.

"What does it mean?" I asked.

She shrugged. "Don't mean nothin' really. It's jus' a funny story you brung to my mind."

I frowned, imagining poor Summer Two, thick face and lip sewn together wrong. I tucked my fists under my arms and looked outside at the garden, now withered and grubby gray with slush. "LoraLee," I said, "how do you know if something's gonna last?"

She nodded. "Mebbe the story got a message after all. My two Aunt Summers, they's buried side by side."

"What?"

"Troubles only last long as you let 'em."

"That's not what I mean." I lifted the figurine she'd been whittling, a man's head like a grotesque growth out the top of a branch. "What if you finally got this one thing you wanted all your life, something you knew all that time you were meant to have? But you also knew there was someone else who thought that thing was meant for her instead. You can't both be right."

"But you can, chile, yes, you can. Mebbe this thing meant for you both, or mebbe meant for you now and meant for Eve when her time come."

"It's not! It's not a sharing kind of thing."

"But it ain't an ownin' kind of thing neither. Ownin' is for God, for fate, not for peoples to decide. Bes' thing you can do is not hold on too tight."

"It's Justin," I said. "Me and Justin."

LoraLee stared at me. "Oh, chile," she said.

I saw then how tired she looked, how suddenly old. Everything on her seemed strangely vertical, from the folds in her neck to the pouchiness under her eyes. I shook my head. "You probably think I'm betraying Eve, or love causes pain, something. The way you live, alone like this, there's nobody can hurt you and nobody you can hurt. It's so much easier."

"You think I choose this? Alone is what God give me and I got no right to complain 'bout what God give. But it ain't my choosin'."

I had no idea what to say to this. It made me want to curl up in her lap. "You're not happy?"

"Oh, chile, that ain't it. All I needs is my own self. All I needs is all I got." She smiled softly. "But thing is, Kerry, when you finds love you got to treasure it, reach for it with both your hand. Could be it make you lose your footin', but in the long run findin' your heart is more important than findin' your feet."

I watched her, the thick ring on her thicker finger, this woman who somehow could take whatever came her way. I knew what she was saying, but the truth was I didn't want to lose my feet. Because I wanted to own Justin and I wanted to own Eve, both. And what I knew was that anything could happen; they could both float away like our mother, like Daddy, like the summer flowers that lost their color no matter how tight you held.

Later that afternoon I returned home to find Eve in the hallway, sitting cross-legged by the attic steps, her newly short hair still a shock to me. It exaggerated the slight difference in her features, the narrow line of her cheekbones where my face was more rounded, the pouty swell of her upper lip, always fuller than my own. She waved me over, gesturing at a banker's box. "Come look."

Inside were old school notebooks, report cards, manuscript paper with rows and rows of capital and lowercase *R*'s. I sat beside her and fingered through it, the innocence of third-grade stories and fingerpainted faces.

"If we could go back, what would we tell them?" Eve said. "I mean about all the stuff they'd have to go through."

"I guess we'd tell them that things'll be tough, but they'll turn out okay in the end."

"Will they?"

I gave her a look but she was staring at a drawing, a blue pond with a fountain in its center, spouting rainbow colors. "When we were little I used to be able to blur my eyes and let the pictures take over," she said. "Sink into them and be somewhere else. Maybe that's the problem with growing up, there's no escape."

I traced my finger across the spirals in a notebook, feeling sorry, but also wanting to show her there was hope. "I guess I don't want to escape," I said. "Things're getting better, getting good for me now, and they'll get better for you too if you just wait. If I had a choice, I couldn't really think of anywhere else I'd rather be."

Eve watched my face for a long minute, then turned away and began to toss the papers haphazardly into the box. When she'd finished she stood and lifted the box, her jaw tight. "Sometimes, Kerry," she said, "I don't know you anymore."

Maybe that was why I let Justin convince me I should lie. It was a holding-on-to-what-I-could kind of thing. And that lie was, in a way, what precipitated everything that came after, which is ironic if you really think about it.

It was a week before Christmas when he suggested it. We were lying on his bed, he on pillows with his writing, me against the wall, my legs draped over his knees. There's an art to fitting two people comfortably on a single bed without cramping. Eve and I had mastered the best positions, this being one of my favorites.

I was trying to work out a budget. Eve had somehow come up with the next month's rent, and I was working through the numbers in our bank account and trying to figure out how she'd managed it. Regardless, I knew that by February we'd be scraping the bottom of the barrel. Maybe if we worked full-time on weekends, we'd make enough after taxes to get by. I tried to convince myself, even knowing it was impossible. There was so little business in the winter that even Mr. Caine didn't work full-time.

Justin gestured at his notepad. "I got an idea."

I smiled, letting myself drift away from the numbers and the worry. "Oh yeah?"

"How 'bout this. On the night they fall in love, Morwyn makes Gaelin soup, a fairy recipe. So after they eat they're sitting together by the fire, their stomachs churning, and they kiss." Justin grinned. "And guess why their stomachs are churning."

"Oh no," I said. "You wouldn't."

"Poisoned strawberries," Justin said. "I like it. It's romantic. She could nurse him back to health."

I punched his arm. "Know what I think? A guy would have to be an idiot to fall in love with a girl who poisons him."

"Not true. I just have to remember never to let you cook for me again. Just wait till I write this, and you'll see how romantic it is." He watched me with clouded eyes. "So listen, Ker. I was thinking if we worked it right, Christmas might be a great chance to spend some time together. Alone."

"Not if you're in Manhattan and we're in West Virginia."

"What I was thinking is, what if we didn't go? Maybe

we get a return of the stomach bug, something incapacitating."

"They're not stupid, Justin. They'll figure it out."

"Bet you anything they don't. You obviously don't understand how gullible my parents are. Look at this innocent face, do I look like I could lie?"

"And Eve would have to go to Bert and Georgia's alone? I can't do that to her."

"Eve wants you to be happy, doesn't she? She might not be thrilled about it, but I'm sure she'd understand."

"Maybe she would." I pulled my legs away, suddenly scared, trying to shake the knowledge that I was risking something important. But of course I was enraptured by the idea, the two of us alone together, our own quiet heaven, and in the end, being me, there was no way I could resist.

And so the day before Christmas, while Eve was still asleep, I slipped into the bathroom. I reddened my nose with blusher, hollowed my eyes with purple shadow, hacked sick coughing noises for good measure, then traipsed back to bed. I watched Eve for a minute, then realized my noises hadn't woken her, so I made a guttural huffing sound somewhere between a sigh and a cough. It didn't sound at all real, but it did work to wake her.

Eve lifted her head and switched on the bedside lamp. She stared at me, her eyes slowly focusing. "Ker?"

I let her get a good look at my bruised face, then buried it into my pillow. "Go 'way."

My stomach twisted as she came to sit by me. *I'm sorry, so sorry.* "I'm dying," I moaned. It was pretty unconvincing, like a kid actor on a Friday night sitcom.

"Kerry, Christ... I'll get someone."

She ran to the phone and I squeezed my eyes shut, kept them shut even after she returned. Minutes later the front door opened and Mrs. Caine strode up to the bedroom. She felt my forehead and smoothed back my hair. "Seems like there's always somebody sick at Christmas. That time of year."

I was shaking, deep shudders that seemed to radiate from my chest. Mrs. Caine frowned. "Heck, Kerry, you're shivering like an earthquake. Must've got it from Justin."

"He's sick?" My voice was unsteady. I had degenerated to a Saturday morning cartoon.

"Fever of a hundred and two."

"Kerry..." Eve was standing in the corner, her jaw tight. I followed her eyes. She was staring at my pillow, faint streaks of red and purple makeup that had smudged from my face. I grabbed the pillow and hugged it to my chest, widened my eyes at her, pleading.

"Guess I should stay home and tend the sick," Mrs. Caine said.

"Oh no, hey," I said, now fully sunk to the credibility of a Teletubby. "You don't have to do that. I know your parents would be all upset."

"I won't," Eve said. She was watching me, a flush spreading to her cheeks.

Oh, I'm sorry. "Eve—"

"I'm not going there alone, dammit. No way."

"This is just awful," Mrs. Caine said. "I was talking to your grandma last week, and she asked me what I thought you girls might want for Christmas gifts. She sounded so excited to have you there." She sighed. "But I guess these two basket cases could use you around, Eve, to bring tea and tissues. Doesn't seem right separating you girls on Christmas."

I felt a soft stretch in my chest almost like relief, until I looked into Eve's tight face, her narrowed eyes and short hair making her look like a stranger.

I narrowed my eyes back at her, and we clenched our teeth, glared silently. Finally, Eve spun away. "Forget it," she said. "Maybe your fever's catching, because I swear, just standing here with you makes me feel sick." She grabbed her purse and strode out the door.

"Eve?" Mrs. Caine glanced at me, then strode after her. "Eve!"

I hugged my knees and my vision blurred. I knew what I'd done. And part of me knew nothing would ever be the same again.

II

I HADN'T SEEN EVE for a week. And now, as the ferry pulled into the dock, I was suddenly apprehensive. Which I told myself was stupid, since Eve and I never held a grudge. Grudges just weren't practical when you lived in the same bedroom and shared toothpaste and tampons. In the driver's seat, Justin tapped his fingers on the steering wheel to the beat of the radio, and I tapped a stuttering rhythm on my seat, four beats to his one.

And then Eve stepped onto the dock. I felt an inner sigh of recognition, the exact feeling of a lost child who finally, after an hour of crying and wandering through aisles, distinguishes her mother from a crowd of strangers. I kissed Justin's cheek and slid from the car to greet her. Eve strode towards me and I flung my arms wide. "Eve, I missed you!"

She reached forward without speaking and thrust her bags at me. I grappled with them as she jumped into the front seat beside Justin. "Merry Christmas!" she said. "God, Justin, what a hell of a week. Yestereday we went snowshoeing. Fucking snowshoeing! Those two old farts gliding around like ballet dancers."

Justin glanced at me. I forced a smile, then opened

the back door and ducked inside, trying to think of something to say. "Wow" was all I came up with.

"I actually thought about buying you snowshoes, Justin, for Christmas, give you some idea what pure hell is like. Too bad I already bought something else."

I watched the back of Eve's neck, the hair fringing her blue scarf, a knot of foreboding in my chest. "Oh yeah," I said. "You'll like her present, Justin, it's really nice."

I'd been with her when she chose the Harleys calendar. *A different bike for every month!* It had made me feel smug that she'd think the repair shop was some kind of career choice. I myself had pored over catalogues looking for the perfect gift, finally settling on a leather portfolio for his papers and a gold Cross pen. Eve had thought they were way too practical to be romantic, the kind of gift grandparents would give when they didn't know their grandkids, like footie pajamas. But he'd been using them every day now, said they helped his words flow.

"Well, you didn't miss much here," Justin said. "At least you had snow. For us every day was like this, fog on top of more fog. Felt like everybody else was off doing something exciting, like some party where we weren't invited."

"Well what did you expect?" Eve said. "She's hardly the party type."

Justin laughed. He laughed like Eve's words were some private joke, then winked into the rearview as apology. "It was okay, though. I guess neither of us is."

It was okay? Okay? I remembered Christmas Eve, how I'd taught Justin how to waltz. And then he asked me to dance alone, so I'd twirled *grand fouettés*, watching him watch me. I was totally embarrassed at myself until I saw his face, his eyes all liquid like he was looking at something awe-inspiring, a foreign city or Niagara Falls. Afterwards we'd lit a fire and just sat, hand in hand, gazing into it without speaking. If I'd died right then and there, I would've felt like my life had been complete. To me it had been as close to perfect as perfect ever got.

Justin glanced again at me. "Anyway, it's good to see you, isn't it, Kerry?"

"At this moment not especially," I said. I couldn't see Eve's face, so I tried to gauge her reaction by the tilt of her head, the thrust of her shoulders. From the back at least, she looked ready to punch someone out.

She sat a minute without moving, then turned, her eyes looking past me, out the window. "Did you even notice I wasn't there?" Her voice was lilting in a fake, overdone kind of lilt.

I shook my head. "How can you ask that?"

"To tell you the truth, I'm surprised you even showed. I was thinking I'd be walking home."

"Jesus, Eve, stop acting like a martyr."

"What, you saying you give a damn? What about while you were here screwing in secret and left me waddling through snowdrifts? You really gave a damn?"

Silence. I tried to think what to say and came up with nothing, so I gave up and hunched in my seat. Justin cleared his throat. "Well, we better get going before we freeze out here."

He started the engine. I smoothed my hands over my legs, up and down, up and down, drowning in the radio's drumbeat.

When the car stopped, Eve jumped out and opened my door. She reached for her bags without even glancing at me and I grabbed at her hand. "Hey."

She looked down at our hands without speaking, jaw clenched like she was considering whether or not to pull my fingers out of their sockets.

"Come on, Eve, get over it. Stop acting so weird."

She raised her head and her face suddenly looked so young, so lost. But then she pulled away. "Acting weird," she said softly. "Gosh, you're right, how awful of me." She lifted her bags and carried them to the house, calling over her shoulder, "C'mon, Jussy, you gotta open your presents."

Justin turned to give me a commiserating sort of smile. "Just give her some time."

I got out from the car and slammed the door, suddenly blaming him as much as myself.

Inside, Eve slipped off her coat and ran upstairs. She returned with a flat wrapped package, which she handed to Justin with a smile.

Justin unwrapped the calendar, wearing a too-polite smile. "A new bike for every month!" he said.

"Hold on," I said, running to the closet. Heart in my throat, I retrieved Eve's wrapped gift, a stone petroglyph I'd bought last summer, two stick-figure women curled around each other, joined.

Eve gave me a smile that showed her teeth, then set the gift down without opening it. "Gee, thanks," she said. "I got something for you too, Kerry, kind of a joke, a gun that shot laser light and made sounds like an automatic. Thought we could freak the hell out of Bert and Georgia, remind them how they almost made me blow out my brains." She shrugged. "But it wasn't so apropos with me there and you here, so I returned it. Bought these instead."

She bent to her suitcase and pulled out two packages. I smiled and reached for them, but Eve handed them to Justin. "Merry Christmas."

My stomach twisted. Justin stared at the gifts with clouded eyes, then turned to me like he wanted me to take them.

"Go on," Eve said. "I promise you'll like these."

Still watching me, Justin tore at the wrapping and pulled out a book. *Tricks and Trends in Writing for Children,* it was called. He flipped the pages and smiled. "This is great, really perfect. Thanks so much, Eve."

He opened the smaller package. I felt a strange rumbling in my chest, as if my insides were being boiled. In the box was a package of briefs with William Shakespeare's portrait on the rear, a fountain pen printed on the fly.

"Been picturing you in those all day," Eve said. "Wanna model for me?"

Justin's face flushed. He rested his hand at my elbow. "That's a little much, Eve, even for you," he said. But his eyes were shining with an undeniable delight.

I found the watercolors in an upstairs closet and the memory washed over me, soft as the paints themselves, of how we used to sit at this table, the three of us, swishing our brushes in muddy water and trying to stay in the lines. It seemed like so long ago, and at the same time so short ago that it hurt.

I brought the kit downstairs and found an old *Boston Globe,* dated before Daddy's death, then sat to obliterate its news with my brush. What had Eve and I been doing back on August 3? Jumping waves, reading *Teen* magazine, braiding each other's hair. Also on that date was a rape, a stabbing, and peace talks between Israel and the PLO. I blotted out each and every one of the stories with a rainbow of colors, red staining to orange to yellow to green. But it didn't help. Not really at all.

There was a tap on the window and I looked up to see Justin blowing on his fingers. I rose to open the back door.

He kissed me on the temple. "Guess our week in paradise is just about over," he said, then lifted the multicolored newspaper. "What's this?"

I shrugged. "Nothing. It's nothing."

"It's a sunset, isn't it? Sun's too small in winter for good sunsets, so you painted your own." He smiled and lifted the brush, smeared a circle of orange inside the wash of colors, then dabbed the brush on my nose. "There you go."

I batted the brush away and Justin held up his hands. "Hey, what's going on?"

"How could she, Justin? How dare she?"

Justin sat across from me. "You're talking about that gift."

"She's trying to prove something, I don't know what. That she can replace me, or she can screw it all up, something."

Justin looked down at his hands and spoke quietly. "Try and think how this has to be for her."

"You think how she's acting is okay?"

"I'm just saying I understand it. You remember back when we dug for pirate gold, you and me? I'd just heard that legend about the buried treasure up by Cow's Cove, so we dug these holes through from the Ashtons' yard to the Sheffields'. We came home completely covered in mud, and we were racing each other to the shower when Eve saw us. And you remember what she did? She went and told Mrs. Sheffield about the holes in her lawn. She felt the same way then as she does now."

"Except now she's ten years older."

He watched me for a minute before he spoke. "You do that, you know, both of you. Things aren't going the way you like and *bam,* you just turn off."

"I'm not supposed to be upset?"

"What I do? I have this image in my head of how I want things to be, and I keep it there whatever happens. Like I tell myself a story and I keep acting and reacting like the story's true, and eventually what happens and what you want to happen meet up. You pretend Eve's okay and eventually she will be."

I shook my head, my throat dry with shame. I'd let Eve travel the same ocean that had swallowed Daddy, the same ocean that had lured away my mother, and for what?

Justin's gift for me had been a red silk nightie with spaghetti straps. I knew what it meant and it terrified me, the eight-year-old part of me that was just hearing about sex and thinking nuh-unh, no way, never. It was only when I'd imagined Eve's eyes, sympathetic and reflecting my same fear, that I'd felt like there was nothing wrong with me. It was only because of Eve that I'd been able to say I wasn't ready.

"Life isn't one of your stories, Justin," I said now. "You can't wish something into happening. That's not how it works."

Justin sighed and gave me a smile that looked half pitying and half exasperated, like I'd just told him I didn't believe the world was round. "Trust me," he said. "Just talk to her like nothing's happened. I know Eve, and I bet you anything she's looking for an easy way to forget she's angry."

This pissed me off a little, that he'd suggest he knew Eve better than me. When the truth was, Eve wasn't that way at all. When she had her mind set about something, she kept it there forever, chiseling herself deeper and deeper into the grooves of it until there was no way out. And even if eventually she might pretend she was forgiving you, she never forgot.

When Eve got home late in the afternoon, she strode right past me like she didn't notice I was there and climbed to the bedroom. I waited a few minutes, then went upstairs and stood at the door.

She was at the mirror straightening her skirt. She twirled, glancing over her shoulder to see the back view. "It's your room too," she said without turning from the mirror. "You can come in."

I stepped inside and reached into my pocket. "We got another brown envelope Christmas morning." I handed her the money. "Twenty dollars each."

She tucked both bills in her skirt pocket. "Now our financial troubles are over."

I watched her, tracing my finger against the door frame. "You're dressed up."

"I've got a date." Her voice was tight.

I sat on the bed. "A date?"

Eve shrugged, reached for her lipstick. "It's really not your business, is it."

I watched her smooth the maroon gloss on her lips. "Listen, I'm sorry I made you go out there alone."

She ignored me, only rooted through her jewelry box. I took a deep breath and went on. "It was nice being with Justin, but I missed you like anything. Christmas wasn't the same, not having you, not having Daddy, in a way it made me feel like I was all alone."

Eve held gold hoops up to her ears and eyed her profile in the mirror. I stood behind her, watching the echo of our reflections. "And I know it must've been ten times worse for you, being all the way out there. So I'm sorry, Eve, real sorry about it. I was being a selfish jerk."

Eve spun suddenly to face me. The twisted anger on her face was like a physical punch, and I flinched back. "Don't you get it?" she said. "It's not that I had to go out there alone, which sucked to high hell, but I would've done it for you if you asked."

Her nose reddened, her eyes filled and I reached for her arm, but she slapped me back. "You lied to me! And you made plans, kicked me out without even caring, without asking if it was okay. I'd never do that to you, Kerry, no matter what. Even if someone was pulling out my toenails, I wouldn't!"

She slammed the door open, hard enough to dent the wall plaster, then strode down the hall. I sank to my knees on the cold hardwood floor, feeling like I'd just swallowed a tennis ball without chewing, and listened to the click of Eve's heels down the stairs and out the door.

It was after midnight by the time Eve got home. I lay in bed waiting as she stamped up the stairs, then closed my eyes, pretending to be asleep. But she flew into the room. "Ker-co," she called. "Ker-eeoh."

She wrapped her arms round her waist, spun in a circle and flopped onto my bed.

She was drunk.

"He's amazing, really totally amazing. I think I could probably fall in love."

I put my hand against her back, part of me alarmed but also flooded with a longing. All was forgiven. "In love with who?"

Eve curled up on the bed. "Mmmghh," she said.

I shook her shoulder. "Where were you?"

Eve spoke into the pillow. "With Brad Carrera."

I gaped at her. "Brad Carrera? Officer Carrera? He's like thirty years old!" Officer Carrera had been one of Daddy's drinking buddies: deep blue eyes, jet-black hair and a perpetual glossy tan, like he'd been dipped in a vat of wood stain and then shellacked.

"Thirty-two," Eve said. "God, can he ever kiss, Kerry. Like this wind rushing through you."

"He's twice your age!"

She turned to face me. "Stop it, Kerry." Her voice was slurred, *Shtop it.* "You're just jealous 'cause I got the hottest man on the island. Hell, the hottest man in the world!" She slapped my arm loosely, then let her hand drop to the bed. "Oh, Ker, it's just so sweet how he looks at me, his eyes all wild like he wants to eat me alive."

I felt sick to my stomach. "Eve..."

She sat up and flung her arms around me, then fell heavily against my chest. "Whoa."

"God, Eve, what's going on with you? What were you drinking?"

Eve shook her head, kept shaking it, slowly lowering herself back onto the bed. "You don't get it, Ker. We were there, we were there at the bar and how it was, all the people were happy and together. They all want you there 'cause they know you're just the freshest thing they ever saw. Best thing they ever seen by far."

She closed her eyes and let out a long sigh, content or rueful, I couldn't tell which. I curled behind her, buried my head in her neck. Her smell of beer and smoke was remotely like Daddy's smell, and so I was obscurely comforted. Until I wrapped my arm around her and felt her ribs, even through her top so prominent that I could've slotted my fingers between them. So like Daddy, this vulnerability in the guise of something strong. And I knew that if she started to love Brad Carrera all it would take was a wrong word from him, a pinch in a sensitive spot, for this shell she'd built around herself to shatter.

THREE

Pulling and Planting

March
2007

12

I STOOD by the bedroom mirror waiting for Eve and Justin to come back from their walk, trying to work out dance moves that could be performed by women with bad knees. I did a sort of modified *échappé,* rising onto the balls of my feet instead of my toes. It seemed to me it might be good for their arches and reduce the likelihood of hip fractures. I stretched into an arabesque, then bent my raised knee. But the whole thing felt stupid with no music, so I stopped and dropped to the bed, then picked up a magazine. It was an old issue of *Highlights.* I opened to the middle and tried to see how many hidden objects I could find that started with the letter *T.*

I was staying in what had once been the left side of Daddy's bedroom, now crammed with a bed and Justin's desk, leaving barely space enough to walk. The room had been divided in two, this half Justin's office and the other Gillian's room. The change was disorienting, and sleeping here seriously bothered me. Because even when things had gotten really bad between me and Eve, still we'd shared the same bedroom because we always had, and because to move Daddy's things would've felt like a betrayal.

So I hated hanging out here, but it seemed like there

was no place besides my bed to sit, no communal area now that the living room held the cold metal of Eve's bed and wheelchair. So I spent my days either in the kitchen or on this bed, waiting for Eve to come home or to wake, to call out, to talk to me, authenticate that I wasn't just a figment of my own imagination.

The front door opened and I walked to the head of the stairs. Gillian emerged from her room and brushed past me, down the stairs, without acknowledging my presence. This had been the routine over the past two weeks, Gillian pretending I didn't exist. She'd come home from school and I'd greet her. If I was lucky, she might grunt back, but most often she didn't even bother. I was ostensibly supposed to be babysitting while Eve and Justin were out, but really I was mostly just sitting.

"Shit," Eve said. She was leaning on Justin, limping perceptibly. "I don't know why you make me do this anyway. When they say exercise adds ten years to your life, they're not really talking about people with terminal cancer."

Gillian jumped down the last two steps. "Hi, I'm home."

"So I see," Justin said, guiding Eve towards the den. "How was school?"

"Not so bad. I got this thing for you, Ma." She held out a sheet of blue paper.

"Not now, sweetie, please? I'm in total pain."

Gillian pulled her arm back. "You okay?"

"She just twisted her ankle," Justin said. "It'll probably be better by tomorrow."

"You want some ice? I'll get you some ice, okay?" Gillian ran to the kitchen.

I started downstairs. "Anything I can do?"

"At least I deserve extra morphine now, don't you think? Let me sleep through the agony you inflicted on me?"

Justin studied her face, then nodded slowly. "You're faking, aren't you. This is a ploy."

"If that makes you feel better about yourself." Eve lay on the bed and pulled off her shoes, then buried her head in the pillows.

Justin watched her a minute, then nodded at me. "She's faking. I'll be upstairs if you need me."

Gillian strode past me, an ice pack in one hand, the blue paper in the other. "Which ankle, Mom?"

Eve didn't answer, either asleep or pretending. It amazed me how quickly she could now transition between consciousness and sleep. Although I was starting to suspect it was all pretend, a way to get away from the world when she didn't want to deal.

Gillian studied Eve's feet, then positioned her ice pack to touch both. "I used two Ziplocs so it wouldn't leak," she said. She stood there with her shoulders hunched, her face expressionless. She clutched the blue paper in her hand, clutched it tighter, then stuffed it into her pocket. "Okay, so I'm going upstairs." She patted the blanket over Eve's legs, stood a minute longer and then turned away.

"Your mom's just tired is all," I said as she walked past me. Gillian shrugged and started to the kitchen. I watched as she pulled the paper from her pocket, tossed it into the trash and then walked upstairs.

Eve sat up, pulled the ice pack from between her

ankles and held it on her palm. Finally she set it on the night table and settled back on the bed.

I felt a sudden spike of anger. "Do you have any idea how hurt she looked just now?"

Eve turned to me, her eyes filled with such anguish I could feel it in my bones. "Fuck you, Kerry. You just try being me. See if you do any better."

You have everything, I wanted to say. *You idiot. You just try being me.* What I really said was, "Let me know if you need anything." And then I turned away. Very gracious of me, I thought.

In the kitchen I retrieved the slip of paper Gillian had stuffed into the trash, smoothed it on the table.

Hello parents!

We're writing to let you know about this year's 1st through 6th grade production! This year we've decided on *Charlotte's Web,* the charming story of a spider who teaches a pig about life. We'll need your help in the following areas:

- Rehearse your child's lines if he or she has a spoken part. Make this a family activity!
- The Book Nook is offering a special 25% discount on *Charlotte's Web*! We urge you to purchase the book for your child to read, or for you to read aloud.
- We will need you to sew your child's costume. Gillian has been given the part of Wilbur the Pig.

Children and teachers will be working together on set and props, but we are also looking for parents with carpentry skills. Call Virginia Brent if you'd like to volunteer.

Thanks for your help, and we look forward to seeing you all at the performance on June 12!

Theodore Allen
Vice Principal, BIS

I folded the memo carefully and walked up to Gillian's room. I knocked on her door, but she didn't answer. "Gillian?" I knocked again, then opened the door a crack. "Gillian?"

She was lying on her bed, wearing headphones and staring at the ceiling. I sat beside her and set the memo on her lap. She looked back at me, unblinking.

"This is great," I said. "I mean, Wilbur's the lead role in the whole play."

She pulled off the headphones with a look of pure annoyance. "Charlotte's the lead role. Besides, the only reason I got the part is because there's only seven sixth-graders and I'm the best reader."

"Well whatever the reason, it's pretty cool."

"Not really. Anyway, I already decided I'm not doing it."

"What?"

She shrugged. "It's just a stupid school play. Every year the little kids mess up their lines or they forget they're on stage and stand there picking their nose. Last year we did Charlie Brown? And Tim Jennings who was Schroeder threw up right on Allie Connor's foot."

I looked down at her bitten fingernails, then glanced at the memo. "I could do your costume if you want. I haven't used a sewing machine for years, but I bet I could figure it out."

She lifted the headphones, started to slip them back

over her ears but then stopped. "I know what you're doing. You're trying to pretend you and me and Dad are a family."

I blinked, shook my head. "What do you mean?"

"I know you used to be in love with him, Mom told me. But you can't just show up here and go back into his life just because she's sick." She was crying now, her voice breaking, the quivering, shoulders-tensed tears of childhood. "You look like her, but you're not her. Maybe you used to live here but you don't belong here anymore."

I reached to touch her arm but she slapped me away. "I'm here for your mom, Gillian," I said, "to help take care of her. And I'm here for you, too, to do whatever I can to make things easier."

"It's worse having you here, not easier." She shook her head against the pillow, wiped the back of her hand against her nose. "When I dream about her? She's normal again, and she has normal hair, and she plays Frisbee with me and Dad and she throws better than anyone."

I took Gillian's hand, sandwiched it between mine. This time she didn't flinch. "That's what I dream, too," I said. "I know I'm not your mom, and I'm really not trying to be her. I'm just me, just her sister, and I'm trying to get through this too."

She looked up at me, then pulled her hand away. "Do you know it's my birthday next week? It's my birthday, but I don't care anymore. It's just a day, and they'll pretend like it's important but really they're just pretending."

"Of course it's important." I tried to remember turning twelve, how a birthday seemed like the most monumental thing. How I'd gone to sleep the night before thinking, *This is the last night I'll be eleven,* and then woke up the next morning and lay there with my eyes closed, trying to see how different it felt.

Gillian lifted the blue memo from her lap. "It's like there's two worlds," she said. "There's the world with me and Mom and Dad, and then there's everybody else who's just out there and they think it's such a big deal that they're having this play." She crumpled the memo and threw it off the bed, then turned to watch it fall to the floor. "How come some people get to have normal families?"

I shook my head, wishing I could find an answer that would help even a little, coming up only with the inadequate life-isn't-fair type of answers used by annoyed parents. I'd learned this long before, that things could go from horrible to wonderful and back to horrible again without reason or entitlement. How even with perspective there was no way to understand it, no matter how closely you looked. "I'm on the inside of your world, too, Gillian," I said. "I know you don't see that now, but I'm there like you, wishing I could get back to where the little things counted."

Gillian stared at me, then slipped the earphones back over her head. She turned up the volume on her Walkman loud enough that I could hear the pounding drums, then spun the tuning wheel up and then back down, the radio voices singing a jumbled, unintelligible blur.

* * *

I'd forgotten the quality of the air on the island, how after a rain it would fill with dusty light. I'd forgotten how the sun shot arrows through branches and clouds, shining spotlights across your path. The rain had turned things muggy, and as we walked the streets holding birthday gifts we'd bought for Gillian, both Justin and I shed jackets and sweaters, our talk growing easy and familiar.

"One of my first memories of you was on the Powells' roof," Justin said, nodding at a yellow-shingled house with a trellis climbing the porch. "You were dressed in this long skirt."

"I was playing a farmer's wife for some skit in school. I had this impression that skirt made me look at least sixteen."

Justin smiled. "And that trellis was like a magnet. I climbed up and you stood here watching, and when you couldn't stand it anymore you stripped off your skirt and climbed up with me."

I remembered sitting beside him, bare legged and triumphant, overlooking an umbrella of trees. A plane had passed overhead and he'd grabbed my hand to keep me steady, hadn't let go until we stood to clamber back to the ground.

"I thought that was so amazing," he said. "If you wanted something, you just went for it. Not too many six-year-old girls you could call brave."

"And plus I had nice legs," I said, feeling unexpectedly buoyant. I had a sudden longing to lean my head on his shoulder, but instead I squeezed fists so hard I knew there must be dents in my palms. I'd been flirting, I knew that.

We walked for a while in silence. He pulled in front of me as a car passed and I forced my eyes to the road so I wouldn't have to look at the line of his shoulders, the pull of his blue-jeaned legs. But after a minute, my eyes forced themselves back to his legs. How vile was I? Completely vile.

When we reached the edge of the bluffs, we stood watching the parade of waves below, each row of crests lined up behind the others, waiting its turn to slip and spread onto the shore.

"Beautiful as ever, hunh?" he said.

But that wasn't what I was thinking, not at all. I was wondering how this spot could be so calm, organized as rolls of folded socks. Only the jagged rocks were the same, visible under the swells, rocks we'd wrongly thought could tear a body to pieces, obliterate. I turned away quickly. "You ever have nightmares?" I said.

He eyed me a second, then turned back to the surf. "Eve does. She doesn't say what it is that keeps her awake, but I guess I know."

"I have nightmares. I mean, sometimes it's enough to literally make me puke. It's scary how you can go about your days and not think about it until something happens to remind you, or until you're asleep and your defenses are down. Which shows it must always be there weighing on you, and the rest of you's just kind of skating above it and trying not to look down."

"Eve says it's like this animal with claws that keeps poking at her belly whenever she tries to sleep. She closes her eyes and this claw pokes at her and says, *Hey, not so fast.* She's so sick and her mind's still holding on to this."

"Well sure it is." I glanced at him. "Isn't yours?"

"No, not anymore. I mean, I think about it." He shrugged, a quick up and down. "But not in the same way." Our eyes met briefly, and I saw a flicker of fear before his face tightened. "We should get back. Gillian'll be home pretty soon."

I kept my eyes on the dirt road as we started home. I didn't want to see anything that would tunnel me back. So many places here on the island were just waiting for me to notice so they could snare my memories like fishhooks, draw them out of hiding.

Justin opened the door without speaking and started in. When he reached the stairs he finally turned to me. "We were kids, Kerry." His tone seemed almost pleading.

But it was such an easy rationalization of something that shouldn't be rationalized. All this time we'd never talked about it, and even now only sketchily: *that night; it; what we did.* Sitting in his car that night, Justin had told us to hold what we wished had happened in our minds until it became the truth. Was that what he'd done all these years?

I studied his face, trying to find some trace, some stain from the past, however faded. His face should at least show remnants of horror, if not guilt, but there was nothing. Just a plea for me to stop talking.

"Could I have some help here?" It was Eve, calling from the kitchen.

I held out the gift bags for him to take. "I'll go."

"You can't live with this haunting you forever. It'll kill you."

"I've lived through worse," I said, then turned away.

In the kitchen, Eve stood over a large mixing bowl. "Where's Justin?"

"He's gone upstairs. What're you making?"

She looked at me, her eyes narrowed. "Tomorrow's Gillian's birthday."

I smiled. "We were actually just out buying gifts."

"Well, thank God. Whatever would I do without you."

I blinked quickly, then shook my head. "Okay. Okay, I'm sick of this. Let's call a truce."

"I didn't realize there was an actual war."

I raised my eyebrows and Eve shrugged. "Whatever," she said. "I'm too tired to care."

"Oh, good. That was exactly the reaction I was looking for."

Eve glanced at me, then away.

I cleared my throat. "So you're baking a cake?"

"And cupcakes for school. Look, I just need you to add the mix. The smell of artificial chocolate makes me nauseous. It has these plasticky undertones that remind me of the hospital. Like latex, or adhesive bandages."

I opened the bag of cake mix and poured it into the bowl of eggs and milk. Eve stood across the room, watching. "God, I can smell it from here. Once it starts baking I may die right then, I'm just warning you."

"We'll keep the kitchen door closed."

She opened the window and leaned out to let the breeze hit her face. "We usually do this together, me and Gillian, make her cake. It's this stupid, fantastic ritual, we each take a beater and toast to her birthday. But I didn't want her to see this, me turning green."

"We used to do that, you and me," I said softly, "toast beaters on our birthday."

Eve watched me for a minute, then gave a tight smile. "Right. I forgot."

Back on the empty birthdays in my Boston apartment, I'd take out the one photograph I had of us and sit with it, sometimes for hours. I wanted to ask her how she'd celebrated birthdays since I'd left, if she'd treated them as something that belonged only to her. For me, it had been the one day I'd allowed myself to remember everything. "You want to lie down?" I said. "I can finish up here."

Eve pulled out a cake pan. "She'll be home any minute. I want her to see me cooking, that at least I tried to make an effort."

As if in response, the front door opened. Gillian's footsteps started down the hall, stopped at the den, then continued towards us. "Ma?"

"Give me that," Eve whispered, pulling the bowl and spoon towards her. She held her breath and began to pour out batter.

"In here, Gillian," I said.

Gillian came into the kitchen, dropped her knapsack and watched. "What's that for?"

"What do you think it's for?" Eve's voice was strained, but she smiled widely.

Gillian's face flushed pink. She didn't speak.

"Did you think I wouldn't remember?"

"How come you used a spoon instead of beaters?" She looked at the packaged mix, then back to Eve. "How come you used Duncan Hines instead of from scratch? How come you didn't wait till I got home?"

"It was a surprise. I wanted to surprise you."

"It's not a surprise, it's stupid."

"Here, let's toast." Eve handed Gillian the spoon, then pulled out a beater from the drawer and dipped it into the batter. "Another year older, smarter, prettier, here's to turning twelve." She clicked her beater against Gillian's spoon, hesitated a minute and then brought it to her mouth. She chewed at the batter a long while without swallowing, a strange smile on her face. "Excuse me a minute." She dropped the beater onto the table and strode down the hall.

Gillian put her spoon back into the bowl, stared down at it, then turned away and started out the door. I reached out a hand to stop her. "Gillian?"

"Everything's different now." Her voice was tight. "Even my birthday."

"Some things have to be different, I guess. But the important things are the same." The words sounded so stupid, so fake, like I was telling her everything would be better soon. I tried to smile. "Wait'll you see what we got you, Gillian. Real grownup gifts."

"I don't want gifts, and especially I don't want a cake. Or a party either, I thought about it and I decided."

"It'll be worse that way. You were just saying how everything's different, so now it's important to make things as much the same as we can."

"What do I wish for?"

"Wish for?"

"On my candles. I know it's dumb and it doesn't really work, but you have to do it anyway. Last year I wished for her to get better because maybe she might've, but this year there isn't even a chance. It's the only thing

I want, and if I wish for anything else it'll feel like giving up, so what do I wish for?"

I stirred slowly at the cake mix, trying to think how to answer. What was left to wish? "There's lots of things," I said finally. "You could wish that however long she has with us is happy."

"I could maybe wish she's still here for the birthday when I turn thirteen," Gillian said, then gave a strangled laugh. "Which is dumb since that's impossible."

"It's not impossible," I said without thinking, then shook my head. "I mean, anything's possible."

"This isn't," she said, then lifted her head to look at me. "Is it? I mean, is there even like a small chance she could be okay that long?"

"She's a really strong person," I said, then smiled. "If anyone could do it, your mom could. We'll tell your dad and we'll all wish for it, okay? If there's a chance wishes work, we'll do whatever we can to make this one come true."

We sat on the lawn watching Gillian open her presents, Justin, Eve and the Caines, with four of Gillian's friends from school. Gillian hugged and clapped at all her gifts, just the way she was supposed to. I couldn't see any trace of her bitterness from the day before.

I reached to stuff the latest round of discarded wrapping into a paper bag, then turned to watch Eve on her Adirondack chair, a blanket wrapped over her shoulders. What had it meant to us, turning twelve? The last year of real childhood, the first year our gifts leaned more toward clothes and music than toys, the year we began wearing bras, the year we got our periods, the year we started feeling the first stirrings of sex. It meant, Eve had said back then, that we'd lived as many years without our mother as with her. And we'd seen that as a sort of victory, like it proved we didn't need a mother anymore.

But this is who we'd been, this little girl with flushed cheeks, now opening the earrings I'd bought for her, her understanding of loss exponentially deeper at twelve than ours had been. And on the cusp of life's biggest changes, needing a mother at least as much.

"They're great," she said, glancing at me shyly. "Really great." Her finger stroked the hoop of tiny pearls, and then she stood to fold her arms briefly around my neck.

I patted her hand, her pink nail polish applied this morning and already bitten away. Across from us Justin watched intently, his thoughts so naked, so exposed I thanked God that Eve couldn't see. He obviously knew what was out there, the ghost of possibility. And like me, he was trying so hard not to want it.

13

JUSTIN'S OFFICE SEEMED to me completely dysfunctional. It was as cluttered as his potting shed had been, papers scattered on every possible surface. Every night before I could sleep I'd have to collect the papers he'd strewn on my bed and arrange them into piles on the rolltop desk, and then the next night I'd find them back on the bed again in the same exact state of disarray. It was funny, in an annoying kind of way.

Justin was at the desk now, hunched over his notepad. Final drafts he typed into the computer downstairs, but first drafts were always written by hand. I watched from the doorway as he wrote in a broad sweeping script, seemingly working simultaneously on three pieces of paper. It was like Mozart composing a symphony, half drunk and half deranged.

I squinted, studying the pen he was using, gold and ribbed, the thickness of a thumb. Could it possibly be the pen I'd given him for Christmas the year I left? I felt a kind of burrowing in my stomach, remembering the thrill I'd felt picking it out, seeing it arrive in the mail, watching him open it and try it for the first time on a scrap of Christmas wrapping: *I LOVE KERRY BARNARD.* Maybe every time he used it over the years I'd been gone, he'd thought of me as he'd held it between his fingers. Or, maybe not. Maybe he just liked the pen.

I smiled with another memory, lying beside Justin on the bed while he wrote. For some reason, needing attention maybe, I'd rested my hand over his notepad. He'd pretended not to notice, had written right across my hand to the other side of the paper. *Across the tree line,* the words had said. And all the next day at school I'd looked down at those words with total and complete happiness, feeling like in a way I'd become a part of his writing.

Now, watching him, I felt a weight on my chest, cramming against my lungs. And I couldn't help myself. My hand had a mind of its own. It reached over his arm and laid itself across the scrawled script.

Justin stopped for a minute, unmoving, then laid down his pen. Without looking up he traced his finger in a faltering S around and between my knuckles. I closed my eyes, angry at my hand but helpless against it. The mind inside my hand held total control.

Downstairs, the doorbell chimed.

I spun back, thrust my fists under my arms. "What're you doing?"

"I'll get it!" Gillian called.

Justin didn't move; he kept his eyes on his desk. "What are *you* doing?"

"I wasn't doing anything." I sank to the bed, forced my fists to loosen. "Dammit, Justin, why the hell did you call me here?"

"You know why I called you. You think it was for me?"

My tongue wanted to say *Yes,* so I bit down on it. Hard.

He turned then, his eyes fierce, his jaw set. "You have

a scent, did you know that? Like lavender kind of, but deeper, not quite as sweet. And every time I come into this room to work I can smell it."

"Justin, don't."

"So my brain gets stuck there and everything I'm writing sounds robotic, like a history textbook." He lifted the scrawled papers in his fist. "I can't use any of this, it's total crap."

"Stop it!" I gripped the blanket as if the swatch of woven cotton could steady me. "I have to go back to Boston."

"You can't go."

"Are you kidding? You tell me you're obsessed with how I smell and what do you expect me to do? Eve already thinks she knows why I'm here. She thinks the minute she's gone I'll just slide right in to take her place."

"Which is exactly why you can't leave." Justin pushed back his chair and strode to the window. "You really think you're irresistible? You really think I'm that weak?"

Oh. Well this wasn't what he was supposed to say. The weight on my chest lifted. I started hating myself.

"I love Eve, Kerry. She's my wife and the mother of my kid and I'm not about to let anything hurt her, not now and not after she's dead. But if you leave now, she'll know everything she suspects is true, that you couldn't stay because you were scared of what one of us would do."

"Hey, Jussy?" Eve called from downstairs.

I hunched over my knees.

"So I'm going to keep writing crap because I don't have any choice. And I won't think about you because I don't want to think about you, and we'll both be here for Eve." He crumpled his papers and threw them at the wastebasket. "I have to go to my wife," he said, then turned and strode from the room.

I sat there, head on my knees. He loved Eve, of course he did. Maybe part of me had held out a twisted kind of hope. But that hope was a tidal wave, maybe exhilarating on the outside but treacherous in reality. We'd played a game, the three of us, and I had lost, and it wasn't the kind of game you could ever play again.

"Firs' the pullin', then the plantin'." The voice came from outside.

I stood to look out the window. LoraLee, Eve, Justin and Gillian were kneeling by the flowerbed, surrounded on all sides by pots of multicolored petunias, fat and round as puckered lips.

"It's gonna look like confetti," Gillian said.

"It's going to look like a funeral home," Eve said, but she was smiling.

"Pssshht," LoraLee said, waving the root end of a weed at her. "I figure you could mebbe use gettin' your fingers in some dirt."

"Pity petunias," Eve said.

"No pity, I don't got pity. Me and the petunias don't know nothin' 'bout pity, we just smile and goes on smilin' till our time is done." She nodded at Gillian. "That there is a none too subtle metaphor for life, part of what I come here to say to your mama. My thinkin' is, these flower smile and you can't help but smile back."

"Well, I'm smiling," Eve said. "Whatever your reasons for bringing them I'm smiling, and you're right about this hands-in-the-dirt thing. It feels kind of fundamental, like it grounds you."

I thought back on the day after I'd come back to the island, the first time I'd seen LoraLee. "I wanted to tell you 'bout it all, Kerry," she'd said. "I's so sorry. You got no idea how my head were bustin' from keepin' it inside. But she made me swear. I tole her it were a mistake and I knows you shoulda been here sooner."

"I don't know if I should even be here now," I'd said. "She doesn't want me here."

"You's wrong 'bout that. I seen her these past years, seen what's missin' in her. And deep down she see it, too. How what's missin' is her one biggest tie to the worl'."

"Not anymore. She has her own life now, which has nothing to do with me at all. And honestly, I don't feel it anymore either, that tie." I shook my head quickly. "I realize I should just spend time with her, give her my forgiveness. It sounds so straightforward, I should be able to just give her what she needs."

"What you mean, straightforward? You been to hell and back and now you say you's wrong to be feelin' the burns? Let me tell you, I know it's a hard thing, but it's harder 'cos you thinks it s'posed to be simple. You thinks there's one singular right way to feel."

She'd turned to sit on the front steps. I'd watched her for a minute, thick-ribbed stockings and pink high-top sneakers, then sat beside her, fingering the ivy-strangled lattice.

"Since far back as I 'members," she said, "you been tryin' to be your sister, like you don't feel there enough of you inside to bother with bein' you own self."

I'd looked out at the dusty road, and it had come back

to me like a dark wink, the grays of my apartment, the city smells of oil and sour milk. What was left of me?

"When you lef', you was at the age most peoples is tryin' to find theyself. But you, Kerry, you muffle your insides with pile on pile of cotton so it don't ever have a chance of seein' the light."

"She took my life away," I said. "It was mine."

"It's hers, Kerry, not yours. Everything happen the way it s'posed to happen, even if it don't seem that way at first. Soon's you unnerstan' that, you be able to go on livin' and learn what you's meant to learn, but till then you jus' be waitin' for time to go backwards. I tell you, you be waitin' forever."

Now, as if she'd sensed my thoughts, LoraLee turned towards the window. "Your sister could use some smilin' too, prob'ly much as you. Where she at?"

"She's not feeling good," Justin said quickly. Eve raised her eyebrows at him and he shrugged. "Some kind of headache thing."

I closed my eyes and wrapped my arms around my waist.

"She'd be better at this planting stuff," Eve said. "She used to help you in your garden, right? But I've never owned a plant that hasn't died within a week."

"Remember the Venus flytrap?" Gillian said.

Eve laughed. "You were what, six?"

"Seven," Justin said. His voice was light now, no sign of distraction. No sign of me. "We suffocated it."

"It was supposed to be a learning experience," Eve said, "like a PBS nature show. But Gillian got a little carried away."

"We wanted it to catch the houseflies," Justin said.

"But after Gillian saw a couple bugs disappear down its throat, she fell in love with it. She treated it like a pet goldfish."

"It looked hungry," Gillian said.

Justin laughed. I opened my eyes in time to watch him slip his arm around Eve's shoulders.

"So I'm passing by the hall table," Eve said, "and there I see this poor Venus flytrap brimming to the roof with bugs. Like some obscene modern sculpture. And little by little it turns yellow and wilts, and there's all these bugs dropping out from the petals. And of all things, Gillian decides to bring it to school for show-and-tell."

"It was totally gross," Gillian said.

"Maybe that could be another metaphor," Eve said. "Too much love can kill."

"Don't like that one," LoraLee said, "but I guess it's maybe true in a sense."

Did Eve realize what she'd said? Had she thought behind it to the people in our lives who love had killed?

Justin wrapped his other arm around her and kissed her cheek. "So let it kill me," he said.

Eve's face flushed with pleasure. Gillian beamed up at them, then rested her head on Eve's shoulder. And as I watched them I realized the reason for the tightness in my throat, that part of me had imagined their life together had been a sham, something invented. That all this time, I'd managed to pretend their real life had only started on the day that I'd returned.

* * *

The gymnasium echoed with children's voices, pounding nails and the clank of paint cans. On the far side of the gym, Gillian and Eve were mastering the art of stenciling, dabbing brushes against a panel of grass blades. Gillian was talking animatedly, stopping now and again to focus on her painting. And Eve was smiling. Beaming. The first real happiness I'd seen in weeks. She was eating more now that the effects of the chemo had worn off and was starting to put on weight in her face. A deceptive, almost cruel, mask of health, the climb before the inevitable crash.

I tried to concentrate, screwing a support beam to the back of a plywood barn, while on the other side Virginia Brent tried to keep it from toppling. Mrs. Brent had been our teacher in sixth and seventh grade, and now taught K-through-twelve art. She'd seemed ancient to us back then, so by all rights by now she should be mummified. But really today she was acting decades younger than I was, flitting from project to project, clasping her hands to her chest with pleasure and chattering away nonstop.

"I'm so glad you're here," she said to me now, "you have no idea."

"I don't know how much use I'll be. I can't draw a straight line, and the most carpentry I've ever done is banging picture hangers into a wall."

"No, no, that's not what I mean. What I mean is I'm glad you're here with your sister. I've always thought it wasn't right with her so sick and you off somewhere else."

I pressed the drill lever, its vibration traveling up my

arms, drilled another hole and another. If this conversation kept up, the barn would look like Swiss cheese. "I wish I had been here."

"Oh, we all knew what had happened between you, and I'm sure no one took a dim view of you for leaving, not back then. But after Eve got sick, well folks started to talk is all. About how you were her only family. We're just so thrilled you're back."

How much did they know? I was glad she was hidden on the other side of the barn, that I couldn't see her face. Since I'd gotten here I'd wondered what the townspeople were thinking, wondered what their eyes were saying when they passed me in the street without acknowledgment. The few people who'd come to the house had greeted me with a hug, but then turned all their attention to Eve. So did they think I'd known she was sick? That I'd just chosen to shut my eyes to it? Most likely it didn't matter that I hadn't known. To the islanders, family was everything, even distant family like second cousins or uncles three times removed. My absence must have seemed to them like the ultimate selfishness.

"Heck, I'm sorry," Mrs. Brent said. "I know I've become an old busybody, sticking my nose in your business. I hate that about myself, but maybe it's a natural part of getting older, like losing your neck."

"Hey, Mrs. Brent?" Gillian called from behind me. "We're almost finished here but we messed up a few times. We weren't very good at it."

"Oh I'm sure it's gorgeous, and besides, mistakes don't matter. They give the scenery character, I think. So you ready for another project? I've been saving it for you,

Gillian, it's the most important project of the bunch. Center stage."

I finished threading screws into the barn supports, while Mrs. Brent showed Gillian how to string white yarn into a web. When she'd left, Gillian came to stand beside me, watching. After a minute she spoke. "I figured it out. Why I got to play Wilbur, and why Mrs. Brent let me do the web, it's because everybody feels sorry for me."

"Oh sweetie, that's not true."

"That's why she said it was okay we messed up on the painting. In art class she just about goes ballistic if some-one colors outside the lines." She shrugged. "It's okay. I mean, I don't really care. Can I try the screwdriver?"

I handed it to her, watched her struggle to tighten a screw. She spoke without turning to face me. "I wanted to ask you something."

"Okay?"

"It's maybe a stupid question but I just thought I should ask. Are you staying with us after? I mean after Mom's not here?"

It took me a minute to answer. Finally I turned back to the barn. "I don't know, Gillian, maybe for a little while."

"Because you could, you know. You could stay even forever, I wouldn't mind. I know I said you shouldn't be here, but I just wanted to tell you I don't think that any-more."

I reached for her, a deep ache in my chest of sadness and sweetness. And then I saw Eve. She was standing be-hind Gillian, trying to look like she wasn't listening, her grin stretched narrow and false. "Eve?" I said.

Gillian spun around, her face pale like she understood the full depth of what Eve had heard and what it would mean to her.

"Well I'm getting tired of this," Eve said. "Think I'll pull up my chaps and wheel on home."

"I'll go with you," Gillian said hurriedly, then glanced at me. "Tell Mrs. Brent it's okay with me if somebody else finishes the web."

I nodded and raised my hand good-bye as Gillian walked her mother to the wheelchair. I leaned against the plywood barn and watched their retreating backs. I wanted to go after them, to say something, explain. But of course I knew there was really nothing that could be said.

I woke that night to a sound echoing through the radiator pipes. I squinted at the bedside clock. Nearly midnight.

It was a moan I'd heard, barely perceptible. I rubbed the sleep from my eyes, reached for Eve's pill bottle and padded downstairs. I turned the corner heading for the den, then stopped short.

Their bodies rocked slowly, silhouetted under the sheets, a tender smoothing of his form on hers like they were spreading butter on something soft. The love hung over them like an aura, a hovering perfume. I stared for a minute, frozen, then spun away.

Back upstairs I reached under my bed for the envelope I'd brought, holding the torn letters we'd written the day I'd left. I pressed the envelope between my palms. All these years I'd known these letters might hold the answer I'd been looking for, the answer to who had owned Justin first.

I lay on my back, my eyes squeezed shut. I hadn't seen their faces, but in my mind their faces were those of children, Eve and Justin the way I'd pictured them so many times, the seducer and the seduced. In those pictures I'd imagined myself standing by their bed and watching. And then when things got hot and heavy, throwing in a live grenade.

But now it was all so different, because I'd seen the love between them. Somehow I'd never let myself think that love might be real.

There was a tight cry from downstairs and I crumpled the envelope and pulled the pillow over my head, every muscle in me tensed. I curled against the wall and imagined Eve's legs around Justin's waist, both thinking of me maybe for one second before they forgot to think. The three of us together there in that one second, a husband and a wife and a woman they thought of only in that glancing moment of shame. While my resentment was still here in the deepest parts of me, hanging over them like foam on the sea, with the sea flowing on unperturbed as if it didn't even know.

Eve gave her a bright smile. "It's only because I'm so thrilled to see you," she said.

Approaching the café, Eve turned to me. "I hate how they pretend they don't know I'm dying. They all do it, like they're trying to keep a secret from me, as if I don't know."

"What, are you looking for sympathy? You want them getting all red in the face and telling you how life is unfair and they've got the whole church praying for you?"

"I could use a whole church praying for me. Do you think they are?" She pulled at the café door, then stopped to read a sign in the window, yellow poster board with letters in tempera paint. "Look at that," she said. "Madame Rosa, palmistry, tarot, answers to every question guaranteed."

"Guaranteed? What's that mean, that she guarantees she'll come up with some kind of answer, or that the answers are right?"

"And she lives over the café. I didn't know we had a psychic. Guess she comes in for the summer."

"A little hokey for the island, God. Soon we'll have neon signs and kids on street corners who want to soap your windshield."

"Let's go check her out."

"Yeah, maybe she'll look at you and tell us you're sick."

"I'm serious. We could ask her how much longer I have. I'm sick of not knowing." She smiled crookedly. "Even if what she tells me is bullshit, at least I'll have something to aim for."

We climbed the side steps to the apartment over the

14

IT ALL CAME BACK to us like retribution, a stranger's glimpse into our past and our future. It was a May afternoon that felt like August with its airless oven heat. The sea breezes were like night breath, moist and fishy stale.

We walked to the Java Café, Eve holding my arm for support. This was our first time out alone together. It wasn't like she'd suggested it; I'd asked if she'd mind coming to help me pick out some clothes and she'd shrugged her agreement, but still. It was something.

As we turned down the road to the café, Audrey Mullin, the town librarian, emerged from Town Hall. She was wearing a bright green sun hat, an orange sweater and orange sweatpants, like a misshapen carrot. She beamed at us. "You're looking good today, Eve!" she said. "Have to say we were all getting worried for a while there."

"Yeah, I had cancer but I'm over it."

I kicked Eve's ankle. Audrey Mullin stared at her a moment, deciding how to react. "Oh, Eve, you're always such a kidder," is what she came up with. She flushed and cleared her throat. "What I mean is, I'm glad to see you looking better."

café. Eve knocked on the faded blue door. There was no answer. After a minute she knocked again harder, and after another minute she turned to me. "I predict a reading's not in our future," she said.

At this, the door swung open. A tiny woman peered out at us, bright red hair, a long scarf draped around her shoulders and a face younger than I'd expected. "You here to see Madame Rosa," she said, her accent thick.

"You must be psychic!" Eve said, then gave an apologetic smile. "Sorry, that was crass. So how much is it? I mean for your basic-reading kind of stuff."

The woman nodded slowly and turned back inside. Eve and I glanced at each other, then followed.

We entered a dimly lit room, purple shag bathmats draped over the sofa cushions and a large abstract painting on the wall. A television was on, tuned to a talk show. "He told me what you done," a woman said. "How you *beep*ed him and then gave him your panties and said he could wear them, and that's how he started buying *beep*ing heels and tryin' to fit into my dresses. Which he busted my favorite skirt and now I say you owe me fifty bucks."

We entered the kitchen. Madame Rosa gestured at the chairs encircling a round table, then began to shuffle through a drawer. I sat, feeling slightly stupid. After a second Eve sat beside me.

"You pay what you think is worth for you. You choose." Madame Rosa swung the drawer shut and held up a pack of cards and a stick tied at one end with a leather tassel. "But first you choose palm or tarot."

Eve held out her hands. "Palm," she said.

I watched as the woman traced the leather tassel

across Eve's hands, amazed that Eve actually seemed to be treating this seriously, her jaw set, watching the woman's face.

"This your life line," the woman said. "Not so long, this line. You don't have much time here left."

"I'm astonished by your brilliance," I said, figuring I needed to do something to break Eve out of her strange stillness.

The woman glanced at me, spoke to my face. "Not so much time as you think you have. It all come much sooner, so is time to do what need to be done to get ready. Not just outside but also inside."

I narrowed my eyes at her. Whether or not she really believed she saw something, her words seemed unbelievably cruel.

"You been through a difficult childhood, done things you ashamed of, many things, and now you playing it out through your body." She closed her eyes and nodded slowly. "But he forgive you. He say it is time to move on."

"I don't believe in God," Eve said.

"Not God, I speak of the man from long ago. The man in your head now, I don't need tarot to see it. He not thinking about you, so why you waste the time you have left still fighting to keep him in your head?"

Eve and I looked at each other silently, and then Eve pulled a bill out from her wallet. "Thanks." She slapped it on the table, a fifty, then stood from her chair.

The woman's eyes snapped open and she stared pointedly at Eve, then shifted her eyes to the money and then to me. "And you? I read your palm?"

I gave her a sharp smile. "That's okay, no thanks."

"You think I am full of shit, yes?" She nodded and

pulled back from the table. "S'okay, I don't need your palm to see. You, you have the same childhood, but you living it out through your soul, not your body. It is healthier through your body though, because when your body gone, the shame also gone. And oh..." She lifted the tail end of her scarf and flipped it over her shoulder. "There something else I tell because I like you. You don't have to pay, but if someone ask you for advice, you tell them about Madame Rosa, yes? And for that I tell you someone return to you soon, you have a visit. Someone who been gone a long time, and that person help you heal. That's all I have for you."

"And I'll meet a tall, dark, handsome stranger," I said, standing.

The woman smiled. "Oh no, you already know your stranger," she said.

Back on the street, Eve walked a ways before speaking. "So what did you think?" she said finally.

"About her? What do you bet she gives everyone the same lines about how you need to heal your insides before you die?"

"How about that man-from-long-ago stuff?"

I couldn't turn to her, couldn't let her see my face. All this time I'd been here we hadn't talked about it, a promise we'd made to ourselves thirteen years ago and were still keeping. Still needed to keep. "I bet she gives that line, too. Everybody needs forgiveness from someone."

"And about someone returning to you? To help you heal? Don't you think she means me?"

"She said returning soon. Which means future

tense." I tried to smile. "Besides, you haven't even come close to helping me heal."

Eve walked on a minute without speaking, then turned to me. "I want to go up on Beacon Hill."

"Beacon Hill? That's private property."

"Do I care? Won't be the first time we broke a law." She focused on the road again, then shook her head. "She said I was going to die sooner than I think."

"I can't believe you bought that crap."

"I want to go up there. You can see the whole island from the top. I mean, I've never really lived anywhere else, this is where everything happened. I need to see it all together, all at one time, get my arms around it."

I knew what she meant. It was the same feeling I'd had returning on the ferry, how all of it, everything that had made me who I was, was balanced so precariously in one place. "Okay," I said.

We drove as far as we could up Beacon Hill and parked. I struggled to push Eve's wheelchair to the top and then stood with her, looking down over the island. Views like this were why humanity had once thought the world was flat; this land at center and the blue cloth of water on all sides, a universe with no edges and no ends.

"Makes you realize how small the island is," I said.

"Getting smaller every year because of the surf. They had to move the Southeast Lighthouse a few years back so it didn't fall off the bluffs."

I sank onto the ground, hugged my knees against my chest. "Remember the studies when we were kids? How in another few hundred years the island'll disappear altogether? That seemed so scary, the same kind of fear I got when I learned about how a giant asteroid could hit and wipe out the human race."

"Made me picture how we'd all have to move our houses to the middle of the island. I saw Daddy lifting the house onto a truck and carting it out."

"And then the water gets closer and closer, and then it's at our doorstep and we have to decide if we should leave or just drown."

Eve gave me a vague smile. When I smiled back, her face hardened. "God, I feel sick."

"You want to get home?"

"Not that kind of sick. You know what I was thinking? I keep thinking, what would we have thought back then if we could see us now? Christ, I would've killed myself, saved myself a lot of trouble."

"Stop it, Eve." I eyed the wheelchair behind her. What would I have done if I'd seen all this? "Look what you've accomplished. Look at Gillian."

"Yeah, I've been a hell of a mother."

"Look how great she is. You've been an amazing mother."

Eve reached into her pocket for a bottle of pills, her face white with pain. "I heard you rehearsing lines yesterday."

"She's not bad, you know, says her lines with lots of inflection. And did you see her in the pig costume I made, with the ears and the twirly tail? You might be raising a movie star."

"God, I hope not." She shuffled backwards and sank into the wheelchair. "I sewed her a cat costume for Halloween last year, she tell you that?"

Shit, what was the right thing to say? "Well, I'm sure

your cat was better than my pig. The only pink fabric I could find at the quilt shop had pictures of cupcakes, so I bought her a leotard and made her ears out of sparkly paper."

"I heard what she said last week, while we were working on the set. About wanting you to stay."

I shook my head. "She was trying to be nice. To be polite."

"Right." She gazed out over the horizon. "Know why I never come to the dinner table?" Her words were slow and steady. "I hear you all. She tells you how Karen's her new best friend. She asks if she can stay up to watch the Sunday night movie, and then she comes to me. She stares with these weirdly big eyes and gives me this shy hug like she thinks I'm going to break." Eve's breath was ragged. She closed her eyes and fought for a minute, trying to get enough air.

I watched her, not sure what to say. "I'm not trying to take your place."

"If you stay after I'm dead," she said, "if you're here when she's fifteen, when she's thirty so she knows you more years than she's known me, don't you think she'll forget she ever used to tell me anything? Or even worse, it'll all run together in her mind. When she tries to remember me she'll think of you."

I watched Eve, not sure what to say, if there was a right thing.

"That's not true. We won't let her forget."

"But it's more than that. More than forgetting. She'll remember she had a mother, but inside she'll replace me." Eve's voice cracked and she swallowed quickly. "I hated Mom for leaving us, and Daddy I hated too. Anything I ever used to feel about them got swallowed up by the hate."

"That's different," I said.

"If you stay after I die..." She closed her eyes. "If you stay, they'll eventually think my death was a good thing. They'll miss me for a while maybe, but they'll remember how I was in the end, and then they'll look at you." She made a disgusted face. "Boobs and all, the vision of the woman I should've been, and they'll think it was a good thing. So you have to promise me."

"Eve—" The word sounded like something scraped against gravel.

"Promise me you'll leave." She spoke in a hoarse whisper. "You won't stay with him, will you?"

I looked out over the hillside, my island, a knot of pain in my chest. "I promise," I said. "I won't stay, I promise you."

February 1994

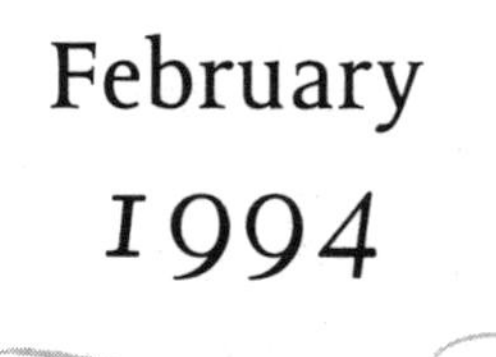

15

WINTERS ON THE ISLAND, the wind never stops. It's a wet wind, a biting wind that eats through clothes and sheets your eyeballs with ice. "The graying gusts," Daddy used to call them because of the crystals the wind feathered through his beard and eyebrows, or maybe because everything in winter—the sky, the grass, the ocean, even the people—looked like they'd been washed too many times in chlorine bleach.

I sat on the shore, watching that gray water, the flurries that danced like dust motes shaken from the dirty clouds. Eve was out again. She'd been out past midnight three times that week and usually came back barely able to walk straight, her eyes glinting with something scary and adult. Seeing how things typically were with Eve, I knew she'd soon get tired of Brad Carrera or he of her, and life would go back to normal again. But I also knew this all must have something to do with me and Justin, so I felt guilty, and angry about the guilt, and guilty about the anger, one on top of the other.

I wrapped my scarf higher on my nose, remembering another beach; was it Delaware? It was one of the few memories I had of my mother, on a lounge chair, feet trailing in the water, her hair a dark cascade down her tanned back.

Eve and I were collecting shells and smooth stones into a paper sack. We ran barefoot along the shore dodging cold September waves, while Daddy lay slumped on his towel, his arm thrown over his eyes. When the sun started to set we ran back to show off a closed clam that was maybe, although realistically probably not, still alive. Daddy was snoring now, in grunts that jiggled his belly. Eve elbowed me and whispered, "I got an idea."

Quietly, stifling our giggles, we'd arranged our stones in a circle around him. Eve grinned at me and crept to set a crab shell in a cap on Daddy's head, then scampered back to me with a whoop of glee. We held each other, doubled over, cheeks aching with the laughter, filled with the lightness of summer, of laughter and of each other. In that one moment I was certain we'd always be like this, the four of us. I felt like we would never get older, like things would never change.

"Momma, look!" I'd called, my voice a screech of hilarity as I ran to her and wrapped my arms around her neck.

My mother took a long time turning, and when she finally did she only squared her jaw. She brushed my arms away. "He's drunk," she said.

Now I watched as the clouds faded to gray emptiness. A seagull strutted after a small black crab, the kind that's more legs than anything else. He poked at it, jabbed it with his beak, dropping and lifting and spitting out shell, so much work for a tiny bit of meat. When he lifted his head there was blood on his beak. I threw a rock and watched the bird flutter back over the shoreline. I stuck out my tongue at him, then picked up my bike and started home.

As I walked along the harbor I saw lights on in Samuel Peckham's Tavern. There were voices, raucous laughter, the whining cry of a saxophone, and I suddenly realized why. It was Groundhog Day. Daddy had come to the tavern every year for the Groundhog Day census, a virtually meaningless activity done more for the sense of tradition than to get any kind of serviceable count of population. When you're stone drunk you more or less forget any numbers after fifty.

Brad would be there, I knew that. Which meant Eve would be, too. I stood by the door, blowing on my hands for warmth, watching men with their beers making phone calls and keeping tally. They'd call out names from memory and phone the inns where off-islanders came in the dead of winter only to be counted and then leave, like being one out of the eight hundred gave them some claim.

It was dim inside, the smoke so thick the room looked out of focus. And yes, Eve was there, drifting around the bar. As I watched she sat with Brad and then, getting no attention, she stole his beer and drifted to stand by someone else.

"Whadda you guys think?" Congressman Maclean said as Eve swung onto a stool beside him. "We count the twins as two or one?"

She smiled and slipped an arm over his shoulder. "This from the politician who comes for summers, for census and Election Day. I'd say they don't count you at all."

"Guess you're definitely a person unto yourself," the congressman said, grinning.

Across the room Brad grabbed Missy, the waitress, around the waist. "A true original," he called.

Eve glanced at him, her face pink. "Enough for two men," she said, then took a swig of beer. She looked like she fit in perfectly here, flirting with these men Daddy's age. In the dusky light she looked like someone I didn't know at all. Someone I'd be in awe of, afraid of, someone I'd watch secretly, trying to learn what it was that drew everyone to her like she exuded some mysterious scent.

"Maybe you've had enough to drink," the congressman said. "You twenty-one yet?"

"Close enough."

The congressman laughed. "I'll buy that. Anyway, I should have the power to suspend state laws at least for one night."

Bill Greer, a man with badly chapped lips and skin the color and texture of Daddy's fake-leather wallet, smirked and slid another beer across the table. "She's got a body that's at least twenty-one. Drink on, sweetheart, and if you need a ride home you let me know."

Eve wrinkled her nose at him. "If it keeps you shelling out for drinks, then you dream on."

I rested my head against the door frame, the vibration from the loud jazz music shimmering through my skull. And standing alone there in the dark, I finally understood that Eve had abandoned my world and was on her way to another. Not caring if it meant she was leaving me behind.

* * *

It was early the next morning, still dark. I sat on Eve's bed huddled against the chill. Eve stared back, but she didn't see me, I could tell that, her eyes as cold and blind as glass marbles. I shook her shoulder. "Hey, wake up."

She rolled to the wall, pulled the covers up to her chin. I'd seen her like this a few times now and it was scary as hell, her deadness, this sense like she'd sunk underneath herself, flattened like a shadow or a paper doll. I brushed back her hair, the pieces that fell in her face. "School," I whispered.

She didn't respond. So after a minute I rose and found some clothes I thought she might wear, a black sweater, a skirt, thick wool stockings. I opened her dresser, frowning as I sifted through underwear I'd never seen before: thong panties, garters, a camisole and an underwire bra with holes cut where her nipples would be. And buried under the hooker lingerie was a bag filled with clanking bottles. Liquor bottles.

I tried to focus on where the hell she might've gotten the money for all of it, so I wouldn't have to think about Eve in porn clothes. But then the question got kind of scary in itself, so I shoved the silky things aside, reached to the back of the drawer and chose a pair of white cotton panties. I laid everything on the bed in order as if she was a little kid. "School," I said again.

She twisted towards me then and grasped, in one abrupt movement, for my arm. Her eyes pulled at me, hard with anger or fear. "I did it," she said.

She'd been out past two the night before, I'd watched her stumble in. Had something happened? My skin felt numb, like a celluloid Halloween mask. "Did what?"

"He's amazing, don't you think? And he loves me, I really think he does."

I pushed her bangs away from her eyes. "What's going on with you?"

"He does." She let go of my arm and stared down at her hand like it belonged to someone else. She smiled at it, then closed it in a fist. "He does," she said again.

"I told Brad it has to be somewhere warm," Eve said. "This snow's getting on my nerves. And no more hick towns either. Maybe Key West or New Orleans, somewhere there's always something happening, you just step out your front door and join the party."

I didn't speak, just mirrored my step to hers, crunching against the gray snow banked at the side of the road. She seemed to have recovered from that morning and I didn't want to ruin it. We were on our way to the Caines' shop, a stopover on Eve's way to the police station so she could "fix herself up." Apparently Brad was doing desk duty that afternoon. Last week Eve had told me how they'd made out on his desk, and I'd squealed because I knew she wanted me to.

"So he says whatever, long as it's with you. How romantic is that? It'd be sappy if somebody else said it, but with Brad it was romantic."

We used to talk about our future before Daddy died. We said we might travel, live a few years off-island just for variety, but then we'd come back and be neighbors. I should've realized that had changed.

"I told him he could make lots more money in the city, plus I said it'd be a hell of a lot more exciting being someplace where there's more for him to do than slapping kids' fingers for shoplifting. He's really wasting his talents, Ker, he could do anything if he just made himself get off his ass." Eve's hair had grown too long over the past few weeks, scraggly, always falling in her eyes. But she never bothered to pull it back or mentioned wanting to get it cut again.

"I was thinking politics," she said, "like mayor or governor. Hell, maybe president. Look at Ryan Maclean, Kerry, what's so great about him that he got into Congress? What makes him any better?" She shrugged. "I was at Samuel Peckham's last night and I was sitting with him. I think it's good for Brad to see he's not indispensable. So I'm sitting with the congressman, talking to him all friendly like. And get this, when I get up to leave he gives me this smile and pats my butt."

"Congressman Maclean patted your butt?" Somehow this depressed me.

"So here I am married to the president, and I could be a performance artist maybe, or lead tours through the Smithsonian, something trendy. And then Brad comes home and tells me about his day and picks out what dress I should wear to somebody's coronation ball."

I stopped at the entrance to the shop and stood there looking up at the faded paint. "I'd rather stay here," I said.

"Then you'll be stuck groveling to the Caines for shit-ass jobs."

"Least it's a little more realistic than thinking you'll be invited to a coronation." I strode past her into the oil scent of the shop. Justin was working on a moped, tightening something with a wrench so huge it probably could've screwed the roof off a house. Eve nudged me and spoke in a loud whisper. "Lookit those muscles."

Justin's face flushed as he turned to us. "Didn't know you guys were coming in today."

"I'm actually here to drop off Kerry and make myself presentable." Eve reached into her purse and pulled out her compact and lipstick, opened the mirror and smoothed deep crimson onto her lips.

I bent to Justin for a kiss, but he scurried backwards on his knees. "You better not," he said. "I'm filthy."

"Like I care." I pressed against him, buried my face in his hair. It was kind of cool holding him like this, like he was smaller than me, something I could protect.

"Much better," Eve said.

We both turned.

Eve had taken off her coat and sweater to reveal a black halter underneath. As she spoke she peeled off her stockings. "Kerry dressed me like a nun this morning."

Beside me Justin froze. His grip tightened on my arm. I glanced at him, then shifted to stand between them.

But Justin pulled away. And all of a sudden I could feel it, this wordless shadow that passed between them from Eve's narrowed eyes to the blanching of Justin's face. "It's twenty degrees out," he said.

"You worry too much." Eve pulled on her coat and nodded at me. "He worries too much. You gotta teach him to have more fun." With that she turned and sauntered out the door.

Justin watched after her, his eyes all hooded and unreadable. I looked down at the stockings she'd left on the floor, then reached again for him, kissed his cheek and then his neck, my lips working against the oil scent of him, working to pull him back.

He sighed and held me close, hands pressed at my back. His erection pressing against me felt like knuckles digging deep under my skin. But it was mine.

16

JUSTIN STOOD THERE NAKED, pink and raw looking, like the skin under a scab. He was ogling me and pulling at his penis. It was getting longer and thinner, like Silly Putty, and he grinned and held it towards me and started twirling it like a jumprope. "It's fun!" he said. I startled and sat up, sucking in my breath, then rubbed my hands against my eyes. Sometimes, I thought, it was better when the symbolism in dreams was more symbolic.

And then I noticed the light was on. I pulled my hands from my eyes and saw Eve huddled on the end of my bed. "Eve?"

She looked up at me, eyes black with smeared mascara. I crawled from my sheets to sit beside her. "God, Eve, what happened? You okay?"

"Sick fucking bastard."

I flinched and she covered her face and spoke into her hands. "He said he loved me, you believe that? And I actually thought that meant something. But tonight?"

I brushed back her hair, smoothed it behind her ear.

"Tonight he says, you know what I always wondered about? He goes, ever since I first saw the two of you last summer rubbing oil on each other's back, I've been thinking about it and thinking about it, can't get it out of my head."

I pulled away, beginning to realize what was coming. The Barbie Twins. Eve wiped her hands in black mascara streaks across her face. "He goes, you know how you guys share a room together and all, how you see each other…" She took a long, shuddering breath. "See each other naked? Well I always pictured the two of you together, he says, with maybe me in between to give you a little of what all girls want."

"Oh God…"

"What all girls want! That's what it was about, Kerry, from the beginning. Not about me. If you showed any interest, he would've been just as happy so he could watch you, and touch you, and make love to you and imagine I was there, too."

I stared at her. "Make love to you?"

She eyed me, then slowly nodded and gave a slim smile. "Guess 'make love' is the wrong way to put it. I'd say we fucked."

My heart plunged to my stomach. "Oh God, you didn't."

She squeezed her eyes shut, tears sheening on her cheeks. "I knew the whole time there was something sick about it, I really did. The words he used, oh lick me baby, so horny for me, can't-hold-back-you-gotta-suck-me. But I thought, I thought—" She pulled off her spiked heel and threw it against the wall, where it left a spiked-heel dent. "God, so stupid!"

I wanted to be able to say the right thing, but I was

still shaking and all I could remember was my eighth-grade Sex Ed and Daddy's halting talk. *There will come a time when you meet a very special man*... "Were you careful?"

Eve snorted. "Careful? Brad didn't like being careful. Could you imagine if I got pregnant? He'd say, Eve baby, I'm real sorry but pregnancy just doesn't turn me on. But hey, though, your sister free?"

I stared down at the bed. She wasn't a virgin, she wasn't a virgin. She'd seduced a man into her bed. She knew how it felt to have him inside her. She was a woman and I'd been left behind, and she hadn't even told me when it happened. I smoothed my hand helplessly over her leg. "It'll be okay," I said. *She's seen sperm,* I thought.

"Yeah, after I bite off his prick." She was silent a minute, then she grasped my hand and looked up at me with swollen eyes. "Could I lie here with you? Just for a little while?"

"Sure," I said.

She laid her head on my pillow and I pulled the covers over us both. She'd left Brad, which was all I'd wanted. And I tried to believe this meant I could pull her back, that we could lie here in my bed like when we were little, and I could watch her fall asleep then close my eyes and try to enter her dreams. I needed to know that things could be the same again. But when I closed my eyes, all I could see was Eve's naked body, legs wrapped around Officer Carrera in his blue-gray uniform.

The next day, Eve and I walked home from school together, something we hadn't done for weeks. The air was cold, but carried a hint of lemon, like it was trying to make it known that spring still planned on coming. Eve pretty much seemed to have forgotten last night. Her stride was strong and she bent to scratch the head of one of Miss Cora's swarming cats. The cat stared up at her, swishing her tail around and between Eve's ankles as if recognizing some kind of shared sensuality.

"I was thinking," I said, "want to hang out tonight? Just us?" I imagined us on one bed in our pajamas with flashlights. We'd talk about makeup and movie stars and who liked who, our conversation slow and fluid, as easy as thought.

"Sounds great," Eve said. "I would, but I have plans."

"Plans?" I stopped walking, feeling like I'd been slapped. She wasn't supposed to have any more plans.

"Hey, want to come with me? I'm going out for a few drinks. You could meet the guys."

"The guys?" I frowned. There weren't supposed to be any more guys. "Could I bring Justin?"

Eve glanced at me, her smile crooked. "You know what they call Justin? White-collar wannabe. They say he washes the dirt out from his nails every night so he can pretend he's somebody else."

I felt a flush of anger. I couldn't look at her, so I brushed by her and strode down the street. She grabbed my arm. "Hey, look, I wasn't agreeing with them, I just thought it would be nice for a change to spend time without Justin around."

Wasn't that what I'd wanted, time together? And if I wasn't sure yet how to pull her back to being herself, maybe understanding wherever she'd gone would help me to do that, like pulling a weed out by the roots.

We turned up Water Street, and as we started down the block I saw a flash of light. I swiveled my head and saw LoraLee sitting on the ground behind a dumpster. She had a large black box camera in her hands, and she seemed to be hiding. "LoraLee?" I said.

She stared at me wide-eyed, then rose, held up her hand in a quick wave and turned away from us into an alley. "LoraLee!" I said again.

Eve frowned. "Well, that was rude."

"It was weird," I said, watching her disappear around a corner. "Was she taking our picture?"

Eve shrugged. "She *is* a little weird. I could tell you other things I've seen her doing too."

"Like what?"

"Nothing you need to worry about. You'll find out eventually. So are you coming with me tonight or not?"

I squared my shoulders. "Okay," I said. "Okay, sure."

"I saw the hottest little outfit you could wear, black leather skirt and this red bodysuit. I almost bought it for myself."

"Black leather? That's not exactly my thing, Eve."

"But maybe it should be." She took my hand and squeezed. "C'mon, Ker, you can't wear lace collars and muumuus all your life. Let's see a little spirit."

"What exactly is so spiritual about leather?" I said, but I followed her down to Water Street and stood outside Eisner's, staring in at a faceless, hipless mannequin wearing a skirt that stopped mid-thigh. I tilted my head to see if it was wearing mannequin undies, then saw the price tag.

"A hundred fifty dollars?" I said, my chest bubbling

with insane-feeling laughter. "That's like fifty dollars a square inch."

Eve stood in silence watching me, then raked her fingers through her hair. "Look, forget it, you don't have to come. You wouldn't like it at the bar anyway. The things they talk about have nothing to do with you, like how when they were kids they were sure they'd play pro football, like the girlfriend that got away. When I'm there with them, it's like I can make them remember what they used to dream. But you, you just wouldn't get it."

"I have dreams," I said, "just I'm a little more realistic."

"That's the point of dreams though, Kerry, you reach for things that're just beyond you. And then once you get them, half the fun's gone out of it and you have to reach for something even bigger."

A foghorn pierced the air, the five o'clock ferry pulling from the harbor. I looked up at the skirt in the window and imagined how it would feel hugging my hips. "I can't, Eve. We're already late paying rent."

Eve nodded slowly, then tapped her knuckles against the small of my back. "Let's try it on."

Mrs. Laurence sat on a high stool behind the cash register, reading a book with a black cover. Her short dark hair fell in strands like claws against her face; the neckline of her black blouse spiked low between her flat breasts. "Girls," she said, barely lifting her head.

"Just browsing," Eve said, lifting random blouses from the racks. She made her way to the window and selected a bodysuit and the skirt.

Mrs. Laurence used a finger to mark her place. "Can I help you girls find something?"

"These purses are totally beautiful," Eve said, nodding at one with blue alligator skin and a huge brassy buckle. "We'll just try these few things."

In the dressing room Eve nodded at me. "Go on," she said.

I pulled off my jeans and struggled into the bodysuit, then the skirt. I frowned at the mirror. With my bangs ruffled, hanging in my eyes, I looked like I was about six years old, like one of those baby pageant stars. "Yick."

"Man, look at you," Eve said. "You got attitude. Who woulda guessed." I began to strip off the skirt, but she grabbed my hand to stop me. "Look, I got a better idea. Let's skip the bar. Those guys, they're Brad's friends anyway, type of guys who have pissing contests."

I made a face. Eve nodded at my reflection in the mirror. "But why don't you wear this for Justin instead? We'll take him out to a movie, think how he'd go for it. God, Kerry, look what it does for your boobs. Look at your butt, you're like every guy's wet dream."

Heat rushed to my face as I studied my reflection, the shimmer of leather at my hips. My butt did look good. "He'd hate it."

Eve rolled her eyes. "Look, Ker, he's not gonna hold out forever. If I can teach you one thing, it's that a man's brains are centered in his pants, and unless you make that part of him happy, eventually he'll look for somebody who can. This is just a little teaser, keep him interested."

"I don't need sex to be interesting."

"So that's all you want? To be interesting? You need sex to keep him passionate."

I ran my hands over the skirt, then pulled my hair over one shoulder.

Eve nodded. “It’s perfect. Now try this on over top.” She pulled off her own cotton skirt and stockings.

I stared at the clothes a minute, then slowly stepped into her skirt. I’d known all along this was what she’d been planning. Of course I’d known. It was like a test.

Eve pulled on my jeans and sweater and I tucked in her blouse. “She’ll notice,” I whispered.

Eve shook her head. “Someone asks her an hour from now who was in her shop, she won’t even remember we were here.”

I tucked my hair behind my ears and tried to smile, but I suddenly felt like crying.

Eve gathered the extra clothes and pulled back the dressing curtain. From the corner Mrs. Laurence eyed us and Eve shook her head. “Nothing really fit, but we’ll put these back for you.”

Mrs. Laurence gave a tight smile, the kind where you just knew her teeth must be gritted behind it. But I helped Eve hang the clothes and then walked to the door, the leather slithering its slinky foreign hands around my hips.

Eve and I stood on line for popcorn, homemade and buttery in large lunch bags. We’d walked to the theater, and I was shivering from the cold air seeping through my thin top. My toes, in Eve’s high heels, were killing me.

The Empire Theater was too tiny for the gathered crowd. From the street the Empire had a kind of romantic charm about it, but inside you could tell the cleaning staff was not the greatest. There was dust on the faded maroon curtain, a sticky cracked tile floor, and a stench somewhere between the smell of pee and of the cheap beer they served in plastic cups.

Parents and children milled around, waiting for the inner curtain to open. In the off-season, Friday was the only movie night, and the one-screen theater was bound to be packed, even though most of us had seen the movie more than once. I saw little Sara Cooper in line behind us, staring wide-eyed, gripping the back of her mother's knee. I wondered if she was seeing up my skirt.

I crossed my legs. "I feel pornographic."

"You look pornographic. I can't wait till Jussy sees this. Just think, he's sitting next to you and you look like this. He can't hardly keep his hands to himself, but he knows he can't be jumping your bones at the movies. It'll kill him."

I rolled my eyes, feeling suddenly sexy, adult. "You're so full of it."

"Yeah, there's gratitude for you."

I grinned at her, then pecked a kiss on her cheek. "Thanks, Eve."

She elbowed me and nodded towards the corner. "They're checking you out."

Two eighth-grade boys were eyeing us, their faces bright, looking just one step short of rolling out their tongues. It was gross. I wrapped my arms over my chest. "I can't believe you made me do this."

"You ever seen a guy pant? Lick your lips and see what happens."

I burst into giggles. Eve waggled her hips. "The power of femininity."

"The power of boobs!" I screeched through my giggles, so loud that several heads turned.

Including Justin's.

He was standing at the entrance to the theater, his face slowly flushing pink. He walked towards us, frowning.

I twirled in a circle, and ended with my arms stretched at my sides. "Ta-da!" Inside, though, I was shaking.

"It's the new Kerry Barnard," Eve said. "Admit it. She's hot."

"Jesus, Eve." He wasn't even looking at me. "What the hell're you doing?"

I stepped towards Eve. "Why does this have to have anything to do with Eve? I can't dress how I want?"

He watched her for a minute, then squared his jaw. "This is about last week, isn't it. Some kind of twisted revenge."

The color drained from Eve's face. She shook her head slightly.

"What do you mean last week?" I said. "What happened last week?"

His lips tightened.

"You think I even thought twice about it?" Eve said slowly. "You really think you're hot shit, don't you."

I watched the look that passed between them, and in it I thought I could see what had happened: Eve coming to Justin dressed more or less like I was now, an attempted seduction and his refusal. And now me and Justin, we'd been playing out a script. Had she been waiting for Justin to react just this way?

A tear of sweat slithered between my breasts. "What the hell's wrong with you?"

"There's something wrong with Justin, Kerry, not me. I'd think you'd get that by now." Her face was pale, almost frightened, but she narrowed her eyes at Justin and slipped her arm over my shoulders. "You want the virgin or you want sex, Justin, make up your mind. Although I guess you were wrong, it looks like Kerry could give you both."

"You bitch!" I shoved her away, then strode from the theater past the throng of people staring at me, my cleavage, my legs, all whispering and wondering. My breasts flounced under my braless bodysuit as I started to sprint, my ankles twisting in the heels. I finally hurled the shoes into the bushes, my bare feet screaming with each pounding step against the rough road.

At home I ran up to the bedroom, pacing to the window and back, window and back, as pissed at myself as I was at her. I wasn't that gullible. I knew Eve always had ulterior motives, so why hadn't I made myself look deeper? It was like trusting a shark not to eat you just because it looks like it's smiling, and because you like sharks.

I imagined Eve and Justin in the tiny darkened theater, eyeing each other in the romantic moments, holding each other's hands at the scary parts. I saw Eve turn to him and shake her head. "What the hell got into her?" she'd ask. And Justin would shrug and then he'd smile and take her hand. "Frankly, I can't deal anymore," he'd say. And then they'd make out.

I tore off the skirt, black buttons clattering to the floor. I went to Daddy's bedroom and pulled his terry robe from the closet, wrapped myself inside it. And I huddled inside its smell of Irish Spring, its pocket still weighted with his sloshing tin flask of scotch.

It was still dark out when I woke up on Daddy's bed. In the light from the hall, I could see Eve's silhouette above me. "I'm sorry," she whispered hoarsely, smoothing her hand against the bedspread.

I slapped her hand away. "What's the matter with you?"

She hunched her shoulders. "I don't know."

"You don't know. Oh fine then, no problem. That explains everything."

"There's things going on, stuff I can't tell you, and I was just..." She shook her head. "I know you don't get it but it wasn't about you. Not to hurt you." She reached to touch the collar of Daddy's robe, then pulled back. She stayed a minute with her arm frozen midair, then brought her hands to her face, dragged her fingers down and squeezed at her cheeks.

I watched her, running my stale tongue against my unbrushed teeth, then finally pulled her down to the bed beside me. There was a quick wet inhalation through her nose, and then a keening from behind closed lips, a cry I'd only heard from small children. What did it mean? An apology? Or was it that she was scared of herself? I imagined her jealousy as a tumor she could only see now that the cover of Brad Carrera had been stripped away. I imagined her seeing that tumor all at once, and I put my other arm around her, cradled her head against my neck and we rocked, both of us hiding inside her sobs.

17

JUSTIN AND I WALKED out to Mohegan Bluffs, the air bright with the scents of apple and salt, road gravel scuffing up into my sandals. In a month this parking lot would be crowded with cars. Tourists would hike down to see the view, how the bluffs dipped and folded before they plunged down to the sea, chokecherry buds dotting the hillside in random patches like a splatter painting. But now the bluffs were bare and there was only us, not speaking, not holding hands, just focusing on the sounds of our feet.

We climbed down the rickety wooden steps that cut into the hillside, took off our shoes and sat on a huge boulder facing the water. I waited for the rhythmic ocean dance to slip me away, take me to the place where the only movement was ebb and flow, tide in and out, again and again and again. "The clothes, they were Eve's idea," I said finally.

"No kidding." He squeezed my knee. The gesture seemed patronizing and I pulled away. Below us a cormorant swooped to perch on a rock and spread its wings to dry them.

"Something's different in her," I said. "Since Brad, I guess. Sometimes in the mornings she'll lie in bed, just lie there. And her eyes are open but they're not really open, not looking at anything."

Justin watched the ocean, his face flat and unreadable.

"And there's other stuff too, Justin. I was looking through her drawer the other day and there was all this... new underwear, thong kind of thing."

"Thong underwear?" Justin smiled crookedly. "Thong underwear."

"And this bag of liquor bottles. So I was wondering where she could've got the money, and how she could possibly be buying liquor underage, and then I realized she hadn't."

"What do you mean?"

"What do you think I mean? She stole them, Justin." I pressed my bare toes against the rock. "She stole them."

Justin glanced at me, then looked back over the horizon. "You stole those clothes."

I shook my head.

Justin bent for a handful of stones and started tossing them one by one into the ocean.

I scanned the bluffs, the Southeast Lighthouse where we'd climbed with Daddy on foggy summer nights to watch how the beams drew their slow-weaving ribbons across the sky. Back then it had seemed like the highest point in the whole world. "I didn't want to, Justin. But she really did, and not like that should matter but the way things've been with us—"

"I have to tell you something." His voice was unsteady. He threw his last rock and watched it skip across the water. "It's about Eve, okay?"

A wave swept beneath our feet, rattling the stones

around us like scattered applause. I brushed the dirt from my feet without answering, then slid them back into my sandals. I needed shoes on because he was going to tell me she'd tried to kiss him, and then I'd have to either run away or kick him.

"Thing is, I think she shouldn't work at Dad's shop anymore."

"What?"

"There's been money..." He cleared his throat. "Missing. There's been money missing. I'm just telling you in case my parents ask about it, so you're prepared with what to say."

I shook my head.

"It started when you first came to work for us. In the beginning it wasn't all that much and we thought maybe it was problems with the books, but recently it's been more. Over a hundred dollars last week."

He watched me, waiting for me to respond, and when I didn't he said, "I know it wasn't you, you wouldn't do that."

"Neither would Eve!" This was, I realized full well, a lie. Because I'd known, hadn't I? Part of me must have known.

"I'm sorry. I didn't know how to tell you. Dad asked me about it the other day and I was scared he'd come to you. I just wanted to make sure I talked to you first."

"It's some kind of mistake."

Justin held my eyes, his expression wide with something I didn't understand. There was something else here, something he wasn't telling me.

I turned away. "You don't know," I said. "It could've

been somebody breaking in, it could be somebody didn't pay what they should've."

"Kerry..."

"You don't know!" I jumped off the rock without looking back and ran up the steep stairway.

But when I reached the top and did look, winded, I saw he hadn't even tried to follow, which is, of course, the real thing a person wants when they run away. I was sure that Justin knew this. But if he did, he apparently didn't care.

I lay with my feet against the wall, head hanging over the edge of my bed, waiting. The front door clicked shut and I sat up and quickly lit a cigarette. I leaned back on my elbow and tried to look casual.

When Eve came in, she raised her eyebrows. "What're you doing still awake?"

I shrugged. "Just thinking." I took a drag on the cigarette. It burned down my throat and I struggled to keep from choking. I wondered if I was going to puke.

"God, Kerry, since when did you start smoking?"

I shrugged and pretended to take another drag. How people got addicted to this was beyond me.

Eve nodded at the line of ash trailing to the bed. "I think you need an ashtray."

"Right." I reached for a hand mirror, tapped the ash onto it. "You want one?"

"Smoking's bad for your lungs." Eve reached into her purse and pulled out a wad of bills. "Before I forget, put this away for next month's rent. I ran into some luck."

The Caines' money? I fingered the bills, a fifty and

six twenties. For months we'd gotten the pity money in blank brown envelopes, placed anonymously on our doorstep. And so I'd been able to rationalize it, had pictured our neighbors pressing the bills into her palm. "Just a little something," they'd say, a bigger something each month. But how many islanders had this much money to spare? Not any that knew us well enough to care if we were broke.

Eve pulled off her blouse and reached into the bureau. I narrowed my eyes and admired the line of her shoulders and the graceful curve of her neck. She was wearing a scarlet underwire bra I didn't recognize, and it made her look globular, like she'd had a boob job.

I sighed. "God, I think I drank too much."

She stared at me. "You were drinking? Good little Kerry?"

"Very funny." I gestured at the trashcan, the empties I'd stolen from the Caines' garbage bin. If you went by the number of bottles in the trash, I should've been dead by now. "Me and Justin, but I think I must've had more than him. It was fun while we were doing it, but now my head's starting to kill."

"Aspirin," Eve said, looking at me funny. "That helps, and lots of water. Jeez, Kerry, what's got into you?"

"Nothing." I lay back on the bed, crossed my legs and looked up at the ceiling.

"Good little Kerry becoming a boozer. Who would've guessed?" She shrugged. "Maybe I will have a cigarette."

"Help yourself." I pushed Eve's money under the blanket so I wouldn't have to look at it, then stared at the tip of my cigarette, the red glow biting through the blackened paper. It was kind of pretty, if you didn't think about it being carcinogenic. I cleared my throat. "So where you been?"

Eve grinned and came to sit on the bed beside me. "I was with this guy."

I took a half drag on my cigarette and held the smoke in my mouth until my eyes started to water, then spat it out. "Really?" I said.

"I think this could turn into something, Ker, I really think. God, is he gorgeous. Movie-star kind of gorgeous."

I gave her a quick hug, trying to think who she could be talking about. "He's an islander?"

"He's so completely different from how Brad ever was. That was a fling, but this..." She shook her head. "I think he's falling in love already. It's the kind of thing, if I could get him I could get just about anybody. But when I'm with him I keep thinking who knows, maybe I'll never want anybody else."

"So what is this, twenty questions? Is it somebody I know?"

"I guess. Yeah, you know him." She glanced at me. "I can't tell you yet, okay? He wouldn't want me saying anything."

"You embarrassed or something?"

She blew a long curl of smoke from the corner of her mouth, a strange look on her face. "Look, I'll tell you eventually, it's just too new."

"Animal, vegetable or mineral?"

Eve ground her cigarette on the mirror and stood. "Tell you what, Ker, you mind your business and I'll mind mine."

"Well, excuse me," I said, stubbing my cigarette next to hers. "You *are* embarrassed, aren't you?"

"Get a life, Kerry. If you had a life, you wouldn't have to try and piggyback on mine."

My face flushed hot. "I know you took the Caines' money," I said.

Eve froze. "What?"

"Justin told me there's money missing from the shop. God, Eve, how could you? After all they've been doing for us?"

"You're crazy. How the hell can you accuse me?"

"Obviously I'm not as crazy as you."

Eve rolled her eyes. "Grow up."

"No, you grow up. Now the Caines are going to basically fire you because of this, and how the hell are we going to pay rent then? Can't steal from the shop anymore, right? Pretty self-defeating."

"What exactly did Justin say?"

"He's going to have you arrested."

"Kerry..."

"Look, he doesn't even know for sure it's you. He just knows there's money missing and Mr. and Mrs. Caine suspect, but what I think is they put on blinders because the alternative, that we might steal from them, is so awful they don't even want to imagine it."

Eve's face was red. She stood a minute facing out at the hallway. "So they trust me more than my own sister does," she said finally.

"That's because I know you better."

"Fuck you." Her voice was unsteady. She swallowed so loudly I could hear it.

I had simultaneous urges both to hold her and to slap

her. She spun away and strode from the room, and I smiled widely so I wouldn't feel the bruising in my gut. And it worked; by the time Eve got back, I felt nothing at all, not even anger. She might as well have been a stranger sleeping in my room, someone I'd put up with until she found somewhere else.

This is where it really started, the night I learned the identity of her mystery man. Everything else was preparation, but this was the first little Big Bang. There's times in life like that, I think, when life turns a corner and then there's no going back.

Eve had left straight after dinner, her fourth night out that week, and after an hour staring blankly at the same chemistry formula, playing the letters across my tongue like they were words, I decided to get away from the echoing emptiness of the house.

Maybe it was luck that led me to Old Harbor or maybe something deeper, Eve pulling at the threads of my subconscious. I walked along the waterfront, hunched against the wind, watching the silvery reflection of moon on water. It had gotten warmer over the past few weeks, but the damp could still cut through to the bones. Spring was like this on the island. It showed its face in daffodils and longer days, but still wouldn't give up on the idea of hibernation until June.

The spire on the National Hotel was lit an eerie, vacant blue. In the dock the moored boats creaked and clucked against each other, a conversation. *Alone,* they were saying, *I'm wet and empty and alone, and covered in slime.* And there was Daddy's boat, *Double Trouble* printed on its side in faded red script. *Double Trouble,* named for his twins. The Caines had suggested that we sell the boat, which would get us a good amount of money and plus we wouldn't have to pay the docking fee. But we couldn't stand to sell it. In a way this was Daddy's tombstone. And his murderer.

The boat was swaying. That was the first thing I noticed, the roll of it heavier than the calm water. I walked closer. The door leading to the hold was closed, but the pole that usually locked it had been lifted. I stepped onto the deck and walked to the door. Daddy had never used the hold, its closet-sized bedroom and side bathroom with toilet and shower. He'd bought this bigger boat five years ago on a whim with money he didn't have, and even though the bed never got slept in, the shower never got run, we'd all thought it was a huge luxury, a sign of having succeeded in a way.

And now it was unlocked.

I crept forward and pulled slowly, *click-click,* at the door, bracing myself, getting ready to confront whoever was trespassing. I peered down the stairs into the darkness, the flicker of candles against the floor planks. And I saw her.

I knew it was her because I saw her L.L. Bean windbreaker. Daddy bought us the jackets a year back, hers a bright greenish blue and mine identical but in red. And now here it was, thrown at the foot of the bed. Two bodies on the bare mattress. Gasps and groans. Bare skin.

The music echoed from Ballard's bar down the street, Mexican or Spanish with castanets and heavy rhythm, *shake-a-shake Arriba!* It made the whole thing seem almost comical, like a scene from a Woody Allen movie.

I ducked behind the door and watched, struggling between horror and fascination. I heard Eve laugh, but it wasn't her real laugh, it was the laugh we used when strangers clasped their hands and squealed over our twinness. It was the laugh she'd used back in the days when I'd reported the details of my nights with Justin.

Her arms were tied above her head with a red silk scarf, knotted on the headboard posts. And he was on her, this man with dark hair and a pale gray sweater, his pants pulled to his knees. As I watched, he untied the scarf and crawled to the end of the bed, kissing down her belly. Eve threw back her head in a moan and in a sudden dizzying shift I saw myself, how I would look under this man, her face my face, twisted like she was in pain. It was horrifying and weird and embarrassing. I felt coated with an opaque sheen, like a skin of soap, and I wanted to turn away but was completely and totally unable to move. She clamped her legs around him, and with a force that shocked me she rolled him over and pulled him down.

And I saw his face. I saw and I stared for a moment of numb disbelief. It was Ryan Maclean.

Congressman Maclean whose sons we'd babysat, whose wife had brought banana bread to Daddy's funeral reception. Mr. Maclean, Rhode Island representative, millionaire and husband and father of two. And as the horror of it sank under my skin, some deep knowing inside of me understood that Eve was on the brink of something that would destroy us both.

FOUR

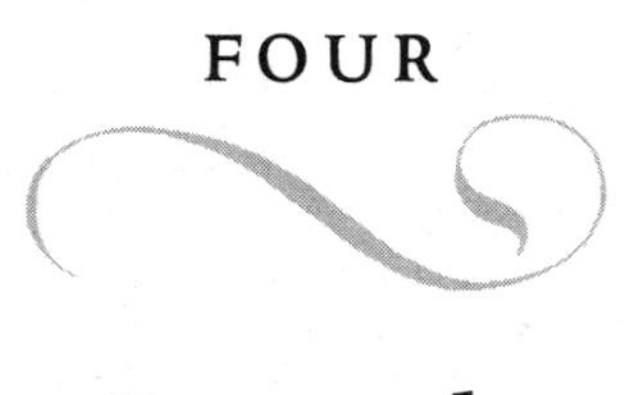

Day Lily

April
2007

18

LET ME PUSH YOU NOW, okay?" I said, my voice sounding desperate and childish, like I was pleading for a turn on the swings. Eve had gotten noticeably frailer over the past couple of weeks, her nausea returning, the trip from her bed to the bathroom enough to wind her. But still she insisted on doing everything herself.

She stopped her wheelchair in front of a store window, obviously working to catch her breath, but pretending to be interested in a set of spangled Barbie dolls arranged against each other in vaguely X-rated poses. Beside us, Gillian patted Eve's shoulder. "You want a pill? I think you probably better give her a pill."

I reached into my pocket but Eve batted my hand away. "I just hate this chair," she said. "It's this contraption that's taking over my body like an iron lung, or that machine for mutes that makes your voice sound like a rusty computer. This thing's too fucking shiny."

"Mom!" Gillian said.

Eve glanced at Gillian, then shrugged. "Listen, let's not kid each other, Gillian. I think the most useful words in the English language are *fuck* and *shit* and *asshole.* I might as well teach you to say them now, because you'll find them extremely valuable throughout the rest of your life."

Gillian widened her eyes at Eve, then gave a sideways smile.

I touched a wheel rim. "We could fix the chair up if you want. It'd be kinda fun, right, Gillian? We could run ribbons through the spokes."

"It'd be...fucking fun," Gillian said, her face pink. An old woman in a flowered straw hat stopped and stared at Gillian, her mouth pursed, and Gillian started laughing.

Eve made a face. "Shit. That'd be about as uplifting as painting polka dots on a fucking colostomy bag." She gripped the armrests, still struggling for air. "Go ahead and push me. Let's go back." She glanced at Gillian, then turned to me. "Asshole," she added.

I grinned and turned the chair around, walking us back through the streets. Already the mainlanders were here, mostly day-trippers who came to shop and wade in the cold May tide. A little girl with a bulbous belly was staring at us unabashedly, running a strand of wet hair across her lips. I thought at first her amazement must be because of our twinness, but then Gillian stuck out her tongue at the girl, and I realized what Gillian already knew, that she was actually staring at Eve. It was then I noticed the people around us pointedly avoiding our eyes, pretending to study their purses or cracks in the sidewalk. I glared at them, hoping they could feel my eyes like knuckles against their backs. The three of us against the world.

As we approached the marsh near home, Eve held out her arm. "Okay, stop. This is good." She slipped from the chair onto her knees.

"Mom? Mommy!" Gillian grabbed for Eve's shirt, tried to balance her so she wouldn't fall forward, and I ran to help her back into the chair. But Eve laughed and pushed us both away. In her hands was a wad of mud.

"You're not," I said.

"Wanna bet?" She smeared her hands over the wheels.

"You're not!"

Eve dug her hands into the ground and painted mud across the footrest. I watched her a minute, then bent to lob a fistful against the chair back. Gillian stared at us like we were completely insane, but then Eve held a wad of mud towards her. Gillian looked at it a minute, then reached for it and gave a tentative toss, and it landed on the ground a foot away.

"In the twelve years we've had you, has nobody ever taught you how to throw?" Eve said.

Gillian gave a panting laugh and grabbed another handful, then heaved it against the seat.

Eve slapped her on the back, making roaring-crowd sounds. And we all reached for more, our hands in the muck, fingers sliding together, mud to our elbows, filled with laughter that felt like anger, felt like tears.

"Wait!" I said, pulling at wheatgrass. I started to weave the strands through spokes when a chunk of mud clocked me on the forehead. I stared at Eve.

She narrowed her eyes and hurled another handful at my nose.

My eyes teared at the cold shock of it. I wiped the mud from my eyes and stared at her, then slowly reached to slime my fingers over her cheeks. Her eyes were wild as she pushed me away, flinging the mud with both hands. Gillian sucked in her breath. "Stop," she said. "Stop it, okay? Aunt Kerry, stop!"

The mud was caking on my forehead, murky tears against my eyelashes. There was grit in my mouth and my belly hurt, really hurt, but I reached for more, then froze.

Eve was breathing heavy, hands flat on the ground. "Okay," she said. "Okay."

I shook my head.

"I'm sorry, okay?" She was watching me.

I shook my head again and stared down at the fringes of dried grass. And I saw it.

Bert and Georgia's house. How old were we? Not old, not at all. Still young enough to make mud pies. Still young enough to have a mother.

She sat on the porch step, an unread *Vogue* on her knees. We brought her mud cookies in a custard dish and she dug in her fingers and pretended to munch, her eyes so bright they hardly seemed like Mommy's eyes.

"My favorite!" she said, laughing as she scampered out to the overgrown lawn. She fell to her knees by a puddle and filled her hands with sludge. "Some chocolate mousse, Eve?" she said, then jumped up to plaster the muck onto Eve's hair.

Eve squawked and hid behind me, and Mommy rose and pitched underhand, hitting my chest. I threw, they threw, mud everywhere, plastering our bodies, splattered on Mommy's cutoff shorts. I ran to her and she swung me, then held me against her chest. And then dropped me. She was staring into the distance, towards Bert and Georgia's house. I turned.

"You," Georgia said.

Eve sidled towards me.

"He just told me," Georgia said.

Mommy stepped towards her and then stepped back, gave a strange, snorting laugh.

"You murderer." Georgia's hands were trembling. "I knew you were no good. From the first time I met you I saw it. You're no good."

I'd glanced at Eve. She was watching our mother, her lips pale. And our mother smiled at Georgia, eyes narrowed with disgust, and she filled her hands with mud and threw.

Now I stood and leaned against the back handles of the wheelchair, and pictures started flashing one by one through my head clear and flat as a series of still lifes. The frenzy in my mother's eyes, a hand slapped across my father's face and then the bloodstained sheets, their diluted pinkish rust smearing on countertops and spiraling down the kitchen drain. I pushed the wheelchair to Eve. "We're going home," I said.

"Look, I told you I'm sorry," Eve said.

I shook my head. "It's okay."

"I wasn't trying to hurt you or anything."

"I said it's okay." I glanced at Gillian, who'd backed away from us like we were contagious, then turned back to Eve. "Can I ask you something? What do you remember about Mom? I mean about anything specific she might've done wrong?"

Eve combed mud out of her hair and tossed it on the ground. "Where'd that come from?"

"I just had this memory of her and Georgia. I just remembered that Georgia hated her and I'm trying to think why."

"From the few things we know about both of them? I'd have to say that is not a surprise." She gave a narrow smile and shrugged. "Look, what I remember most is her leaving. That's what's important."

"But why did she leave?"

"Does it matter? Look, Kerry, you know the way most of my life's been? I had parents who left and grandparents I left, I lost you and now I'm losing everything else. She's just first in a long line of failures." She lowered herself back into the chair.

Gillian and I stared at each other, and then Gillian started to clean off the wheelchair arms with her shirt.

"Stop that, Gillian," Eve said. "You're too clean. Real kids are not that clean."

Gillian frowned at this, then said, "You didn't fail, Mom."

Eve flashed her an overly wide smile, then said, "Let's go home. I think we could all use a shower."

Back in the kitchen I washed my arms and face in the kitchen sink, listening to the hiss of the water from Eve's shower. My hands still wet, I stared at the phone, suddenly realizing what I should do. What I had to do. "Okay," I whispered, reaching for the receiver. "Okay."

I had no idea what I was going to say. What did you say to grandparents you hadn't bothered to call in a decade? "Still alive, hunh?" or "You may not remember me, but..."

"Hello?" Georgia's voice sounded impossibly old.

"Georgia?" The word came out high-pitched, anxious. I concentrated on the pipe squeal as Eve shut off the water. "It's been a long time. This is Kerry."

Silence. I clutched the phone harder. "Barnard. Kerry Barnard."

"My goodness," she said finally, "it *has* been a long time."

"I'm just calling because there's things I need to know. Things you can tell me." It sounded awful when I said it. Here I was, calling not to apologize for avoiding them or to ask about their lives, but to extract whatever pieces of information they might have about someone who didn't give a rat's ass about us.

"Excuse me?" Georgia said.

"About my mother. There's something bad she did, and you know at least some of it. Daddy told you some of it."

"I'm sorry, I'm not sure what you're asking about." She sounded so far away and so weak. I imagined her with jowls and pale, plucked-turkey skin, hair gone a linty gray.

"This is important, Georgia, please. If there's something she did, some reason she left us, I have a right to know."

Georgia was quiet a minute. I could hear her breath in my ear. "Your mother wasn't a good woman, Kerry," she said finally. "That's all you need to know. She was very beautiful, stunning actually, but she wasn't a good person."

I lowered myself into a chair and waited.

"Look, Kerry, there's nothing about her that you really need to hear. Just know that she destroyed your father. She chewed him up and spat him out. The man you remember wasn't the man I raised."

What was I supposed to do with this? How was I supposed to feel? "Okay," I said. I didn't have to believe her. Probably I shouldn't. A son dies of suicide or stupidity, and his mother needs someone to blame.

"So how are things with you?" she said.

I nodded. "Fine, I'm fine."

"We do think about you, dear, you know." Her voice trailed off and she coughed, then continued, louder. "We were in touch with Abigail Caine, of course, even after you left the island, and then I tried to call Eve several times, left messages on the machine, but I never heard back. So Bert thought you'd both probably rather if I stopped calling."

She sounded so kind, so grandmotherly. How had I built her up in my head to be someone heartless? "I'm sorry. I wish things had been better between us all." My voice broke as I suddenly realized she must not know. I inhaled deeply, then released the words in a rush of air. "Eve's sick."

"Oh? Well, that's a shame."

"No, I mean she's very sick, Georgia. She's dying."

There was a shuffling sound from across the phone lines, the sound of something settling. "My God."

"She has cancer, ovarian cancer. She stopped treatment a couple months back and she's not doing so great. I just thought you should know."

"Oh Kerry, God, so young? We have to do something, Bert and I, come up and be there for her."

"Maybe," I said. "Maybe but not yet, not now. Let me talk to Eve first." I squeezed my eyes shut. "I promise I'll be in touch."

Georgia didn't respond. Had I hurt her? But then she cleared her throat. "She should know."

I sat a minute, waiting. Had I missed something? "Excuse me?"

"Your mother. Your mother should know."

"There's a lot she should know."

"I've got her number."

I blinked. "You what?"

"Somewhere, I've written it somewhere. Bert! Just a minute..."

The receiver clicked against my ear and my mind raced. What did she say? She had a phone number? How could she have a number?

Georgia came back on. "Bert is wonderful. I swear without him I'd lose my own nose."

"How could you have her number? Did you talk to her? Why the hell didn't you tell us?"

"I'm sorry. Oh Lord, Kerry, I know, but we thought we were doing the right thing, we really did. We called her years ago when your father died—"

"You said you couldn't reach her!"

"She didn't want to see you, Kerry. She knew she couldn't be a good mother, I guess, and truth is I agreed with her. How could I tell you that your mother had refused to even come visit? It would've broken your hearts."

My back and arms went weak. *She hadn't wanted to see me.* We were silent for a minute and then Georgia spoke. "Will you call her?"

"I don't know. You can give me the number, and then I don't know."

Georgia began to read off the number and I grabbed

for a pen, copied it down on a napkin. I stared at it, barely comprehending. "Six-one-seven area code. She's in Boston."

"I think so. Or at least she was when we talked to her. That was years ago, but it's the last I heard."

It had to be a joke, God up there belly-laughing. Could it be that all this time I'd held the question, a constant pressure like a kneading fist behind everything, all this time she'd been just minutes away? Why hadn't I felt it? How hadn't I known? "Thank you," I said softly. "Thanks, Georgia, and I'll be in touch."

I dropped the phone back on its cradle and lifted the napkin with my mother's number, folded it and tucked it into my jeans pocket. I knew that of course I'd call her. And I knew I couldn't tell Eve.

I waited until Justin left for the mail, then sat in the kitchen, stomach churning, one hand on the phone, the other holding my mother's phone number. I tapped my foot four times, lifted the receiver and listened to the dial tone. I tapped my foot four more times and dropped it again. I rose and paced to the window. Such a beautiful day outside, and I was reverting back into a froot loop.

Without letting myself think, I lifted the receiver again and dialed the number. I let the phone ring once, twice. Heart stuttering, I slammed it down. What would I say? What would I call her even? Mom? Mrs. Barnard? Did she use that name anymore? Diana. Hello, Diana, this is Kerry Barnard. Oh God.

From the den I heard Eve's hacking cough and her struggle to regain breath. She'd been getting winded more easily, had almost given up on walking. Our mother should know, Georgia had said, but if she saw Eve now what would she know? She'd see a shadow, not a daughter, not a person worth her time.

I closed my eyes until I heard Eve's breath steady, then timed my own to match it, reassuringly rhythmic and slow as I dialed the number.

A click and a hiss, then a voice. "Hello, I can't come to the phone right now—" I slammed down the phone and stood, staring at the receiver. That was her. That was my mother's voice. I dialed again.

One, two, three rings, click-hiss. "Hello, I can't come to the phone right now—" I hung up.

She had a thick Boston accent that made the hair prickle on my arms. She sounded harsh, citified, almost masculine, like a used-car salesman. Not what I'd expected. Really not at all.

I dialed again, tried to get used to the voice. "Mom," I whispered, "Mother," trying to ingrain it. Then the answering machine played a grating computerized song, the kind you might hear once after buying a machine and then realize you had to erase it. When the song ended, without thinking I whispered, "Hello."

The phone slipped to clatter against the table. I grabbed at it and hung up, then sat gripping the receiver. She would listen to that message. My mother would listen to my voice and maybe even wonder if it could be me. I inhaled deeply. One last time.

One, two, three rings and then the voice. "Who the hell is this?"

Oh my God.

I slid down the wall onto my butt and focused on a

thumbprint smudge against the yellow wallpaper. "I..." My voice was a hoarse croak. I cleared my throat. "Hi." I shook my head. "Hi, this is me. This is Kerry." I curled my toes inside my sneakers. "This is your daughter Kerry."

I could hear her breath on the other end, every sound intensified. I heard everything, from the click of settling walls to the hiss of a radiator. I thought I heard her brain searching for words, pictured the shock on her face, the joy. I thought I heard the fluttering excitement in her heart and the tears filling her eyes.

"Oh," she said softly. "Oh man, you made a mistake."

I dug my nails into the skin of my knee. Damn her. Damn her to hell. "Damn you," I said.

"No really, Kerry, I mean I'm not your mother. Diana you want, isn't it? I'm a friend of hers, lived with her until she left five years back. She got married to this guy, a developer, Joey was his name except now they're not together anymore."

I pulled my knees up against my chest, tears drying tight on my skin. "Joey?"

"I got her number here if you want it. Well, of course you want it, I mean of course you do. I can't believe you're calling after all this time. Diana used to talk about you girls, talked my ears off."

I wiped at my face, half expecting the skin to come off in my hands. "She did?"

"I got her address too, if you want it. I was just there last summer for a visit. Nice big condo place she got when she left Joey, oak library, tub with jets, all that. Moved down to Miami since it made sense for Joey's job and never came back."

I stared at the smudge on the wall until it blurred into nothing. "Okay," I said. "So give me the number."

The woman made an odd humming sound. "Maybe I should call her first and let her know I talked to you. I got the number here, but you best wait till I can give her a little warning. Big surprise you're about to drop on her."

I nodded as if the woman could see me, kept on nodding as if convincing myself to go on listening. When she continued, her voice was softer, strained. "Was it you that's sick? Was that you or was it your sister?"

"What?"

"She wanted to come up there when she heard, I swear she did. But she didn't want to get you all upset."

I shook my head. "Who told her Eve's sick?"

"Oh." There was a beat of silence. "So I'll tell her you called, okay? I bet she calls you back."

"How did she know? Who told her?"

"So it was good to speak with you. Your voice sounds like hers, you know, deep like hers. I'll tell her that."

There was a click as she hung up. I held the receiver against my chest, held it through the dial tone, held it through the operator's voice and the blaring alarm. It was only when the phone clunked to silence that I was able to rise.

19

I MADE EXCUSES all week not to leave the house. I jumped each time the phone rang. I practiced, like I was waiting for a boy to invite me to the prom, how to answer with the right degree of apathy. *Hello, Mother, I didn't think you'd call.* But in the end she sent a package instead of calling, as if she didn't care enough to hear my voice.

It was our thirtieth birthday. The Caines had invited us all for dinner, and Eve dressed up for the occasion, the first time that I'd seen her in anything but sweats or cotton nightgowns. She wore a dark pantsuit, seventies-style, and she had a wig, shoulder length, in an odd burgundy color that at first made me wince. But with deep red lipstick, her hollowed cheeks and pale skin, the final effect was strikingly exotic.

Eve eyed herself in the bathroom mirror. "Anorexic chic," she said.

"I think you look great. You could be the diva in a James Bond film."

"Or an alien invader. She can cut steel with her cheekbones and see the sky reflected off her head." Eve sighed and fingered the rust stains in the sink. "I hate birthdays."

"You hate bunnies, too? And world peace?"

"Since you left I hated them. But now it's my last birthday, and I'm suddenly realizing how much I love birthday cake, the fluffy white kind with jam filling. Isn't it stupid? I want fucking birthday cake every day for the rest of my life."

"We could do that," I said. "We could celebrate the days."

Eve laughed. "Like now each day of life is a gift? Man, that's pathetic." She looked down at the bathroom tiles. "I made a deal with God, you know, back last winter when they stopped treatment, if I could just make it to thirty, just make it to real adulthood, I'd try my hardest to be accepting about this all. I wouldn't get mad."

"And you made it," I whispered.

"It was a stupid bet." She closed her eyes and weaved slightly. "You better get me back to bed."

I gathered her in my arms and carried her down the stairs. She was surprisingly heavy, and by the time we made it to her bed, we were both exhausted.

"My bones hurt," she said. "Shit."

I began to rub her shoulders but she winced. "Pills?" I asked.

Eve grimaced. "I'd rather not fall asleep at dinner." She lay back and smiled weakly, then reached under her pillow to pull out a small wrapped box. "Just distract me. Happy birthday."

I raised my eyebrows and took the box. She shrugged, then wrinkled her nose and slid her hand beneath her back.

I pulled at the childish birthday wrap and found a gift box lined with velvet. Inside was a tiny gold leaf. "For the birthday bracelet," I said softly. Ever since we were little, on birthdays we'd exchanged tiny charms for the bracelet chain our mother had given us. And then the year we'd turned seventeen, I'd thrown my chain over a cliff.

"I got that for your birthday the year you left," she said, her teeth still gritted against the pain. She winced as she leaned back onto the bed. "We weren't doing so great, I guess, barely speaking, but I bought a charm. I thought if you had one for me, I'd be prepared."

I felt a notch of pain in my chest. "I did get you a charm. But I was waiting to see if you'd get something for me."

Eve exhaled a short laugh. "Son of a bitch."

The front door opened, and Justin walked into the room, a package in his arms. He watched us a moment, then held it forward.

"Gee, you remembered," Eve said, grinning at him.

He shook his head, stepped forward and placed the package in my arms. I stood with it, reading the return address.

"For your birthday, I guess," he said.

I looked down at Eve, then set the package on her bed. Eve stared at it and then up into my eyes. "You found Mom?" she whispered.

"Bert and Georgia gave me the number. I called a couple weeks back, talked to a friend of hers, that's all."

"A friend of Mom's?" Eve huddled against her pillows. "What did she tell you?"

"Not much. Just that she was married and divorced again and now she lives in Miami. And also that she used to talk about us."

"How would she talk about us? What would she say?"

I shrugged. "Her friend said she used to talk her ears off. I can't see how six years with us could've given her enough material."

"Did you say anything about me? Say how I was dying?"

I tried to read Eve's expression, the creases deep at her eyes. "Her friend said she knew already. Somehow she knew."

"Is she coming to see me?"

I watched her for a minute, then reached for the package, but she pulled it back. She traced her finger over the return address, back and forth, back and forth. "Bitch," she whispered.

"You okay?"

"Let me tell you." Eve smiled crookedly. "You know what it was like when I went for my last CAT scan? The doctor's sitting there, holding up pictures of my lungs, my liver, my brain, with these white blotches everywhere, like cultures on a petri dish. And he says it's gone too far, says it's in too many places and there's nothing he can do. And all I'm thinking about is Justin and Gillian. I didn't think of myself, like how unfair and I'm so young. What I thought is, if there really is a God, how dare he do this to my daughter?" Eve's eyes fogged over. "We were six years old, Kerry."

I slipped onto the floor. "I know." I brought my knees to my chin and hugged them, looking up into her face.

"Go on," she said, nodding. I stared at the package a minute, then pulled at the brown wrapping.

Inside was a shoebox. I lifted it, studied the outside as if it could tell me something: Nike cross-trainers, size seven, white and teal. Just like me she kept important things in shoeboxes. I lifted the lid.

The box was filled with cards and letters, all sizes and colors. They were placed in chronological order, the top card dated the summer after my mother left, the bottom postmarked the year before Daddy's death. I lifted the top letter, unsettled at seeing Daddy's handwriting, so instantly recognizable, sweeping capital letters flattening into scrawled script. I gripped Daddy's key necklace as I read.

Diana,

Just so as you know, I'm not writing on account of me, I'm writing on account of your two little girls, in case you forgot you had them. Of course I can't forget because I hear them every night crying for their momma, and what am I supposed to say? So I tell them you're off sailing around the world, you're having a big adventure and you'll be back soon as you do what it is you have to do. I hope to God I'm telling them right.

You said you weren't meant to be tied down to a family. Well fine, I get that, and it's not like I would have chose this life either to tell the God's honest truth. But I'm not about to turn my back on our kids who never asked to be born. Because the way I see it, we made our choices a long time ago, and we just don't have the right not to stick by them at this point.

I tried hard to make a good life for you. We weren't rich maybe, but we had enough to get by. If you ever wanted for anything you should have said it. So maybe you were right, it wouldn't have worked to have another, but if that's why you left, you know I never would've forced you into anything. I didn't yell at you so much for what you did, Diana, just how you didn't think enough of me to tell me about it beforehand. I would have forgave you even if it tore my heart out to kill one of God's most helpless souls.

But anyway, it's too late for that now, so I'll just tell you that when you come back we'll start again from scratch. Because what you have here is pretty damn good, even if you don't see it.

I have to go because one of them is crying. You have the new address, our house is right close to the water the way you always said you dreamed. It's a good house and we have good neighbors and I found a good job cleaning fish which makes decent money, enough that I'll be looking to buy my own boat someday soon, maybe start up my own business. There's a real nice neighbor lady, Mrs. Abi Caine, who's kind enough to watch over them when I'm working, but children do need their real momma. If you'd stop looking only at yourself for one minute, you'd see that was the truth.

As always,
Thomas

I read the letter again, then handed it to Eve, sat in silence until she turned to me. "There was a baby."

I wrapped my arms around my shoulders.

Eve smiled shallowly. "I remember him telling us she was going on an adventure. And we waited for her to come back, a day, a week, a month, and then we stopped waiting."

I looked down at the shoebox, the litter of cards and envelopes. "Actually, I guess I never stopped waiting." I shook my head. "Why would she send these? I mean, what's the point?"

"We were right all along," Eve said softly. "It was

our fault. She left because she was trying to get away from us."

Justin brushed back the hair at her temple. "She left because she was selfish and a shitty mother."

"We could've had a sister or brother," I said. "Part of me felt like there should be someone else, especially when things started going bad, somebody else to turn to who could pull us away from it." I blindly stuffed the letter back into the shoebox.

Eve's face twisted. She batted the box away. "I had this idiotic fantasy about it, you know? A while back when I found out I was dying, I had this fantasy about her up there waiting, I'd drift out of my body and find her and Daddy both. Like it would mean all this time she wanted to come back, but just couldn't."

I gazed blindly at the floor for a minute, then lay on the bed beside her. Justin rested his hands on both of us, stood a minute unmoving and then squeezed our shoulders and backed away. And pressing my face against the scratchy tickle of Eve's wig, I realized that for all these years when I'd thought we'd lost everything that we'd once shared, this is what, in a twisted way, had always bound us together. Not our childhood. Not our twinness. Just the vacuous ache of everything we'd lost.

April
1994

20

IT WAS PAST MIDNIGHT when I returned to the house. For almost an hour I'd been running up and down the same streets trying to pound away the image of Eve with Mr. Maclean, but of course it followed me everywhere.

I walked up to our room and lay in bed, staring up at the ceiling. I didn't know what was the right thing to feel. Should I be angry? Alarmed? Ashamed? I was all of these, but most of all and worst of all I realized I was jealous. Some insane, irrational part of me was jealous of Mr. Maclean, because in those nights he spent with her, he was closer than I'd ever be.

On impulse I slid to the floor and crawled under Eve's bed skirt. I lay there in the dust and bed-skirt shadows, staring up at springs and imagining the way he must look at her, the things she must say to make him forget the wife he'd left at home. *You're so hot,* she said. *You make me all wet.* I grimaced and slid out from under the bed.

My foot brushed against a crinkle of plastic. I pulled at it, a heavy shopping bag, and looked inside. On top were two photographs: one of Daddy piggybacking Eve, the other a picture I hardly remembered, Eve and I at the shore, hand in hand in matching pink bathing suits. I fingered this picture, trying not to see inside the bag, the stacks of green. Maybe it was tens, maybe hundreds, maybe thousands, I didn't want to know.

I set the picture back and pushed the bag under the bed, then crawled onto my own bed, closed my eyes and waited.

Eve got home at two A.M., her eyes red, face shadowed. She slipped into the room and raised her eyebrows at me. "You're still up?"

"Couldn't sleep." I hugged my arms over my chest. After a minute I spoke, my voice nonchalant. "So, you have a good night?"

"Real good. It was pretty amazing." She sat on the bed beside me, lifted her foot. "Like my anklet? He gave it to me tonight. That's real amethyst."

I tried to smile. "Nice," I said.

"You can borrow it if you want. Guys love anklets for some reason, I guess they help define your leg."

She unclasped the chain and started to fasten it around my ankle, but the feel of it made me shiver as if it were alive, a snake. I pulled my leg away. "Hey, I'm starving. Wanna check out the fridge?" My voice had a shrill edge to it, kind of like a parrot.

Eve watched me for a minute, finally smiled. "Okay, sure." She stood and rooted through her underwear drawer, pulled out a brown bottle. "Let's make it fun. You'll like this, it's Kahlua. Mix it with milk and it's just like a shake."

"Sounds good," I said. "Let's bring it down."

Downstairs we found Doritos and salsa, cold chicken and a bag of Oreos. We ate with our fingers, whispering like we once used to, hiding our midnight snacks from Daddy. Together in the dark and whispers and milk laced sweet with liquor, I knew I should feel all close and connected, joined by secrets. Instead I felt like I was tiptoeing, trying to ignore a truth so huge it pressed against both of us, constricting the space between it and us like an expanding hot-air balloon.

"You're staring at me," Eve said.

I shrugged. "You're so gorgeous I can't help it."

"And you're so full of crap your eyes just turned brown."

This exchange filled me with a wash of loss. I reached for the Kahlua bottle, poured myself another splash.

Eve leaned back in her chair and closed her eyes, and something about the way she looked, her slightly protruding belly, her faint milk mustache, reassured me enough that I could ask. I made my voice relaxed, almost slurred as if I was drunk. "So tell me about the new boyfriend."

"C'mon, Kerry, I promise I'll tell you when I'm ready."

Is he married? In his forties? "Do you think you could marry him someday? I mean hypothetically speaking."

"I've thought about it." She took a swig of Kahlua, straight from the bottle, grimaced as it went down.

"You think he could marry you?"

Eve sat straighter. "Just get off this, will you?"

"Seems like you've been with him every night this week. I was just wondering if you think there's a future in it, or if you're gonna just keep letting him screw you in exchange for jewelry."

Eve stood to put the salsa in the refrigerator, then

turned to me, her eyes cold. "Listen to your voice, Kerry. Just because you think you're dating Mr. Wonderful gives you the right to be sarcastic? Can't you just be happy for me?"

"I'm just trying to understand what's going on with you." My eyes began to fill. "You've been out every night, and now you don't work at the shop I hardly see you anymore. You've never kept any secrets from me before, not anything important like this. So I'm just trying to get back to normal, how it used to be."

Eve leaned against the refrigerator, staring at the dark kitchen window. Finally she shook her head. "There's things I can't tell you, Kerry. You wouldn't get it. Too much has happened."

I steeled my shoulders. The words came before I could stop them. "You're sleeping with Mr. Maclean."

Eve stared at me. I watched the flush spread into her face and felt an obscure kind of triumph. "Who the hell told you that?"

"It's true, isn't it? He's the one gave you that anklet, you go to him every night, behind everyone's back. God, Eve, he has a family, two kids!"

"Shut up. You don't know anything."

"How could you?"

"You have no idea what you're talking about!" Eve strode to the door. She stood a minute, her back straight and stiff, then slowly turned to face me. "You want to know what's going on? You really want to know? I got an idea how we can both find out."

She gave me a crooked smile and reached for the phone. Shell-shocked, I poured myself a glass of straight Kahlua, swigged it down.

"Justin? Listen, there was an accident."

I widened my eyes and jumped up, grabbing at the phone. "*Stop* it!"

Eve wrestled me away. "We need you here, it's an emergency. Pretty serious." She winked at me. "God, thanks, Jussy, you're awesome."

She hung up the phone and smiled. "Let's see how long it takes the hero to rescue us."

"What the hell are you doing?"

"Like I said, I got an idea. Because there's things you want to know about me and things I want to know about him. So we'll swap questions, give something and get something, it's only fair."

"Questions for Justin?"

She raised her eyebrows in reply. I hunched forward, feeling the liquor burning in my stomach. "Like what?"

"Oh, you'll see. Things I'm sure you'd want to know yourself."

The front door slammed open. "Eve? Kerry? What's going on? Where are you?"

"In here!" Eve called.

Justin ran to the kitchen, wearing only a jacket over pajama bottoms. "What is it? What happened?"

"Glad you could come."

Justin stared at her. "What're you doing, Eve? You said an emergency."

"Well, in a way it is. Kerry was about to drive me crazy with her questions, and I think none of us wants me going insane." She sat across from me. "So I thought instead we could play a little game, I'll tell you if you tell me. Truth or dare. I'll answer anything you want."

"It's the middle of the night," Justin said. "What's wrong with you?"

"C'mon Jussy, it'll be fun."

"Fine," I said, "but I go first."

Justin stared at me pointedly. "Kerry—"

"We'll do what she wants. Truth or dare?"

"Dammit, Kerry, you're acting like two-year-olds."

Eve rolled her eyes to the ceiling. "I'll take truth. That's the point of this all, isn't it?"

"Okay." I watched her face carefully. "Okay, Eve, are you having an affair with Ryan Maclean?"

"Jesus," Justin said. "What?"

Eve smiled. "The answer is yes. Now you, Justin, truth or dare."

I shook my head. "Wait a minute."

"Yes, I'm sleeping with him, okay? That's it, now it's my turn. Truth or dare?"

"Mr. Maclean? Congressman Maclean?" Justin stared at her. "Holy Christ, Eve."

"Here, have a drink." Eve poured a shot of liquor into my glass and pushed it at him.

"I'm going home."

"No, don't," I said.

"You better keep playing or we'll go on a drinking spree, me and Kerry, and I'll start making up stories that are maybe or maybe not true. Bet I'm as good at thinking up stories as you."

Justin narrowed his eyes, gave her a long and steady gaze and then sat and swirled the glass agitatedly against the table. "This is ridiculous. What the hell do you want?"

Eve glanced from Justin to me and back. "Okay,

Justin, what I want to know is why Kerry? Why did you go for Kerry?"

I sucked in my breath. Held it, watching Justin.

He blinked twice, rapidly. "You're sleeping with Congressman Maclean and you act like you have the right to question me? Because I love her, what do you think?"

"Who would you say is sexier?"

Something squeezed at my stomach.

Justin shook his head. "What?"

I pressed my toes against the floor. "You can't ask another question."

"But don't you want to hear the answer? I'm just wondering who you think is sexier, Kerry or me."

"This is ridiculous. You're both sexy, okay? God, Eve, what do you want to hear?"

"I just want to know why." Eve was looking at him, her face tight. "How come you chose her?"

Justin started to speak, then stood. "I'm going to bed."

"There's got to be a reason." Eve's voice was trembling slightly. "You made her fall in love with you, Justin; were you lying to her just a little? Did you really want her or was it because you thought you couldn't have me?"

"Stop!" I couldn't listen to this, even though part of me had examined the same question so many times. I was scared Justin wouldn't have an answer. And if he didn't have an answer, nothing would ever be the same again. "Just stop. It's a stupid question."

But Justin shook his head. "I love you both." His voice was even and slow. "But I'm in love with Kerry, I was probably always in love with her, even before I realized it. How can you be so conceited to think it has anything whatsoever to do with you?"

Eve gazed at the wall above Justin's head, her shoulders stiff. When she turned back to me, her eyes were red. "Okay," she said. "Sit down, Justin. It's Kerry's turn."

I felt like burrowing against him, covering myself with him and never coming out. I couldn't look at Eve, but it was my turn to ask a question and there were so many things I needed to know. "Truth or dare?" I said.

"Truth," Eve said. "Let's get this over with."

"How—" I started, then shook my head. "How could you?"

Eve kicked her foot rhythmically against a table leg. "What kind of dumb-ass question is that?"

"He's married! God, Eve, what are you thinking?"

Kick, kick, kick. "He's the one that started it. Not everyone's virtuous as they seem. Look at Justin, for example."

"You're not funny, Eve," Justin said.

I took the glass from him, sucked at the Kahlua and felt it burn down my throat.

"I'm not trying to be funny."

"No, you're just trying to justify adultery."

Eve smiled at Justin, her eyes fierce. "What are you, jealous?"

"Jealous of what!" My voice choked and I looked to Justin for help. "He buys you jewelry and you sleep with him? You'd sleep with anybody, wouldn't you. Like a hooker."

"Oh, stop it, Ker. You have no idea how fun it is. Men are like boys inside, you hold up a Snickers bar and they start to salivate. I'm like a grownup version of a Snickers, maybe just chocolate and caramel and a few nuts, maybe that's all you see in me, Justin, but that's what I'm trying to find out." She squinted at Justin, then shrugged. "Just trying to learn about your sweet tooth. Okay, Jussy, you guys wasted that question. Now, truth or dare?"

Justin glared at her. "I can't believe you, Eve. What the hell are you trying to pull?"

"It's only fair. You can't cheat now, this is just starting to get fun."

Justin poured more Kahlua. His hand was shaking. "Dare."

Eve smiled slowly, stretched out her legs. "Matter of fact, I was hoping you'd choose a dare, because I know already what I want you to do. You'll like this. See, I've heard so much about your technique." She raised her eyebrows at me. "Your kissing technique. So I was thinking just for fun, I dare you to kiss me."

Justin choked on his drink. Apprehension sunk into my stomach like cold mud.

Eve leaned forward. "Not just a peck, either. I want you to use your tongue."

"No way." I grabbed Justin's hand. I felt like slapping her. I felt like crying.

"Or you can pick truth, but then you have to answer two questions, not just one. That's the rule. Your choice."

Justin swallowed his Kahlua in three quick gulps, then coughed and wiped at his watering eyes.

"Well?" Eve said.

"I can't believe this. I can't believe I'm doing this. Go ahead then, truth."

Eve traced her finger down her neck to the collar of her V-cut blouse. She smiled wryly. "Okay, truth. I can see why you maybe wouldn't want to kiss me in front of your girlfriend, but I bet you're curious who might be a better kisser. So tell me, Justin, you ever have fantasies about it? About kissing me?"

"What?" Justin said.

I squeezed his hand so hard he winced and pulled away.

"Why so upset, Ker, you scared of the truth? Look how his face is flushed. I think that's your answer."

"This is ridiculous." He started to rise but I pressed him back down. I felt strange suddenly, drifty with sleep or with alcohol, as if none of this was quite real. "Ask something else," I said.

"Okay." Eve looked into my eyes while she poured Justin another glass of Kahlua, kept watching me as she spoke. "And you better tell the truth, or we'll both know you're not. We can read your face like a book, can't we, Ker." She grinned sideways. "I'm gonna give you something, Jussy, and you tell me the truth, tell me what it does for you. No holding back, right? Just first impressions." At this she bent to Justin and pressed her lips against the side of his mouth, her hand scrabbling in his lap.

Justin cried out and pushed her away, fierce enough to send her spiraling to the floor. And I, for some God-knows-why reason, began to laugh. I couldn't stop myself. Maybe it was embarrassment or anger, or the absurdity of the situation, or maybe it was just intoxication, but the laughter exploded in painful waves from my chest until my eyes were running. And then, suddenly as it had come, my laughter choked to silence.

Eve stared up at me from the floor. Justin's face was

flushed with sweat. I slapped my hand on the table. "You're such a slut!"

Eve pulled herself up and eyed me. "He has a hard-on."

"Dammit, Eve, what's wrong with you?" Justin spun away from the table, knocking over his glass, his chair clattering to the floor. He strode from the room and the glass rolled from the table with a sickening crash.

I looked down at the splattered liquid and shattered glass as the front door slammed shut. Eve was watching me, I knew, and I couldn't stay there, couldn't stay with her. I started to rise, and a wave of dizziness hit me. I leaned against the table, held my palms flat on it until the spinning stopped. "How could you?"

"It's for your own good." Eve's eyes were red with tears, her jaw firm. "Don't you get that?"

"You bitch." I didn't recognize my voice, pitched low and dark. I whirled away and left her sitting there, ran outside in my bare feet to the Caines'.

Justin was sitting on the edge of his bed. He looked up when I entered, held out his hand. There was an awful fire in my gut as I crawled onto the bed beside him. He took me in his arms and crushed me against his bare chest. But I knew nothing would ever be the same again, not with me and Justin, not with me and Eve. And even surrounded by his warmth, his hushing sounds in my ear, I felt alone.

21

MY HEAD WAS THROBBING, had been all day. More than throbbing, it was like firecrackers, like a little man with a sharp little axe. I huddled under my bedcovers and buried my nose inside the pillow. My pajamas were folded under the pillow and I fingered them, considering slipping them on over my clothes, but then I heard the front door. I curled onto my side and pulled the covers up to my chin.

Justin came up the stairs, calling my name as he entered the room. "Kerry? I was waiting outside school for you. You stayed home?"

I rolled to the wall, skillfully managing to bonk my forehead against it.

Justin sat beside me. "You okay? Have you talked to her?"

"I can't talk to her." New tears filled my eyes and I rolled onto my back and swiped my arm across my face.

Justin watched me and nodded, kept nodding like he expected me to continue.

"Now I know," I said. "All this time it's you she wanted?"

Justin nodded again and anger bubbled hot in my chest. "Say something!"

"You know she wouldn't choose to hurt you."

"Oh yeah, that's obvious."

He sat there a minute, his eyes distant. "Look," he said. "Look, she knows I'd never leave you. She knows how I feel, so really she's just crying out for something. What's she getting from Ryan Maclean? There's no future in it. She doesn't love him."

"It's for the sex."

I could feel Justin stiffen. "You really believe that?"

"It's because of you," I said, "because of us."

He was quiet a minute, then said, "That doesn't make sense."

"Of course it makes sense. When did this all start? Soon as I lied to her so we could be together on Christmas, she turns around and sleeps with Brad Carrera."

"It started with your father. She changed when he died."

"She didn't give a damn about Daddy!" I was openly sobbing now, the tears clogging in my nose.

Justin pulled me against his chest and stroked my hair. I struggled for a minute but then I let myself become swallowed in it. And then something rose in me, a burning need. I brushed my lips against his.

He pulled away and watched me, then shook his head. He traced my lips with his finger, and I let myself sink into that place he brought me, a safe escape where I pushed away everything but the feel of him kissing me once softly, twice, then harder, grasping, pulling me back against the bed.

The little axe-wielding man pounded a rat-a-tat-tat in my head, and Justin clawed his hand over my blouse, pulling at buttons, scraping his nails against my skin. I could feel him, the hardness of him against my leg. I put my hand against it and he gasped; his body tensed. My heart stuttered but I unzipped his jeans. He moaned, *Oh yes, oh please*... and I reached inside with numb fingers.

His hand clutched my shoulder, breath heavy in my ear. He wrenched at the button on my jeans, pulling me up, off the bed, and suddenly the hardness in my hand became a fist. "Wait!"

He moaned into my ear, "Oh please..."

He pressed against me but I slipped out from under him. "I'm sorry, Justin, I'm sorry, I—"

"Why? Why not?" He rolled onto his back. "Oh God."

How could I tell him so he'd understand? How could I tell him when my reasons made no sense even to me? It was because of last night, a feeling that Eve had gained some hold over that part of him. And it was because I'd seen her come home from nights with Brad and Ryan, smelling like sweat and beer and men's cologne, hair matted and red bruises on her neck. And this was what I'd come to associate with sex, the soiled look of her face and stunned glaze in her eyes.

I looked up at the ceiling. "You know I love you more than anything."

"It's okay." He zipped up his jeans, looking suddenly embarrassed. "I'm sorry, too. I just got carried away." He watched me for a minute, then swung his legs to the floor. I put my hand on his arm, but he didn't respond, so I pulled it away again.

"You hungry?" he said. "I'm starving. Think I'll go home and grab something."

For a minute I felt disoriented, like I'd been snatched

from somewhere vaguely dangerous. "We have sandwich stuff in the fridge," I said softly. "If you want it."

"Sounds good. Okay, so I'll go down." Justin rose. He stood a minute, then nodded and walked down the hall.

I sat a moment, listening to his steps down the stairs, then followed him to the kitchen. I helped him make sandwiches, working in silence, unwrapping bologna and cheese. I wanted to say something, but the time was past and there wasn't really anything to say. I cleared my throat a couple of times and then just gave up.

When the front door opened, something crinkled inside me. I tried to concentrate on spreading mustard as if sandwich-making was like neurosurgery, something demanding ultimate attention.

Eve walked into the kitchen acting totally nonchalant. "Hey, Ker. Hey, Jussy," she said, tossing a brown envelope on the table. "We got our monthly envelope, ten bucks. If we split it, we could just about each buy a burger."

Her indifference was like a slap. Didn't she realize what she'd done? Didn't she care?

"God, I was so drunk last night," she said, opening the refrigerator. "How much did we drink? And plus I had like three beers before I got home." She pulled out a jar of peanut butter, reached into the drawer for a spoon, then turned to me. "What with all I drank, I hardly remember what we talked about. I remember coming upstairs to show you my anklet, but then after that, *whoosh,* my whole mind's just a blank."

Before I could stop, I found myself trying to believe it might be true. She'd been drinking too much, ran off at the mouth, grabbed at Justin so she wouldn't have to say any more about Mr. Maclean. But then I saw her one eyebrow raised, like a question, *Please?*

I shook my head. "I can't deal with this now."

"Deal with what?" Her voice was too bright.

"Deal with you, Eve." I started for the door. "I'm getting out of here."

"Kerry—"

But I didn't let her finish. I was out the door before she could stop me.

Outside, I stood on our front walkway partially hidden by the porch, and looked through the kitchen window. I could see Justin talking, first facing his sandwich and then the ceiling. I leaned closer, tried to hear. "I know that," Justin said, and then something that sounded like *Go for bumping,* and Eve shook her head and said something like *She's no mobster.* Justin bent to give Eve a quick hug, collected the sandwiches and raised his hand in a wave. I strode across the lawn to the Caines' and slammed the front door behind me. I stood in the dark hallway for a minute, watching out the window as Justin walked to the road, searching for me, then turned towards his house.

He pulled at the door. "There you are," he said.

I shrugged without turning to face him.

"You guys'll be okay, you just have to talk it out."

He held out a sandwich but I shook my head. "Did she offer you a hand job?"

"Kerry..."

"You know whatever she told you is a lie. She knew what she was doing last night."

"She didn't tell me anything, and I didn't ask. But if

she's getting herself into trouble, you owe it to her to try and help."

"I owe it to her? She had her hand in your lap!"

Justin flushed. "She was drunk."

"Like hell."

He pulled me close and rested his chin on my head, but I shrugged him off and focused on the shadows cast by branches weaving against the hall floor.

"Jesus," he said suddenly. I glanced at him but he was staring out the window, his face pale. I turned back and my breath caught.

It was Ryan Maclean. He was sidling up the driveway, edging along the bushes like he was dodging gunfire, glancing now and again back to the road.

"Holy fucking crap," Justin said.

I held my breath, watching. Mr. Maclean pounded the door with his fist, turning back to watch the road. He leaned on the doorbell, pressing his lips between his teeth, a painfully childish, girlish expression. Eve had made Congressman Maclean into a girl.

"Why?" I whispered.

We watched as the door opened and Eve stood there, talked to him. She tilted her head and smiled, and he brushed the hair out of her face.

"Why?" I said again. "He's married, Justin, he's been married how long? What did she do to him?"

"That son of a bitch! She's sixteen years old!"

Eve stood on her toes and tapped a kiss on Ryan Maclean's lips. She said something, then closed the door, and Mr. Maclean stood on the porch without moving, watching the closed door, his shoulders slumped. After a minute he turned and walked back down the drive.

I watched Justin's face, trying to read his expression. "Who's taking advantage of who?" I said. "It must make her feel so powerful, hunh? Messing with a ten-year marriage."

"What's wrong with you?"

There was a grinding inside me, so hard I was pretty sure I could hear it. "Do you want her too, Justin? Is that why you're defending her?"

He grabbed my shoulder and our eyes locked. After a minute he pulled me towards him, crushed me against his chest. "What're we doing to each other?" he said hoarsely. "I swear to God, Kerry, I won't let her do this to us anymore."

I shook my head against his chest. I listened to the beat of his heart and the gritty rasp his words left in the air, and I tried to believe. I had to believe him. He was now the only thing I had left in this world.

22

IT WAS OUR SEVENTEENTH BIRTHDAY. I was in LoraLee's garden, helping her pull new weeds and prune the roses, a job that always seemed a little mean. I was waiting for Justin to come home. This day had been like every day this week. Eve and I had woken up, gotten dressed, and stared at the cereal boxes while we ate. I'd tried not to knock four times on every item I passed, mostly unsuccessfully. We'd gone to school and sat on opposite sides of our small classroom, her the last row to the right and me front left, trying to pretend I didn't feel her eyes on the back of my head.

I'd bought her a gift, a gold charm in the shape of tiny twin cherries. It was in my pocket now, tucked inside a padded box, ready to be whipped out with a smile of forgiveness. "Even though I'm still pissed off at you," I'd say.

But we hadn't said happy birthday. All day I'd tried to ignore the words pressing just behind my lips, waiting for a glance, the glimmer of a smile. All I needed was a little evidence that the words were behind her lips too. But she gave me no evidence of anything, so I pretended I didn't care. I didn't care.

LoraLee was watching as I tore stems from roots, fierce enough to scatter the earth. I thought she knew that something was wrong, but I couldn't tell her about Eve. Because if I did she'd come up with some story or metaphor that was supposed to be an answer, when there was no answer. Not to this. Instead I spoke around the truth, told her Eve had found a new boyfriend only a week after she'd broken up with Brad. "She just blinks her eyes and they go after her," I said.

LoraLee laughed and shook her head. "That Eve, she like a day lily, burst into color and sing for all she's worth, and you can't help but listen."

"She doesn't love him, I know she doesn't."

LoraLee patted my hand. "In the end it for her to make her own choice and find her own way. Deep down she the only one know what's bes' for herself."

"But if she's doing something completely wrong?"

"You think you can reason her into changin' her notion 'bout what's wrong? It ain't right, she find that for herself. It's hard puttin' on a show you doesn't believe in. Day lily, they only hold they color for so long."

"And then they die."

She sighed and brushed the dirt from her hands, then rocked back on her heels to watch me. "When you gonna see it ain't for you to pull her back? It's like a bush what you cuts back so's it won't block out your view. You can trim it but you can't do a thing 'bout the smell of its flower or shape of the leaf. And in the end, the bush still allus want to keep on growin'. So you either has to keep battlin' nature or you jus' work with it."

"You're trying to say there's nothing I can do."

"No, that ain't it at all. I's sayin' you got to be careful, listen careful to how the bush want to grow. Work with it and it jus' may grow fuller stead-a taller. In the end it still grow, but if you's lucky, it also won't block out the view." She tilted her head. "You know she need you to unnerstan' more than she need you to tell her what's right."

My throat tightened and I turned away to the colorful pots of new annuals that would soon inherit the garden. And part of me wanted to kick them, to shatter their pots and trample their buds. Eve thought I was weak enough to accept anything she did just to keep the peace. But I'd show her that times had changed. I had changed. I didn't need her anymore.

When I returned home, Justin was sitting on the front step waiting, a small gift-wrapped box in his hands. He jumped to his feet when he saw me, lifted me from the ground in a hug.

I made a choked sound and pushed at him, and he set me down. "Hey, I thought you'd squeal for me. You know I love to hear you squeal." He backed away and looked into my face. "Something wrong?"

I turned away and opened the door. "I'm okay."

"You should be ecstatic. You're sweet seventeen and soon to be kissed." He brushed back my hair and planted a kiss on my forehead. "Seventeen and about to be gifted, look!"

I took the package from him, pulled at the wrapping and opened the flat box. Inside were two ferry passes, two Red Sox tickets and a hotel brochure. "Wow," I said.

"Don't you get it? We're driving to Boston. We have to get away from here for a little while, start fresh. We'll go in June the day after school ends, hang out at Boston

Commons, see the waterfront. You guys need time together, away from all this, away from Ryan Maclean and Brad Carrera and memories."

I stared at him. "This is for me and Eve?"

"For the three of us, actually. I gave Eve her ticket already."

"The three of us," I said. I pictured the three of us at Fenway Park, Justin in between. I pictured a foul ball soaring our way. And hitting Eve in the head.

Justin tilted his head at me. "Did you and Eve..."

"No," I said. "Me and Eve nothing. We're not talking."

"Come on, Kerry, you have to stop this. Eve's hurting too, you know."

"I'm not hurting."

Justin gave me a pitying look and I clenched my jaw and turned away. "Forget it. You don't know anything, Justin. Eve's exactly where she wants to be."

I pushed past him up the stairs. With a shock I saw Eve standing in the hall, watching down. I strode to the bedroom, kicked off my shoes and sat on the bed, squeezing my eyes shut and waiting to see what she'd do.

A minute later she came to the bedroom door. I pretended to be inordinately interested in my socks.

"Hey," she said.

"Hey." My voice was rough and masculine, someone else's voice. I could feel the sharp edges of Eve's gift box through my jeans.

Eve reached into her drawer for a can of beer, then sat on her bed, gripping it without pulling the tab. "So you think we'll get a birthday envelope? Five bucks this time? Maybe ten?"

"Guess you'd think ten bucks is pretty lame." I smiled thinly. "When you take into account that money under your bed."

Eve's shoulders stiffened. "What?"

"I saw it, Eve, must be a thousand bucks stashed there. You steal money from friends and you steal other people's husbands. It's inspirational."

"I'm not stealing anything."

"Or is Ryan Maclean paying you for sex? For a good fuck call Eve Barnard, weekends half-price." The words were coming from somewhere outside me. A sweat broke above my upper lip. I couldn't look at her, only watched her toes clench and unclench in her sandals.

When she finally spoke, there were tears in her voice. "I can't believe you."

"You can't believe *me*?"

"What right do you have to preach? You think you have this Ward Cleaver boyfriend who writes fairy stories, this perfect septic-sweet relationship. But what you don't get is it's not going to last because you have no idea about passion."

"You think you and Mr. Maclean have passion? Maybe like a mutt and a bitch in heat have passion."

She glared at me, then shook her head. "Maybe you don't get it, but Ryan needs me. He loves me."

"You're really that clueless."

"He's an important man, Kerry, he wouldn't risk his career if this was just about sex. You know what he does to be with me? What he's been doing? He says he has to be in Washington, that Congress is in session and he has to leave. So this is what he does, he drives out to the airport, takes the plane out and then he takes the next one back, and when it lands he leaves his car and walks out to Daddy's boat."

I stared at her.

"You know how cramped it is in there?" she said. "How tiny the hold is, but he spends half those in-session days on Daddy's boat."

"You let him stay in Daddy's boat?" So many things were rushing through me, words and images on fire. "Daddy's boat!"

"We've fucked on Daddy's boat," she said.

Heat roared under my skin and I jumped to slap her face, slapped at her before my mind could fathom what my hand was about to do.

Eve raised her hand to her cheek, then looked at her fingers like she expected to see blood. And then, slowly, she held out her wrist for me to see. A thin gold chain of diamond-studded hearts circled where her birthday bracelet used to be. Where the birthday bracelet had been for seventeen years. "He gave me this," Eve said. "He loves me."

Where had she put our bracelet? Was it tossed in with the cheap earrings in her jewelry box? Or in the trash? "You're paying for his attention with sex, don't you get it? You can't get anyone to love you for real, so you're pretending that those few minutes he's screwing you mean something."

Eve shook her head slowly, her eyes fixed on my face. "How do you think it is with you and Justin? I could have Justin any time I want, and that's the truth. He's not better than any other man, Kerry, and he's always wanted me."

"Shut the fuck up!" I raised my hand to hit her again,

but then slammed my fist against the wall and strode into the hallway. Justin was standing at the head of the stairs, his eyes wide. He reached forward but I batted him away. "She's a whore!" I choked, and raced past him.

I ran outside and down the street, ran all the way out to the bluffs, where I pulled Eve's gift box from my pocket and threw it into the ocean. After a minute I tore the birthday bracelet from my wrist. It broke, scattering years of birthday charms like tears, and without a moment's hesitation I flung it out into the water. I watched it fall, a glittering sliver like a wish until it vanished beneath the waves.

23

I SLEPT IN DADDY'S ROOM the night of my birthday and woke early, well before Eve. I couldn't face her, I knew I couldn't, and so I pulled on a shirt and jeans and went outside. I walked, not quite sure where I was walking to, up north where the houses were grander, with walls of windows that gazed blankly out to sea. And even when I reached the Macleans' it took me a minute to realize why I was there and what I was going to do.

I slowly undid the top two buttons of my blouse and tucked my hair under my collar to hide its length. I lifted my chin, stretching my neck. I knew how to play Eve, a tilt of the head, a slender smile, that was all it took. No magic in Eve, not really. *Honey,* is what I'd call him, no matter how weird it felt. *I'm sorry, Ryan, honey, but this has to stop.*

I hid behind a neighbor's bush and waited. The flag masted against the porch rail hung limp and still. Congressman Maclean. All-American Adulterer.

Through the front window I could see the Maclean boys with popsicle-blue tongues outstretched and comparing, Mrs. Maclean facing the television and hugging a coffee mug in both hands. I watched them. I watched and the guilt was mine, the sourness in my belly. How could

Eve do this to them? Knowing what it was to lose a father, how?

I'm sorry, honey, but I'm getting sick of this. If you even look at me again I'll tell your wife, I'll tell the news and you'll lose everything you worked for just because you couldn't see past your own stunted prick. And then I'd give him one of Eve's disparaging sneers. *By the way,* I'd say, *you were by far the worst fuck I ever had.*

I was there less than ten minutes before Ryan Maclean appeared at the window to kiss his wife and ruffle his sons' heads on his way out the door. He closed the door behind him, a paper tucked under his arm, and headed for his car. I watched him walk, his brown hair streaked with gray, his deep-set eyes, the things that made him a grownup. I watched the confidence of his stride, a man who knew what he wanted and where he was going, and then made myself remember how his face had looked trapped in a helpless moan.

I stepped out from the bushes.

The flush on his skin was instantaneous, would have been kind of fascinating if I'd been in a different mood. The color rose from under the collar of his blue shirt, up his neck and to his cheeks. And in that minute, with the wide grin on his face, he might've been a little kid thrilled with the weight of a fish pulling at his pole. In that minute I thought I understood some of what Eve might see.

I gave him Eve's narrowed eyes and uptilted nose. "I'm sorry," I said. "But this has to stop."

He stepped closer, and the flush drained from his cheeks as suddenly as it had come. "Holy Christ," he said, backing away. "What the hell!"

He knew it was me. What was it he hadn't seen? There was a time when even Daddy couldn't tell us apart. But times had obviously changed. "Congressman," I said.

"What do you want." Not a question. A threat.

"What do I want? What *do* I want." This was all feeling too adult for me. I knew what I wanted, but I was suddenly reasonably sure this wasn't the right way to get it.

He glanced back at his house, then shook his head at me. "Not here." His voice was dark with disgust. He wiped his hand across his mouth and walked down the street without looking my way. I followed.

"I guess they don't have any idea," I said.

He didn't answer, just kept his eyes on the road ahead, the brambles overhanging the gravel, the rambler roses smiling blankly up at us.

"What're you doing, Mr. Maclean?" The musical tone of my own voice scared me. I was pretending to be Eve, and I wasn't Eve. I didn't know how long I could keep on with it before I did something stupid, apologized or ran away. "Do you love her?"

He walked faster. "What do you want from me? If you want something from me, Kerry, you tell me now."

"It's a legitimate question, isn't it? Do you love her?"

He was quiet for a minute, then suddenly burst into laughter. It hit me that he might actually be insane, but then he turned to wave at Nora Beaufort sweeping the front porch of her Victorian inn. "Morning, Nora," he said. "How many today?"

"Three couples," Nora said, "plus a single man in the Wyeth Suite. You imagine one man wanting a whole suite?"

"All filled up then!" Mr. Maclean rested his hand on my back, pushing me along.

"You better be careful," I said brightly. "People are going to start to think we're having an affair."

He threw back his head in another hearty laugh as he pulled his arm away. The laughter stopped abruptly as it had started, an actor leaving the stage. "Look," he said under his breath. "I don't know what kind of game you're playing. I hope you can be adult enough to have some kind of sense."

"You hope I'm adult enough. And if I'm not, then I guess Eve's not, and what does that mean exactly? That you're screwing a kid? Who's got more sense here?"

"I'm repeating myself, Kerry. What do you want? You want me to tell you I love her?"

But what I wanted, what I really wanted, I realized, was for him to tell me he didn't love her at all. To tell me she was just this fling he was having, that all his life he'd been having these kinds of flings with pretty girls. Did the fact that he hadn't said anything to deny it mean this was actually something more?

"Do you want to marry her?"

This question stopped him in his tracks. He pulled the newspaper from under his arm, eyed it as if he was scanning the headlines. "I know you're concerned about your sister," he said. "I understand you'd be concerned."

Of course he didn't understand anything, but I'd let him go with concern. It was more acceptable than rage and disgust and fear. And jealousy of him.

"Eve knows how things are, we've talked about it many times. In my career, unfair as it is to either of us, appearances are everything."

"Unfair? Seems to me like appearances should be everything. Seems like cheating on your wife to sleep with someone who's in high school says a hell of a lot about the kind of person you are."

He ignored me. "No matter how I feel about her, no matter if I love her—"

"Do you love her?"

He was silent for a minute, then looked back at his newspaper. "Are you going to talk to her?" he asked. "To Eve, will you be telling her about this conversation?"

"Probably not. There's no reason to tell her."

He gave a single nod and then something changed in his face, a tightening behind the skin. "Does anyone else know? Did you tell anyone?"

"Justin knows," I said, "that's all."

"Justin. Justin Caine? The mechanic?"

This made me want to slap him. "The mechanic knows," I said, tightly.

"Dammit," he muttered. "She knew better than to say anything."

"Us kids like bragging to our friends about the men we're sleeping with. It bonds us."

He flinched. Congressman Maclean, Rhode Island elect, flinched at my words and I smiled. This was the power Eve felt. This is how it felt to be an adult. "Look, I won't tell anyone and neither will he. I don't give a damn about your career, but I know what it would do to your kids."

He nodded. Not grateful but calculating, a politician's nod. "I don't know if I love her," he said after a minute, his voice so low I could hardly hear. "But I'd do anything for her, I'll tell you that much."

I narrowed my eyes at him, hoping he could see my disgust, wishing it would at least make him listen to himself, to think. But then Mr. and Mrs. Lynch approached with Sheila Jessup, and Mr. Maclean broke into a roar of greeting, slapping backs and shaking hands, no sign of anything else.

I listened as he spoke to his constituents, a light and limber filibuster, and after a minute I turned away. Knowing the only thing I understood of people was the lie of them.

My stomach was complaining, and so as soon as I returned home I searched through the kitchen cupboards. In the back of an up-high cupboard I found a bag of Daddy's pork rinds and I opened them, imagining him with the bag between his knees, telling us about the lady who'd been so terrified of the parasail that she'd pulled off her husband's toupee as her feet left the ground. I sat with the bag on the chair that had been his and inhaled the onion salt of it, and I imagined his laughter and the red crumbs in his beard that would stay there until someone reminded him to brush them away. It was eight months since anyone had sat here. I swept my hand across a spider web between the chair's legs, and then on impulse I began to clean.

We hadn't cleaned for quite a while. In fact, except for random tidying, we had never actually cleaned at all. So now I wet rags and went over every surface. I pulled our childhood drawings from the walls, fingering each one: Eve and Kerry, age three, age four, age five. A BAD GUY, some adult had printed on one. PRETTY FLOWERS; A

BIG MACHINE. Each picture I removed uncovered squares of too-dark wallpaper, like vacant eyes that watched me no matter how hard I tried to ignore them.

I set the paintings in the hall and moved out to the den, retrieving some of the kitschy things Daddy had bought either to make us laugh or because he had exceptionally bad taste. Rocks with googly eyes, shells painted with stripes, a furry stuffed eyeball and a Sylvester-the-Cat clock; I set them all out in the hall. I rolled up dark rugs that looked like winter to reveal the shiny, protected hardwood and then began to sweep. When I was done I sat cross-legged on the floor and fingered the sweepings: a dead leaf, an earring back, a mat of curly black hair. Daddy's hair. I tucked it into my pocket.

The momentum of the cleaning was soothing in its way, but with each old thing I piled by the door I felt myself sinking, no way to stop, the empty floors a sign of transience, one step closer to blowing away.

The afternoon grew long. I ate stale saltines and some spaghetti strands straight from the box. Returning to the den, I gasped. Eve was at the window.

She was watching me, her hair uncombed and greasy at her neck, so long now it hid her eyes. We stood for a minute, face to face, expressionless, and then Eve started to the door. I stood there, numb and nauseous. I didn't think I'd be able to lift my legs.

I watched as she knelt to sort through the things I'd left by the door. She lifted a TV tray, examining a stain from a long-ago dinner. "You're going to throw this all away?"

I looked down at the floor. "I don't know. Yeah, I guess I am."

She nodded, kicking at a footstool shaped like a turtle. "Can you imagine buying crap like this? I mean seeing it in a store and paying actual money?"

I smiled at the floor, suddenly wanting to stop, to drop everything and grab onto her, but instead I shook my head. "No accounting for taste."

"We should keep them," she said, without looking at me. "I mean, there's room in the attic, so why not? In case someone ever wants to know who we all were. I always wanted that when we were kids, some kind of history."

"Okay." There was a sharp squeeze in my chest. I lifted a plastic goldfish bowl, its multicolored plastic fish swimming through blue gel. I glanced at her, then started up the stairs to pull out the ladder to the attic.

We went down for more, and then again. And with each trip I felt something in me settling as our childhood found its place. When we'd finished, we sprawled onto the bottom stair exhausted. We didn't speak, just watched the dust we'd stirred swirling in the fading afternoon light. And then slowly I bent my knee so it touched her leg. I knew she must feel it but she didn't move away.

After a minute, she nodded at the window. "Take a look."

Through the front window I could see LoraLee marching towards our drive. I started to get up but Eve pressed me back. "Just watch."

LoraLee strode to our doorstep, then glanced up and down the street before reaching into the pocket of her skirt. She quickly slid a brown envelope onto our porch, lightly touched the porch rail, then traipsed away.

"Birthday money," I whispered. "She's the one been giving us money."

Eve nodded. "I saw her a while back."

"Why didn't you tell me? How can she give us money when she hardly has enough for herself?"

"It makes her happy, can't you see that? People want to help us, Kerry, like the Caines. They do it for themselves as much as us."

I leaned my head against the banister rail, tears filling my eyes, tears for us, for LoraLee who thought ten dollars could make a difference, for the pieces of the past I'd almost thrown away.

"That money under my bed, it's not what you think. I didn't steal it."

I nodded without turning to face her, wishing she wouldn't talk about this, not now.

"It is the Caines' money, Kerry, but it wasn't stolen, it was given. I don't know why Justin told you I took it, maybe he was embarrassed. But the truth is he gave me the money because he knew you were too proud to take it. We've been planning, me and Justin, for our future, all our future."

Her voice hitched and she blinked quickly before continuing, her words too fast. "We were thinking maybe we could open a bed-and-breakfast, it could be perfect for us. I know you always talked about us running some kind of shop, but really this might make more sense. We'd meet people from all over the country, all over the world even."

I looked up at the small circular window above our door, feeling the breath rush through me, through the earth, up through my legs and chest like I was a hollow pipe with solid, echoing walls. I didn't believe her. I didn't believe a word of it, but at that moment I didn't care. I tilted my head. "You'd dust and change sheets and I'd learn how to make five kinds of French toast."

She glanced at me. "I'm not going to see Ryan Maclean anymore, I'm telling him that. He's getting too psycho for me, wants to be with me every minute it seems like, and I'm bored of it. He doesn't even know who I am really." Her voice trailed off and she clutched at the step.

Without thinking I reached for Eve's hand. She flinched but then, her eyes on the floor, she slowly interlaced our fingers. Her fingers pressed against mine, then harder, gripping me as if my hand could save her. And my fingers were tingling to numbness but I held on.

24

THE FERRY RIDE on our way to Boston was the last time I can remember truly being happy. It was the week before everything went bad.

The afternoon was the kind that brought tourists on day trips, clear skies, the solstice sun as high as a New England sun could get. As the ferry gathered speed, I watched a little boy running hard along the jetty. He was waving frantically as he ran, chest heaving, his face tense with determination, as if he knew he could catch us if he just ran hard enough. When he reached the end of the jetty he stopped, gathered a breath and turned, then raced back to shore with that same fervor.

Watching from the deck I thought I knew how he felt, like almost anything was possible if you only ran hard enough. School had just ended, the worst year of my life in so very many ways, and the summer stretched out in front of me like a lanky, purring promise. We'd both found new jobs, Eve in a gallery on Water Street and me as a shelver in the town library, but even with these responsibilities, still I saw the three of us floating free along that summer promise, with a clear view on all sides and only a gentle dip and sway.

The ride to Point Judith was barely an hour long, but

in that hour we ate enough junk food to make us sick. Eve made friends with the boy behind the snack counter and I watched his face redden each time she ordered, watched Eve's flirting and felt an insane kind of pleasure. This was how life was supposed to be. Here Ryan Maclean didn't exist, or existed only as a name in a list of four hundred congressmen. This was the Eve I'd known all my life, a girl who'd only pretended to be world-wise.

After reaching Point Judith we started the long drive north. I sat in the front seat of Justin's Ford with Eve in back, leaning forward to talk, elbows draped over our seats. "This is it!" she said as the Boston skyline came into view, cement monsters with glistening, lidless eyes. "I'm serious, I'm gonna live here someday, go to museums, eat out at French restaurants, open a coffee bar."

We drove past the harbor, its rust-coated ships ten times larger than anything on the island, its black and still water more like a huge stagnant pond than ocean. Even under the steady sun, the city seemed dark and brooding. I glanced at Eve but didn't say anything. Already part of me was homesick.

"Holiday Inn," Justin said, pointing over my shoulder. He glanced at the hotel brochure, then pulled off the interstate, but the streets kept twisting, and the hotel kept appearing in places it shouldn't.

In the backseat Eve was providing a running commentary. As we passed a huddle of unshaven men in stained T-shirts and ragged jeans, she grinned and tapped on the window. "Forget Harvard Square, there's plenty of eligible guys right here. Hey, what's that girl think this is, an alien parade? Whadda you think, Jussy, think I'd look good with purple hair?"

"This is ridiculous," Justin said. "Let's get directions."

He slowed down and Eve stuck her head out the window, calling to a man in a navy suit. "Hey, sweetheart, how do we get to that hotel? We been driving around for hours."

As he turned towards Eve, the man's eyes softened. He flashed her a grin. "That's Boston for ya," he said in a thick accent.

"Baahston?" Eve said, grinning back.

"Try going thataway," the man said, pointing the opposite direction from the hotel. Eve raised her eyebrows and he shrugged. "You'll get there, trust me. So what room you staying in? I'll look you up."

"Just go to the front desk and ask for Kerry," Eve said. Justin pulled away and we all burst into laughter, our first genuine laughter in what seemed like months.

The road he'd sent us on turned sharply, leading us directly to the hotel's parking lot. We checked into the orange-carpeted room, where Eve and I would share one double bed and Justin would take the other. Eve, who wore her thin silk nighties every summer night at home, had instead packed flannel pajamas and her terry robe. The sweetness of this, her unexpected guardedness around Justin, made my insides ache. And I longed for that night when I'd curl with her in our shared bed and we'd breathe each other's breath, take back our world.

We walked out to the T station through streets lined with traffic and honking horns. The people were everywhere, bustling home from work with their heads down, eyes on their feet. We sat waiting for the train, the three of us squashed in a seat meant for two, until we saw a foot-long rat scuttle under the tracks. Eve made a face and jumped to her feet. "I'm going for a walk," she said.

A man in a torn sweatshirt, his face ragged with stubble, sidled his way across the platform. He walked towards me, caught my eye before I could look away and gave a gap-toothed grin. "'Scuse me, honey, you got some spare change? I didn't eat today or yesterday neither." He watched my face carefully, then shook his head, speaking with a practiced despair. "And the thing is… Thing is, it's my *birthday,* see."

"Well, tell you what," Eve said, appearing from behind a post.

The man startled away, staring from me to her and back, like he was regretting that last bottle of cheap vodka.

"We don't have any money, but since it's your birthday, we'll give you a song." She pulled me from the bench and jumped up onto the seat. "Hey, guys, guess what!" she called, her voice echoing off the cement walls. "We got a birthday boy here. How 'bout we all sing!"

Everybody turned, and a laugh rippled through the crowd. I stared up at Eve in disbelief as she raised her arms, even more shocked as the crowd began to join her, the voices gradually swelling into a cacophony of disjointed song. "Hap-py birth-day to youuu…" Beside us, Justin gazed at her in awe, then turned to me and joined in with a laugh.

"Hap-py birth-day dear…" The voices trailed off as the crowd looked to Eve expectantly. Eve just grinned back, glanced at the man and shrugged. She raised her arms again and the crowd started back up. "Hap-py birth-daaay to youuu…"

The crowd cheered and the man walked away, shaking his head, his eyes wide and dazed. I looked into Eve's face, trying to read her expression. As the crowd turned away her shoulders dropped and she stepped down from the bench. And I suddenly had the strange sense that I should find some way to comfort her. I smiled widely. "That was hilarious," I said.

But even though she smiled back, her eyes seemed glazed, like they were trapped in some far distant place.

By the time we finally got to Fenway Park the game was in the second inning, the Yankees winning by four.

"Think I'll root for the Yanks," Eve said, grinning at Justin as we took our seats.

He shook his head. "You looking to get beat up or something?"

"What's it been, seventy-six years since the Sox won the World Series?"

I stared at her. When had Eve ever watched baseball?

She shook her head. "It's like they're some kind of low-budget running tragedy. Maybe the actors and the plot change a little each year, but you know what's gonna happen in the end. Ask me, I'd rather laugh with the winners than cry with the losers."

Did she look this all up before we came? Justin smiled at her. "I'd rather not get beat up," he said.

The Yankees led most of the game but remarkably, in the bottom of the ninth inning with bases loaded, the Sox shortstop hit a fly ball that arched over the Green Monster. The crowd exploded and Justin grabbed me round the waist with a cheer. I let the crowd's electricity surge through me, as if it could discharge everything that had happened in the past few months.

As we got up to leave, a man turned to Justin. "I think you should tell your friend there that this is gonna be the Sox year."

"I bet you're right," Justin said. "I think this is going to be the year."

"Let's hit the bars," Eve said as we left the stadium.

I made a face at her. "How you planning to get in? Last I heard, the drinking age is still twenty-one."

She smiled slowly and kissed her fingers, tapped them on my cheek. "Silly girl," she said. "Don't you worry, I'll take care of it."

Back at the hotel she hitched her skirt in half so it fell well above her knees, grabbed a black leather jacket from her suitcase and slipped it over her T-shirt. She went to the vanity, and Justin and I both watched mutely as she darkened her lipstick, deepened hollows in her cheeks, then smoothed back her hair with gel and a headband. She smiled at her reflection, tilted her head one way and then the other and grinned. "Voilà, twenty-one," she said.

The block by our hotel was lined with bars, all themed in one way or another: sports bar, gay bar, bohemian and artsy, and then a neon-lit window fronted by yuppies in business suits, busy even on a Monday night. This, of course, was the bar Eve chose.

We were on our way in when a man in black grabbed Justin's shoulder. "I'll need ID," he said.

Eve, who had already made it inside, turned around and gave him a slow, slim smile. "They're with me," she said. "There's not a problem, is there?"

The man eyed Eve, a look that slid from her lips to chest to legs. Finally he flicked his chin in a quick nod. "They'll card you all if you try and get drinks, you know that."

Eve winked at him. "S'okay. There's other ways to have fun."

We sat on barstools amid the smoke, the rock beat so loud you had to shout to hear your own voice. And the men were drawn in right away, came to stand behind us, order us drinks, red-faced and feverish, making twin jokes and thinking they were funny.

But Eve was the one they ended up talking to. After a few minutes I became as uninteresting as belly button lint. They grew more and more animated, began to laugh at everything she said before she even finished saying it.

Justin and I sat with our stale beers and watched. It was incredible to see, even though I'd been with her every day of her life. Was it a scent she had? A pheromone? Was it the way she threw back her head when she laughed? Really it was all of these and more, something indefinable but everywhere. I looked the same, could say her words, I could carry myself in the very same way but I'd still only seem like a shadow.

As the room started to thin out, Eve slid her butt up onto the bar. "I want to make a toast," she slurred.

Heads turned, the men gave their lizard-watching-a-fly grins. Justin whispered between clenched teeth, "Eve! Get down!"

Eve beamed and hiked up her skirt. Raised her beer mug. "Here's to the Red Sox," she shouted. "Here's to staying up past three and tongues that are long enough to touch the tip of your nose."

Someone hooted from the back of the room. "You go, girl," someone else called.

"Here's to German beer and Marlboros, and the feel of a guy's you-know-what when you dance."

Justin's face tightened. "That's it," he said. "You can stay with her if you want, but I'm going back."

"You're leaving me here?"

"I'm leaving Eve. I can't watch this, it's making me sick."

I looked up at Eve. She was high-fiving men with both hands, and as I watched, one of them intertwined his fingers with hers as another lifted her by the waist.

"Okay," I said. "You go on. I have to see her back."

Hours later I walked Eve up to the hotel. I helped her into her flannel, squeezed toothpaste on her brush. I lay with her, breathing the liquor-sweat of her neck and the baby whisper of her hair, and the thought rose to cover me fine and gossamer as a veil, that I was the only one that knew. I was the only one who understood the truth of her.

25

THERE WERE SEVEN STUDENTS in the graduating class, and as we watched the small procession, Eve on the folding chair to my right and Justin to my left, I didn't think of my own future a year away. What I felt was the fragile shell that was finally forming again like a cocoon around the three of us. I knew how to be careful. I knew how not to break it, and in time we'd all be able to be ourselves again.

Ryan Maclean was there to give the commencement address. He sat in front of us with his wife and his two sons, and every few minutes when he turned to us, face red and slick in the hot June sun, it was me who caught his eye and slapped him back with my tsunami-strength hatred for what he'd almost taken away.

Eve felt it too, felt his eyes. He'd turn and I'd sense her stiffening beside me, but her eyes stayed on the stage. I wondered what he could be thinking, sitting there with his wife but turning to Eve. Maybe it was only that he was scared, but in his eyes it looked like more. Sitting there I began to understand the truth he hadn't been able to tell me, the unthinkable fact that in a way Congressman Maclean actually had loved Eve.

He rose and approached the podium to a watery rush

of applause. He stood for a minute, looking out over the audience, smiling and nodding, acknowledging admirers like the applause was for him rather than the occasion.

"I watch these bright young faces," he said, "so beautiful, so full of promise. I look at you all and I wonder." And then he turned to Eve, looked straight at her with his piercing eyes, his serene and fatherly smile. "You have so much confidence in what you've done so far, in the steps you've taken to leave your old lives behind. But before you leave, make sure you stop to reflect on the magic of the life you're leaving, the beauty of the island, the community, and especially the people. The folks who love you more than anyone you'll ever find on the outside."

His gaze lingered on Eve and then shifted away. He stretched an almost mocking smile. "Remember that, remember what I've said as you continue on your journey. You remember the magic you walked away from and mourn the loss of it, and when you're done with that journey just remember it's still here for you, whenever you decide to come home."

Eve's face was pale, her eyes wide and startled. "Son of a bitch," I whispered, hoping he could read my lips.

Eve stood and slipped out from the row. I squeezed Justin's knee and followed.

She was walking so fast I had to jog to keep up, but when she reached the road she stopped, facing away from me. "You okay?" I said finally.

"Wasn't it romantic? I think I'm in love."

"It was disgusting, really," I said, then glanced at her. "Do you think he really does love you?"

"I don't know." She looked back at the white graduation tent and shook her head. "I think he might be crazy, though. There with his wife, his kids, I think he might actually be clinically insane."

We listened to a smattering of applause, and then the reading of the graduates' names. More applause and the throwing of caps, then Principal Greene's congratulations.

"We should go back, I have to do something." Eve pulled at my arm. "Come with me."

I let her drag me until I realized where she was going. "Eve?" I said, pulling away. "Eve!" I stared at her a minute, stunned, then rushed forward.

"You too!" Eve was saying. "And how old is Tim now?"

"He's almost seven," Mrs. Maclean said. "Can you imagine? It seems like the last time I looked we were still trying to potty-train." She leaned forward conspiratorially. "We had the hardest time with it."

"Mo-om!"

"And Billy's what? I'd guess three years old?"

Billy Maclean held up three fingers. "And a half."

Mrs. Maclean put an arm around him and beamed. "And you girls are going to be wearing the caps and gowns soon, right? Is it next year? I still remember when you and your dad first came to the island. You were hardly knee high." She turned to Ryan. "What is it the Psalms say, sweetheart? Days consumed like smoke."

Mr. Maclean was watching Eve's feet mutely as his wife spoke. Or was he actually watching her bare legs? I narrowed my eyes at him, pulling Eve's arm to get us out of there. "There's a party at Jill Stanton's," I said. "So we should probably get ready."

"Ryan was planning to stop by too, weren't you, honey? Congratulate the grads and he bought gifts, plaques with an Emerson quote."

"How sweet," Eve said dryly.

"Should I tell you what happened the night of my graduation? It was the night we first kissed and five years later we were married." She chuckled and squeezed Mr. Maclean's arm. "So you have fun then. But not *too* much fun." She laughed again and waved as I pulled Eve away.

"What're you doing!" I whispered.

She shrugged. "I just wanted to let him know how things would be now. How it means so little to me now that I can talk to his wife without even flinching. And really, how much easier it'll be for him, too."

Justin came up behind us. "What were you doing, Eve? You weren't—"

"Why're you guys making such a big deal? Look, we're going to have to live in the same town for how long, so we have to learn how to deal with it."

Justin raised his eyebrows at me and I shook my head.

"So we going to the Stantons'?" Eve said.

I eyed her for a minute, suddenly realizing it would ruin something in me, seeing Eve in the green silk dress she'd bought with the Caines' money, its low neck and spaghetti straps. All night, I knew, I'd be watching how the boys all looked at her, how she pulled back her shoulders when she sensed them looking. "I think I'm not in the mood anymore," I said. "Could we just walk, Justin? You mind?"

He watched me carefully. "They say it's going to storm tonight."

I widened my eyes at him pointedly, and he shrugged. "Guess I don't mind getting wet if you don't."

So we spent the evening walking through streets and watching the mainlanders with their after-dinner ice creams, hair wet from their after-beach showers. They clustered like carolers around posted dinner menus, pondering whether entrée descriptions justified their prices. They stood under streetlamps studying maps and deciding what to do tomorrow, and I felt a sort of ache watching them, their only concern whether the clouds would blow over by morning. As we walked I realized what had bothered me since our trip to Boston, that I felt like I couldn't speak my mind to Eve. For my own sense of peace I needed to pretend she held none of the blame for what she'd done, when inside, this was how I felt: If Congressman Maclean had become crazy in love with her, to the point where he couldn't leave it behind even in the presence of his family, that was her fault. Eve had known exactly what she was doing.

"Next year it'll be you," Justin said suddenly.

I looked across the harbor to the emerald lights tracing the Newport Bridge, following its rise from the blackened sea, its long run and dip back into the ocean. "It's weird," I said. "I feel so much older than them in a way. Like there they are, thinking how walking past that podium and taking that diploma is the most important thing. When I know it's just one foot in front of the other going nowhere. Just this piece of paper with their name in fancy writing, but what does it change about them, really? If their life sucked before, then it still sucks."

Justin stopped short, turned to face me. "Where's that coming from?"

I raised my chin. "When I graduate, are you going to ask me to marry you?"

Justin blinked. "What?"

"Mrs. Maclean told us that when she graduated was the first night they kissed. And then they got married and now here he is screwing Eve." I tilted my head to the dark sky. "I don't know what I'm trying to say. I don't even know, just all these thoughts are jumbled up inside me. I feel like there's only a few really important things in your life and you have to take them when you can because you never know when they'll go away. I need to find out if you'll ever want to get married."

"Well of course I will, of course I do."

"To me?"

Justin watched me a moment, then took my hands. "Of course I do," he said again. "That's what I've been planning."

My eyes stung as he brought my hands to his lips, whispered against them. "You are older than those kids," he said. "Older than them and in some ways you're older than me." He kissed my fingers, smiled crookedly. "Of course I want to marry you."

I slid my hands up to his cheeks. His face was flushed, his eyes full with something swollen and guarded.

I kissed him then, me and Justin in the middle of Dodge Street, off-islanders watching from the wraparound porch of the Surf Hotel. The air around us was hot with summer laughter, the yearning scraping at my insides. But somehow, I knew something was missing. A tiny chip I couldn't name that kept the picture from coalescing, from being wholly complete. So I pulled at him, clutched his shirt in my fists and his tongue against my teeth, as if I could stop him from leaving the ground and drifting away.

It was fully dark when we got back home, the moon hazing yellow between the clouds. The rain had started, just a drizzle, but the winds were picking up and promising more. "Better not take too long saying good night," Justin said. "I'm gonna have to make a dash for it."

I reached for him. "What's more important, getting wet or getting kissed?"

He laughed and pulled me close. It was then I saw the window.

The pane of glass beside the door was shattered, an approximately fist-sized hole. "Justin?" I whispered.

As if in response, the blustering wind blew the door open, then clicked it back to the latch. There were no lights on inside, no sounds. Justin put out his arm to stop me from coming closer, lifted a potted plant. "I'm sure it's nothing," he whispered. "But you stay here until I say it's okay."

He pushed the door and stepped inside. I waited on the porch wishing for light, something brighter than the sickly yellow moon. The rain was hitting nails against the tin roof; it was all I could hear. There could be anything out here, anywhere, behind the bushes, under the porch grating—really he shouldn't have left me there alone.

I walked into the hall. Footsteps. I pressed myself against the wall, hand over my mouth. Something ran out from the kitchen towards me, arms raised over its head. I shrieked.

"Christ!" Justin said. "Jesus, Kerry, I told you to stay outside!"

I stared at him, then suddenly exploded into laughter. "You almost creamed me!"

Justin shook his head, then snorted. "Can't you see the headlines? Girl bashed into coma by man wielding a dead clematis. I'd never live it down."

"Well if there was anyone here, I'm sure they got scared off. You see anything missing?"

It was then we heard the muffled scream.

Justin and I stared at each other over the dead vines. Suddenly Justin backed away. "Eve!"

We raced up the stairs and down the hall, swung round the corner, darkness, darkness and then I saw the bodies and the flash of pale skin on tanned skin. His hand plastered over her mouth, the other round her neck, his groin grinding against her, pushing her down against my bed.

Eve screamed when she saw us but somehow Mr. Maclean seemed oblivious, hadn't heard us, so intent he was on his grinding and thrusting, his words pitched high and wild with frenzy, maybe also with drink. "You little cockteaser. Stop pretending you don't want it, you said!"

"Get off me!" Eve hit at him. "You son of a bitch!"

"Please," I whispered, "oh, oh, please…"

"Stop it, stop it…" She was sobbing now. "Stoppit, stoppit!"

Beside me Justin had frozen, watching the legs and flailing arms, the black lace of her underthings and torn silk of her dress. He stared like a deer blinded by headlights and then with a roar he lunged at Mr. Maclean with strength I didn't know he had, strength that lifted the heavy flowerpot and rammed Mr. Maclean's shoulder, sending him stumbling against Eve's bed. Mr. Maclean shrieked, hitting back at Justin, kicking, catching him under the chin, but Justin didn't seem to feel it. He swung the flowerpot at Mr. Maclean's head.

Time is elastic; Einstein proved it and everyone can feel it, how a clock tells you nothing about how long a nightmare lasts. Time stretches and each second sticks to the last: a smash of terra-cotta against bone, blood spraying from Mr. Maclean's nose, the panic in his eyes and heaving of his chest, I saw it all. The pot lifting and battering again and then again, the rage on Justin's face fiercer than anything I'd ever seen before. Justin, who was never angry, who wore his calmness like a badge of honor, now seemed raw and red, unhinged. Still blindly battering as Mr. Maclean gaped up at him, gurgling, his face twisted in horror. Eve gave an ear-piercing shriek and I dove for Justin's arms, wrapped myself around his body and pulled him to the floor.

The sound of our breath. Silence. He was lying there, Ryan Maclean, with open eyes and open zipper, his penis, the first I'd ever seen, deflating slowly to curl purplish blue against his beige dress pants.

I covered my face and backed against the wall, my chest heaving, gagging, bringing up nothing. Eve staggered backwards, cowering in an identical huddle against the wall, her hands pressed over her mouth.

"Justin?" I whimpered. "Justin?"

But his eyes were on Eve, her huddled near-naked

form. "Oh God," he said, striding to her, cradling her head against his neck. "Are you okay? Did he hurt you?"

"He's dead," Eve said. "Is he dead? Is he?"

I watched them, hands still cupped over my mouth and nose, watched how Justin pressed his hands to her bare back, his fingers under the black straps of her bra.

"Did he rape you?" Justin said.

She shook her head and wrapped her arms around him, sobbing against his chest. I watched them a moment, then bent to the floor, trying not to look at Ryan Maclean's penis or his staring eyes, the blood now pooling on the hardwood floor, lining veins into the cracks and ridges. I pressed his eyes closed and reached for his neck, wet and still warm, felt nothing but the sheen of sweaty skin. "I..." I inhaled a quick, hiccupping breath. "I..." I said again, then gagged, a sickly bile that burned my mouth.

"He's dead," Justin said. He touched a cut on his own chin, stared at the blood on his fingers. "He's dead, isn't he."

Eve pulled away and stared down at Ryan Maclean, trembling. "No," she whispered, then slowly slid against the wall, down onto the floor.

"We have to call the cops," Justin said.

Eve stared at him, wide-eyed. "No!"

Justin sank to the bed. "We have to, Eve, we can't just leave him here. Nobody can blame us for this, you know that, right?"

I crawled to sit on the bed, hid my face against Justin's shoulder. "You kept hitting him," I whispered. "He was down, he was down and you kept hitting!"

"They'll blame me," Eve said. "He's married, famous,

whatever the fuck that means, but to them it'll mean it's all my fault." Her voice broke and she shook her head. "Don't you know how it'll be? The rest of my life that's who I'll be."

We sat there, the three of us, watching the spreading blood as if waiting for something to happen. We sat there knowing who Eve and Justin both would be. We knew how it was on the island, how sins followed you everywhere and always, a sour-scented shadow.

"You kept hitting him," I said again. "Even if he was the one who came here, whatever he did to Eve, look what you did to his head, Justin. Look at—"

"Stop it!" Eve's voice was a shriek. She hugged her knees, rocked back and forth, back and forth.

Justin stared down at the blood spattered on his hands and his jacket. He wiped his hands against his jeans, then slowly rubbed his sleeve at the streaks they'd left behind.

"Please," Eve whispered. "We have to get him out of here. If he just goes missing, if we buried him..."

I noticed suddenly that Eve's feet were still encased in green satin pumps. I stood, pulled a robe from the closet and draped it over her shoulders. "The blood's stopped," I said, the words coming from someplace else, my head feeling drifty as if it hovered somewhere above my body, watching down.

Eve started to rock faster, crooning to herself, her hair limp in her face. Justin stood and threw a blanket over Ryan's body, then knelt to pull the robe tight over her shoulders. "I'll take care of you, okay?" he said. "Whatever happens, whatever we do, I promise I'll take care of you."

* * *

This is the good thing about growing up so near the water. You know where to take a boat so that the tourists out late can't hear the noise of your engine. You know the framework beneath the waves even though you can't see it, know where the craggy rocks can catch a body, hold it down, tear it to pieces in the squall so that if it ever finds the surface there will be no sign of what it once had been.

We hauled the steamer trunk that Daddy had used for his tools into Justin's car, then carried the body, wrapped in my blanket. Justin held his shoulders and I held his legs, the dead weight of him reminding me of the ten-foot swordfish Daddy used to clean. We sat him upright inside the trunk and then folded his chest over his legs like he was stretching or doing sit-ups.

We drove in silence and parked at the ferry landing, then sat there in the car, waiting. Behind the hushing sound of the wind, we could hear the music from the bar, the pounding drumbeat so muffled it almost seemed like a heartbeat. On the dock a couple, holding hands, stood gazing at moonlight on water. We watched the man bend to kiss the woman, then wrap her in his arms and rest his chin on her head. We waited as they rocked foot to foot, a slow dance that seemed to last an eternity before they finally kissed again and walked back to the street, his arm around her shoulders. Justin nodded. "Okay," he said. "Let's go."

It took three of us to lift the trunk from Justin's car, Eve's fingers gripping the handle beside me. We carried it down to the harbor and hoisted it onto the deck. None of us spoke.

It was the first time I'd been on Daddy's boat since

the night I'd seen Eve in the hold with Ryan Maclean. And on this night I believed in fate, in rightful destiny.

I rowed from the dock with a loose plank, the gulp of the wood on water and the hollow thud as the plank hit the hull eerily magnified. A cold drizzle glazed my cheeks as we passed the breakwater and pulled into the vast blankness away from shore, the dark sky indistinguishable from the dark water, one yawning mouth. I started the engine.

Eve huddled in the corner, Justin beside her, enfolding her in his arms and staring out at the choppy waves. I began to steer, pressing the cold kiss of Daddy's key necklace against my lips. The picture in my mind was the photograph of me and Eve in new pink bathing suits, the picture I'd found hidden with the Caines' money in the bag under Eve's bed. I thought now I could remember that day on the beach, holding Eve's hand as Daddy grinned. "Such beauties," he'd said, the camera at his eye. "Who woulda thought a guy like me could make such beautiful girls."

The boat weaved in the storm. Though the rain had stopped, the wind was fierce and biting once we left the shelter of the harbor. I kept my eyes on the land, trying to avoid my qualmishness while Eve was sick over the edge, Justin holding back her hair.

This was the northeast side of the island, an isolated stretch accessible only by boat or long walks on the Clay Head Trail above the shoreline. Isolated enough that you might imagine it an ideal place to stroll while composing a congressional address. The ocean close enough to the low hanging bluffs that a man might climb down to watch the evening surf. Might lean too far. In a drunken fog might fall. I cut the engine.

The boat pitched even more violently and I had to fight to keep my feet. I watched Justin's face, wet with sweat or rain, and he watched mine, wearing no expression that I could read. Finally he nodded sharply and the two of us opened the trunk. We unwrapped the body from the blanket and it hit the deck with the thunk of flanks on a butcher block. We lifted the body and heaved it over the stern.

Eve stumbled to stand beside me and watched as the body hit the water: head, then torso and legs. I knew her thoughts were the same as mine, knew she, like I, saw another man lean over that same stern, either too drunk or much too sober to stop his knees from climbing, his body from hitting the water and floating there without a fight. He bobbed above the water as we watched him, knowing there was no hope, no saving. We watched as the water judged and claimed him; we fought to keep from lunging to pull him back. We watched his pant legs billow and his mouth fill, watched his arms float towards us as if with the pain of leaving. We fed the ocean this one last piece, and wondered what we had left.

FIVE

Bloodroot

June
2007

26

I'D BEEN PLAYING with the torn letters I'd brought, shuffling them on the bed, piecing fragments with fragments. It was a difficult process because Eve and I had written our letters in similar blue pen on plain white paper, like those annoying thousand-piece jigsaw puzzles of popcorn kernels or baskets of golf balls. But our handwriting was different enough to identify, her print straight and blocky, mine slanted and slim. We'd once read a *Cosmo* article on handwriting analysis, and it basically said that Eve was headstrong and I looked towards the past rather than embracing the present. Surprisingly accurate considering the article was probably written by a twenty-year-old communications major, hoping for a reference on her resumé and five hundred bucks towards her tuition at Podunk State.

I began with Eve's scrawled signature and worked my way up, joining lines into letters into words. So many mangled, furious pieces. This was a mindless task that was not at all mindless; my hands were still but my insides were shaking. This in itself could bring a sort of answer, the words Eve had used, the lies to take him away from me. But playing with the scraps, all I could think was how incredibly young and stupid we both had been.

When I finished the bottom two rows of Eve's words, I stared at them, trying to figure out what they meant. *up now for the first time. I'm in my Dad's room if you want to talk it out.*

I laid a strip of Scotch tape over the line to hold the pieces in place, then slipped it all back into the envelope. There was no point in this. It wouldn't change anything.

I glanced at the clock. Two-thirty. Usually by two Eve would have woken, asked for her bedpan or for the pills she knew I couldn't give her yet. I slipped the envelope under my pillow and started downstairs.

Eve was propped in bed, looking unusually alert. Her eyes were quick and nervous, and for a minute I wondered if she might somehow know what I'd been doing.

"Kerry," she said.

"You want some water?"

"Sure. Yeah sure, that'd be great."

When I returned with the water, her eyes were closed. I set the water on the night table next to a pair of nail scissors, then sat on the bed and lifted the scissors, cradled them in my palm. How pointless that her body would waste its energy on growing nails when it had already given up on everything else. "You want me to do your right hand?"

"Really what I want is just to sleep." Her eyes were still closed. "Please."

I nodded and bent to tuck the blanket under her chin. It was then I saw the blood. I screeched and jumped away.

Eve's eyes snapped open.

"You're bleeding! Eve, oh God..." The blood was spreading, seeping across her sheet. I yanked at the sheet with a strangled cry, expecting to see some sort of monstrous, oozing growth, her cancer saying, *Hello there! Here I am!* But what I saw beneath the mire of blood was a deep slash at her wrist.

"Oh...oh...oh..." I pressed the blanket over her wrist. Tourniquet, I needed a tourniquet. I stripped the scarf from Eve's head and tied it around her emaciated upper arm. So much blood. If she weighed a hundred pounds, at least half of them must have leaked onto these sheets. "Oh God, help!"

Eve's face was calm, her shoulders hunched as she looked down at her wrist. "It's not deep enough."

"I have to call. I'll call an ambulance."

"Five more minutes, maybe I could've done something."

I began to run to the kitchen, then stopped and gathered her in my arms. In the kitchen I reached for the phone but Eve batted me with her head. "Don't."

"I'm getting the doctor. You need stitches."

"No I don't, Kerry, stop overreacting. I'm fine and I'm not leaving this house. I'm not letting anybody see me like this."

I lowered us into a chair and looked under the blanket. The cut was already beginning to heal, blood curling slowly over its edges. I awkwardly cradled the skeletal length of her, rocking back and forth.

"Shit, that stings," she said.

"What are you doing, Eve? What did you do?"

"Look, you're hurting me, okay? I don't fit in your lap, and this—" She tugged at the headscarf tourniquet. "What're you trying to be, Clara Barton? Just get me back."

"You think this is okay, you can just do this, no big deal?"

Eve made a face, sarcasm or pain, I couldn't tell. "Get me back," she said. "Before I puke all over this impeccably dressed wound."

I held her eyes a moment longer, then carried her on shaking legs back to the den. The sheets were wet with blood, and so I set her on the wheelchair and began to change them. She stopped me with a hand on my arm. "You won't tell Justin."

"I don't know what I'll do."

"I'll tell you what you'll do. You'll throw away the sheets, help me change my clothes, and then you'll just forget this ever happened."

I reached again for the sheets, heaped them in a pile on the floor.

"What?" Eve said. "I won't do it again if that's what you're scared of. I was just hurting so bad, and for a few minutes it was like a release, a way to stop hurting. But this, this is worse. Feels like someone's trying to press wrinkles out of my arm with a curling iron."

I sat on the bare mattress. "I don't know what to do," I said. "I don't know what to do for you."

"I don't want to die, Kerry, not really, not yet. It just helps me sometimes to think about it ending, that it could end when I want it to."

I looked down at my scarred wrists, the memories running through me like slivers of glass, my blood and Ryan Maclean's, and then another kind of blood that had stained my hands so persistently I'd found it even a week later under my nails. It was more orange than red and as bitter as bile, and although I'd meant for Eve to drink it, I would later end up drinking it myself. So much blood; too much for one lifetime. "I've thought about it too," I said. "I mean, not seriously maybe, but yeah I've thought about it. More than once."

"Then you're a fool." She raised her chin. "Look, let me tell you something, Kerry. Since last winter, what I keep thinking all the time is all the things I'll never do again. Some of it's stupid, last President's Day, last spring we'll put up window screens. But then there was my last snowfall, last daffodils, Gillian's last birthday."

I lay down on the mattress, curled up and closed my eyes.

"It's not like I'm a big fan of Christmas, but when I realized I'd never see it again, all I kept thinking of was all the Christmases I'm missing. I could've given Gillian and her kids and her kids' kids these incredible Christmases if I'd just got the chance. And then there's other things, too. I'll never have another kid, I'll never have a career, I'll never... see Italy."

"You want to see Italy?"

"I want you to see it."

I shook my head and she grabbed my hand. "Since you came, that's the only thing that made it easier, realizing that you'll be here to do all the things I never got to do."

I pulled away. "I can't."

"Because you're weak and you're used to being weak."

"You want more than me, Eve, you always did. I don't need anything more than what I have."

"That's bullshit. You're like me, Kerry, you haven't given yourself a chance to live because you feel like you don't deserve it. You just crawled into your hole and waited to die, and I'm holing up here and dying."

"Maybe I don't deserve it. Maybe neither of us does."

Eve narrowed her eyes, her voice tight. "You think I don't feel guilty every day of my life for what we did? Every single fucking day? So maybe I won't live long enough to get past it, but I've lived long enough to at least help you see past it. It's been thirteen years, Kerry. That's long enough to hate yourself."

I fingered my scars, once raised white ridges, now only visible when I tanned, hard to feel against the veins in my wrist. She could forgive herself, but I had more in me to hate.

"I'm sorry," I said, then turned away, strode out into the hall. I gripped the stair rail, pulled at it as if I could bring the roof, the house into shambles around me. I listened to the sounds, the humming fan, the clack-clack of settling walls, and my mind ran with dry laughter like a little dead voice, trilling with all the things I'd once had inside me, the pictures of a husband, a child, a home, and hopes and colors and dreams. It was gone, all of it, and I didn't know how to get it back. It had been so long, I'd forgotten that I'd ever wanted it.

27

DR. KRAMER CAME to insert a catheter to drip morphine from an IV into Eve's arm, allowing her to dose herself once every two hours. She made him use her right arm so he wouldn't see the scars on her left wrist, which left her helpless, awkward, hardly able to feed herself or brush her teeth.

She slept more, but began calling out in her sleep, like she was conjuring a new world in her dreams to make up for the waking world she was missing. She would cry out and we'd come running, me and Justin, only to see there was no awareness behind her opened eyes. And each time it would raise the nerves to the surface of my skin, this creepy stillness, this dead-eyed gaze, foreshadowing.

And then one morning I woke to the sound of an inhuman screech. I sprang up and sat a minute, trapped in a blind post-sleep confusion. There was a thunderclap outside and then an answering guttural wail. "Eve?" I said, then jumped to my feet and ran downstairs.

Gillian was standing at the entrance to the den, barefoot, her shoulders trembling with tears. I pushed past her to the bed where Eve lay writhing, her face contorted and deathly pale. Justin, just as pale, was fumbling with the morphine pump, his hands shaking. "What do I...? Oh God, Eve, please, oh God!"

I ran to Eve, threw myself over her body like I could stop her writhing, muffle the pain. Justin pulled at me. "She's dying! Is she dying? Is she—?" His voice broke into a sob.

"The pills, get the pills!" I said. I pushed the button on the morphine pump but it gave a dull beep and wouldn't deliver more. "Dammit!"

Justin ran in with a pill bottle, pulled at the cap, spewing tablets across the bed. I grabbed one, lifted her head and reached for water, but she gagged before the glass touched her lips, spit out the pill and swung at me. "Just go 'way," she croaked. "Go 'way!"

Justin lifted her in his arms, cradled her, rocking, the tears glassy on his cheeks. He looked up at me and I backed away, my hands pressed to my mouth.

Gillian grabbed my waist and I wrapped my arms around her as if I could hide her from it. "It's okay," I sobbed. "It's okay, it's okay..."

I pulled her into the hall and we slid to the floor, her head against my breasts, my face buried in her warmth. "No, no, no..." Gillian whimpered with the voice of a girl half her age, as behind us Eve wailed, pleading for an end.

The rain started, first slow, then heavy, and I sat on the front porch trying to remember the last time I'd listened to the rain from this porch swing. Storytelling afternoons, Justin sideways on the top step and Eve on the swing beside me, nudging at my arm to mock the passion of his voice. But this rain sounded different. They'd replaced the corrugated tin roof with slate and the rain knocked like pebbles, unrelenting. Not magic anymore.

Justin found me there and stood beside me, and I watched him out of the corner of my eye, not speaking.

"That was bad," he said finally.

"Yeah," I whispered. "Yeah."

"They want to up the morphine and put her in the hospital, but I can't. I won't." He walked to the porch railing and leaned against it. "You know she asked me to help her."

Wind gusted rain into my face, and I focused on that, the cold insult of it, rather than his words.

"Asked me to end it for her and sometimes, I don't know." He sank to the rocking chair, rocked back and forth, back and forth, a centered, schizophrenic rock. "She has these clear times once in a while, where she hardly seems to hurt. She talks about us, about Gillie, about the time she was training for the marathon. You know she ran the freaking Boston Marathon two months after she was diagnosed? She talks about our life with so much energy and I know there's still so much living she has left to do. But what comes after the clear times is that helplessness, the pain in every muscle and bone and every pore of her. Nobody should have to hold out against that, and I think if it was me... Sometimes I think about it."

I turned to watch his face, his hair strung with sprayed rain, cheeks glossy with tears. And I don't know what made me do it.

Just an emptiness, my aloneness, maybe a need to mourn with him that made me climb onto his lap. He inhaled sharply, and after a minute wrapped me in his arms and we rocked together, rocked. Rain sprayed softer now, or at least it seemed softer; there was a splash of thunder and faintly I felt his lips brushing at my hair. That's all it was, innocent maybe, but it felt like so much more, an aching, awful burning. I couldn't move.

It was he who stood finally, spilling me to my feet. I kept my eyes where they'd been, down on the floor. He touched the back of my neck, then walked away.

I stood for a while, looking out at the puddles pooling in the divoted grass, and then I sat in the chair he'd just left, feeling his warmth.

I sat there, not thinking, my mind centering only on the squeal of my rocking, the spattering on the roof. I waited until I heard sounds from inside, then rose and watched through the front window.

Gillian was lying curled against Eve's legs, head on her lap, stroking the side of Eve's thigh. And Justin was hovering over Eve's bed, combing his fingers through the fringes of her hair. I watched as she gazed up into his face, trusting him, trusting me.

When I couldn't stand to watch anymore, I turned and began to walk. I walked down the hill, not bothering with roads, tramping on weeds and over lawns, the rain so blindingly heavy it seemed like I was swimming, my legs gliding, kicking and carrying wherever they wanted me to go.

When I reached the shoreline on the island's north side, I turned onto the Maze, a tangle of twisting, branching, interconnected paths. I startled at the sight of the stunted pines, once full and arching between paths but now stripped by blight, their branches curled and bare like tentacles. The Maze was nothing special, listed in the Block Island guidebooks but really just a thing to do when you'd already done everything else. To us, though, it had been an adventure. We'd come out here sometimes with Daddy, pretending to get hopelessly lost, and then later, with the thrill of newfound independence, we came on our own and found a secret place hidden under a stand of cedar. We'd sit against the trunks and build tiny homes, sticks forming walls, moss for carpet, sand piles for beds, flint chips for twins, a smooth gray rock daddy and foggy quartz mother. She was rolling dough from an acorn cap as the twins sat beside her, all of them laughing at how perfect their little world was, pressing circles and stars.

I crawled now beneath the overhanging branches and closed my eyes, feeling the closeness of the branches dripping rain over my head. The flint chips were everywhere and I lifted them, sifted the stones through my fingers, cradled them and let them fall. Again and again I lifted and let fall, as around me the rain dwindled, the sun cleared the clouds, and the shadows shrank, then lengthened again. And when my vision blurred too much to see the stones between my fingers, I curled against the craggy ground and slept.

The sun was fully out when I woke up. I stared blindly at the brightness. Outside, why was I outside? And then the pictures came at me: the shrillness of Eve's screech, her twisted face, lips nearly blue with pain. Dying.

My shoulders ached; my clothes and hair were damp and sticky. I pulled to my feet, grasping onto a branch to keep from falling. The path was rambling and abstract in the haze of sleep, each turn like every other, the bare bark-stripped trees leaning in rows of skeletal silhouettes. I started for home, thinking only of the comfort of the bed that had been Daddy's, a flannel nightgown, the hiss of steam pipes and the inky scent of Justin's papers.

There was a strange car in the drive, a red Nissan. And when I stepped inside I heard Eve's voice, seeming fully recovered, cautious but questioning, the voice I'd looked out for in my telemarketing that told me there was potential for a sale.

And then a stranger's voice. "I could understand hating baths," she said. "I have to agree it's much more fun playing dress-up or whiffle ball, but still."

I stood by the stairway listening. The voice was somehow so very familiar, stretching a dusty, forgotten splinter of my mind.

"You used to run away and hide, and one time I actually thought you'd gone out the door and I called the cops. But when they showed up, there you were behind a curtain. You were all excited. One of the cops let you wear his hat."

I shook my head slowly. I wanted to go upstairs and lie in Daddy's bed. I wanted to comb the pine needles from my hair. I wanted to soak in a deep tub, breathe in steam until I wasn't sure where I ended and where the water began. But my feet walked forward without my will. I stood in the doorway and watched.

They were sitting on the bed, Eve in her nightgown and the woman in a raincoat and heels, wearing a face that looked more like my face than Eve's did now. She looked up, her eyes wide as a child's, holding more fear than joy. Or pain. Or love. "Kerry," she said.

I shook my head. "You . . ." I inhaled quickly. "You?"

She gave me a smile, again more fear in it than anything else. "Kerry," she said again.

I looked to Eve and then back again, almost expecting her to disappear while my head was turned. I reached to touch the tendril of brown hair that fell across her ear. The hair was stiff like spray, not real, not my mother's hair.

She started to speak, then stopped. "You're wet," she said finally. "You were out in the rain?"

Our mother was supposed to have warm eyes that crinkled when she smiled. She'd be attractive but in an earthy way, like she could hold you when you scraped your knee and could, with that holding, make everything better. But this woman had her hair up in a chignon, and her lips were lined deep red. She was so young, too young; she could have been my age, the kind of woman men turned their heads at. Not my mother.

"But you look good," she said softly. "You grew up to be so pretty."

She was wearing makeup. What kind of person would think of makeup when going to her dying daughter? This woman was untouchable, glossy like someone out of a magazine, like someone you could wrinkle in your fist and she'd still come out looking the same. I felt a sudden fierce ache for Daddy. "You're here," I said.

"I needed to see her," she said slowly. "I wanted to see who she was before it was too late."

Eve's face contorted slightly, expressing everything,

every knot and fold of my own tangled insides. "How did you even know I was sick?" she said.

Our mother stood and walked to the woodstove, stayed there staring at the blank wall above it. "Just know I've kept track of you, both of you."

"Kept track of us how? I mean, was it the Caines? Bert and Georgia?"

"It doesn't matter who. The important thing's that ever since the beginning, I've done whatever I could to make sure you were okay."

I watched her, thinking how all this time she knew where we were, all this time we were waiting. And just then I wished we were still waiting; it would be better than this, better to think of her as something in our heads, something we'd cradle there like a hope, a piece of our past and our future still on hold rather than this real woman I didn't know.

I sat on the bed, the spot she'd just left, feeling the warmth from her body. I spoke in a whisper, it was all I could manage. "We were kids," I said.

Eve took my hand, intertwined her fingers, and suddenly, with the two of us on the bed and our mother on the outside, I saw her for what she was. A fringe of us, something dangling and mostly disconnected, not some defining moment, not some answer. Only a woman. A woman who didn't know how to be a mother.

"You know what we used to do?" I said. "Daddy told us you were sailing, you'd be back after you saw the world. So we'd wait out on the harbor, me and Eve, looking for you."

Her eyes flinched. Just a second of confusion, a confession that she did know how she'd hurt us. But the pain was fleeting, soon glossed back over into that picture-perfect poise. "I know," she said. "I know how it must've been."

Eve smiled softly. "In the beginning it was almost every day we went out there, summer, fall, in the winter wearing our ski parkas, just standing out there holding hands and looking."

Our mother blinked quickly. Scared? Fighting back tears? Something stuck in her eye? I couldn't tell which. "I thought all the time about coming to see you," she said, "but I couldn't take you back with me, I just couldn't. And I didn't want to hurt you by telling you that. Besides, I knew you had your dad. And then the Caines."

"The Caines weren't our parents," I said.

"I'm not a parent either, not like you mean it." She stepped closer, raised her arms and then dropped them. "There are people who are meant to be mothers and then there's people who give birth and feel like there's been some mistake, no way could these babies belong to them. I know I can't explain the kind of person I am, because I'm not like other people, I'm just not. But I tried, sweetheart. God, I tried."

The endearment echoed through my head, *sweetheart, sweetheart.* I turned away so I wouldn't cry. I wouldn't.

"I wanted to be here," she said, "for six years I tried but it was killing me little by little. And the fact that the things which should've made me so happy were killing me, that hurt even more. I needed to start fresh, make something better of myself."

"We were killing you," I said, and smiled widely.

"Your father never understood it, he was such a simple man. He drove a rig back then, and he'd be gone maybe five, sometimes six days a week." She gave a flat, single-note laugh. "Hell, I was so damned jealous of that time he had, and part of me hated him for it. And then he'd come home and expect me to be this loving wife, totally there for him, like the days in between never happened."

"He loved you, Mother." The word "Mother" came from my lips without thought, sounding cold and awful. I shook my head quickly to lessen the sting of it.

"He loved his vision of me. I got pregnant and then we got married and he thought I'd turn into this mom and wife. But he never really understood me or he never would've married me. He would've known I'd leave someday."

The front door opened. "I'm home!" Gillian called. She tramped into the den, one hand behind her back, then stopped. "Oh, hi," she said.

Our mother looked at her, then slowly, tentatively, raised her hand for Gillian to shake, held so tightly and so long that Gillian finally pulled away. "I'm Gillian Caine," she said, wiping her palm against her leg.

"Pleased to meet you," our mother said, then hesitated a minute before smiling. "I'm Mrs. Evans."

"Good to meet you. You feel better now, Ma? Because I brought you something I thought might help. The petunias are going crazy." She brought her hand from behind her back to reveal a fistful of multicolored flowers. "They're escaping all outside the edges of the bed, so I just brought the extras. I thought maybe they'd make you happy."

"They make me very happy," Eve said. She sat forward to kiss Gillian's head, then set the flowers into her water tumbler.

Our mother gazed at the flowers a moment, then bent to touch the spot Eve had just kissed.

Gillian stumbled back, then gave our mother a wide, fake smile. "Well, I got homework, better go. Nice meeting you."

When she'd left, the three of us stayed motionless, eyeing the petunias, their stunted stems and brilliant heads crushed inside the glass. Until I spoke. "You didn't introduce yourself to your granddaughter."

Her shoulders stiffened. "I would've. I would've but I think it's best if I don't just now."

"So how long are you staying?"

Silence, one of those silences louder than any answer would have been. She didn't talk for so long I almost started babbling, saying anything to keep her from giving the answer I knew she'd give. But then she turned to me, her eyes sharp with a sort of fear, and spoke in a near whisper. "I'm not. I mean, I can't. I don't think it would be good for any of us if I stayed. I'll give you whatever I can, whatever you need from me, but then I think it's best if I go."

"You're leaving. You mean today?"

"Kerry..."

"You just breeze in like you're delivering some gift and then breeze away. Then why did you even bother coming? What good does it do us?"

"I'm not sure why I came here exactly. I don't know, for selfish reasons, maybe. Franny told me you called and I just got to thinking about life, about dying, about my life and these two pieces of me out there somewhere, and about what I'd been looking for all this time."

"Looking for us?" Eve said. So much desperation in her voice, like we'd been at six, at sixteen, so much we wanted the hole in her to be as big as the hole in us.

"I don't know. I think you were a part of what I've been looking for, trying to find what I should've felt for my family but for some reason couldn't." She smoothed a hand over her hair, her eyes distant, smiling a strange smile. "I've gotten everything else I wanted, put myself through school working two jobs, a few years back I married a great guy and then left him after three months. And I won this huge award last year, the Presidential Award at my PR firm." She shook her head as if amazed, then walked to the window and leaned forward, resting her forehead against the pane. "Everything I ever tried for comes to me, except that I didn't know how to love you. Not enough."

I held my breath and felt a bubble in my chest, expanding and hardening, crowding out my lungs.

"It's okay," Eve said. "You tried."

I stared at Eve. Her face was calm, almost sympathetic.

Our mother turned back to us, smiling. "I wanted to show you something," she said, reaching inside her slicker for a large manila envelope. From the envelope she pulled out a photo of Eve and me, walking on Water Street, taken in what looked to be the year I'd left.

"How'd you get this?" I asked.

"Your dad sent pictures every year." She handed it to me and smiled. "And after he was gone I got this from a friend, a mutual friend who thought I should know what you looked like. It was the last picture they ever sent."

I studied the photo. Eve's hair was short, but shaggy. I had a startled look on my face. "Who?" I said.

She ignored me, reaching again into the envelope. "I wanted to give you this." She held out her hand. A gold locket, the size and shape of a pocket watch, fell onto the bed. I lifted it.

"Your father sent it to me the year I left. There was a key on the same chain, and after I filled the locket I locked it and sent the key back for you and your dad. I sent it back and all this time I thought of you across the ocean, the three of you, me having the filled locket and you having the key like it would mean something was waiting to happen. It wasn't over."

I flipped the locket to look at the back. It was inscribed in graceful script above a tarnished keyhole. *You will always be inside me,* it said. I stared at the inscription, fingering the lock, and then wordlessly, I pulled the key from my neck.

It was worn by time but still a perfect fit. I turned the key and the clasp sprung on its hinge, emptying two tiny teeth and two locks of baby-fine hair onto the bed. Eve glanced at me, lifted the teeth and cradled them in her palm.

Inside the locket were two small photos, one of my mother in a gown and veil with Daddy beside her, the other a family picture, taken when Eve and I were four or five. We wore matching dresses with sailor collars, and sat in front of our parents who stood hand in hand, Daddy beaming in ignorant bliss.

"Here." She set the envelope on the bed. "Look at it when I'm gone, okay? It'll explain everything."

"You saved our teeth?" Eve whispered.

Our mother gave Eve a smile that looked more like a grimace. "I named you, you know that, Eve? Kerry was your father's but you were mine. You were the first baby out, and I said to him, that's Eve."

Eve squeezed a fist over the tiny teeth. "I recognized you standing in the window, you know. I saw you standing out there and at first what I thought was you were some tourist hiding from the rain." She gave a strangled laugh. "Damned mainlander come to see the sights, the freaky bald lady, world's skinniest surviving being, but then I saw your face and I knew you."

There were tears in our mother's eyes. Real tears and I locked onto that, played the image of those tears over and over so when I thought back on what she'd said to us, this was the picture I'd see. She turned to me as if waiting for some confirmation, but I had nothing I could give. I just fixed my eyes on hers, and waited for her to leave.

Our mother stayed through the afternoon. I hardly spoke, I couldn't speak, just listened to her voice, calm and deep and distant, the only part of her I really remembered. I let Eve condense our lives into flat, emotionless snapshots and I listened as our mother tried to explain her life, not answers, only words. But they were the only answers she had, and not even close to what I needed.

By the end it seemed like we'd run out of things to say; we sat there uncomfortably as if waiting for some event, some understanding that never came. When it was time for her to leave, she turned to Eve. "You know that I probably won't ever see you again."

Eve nodded slowly. "It's okay."

"I'm sorry," she said.

Eve smiled. "I know. And that's enough."

After she left, I stood at the window, watching the slip and sway of her hips as she walked, even beneath the coat so unmistakably Eve's walk. She'd left without ever taking off her coat, without giving us a hug or a kiss. And part of me wanted to stop her, tell her all the things I'd wanted to say, twenty-five long years of things. Eve was leaving and she'd come back and there should be some sort of balance, a serendipity in it. When instead it was like a flash in the darkness that leaves you even blinder than before.

"What did she talk about before I got back?" I said. "Did she say anything?"

"Nothing about herself. She talked about me a little, the things she remembered when I was a kid. About both of us."

"What kind of things? Good things?"

"Of course good things. And she seemed so happy when she was talking about it. I do think she loved us, Ker, in her own way."

I watched her for a minute, then reached for the locket, fingered the tiny teeth inside. On the nightstand was the manila envelope our mother had left. It was bumpy, full with something. I lifted it and emptied it on the bed, spilling letters, maybe twenty-five or thirty, written in an uneven print.

I unfolded one, and as I saw the signature the realization came slowly and heavily. "This is how she knew you were sick," I whispered.

Eve took the letter from me and scanned it slowly, her eyes filling. She looked up at me with a wide, flat smile. "Holy crap," she said.

June
1994

28

WE SAT AT THE HARBOR in Justin's idling car, looking out over the ocean. Only the crests of distant waves were visible in the dark, ragged and unpredictable, lashing rocks and licking slantwise to the shore. Every so often the engine coughed and gave a shudder, like it was preparing to speak.

"Okay," Justin said finally. His face was gray under the dim streetlamps. There was a smear on the arm of his jacket and I stared at it, unable in the dusky light to tell if it was dirt or blood. "What're you doing tomorrow?" he said. "Were you planning anything?"

I glanced at Eve in the backseat. She was hunched against the car door, her head wedged against the window. When she didn't respond I turned to him, needing something, some kind of reassurance, but he kept his eyes on the dark windshield.

"When do your jobs start?"

"Next Monday."

"Okay." He gripped the steering wheel. "I'm going into work tomorrow. And you have to do something, it doesn't matter what. Go to the beach, buy a magazine, whatever, just so somebody sees you."

I stared at him blankly. How could he be so calculating? "You think anybody who looked at us now wouldn't realize there's something wrong?"

"I know." He was quiet for a minute, then turned to me. "But what you're going to have to do, both of you have to put on the best act of your lives. Tell yourself a story about what would've happened if the day just ended at graduation. You and me, we walked around until real late at night, and then we went home to sleep." He turned to look at Eve. "And you, Eve, after the Stantons' party you came home and crashed."

"You know something weird?" Eve said, her eyes empty. "They injected rum into a watermelon with a turkey baster. And when you take a bite it just slips down your throat like candy."

We both stared at her. Finally I climbed over the seat and sat with my knees bent on her lap and my head tucked against her shoulder.

"See what happens," Justin said, "you get your head inside that story and live like it was true. And it becomes true in the end, that's how it works. For you and everyone else out there, it becomes true."

Eve's neck was damp. I burrowed against it so all I knew was her salt smell. I wanted Justin to stop talking. I wanted him to go away, to leave us. All I wanted was Eve's smell. Her pulse against my lips. Just us.

We lay in Daddy's bed that night, Eve and I, huddled together like we used to, my hand clutched at her sleeve. I drifted time and again to the edge of sleep, jerking back to consciousness as soon as the fall tried to overtake me and then lying with my eyes squeezed shut. Behind my lids the pictures swam, so I cluttered them away by reciting a nonsense poem memorized long ago. *'Twas brillig, and the slithy toves did gyre and gimble in the wabe; all mimsy were the borogroves, and the mome raths outgrabe*... And after several times through it started to work, the pictures blurred to no more than a half-remembered dream, when suddenly Eve cried out and sprang to her feet. In the moonlight her eyes glistened wide with terror.

"Eve?"

She covered her mouth and shook her head quickly, backing from the room. I followed her into the hallway, listened to her heaving choke behind the bathroom door. When she was done I knocked on the door and entered, wet a washcloth and wiped at her mouth, then held it to her forehead.

She clutched at me silently, her head buried in my neck, her breath hazing sour around us. "It's okay," I whispered, stroking her hair.

"I dreamed him," she said, her lips tickling my skin as she spoke. "I dreamed it all, his face, his eyes..."

"It's not real, Eve. Like Justin said, for tonight none of it's real, okay? Just for now."

She shook her head and stumbled away from me, backed into the hall and down the stairs. The front door slammed open and I ran after her, watched from the door as she reeled down the drive barefoot, dressed only in Daddy's flannel shirt. I closed the door and laid my cheek against it until the dizziness in my head cleared, then climbed back into Daddy's bed.

I don't know how long I lay there staring up at the

ceiling. Waiting for Eve, waiting for morning, the seconds pulsing slow and torturous. *'Twas brillig, and the slithy toves did gyre and gimble in the wabe.* And when I knew I couldn't stand it, I rose and started for the Caines'. The light was on in Justin's office. I tried the door but it was locked. I heard shuffling behind it, but when I called to him in choked, pleading whispers, he didn't respond. I stood there, my hand on the door, gravel cutting into my feet. After a minute I turned and started back home. I lay on Daddy's bed, grabbed onto his pillow and curled against it. I wrapped myself in his quilt and began to rock slowly side to side. *'Twas brillig, and the slithy toves did gyre and gimble in the wabe. . . .*

It was the front door that startled me back awake, clicking softly to the latch. I listened to Eve's footsteps on the stairs, waiting for her to come and curl against me. It took me a minute to realize she'd gone back to her own bed instead.

I rose and padded to the doorway of our room, watching, wondering how she could stand to sleep there. On the floor, dark lines of blood still streaked between floorboards. The blankets had been stripped from my bed; Eve's torn dress and heels were heaped in one corner. I shivered, wishing I could go to her but sensing she needed to be alone. So instead I left the house and walked back outside. The office door was open on its hinge. Empty.

I walked to the Caines' house, started upstairs. Justin's bedroom door was closed. I knocked softly and then entered, crawled into bed beside him, ran my lips across his ear to wake him.

Justin flinched away with a gasp. He fumbled with his

bedside light, then huddled back. "Please," he said. He didn't look at me. His eyes shifted from wall to door to window. "Please," he said again.

"It's okay," I whispered. "It's just me."

"Please, Kerry, you have to go."

"I need to be here. I can't stand this by myself."

Justin shook his head. "We'll talk tomorrow, I promise we'll talk, okay?"

"Couldn't I just lie here with you?"

"I can't do this!" Justin squeezed his eyes shut and curled against the wall. "Please."

My eyes filled as I watched him, a huddled lump beneath the sheets. I reached forward, then pulled my arm away. "Okay. Okay." I stood and looked back at him. "I'm going now." I bit my tongue and backed away.

At home I stood in the hallway shivering, the weariness draping over me like a lead blanket. I stumbled to the living room and fell onto the couch. I was asleep before I finished closing my eyes.

It was a fitful sleep, and when my mind drifted to consciousness, I fought off waking. I lay still with my eyes closed until I realized there was a weight on my lap, a warm and steady weight like a curled cat. I slowly lowered my hand to Justin's hair.

He looked up at me, eyes red. "I'm sorry, Kerry. I'm sorry..."

I wiped a tear from his cheek. "I know."

He sat on the couch beside me and slipped his hand around the back of my neck. He watched my face for a minute, then suddenly his eyes hardened. He pulled me to his lips and kissed me, his hands clutching, his teeth crushing against my teeth, then pulled me against his body so fiercely that it hurt. "God, I love you," he said hoarsely. "So much, you know that, right?"

I heard steps from the hall and looked up. Eve was watching us, her face tight and pale. Our eyes met and I reached my hand to her, but she shook her head slightly and slipped back down the hall. So I turned back to Justin. I kissed him, first soft and then deeply, running my fingers down his chest, pulling at buttons and belt, letting myself slide to the floor and pulling him down beside me. My mind was fluttering and swirling as I reached inside his briefs, grasped the smooth flesh that fit so perfectly in my palm. The image assaulted me, Ryan Maclean's open zipper, the bluish sheen of his penis against his leg, but still I pulled Justin to me, opened my legs to press him inside me. I wanted it; it was all I wanted.

And then the front door swung shut.

Justin rolled away. He hunched on his side, jeans pulled around his thighs. "I'm sorry," he whispered, "I love you, please know that."

"I do know," I said. "It's okay, I do."

He stood and straightened his clothes. "I have to go to work."

"You're really going to work?"

He stood without answering, then turned and walked away. I looked down at my bare legs, at my nightshirt pulled crooked to expose my breasts. I looked down at the pale strap lines left from a suntan almost a year ago and began to sob.

29

WE NEVER DISCUSSED that night on the boat. I let the long days of summer roll against each other like fog on fog, smooth and opaque. But always it was there, as if the body followed us room to room, lay by our feet so we were forced to step around or over, pretending not to see. The national papers carried stories for days. The body hadn't been found but rumors flew, Mrs. Maclean was questioned and questioned again, but no one questioned Eve. No one seemed to know there might have been anything to question.

We'd both quit our summer jobs before even starting, and I'd begun to wonder if that had been a huge mistake. Because Eve rarely left the house. I'd come home to find her on her bed, her breath sharp and words slurred with drink. "What's going on with you?" I asked again and again, and there was anger in my voice, much as I tried to swallow it. At the core this was her doing. She had changed who I was forever, the way Justin and I would look back at our lives, the body intruding in every memory of our first year together. What would I tell our children about the night Justin said he'd marry me? The sky was thundery and romantic, he kissed me and told me how he'd be with me forever. And then we went home and committed involuntary manslaughter.

"You know it's not your fault," I'd tell Eve, and each time a hitch of pain scarred her face, showing she knew the lie that was. So much pain that I started to wonder, started to realize there must be more going on than she'd told us. I knew she must've seen Ryan Maclean at Jill Stanton's party. What if she'd led him on, brought him into the house? And the more I thought about it, the more sure I was, and the more twisted my thoughts became. They'd been playing out some rape fantasy, her tears from laughter and then passion rather than pain, and when she heard us come in she played even harder, wanting Justin to see her as vulnerable but kinky, wanting him to see how good her boobs looked in her black lace bra. Why would she have worn her sexiest underwear if she hadn't known someone would see it?

"You have to stop thinking about it," I'd say, when inside me the thoughts dug roots and branched and grew. The guilt hung everywhere around her, Eve, who'd always been able to justify everything she did. Her eyes were hooded, her hair wild as a rag doll's, her skin flushed in the closed-window heat. I'd sit by her and she'd grip my hand. She wouldn't meet my eyes.

And then, after almost a month of avoiding, came the day it all slapped us in the face.

Eve and I had walked down to the corner store for groceries. I'd been shopping alone; Eve seemed to have forgotten the necessity of buying food, of doing laundry, of things as simple as showering or changing out of her nightgown. So after weeks of this I decided not to accept her excuses. She needed to leave the house, I knew that, to see there was an outside world. And so I made up a list of things we didn't need, and I walked with her to the grocery.

We strolled through the narrow aisles and I filled our basket, keeping an eye on her to make sure she looked sane enough not to draw attention. It was working, I could see that. Eve's shoulders began to loosen, there was color in her face. She flipped the hair from her eyes in the way that made men stare, even though her hair was unwashed and stringy and her eyes were hooded and ringed with gray.

We were comparing prices on canned vegetables when Eve suddenly reached for my arm. It was Mrs. Maclean.

She looked awful, unkempt and slightly bewildered, wandering the aisles with her sons in tow. One of the boys wore mismatched socks, the other wore too-small shorts and a stained shirt. The older boy carried the shopping basket in his small fist, and Mrs. Maclean strode ahead without checking to see if they were following.

The other shoppers stepped back to let her pass, none speaking to her but all of them watching. I wanted to take Eve's hand, to give some kind of reassurance, but it was like my arms, my legs, my tongue had been petrified, a rod through my spine fixing me to the ground.

We watched without moving until she reached the checkout counter. Eve dropped our basket. "We have to get out of here."

"We can't now," I whispered. "She's checking out."

"I have to." She turned to me, her eyes liquid pools of dread. "Look at them, we did that. I did that."

"Stop it," I said through my teeth.

"There's stuff you don't know, Kerry." She made a hiccupping sound and the can of baked beans she was holding dropped to the floor and rolled across the aisle.

I stared at her, then bent to retrieve the can. "Not now," I said.

We watched Mrs. Maclean unload her basket and pay, watched the boys pack the bags and lift them, staggering under their weight. As soon as they disappeared out the shop door, the whispers started.

Behind us, Carol Venton hissed to Martha Franks. "You read the paper today? About the investigation? Linda told the cops he was drunk as a skunk the night he disappeared. Would you ever say that about your own husband unless you wanted revenge?"

Martha narrowed her eyes. "Can you imagine it? A man like that?"

I glanced at Eve. She was backing away from them, her face pale. I clamped my hand on her arm, willing her to stay calm.

"It goes with the power they get out of being elected, even the men who seem so honorable. Think of Kennedy."

"At least Kennedy didn't run away from his family."

"Oh, I don't think Ryan ran away," Carol said. "He was looking at the Senate someday, and he still thought this would die down over time. He wouldn't disappear while there were black marks on his name anyway, not the man I know. He'd want to be remembered the right way." She lowered her voice to a whisper. "I remember when he was in school. A playboy through and through, the girls loved him and the boys despised him. He used to crib answers off my Melanie's papers, and she'd just let him."

Suddenly she saw Eve and me standing there, noticed our expressions. She rolled her eyes at Martha, then smiled at us. "Do you girls always eavesdrop on personal conversations?"

Eve's face was tight, an odd shade of pink. She blinked slowly and spoke. "You always talk about things that aren't your business?"

I was stunned at the strength in her voice. The words seemed to come from somewhere outside her. Martha narrowed her eyes. "Excuse me?"

"Listen," Eve said. "He didn't rape anybody. Maybe some girl's accusing him because she wants publicity, but it's a total lie. They didn't even sleep together."

I stared at her. "What're you talking about? What rape?"

"Stupid rumors start and bags like you eat them up. You believe in UFOs? That you can lose ten pounds in ten days? What bullshit."

Both Martha and Carol raised their eyebrows in unison and turned to each other. "Listen to that!" Carol said.

Martha shook her head. "Eve Barnard! What would your dad say?"

"He'd say tell the bitches to shove the rumors up their asses. How 'bout this? Why don't you start a rumor that he raped me and I wanted it? Hell, why not. Have a ball." She spun away and ran out onto the street.

I watched after her, my heart stuttering so quickly I thought I might faint. Should I follow her? Would that make it look better or worse?

Carol glanced at me and then bent to Martha, spoke

under her breath. "Have to let some things slide, I guess, what with the way her father left. Those things can change a person." Both of them gave pitying nods. I could see it in their eyes as they turned to me, the grief over what, in the past year, their island had become.

I strode to the newspaper rack and picked out the *Block Island Times.* There on the front cover of a paper that was usually headlined with stories like "Carl Lawrence Catches Forty-Pound Bass!" or "Delores Miles Wins First with Scrumptious Pumpkin Cheesecake!" was a large photo of Ryan Maclean shaking Ronald Reagan's hand. And above the photo the headline: "Is This the Face of a Rapist?"

I reached for the *Boston Globe* and searched the front page. The article was in the bottom right corner. I sat down on a shelf of canned soup, heedless of the stares around me, and read.

That afternoon I biked up the hill to the cemetery, letting the pull in my legs drown out my thoughts. I rounded the path to Daddy's grave filled with the ache I always felt here, like coming home.

When I was little I used to spend time with my mother like this, just close my eyes and try to remember her sweet-bitter smell of coffee and cigarettes. I was sure that she was listening, wherever she might have voyaged to on that particular day.

But then I started to lose her. First her smell disappeared and then the feel of my cheek on her breast. I lost that and then Daddy tore up every picture of her we'd ever had, so there was nothing left to remind me of her face. It was almost like she'd been this fantasy, something I'd held on to for as long as naïveté let me, like Santa Claus. I wouldn't let that happen to Daddy, and so I came almost every day to etch the feel of him in repeated strokes.

I leaned my bike against the low stone wall and walked towards Daddy's grave, then stopped short. She was kneeling by the headstone, hidden in shadows. "Eve?" I said.

She startled back, stared up at me, looking terrified even through her tears. It was the first time I'd seen her here since the funeral. I'd tried to bring her last fall on our father's birthday, and again the next month when they'd set his headstone, but she'd adamantly refused, like seeing the gravesite would cement the fact that he was buried there in the dirt.

I knelt beside her and she stiffened, scrabbled backwards. I rested my hand against her arm. "It's pretty here, isn't it?"

She didn't answer, just sat there with her fists clenched between her knees.

"Remember how he used to let us roll down that hill? How inappropriate was that, two kids rolling in a cemetery? But he said how the dead people were sitting up to watch us and laughing in their graves."

Eve turned to me, her eyes wide. Suddenly she reached for me and buried her forehead against my shoulder, both hands clutching at my arm. I sighed and held her, remembering how it had been, hanging on to her waist just like this, our fear the same, the aching love the same as when we'd roll, her on top then me, over and over. Like we might free-fall if we ever let go. Like we might lose each other.

She pulled away, her face red and swollen, then shook her head and stumbled to her feet. I watched her run back up the hill and disappear round the other side, then looked down at my arm, at the fingernail marks left in my skin. "You'll be okay," I whispered, then wiped the tears from my cheeks with the back of my arm.

I closed my eyes so I could feel Daddy, his burliness, his throaty laughter, the sandpaper of his thick-callused fingers. I ran my palms over the prickles of newly seeded grass. "We're okay," I whispered. "We're getting through okay." Soon it would be nice here, not so bald. I should plant a circle of flowers around the headstone, his favorite hydrangea, LoraLee's purple phlox. It used to make me feel a little creepy sitting there with the dead people, but now it was actually almost cozy, like a big family. I imagined the people around us: Terrance "Tippy" Fielding and Samuel S. Crawley were Daddy's new drinking buddies, having a jolly old time under the ground.

Ryan Maclean would never have a headstone. The thought sliced through me like a swallow of icy water. Unless he was found, no one would even know for sure that he was dead. His casket would be the lashing waves, his headstone the algae-sheeted rocks that impaled the north shore. But maybe even that was more than he deserved.

The paper said he was being accused of raping an eighteen-year-old runway model. The House had opened a subcommittee investigation months ago, around the time the congressman started sleeping with Eve. He'd denied it and Mrs. Maclean had stood by his side, and since there was no real proof beyond what the girl had said, it had looked like the charges would be dropped. But his disappearance had made the controversy public.

"We're doing great," I said. The tears started again and I squeezed my eyes shut against them. "Everything's—" My voice broke and I inhaled quickly. "Okay, everything's okay. But if he's there, Daddy, if he's up there just tell him we're sorry. And we'd tell his family about where he was, we'd tell if it would help and if we could, but right now we don't know what else to do."

The warm breeze rustled my hair like a stale breath. I watched the headstone for a minute, actually hoping he'd give me some kind of sign, maybe send up a daisy or print words in the dirt. When none came I wiped at my eyes and stood. "I'm sorry," I whispered, then shook my head. "If there was anything that could take it back, we'd do it, but there just isn't. It's too late."

I rested my hand on the cold damp of Daddy's name. "I love you," I whispered. I turned away and started for home.

As soon as I opened the front door I heard Eve's voice, wild on the edge of exploding. "Of course I should have a say in it! It affects me just as much as you. You really think broadcasting it to the world'll change anything?"

I hurried upstairs without closing the door behind me, up to the bedroom. They were there on the bed, Eve huddled against the wall, Justin staring at the quilt and looking lost. I stood in the doorway, watching, scared to enter.

"It won't change what we did," he said, "but maybe it'll help us come to terms with it."

"Come to terms! So you've come to terms? Do you feel even the slightest bit responsible?"

"Of course I do. We're both responsible."

I stared at him. How cruel he sounded, how unlike himself.

"You're blaming me?"

"I'm not blaming anyone! I've never felt this awful about anything, Eve, but what I realize is you can't change the past. What happened happened and there's no going back."

"What the hell does that mean? How can this be so fucking easy for you?"

Justin stared down at his knees, his shoulders hunched. "You think this is easy? And I don't even care how hard this has been for me. What makes it hell for me is knowing how it'll hurt Kerry."

"She'd never forgive us if we tell what we did. Christ, Justin!"

I shook my head slowly. He wanted to confess? He couldn't. He couldn't!

"I just hate how this feels, living a lie. And the thing is, the thing is, Eve, I've replayed that whole night over so many times in my head. And what I think is maybe it wasn't a mistake, maybe it was fate. We didn't do anything wrong, not really, not morally wrong. And the truth of it is if I had it to do over again, I don't know that I'd do anything different."

"Neither would I," I said.

Eve gave a little yelp and scooted back against the corner. Her cheeks flushed a ruddy pink at the same time Justin's drained pale, like she'd sucked the blood from his face. He glanced at Eve, then back at me.

"I don't think I would," I said, my eyes on Eve. "He wasn't a good man, Eve. And maybe he didn't deserve to die, but truth is, the world's a better place without him."

Justin's shoulders loosened and I reached my hand to him. He stared at it, then finally took it. "You can't really be serious about telling anyone," I said. "Not now. It's too late now."

Justin was quiet a minute, then nodded. "You're right. Of course we can't."

I looked back at Eve. Her eyes were wide, the guilt hanging over her whole body like a scent. She nodded sharply.

"And you remember what I told you," Justin said. "Things won't always be like this."

I reached for Eve, but she flinched away. So I slid onto Justin's lap, let him wrap his arms around me.

"We'll all be okay," he said. He squeezed his arms so tight around me that my elbows jabbed against my ribs. "Whatever happens, whatever we do, Eve, we'll all get through this."

30

JUSTIN HAD SPENT most of his free time in his office that first month of summer, writing feverishly. He was escaping perhaps, or fencing off his thoughts within the safe skin and skeleton of pen on paper. Every night now he came home late. I'd watch for his car and then go to his room to hold him. We'd kiss so deep, so passionately it made me dizzy. But each time I tried to move past the kiss he'd recoil, and then he'd apologize: *I'm just so tired, just can't stop thinking, can't shut it off. But you know I love you, don't you? You know how much I love you.* And I'd nod and pull away, let him escape back to his writing, his world. There next to him, that was all I needed on those foggy days. The long blank page of an island summer and a man who could keep me from looking past it.

And then one night he returned from the shop with a flat box. "This is it," he said.

I raised my eyebrows. "This is..."

"My story. I've weeded it where it needs to be weeded, added what needs to be added and I put it in some semblance of order. I wanted you to be the one to read it first. It's as much your story as mine."

I took the box, smiling widely, then pulled him into a hug. It was done. Morwyn and Gaelin and our future were all in this bundled box of notepaper, and waiting to come true. We could separate our lives into Before the story and After the story, like before and after a marriage or a birth, when the before hardly seemed to matter anymore. What happened was awful, it was hellishly awful, but it was done, and it was time to reclaim our lives.

"I'll read it now," I said.

What I did was bring the box up to the bedroom. Eve was on the bed in a stained T-shirt and nothing else. I showed her the box. "Justin's story," I said. "He brought it to me. I thought we could read it together."

"Justin's story." She stared at her bare knees. "Maybe not tonight, Ker. I'm not feeling so great."

"This'll help, though, I know it will."

"Yeah, right."

I sat beside her and said, "What did you mean in the grocery store when you said there was something I didn't know?"

She gazed blankly into the middle distance. "I keep seeing him," she said. "Do you keep seeing him?"

I searched her face then said, "Sometimes. A little. I try not to." This was the dream I'd had the night before: I was wading on the beach, jeans rolled to my knees, with a red plastic fishing pole. And the hook caught in his mouth and dragged him to the surface, all bloated cheeks and blue lips, rotting pustules of flesh.

"He's floating there," she said. "Peaceful, you know? Like he's suntanning or stargazing. And he starts..." She cackled with a strange, dry laugh. "He's lying there and he starts reciting the fucking Declaration of Independence. 'We hold these truths to be self-evident, that all men are created equal...'"

I sat there facing the wall. I couldn't turn to her.

"'...that they are endowed by their creator with certain inalienable rights.' Did you know I have the whole freaking thing memorized? I could recite it for you."

"How did you know about the rape, Eve?"

She was silent for a minute, then pulled her knees up to her chest. "He told me. A warning, I guess. He told me about it on the first day we were together. He said he couldn't believe he was letting himself fall in love with me, how risky it was." She laughed sharply, a sound like splitting wood. "He said the last time he let himself get close to a girl, just as a friend he said, she turned around and accused him of rape."

I watched her, unblinking.

She wiped her palms across her eyes. "And brilliant as I am, I thought he was telling the truth. Part of me's still trying to rationalize it, because if it was rape then what was he doing with me? Fucking asshole ruined my life, you know that?" She tilted her face to the ceiling. "You fucking shithead son of a bitch!"

I smoothed her hair behind her ears, pushed her bangs to one side and kissed her forehead. When she didn't respond I pulled the stack of paper from the box. "I wonder if it's some kind of record, to spend ten years writing a children's book. You haven't heard any of it since we were kids, right?"

"He's finished with it," she said. The words sounded stilted, ragged, like they were pieces torn off some other stream of thought flowing through her head.

"We'll read it and it'll feel like going back. You remember how it was those days on the porch? You and me sitting there listening, and it became everything. Everything else disappeared."

Eve smiled crookedly. "And when Justin left we'd act it all out. The porch beams were princes. We kissed the porch beams."

"Sluts in the making. But for me it was a porch beam with Justin's face."

Eve's smile faded. She flipped through the notepaper in the box. "Okay, let's read."

So Eve and I leaned back on the bed and started to read aloud, alternating chapters. Something loosened as we flipped the pages. Justin had written quite a bit over the past weeks, and it had come together, incredibly beautiful in places. There were new characters I recognized: Arianne, the soulful hippie-child, who I knew was Justin's mother; Kaltos, the gruff, tough-talking, tattooed palace guard, was Daddy. There were the townspeople we'd grown up with: the Hudsons, the Knights, the Barringtons, now become talking bats and cats, and birds that spoke in rhymes.

And then... then there was Eve. I flipped through the next pages, skimming through the words, my throat closing as I read.

Morwyn newly married to Gaelin, both of them living on a glass mountain that only the virtuous could climb. Beautiful, enchanting Esmerelda, queen of the elves, with her thorned crown of roses and her seductively piercing eyes, who sees Gaelin only once but once is all it takes to fall in love. Who claims to be Morwyn's long lost sister and lures her with a potion of sleep. Then calls a flock of crows who fly up the glass mountain, past the sleeping Morwyn to where Gaelin mourns over his lost bride. And they carry Gaelin away.

"She's you," I said.

Eve pushed the box away. "Don't be stupid."

"Stop it, Eve, don't even say anything. This has to do with you trying to take Justin away. Which upset him so much he had to write about it."

"You don't know what you're talking about." Her voice shook, the voice of truths held back.

The images were coming at me, one on top of another, slicing like whiplashes across my back: Justin holding Eve in her lace panties and torn silk dress; Eve peeling her stockings to her knees, twirling in a black halter as Justin gaped; Eve at the kitchen table, lips pressed against his lips, her hand reaching for his crotch. "You slut," I said, my voice guttural.

She watched me, her eyes red. "Kerry, stop."

"You goddamned slut!" I grabbed Justin's box and it happened before I knew what was happening, in a blank second that flashed heat up my arms, that slammed the box at the side of her head with a dull clunk of bone, her rush of startled breath echoing my own.

She skittered backwards on the bed, her hand pressed to her temple. "I can't believe you just did that."

"*You* can't believe *me*?"

"You really think I'm the one after him? You really think..."

I stared at her, saw so much, too much. "I can't believe you," I whispered. "I can't believe you!" I spun away.

Mrs. Caine was out back, pulling in the wash. She waved to me but I pretended I didn't see, clattered up the stairs and burst into Justin's room. "She tried to sleep with you, didn't she."

Justin was sitting on the bed clipping his toenails. He flinched as the door slammed back against the wall.

I held the box towards him. "It was in your book, Justin, all of it. They're happily married and here comes Esmerelda to steal you away. Tell me she's not based on Eve."

He dropped his nail clippers, stared at me, then raised his eyebrows. "Christ, Kerry, would you listen to yourself? You're freaking out over what're basically cartoon characters. You're getting jealous about the goddamned queen of the freaking elves!"

"Why are you protecting her?"

"I can't stand you when you act like this. If we don't have trust, we don't have anything! If you don't trust me, Kerry, it means our whole relationship is a sham."

My eyes stung. I spun from the room, ran down the steps out to the drive, down graveled streets and on. I ran down to the water, clutching Justin's box, out to the dock, past the bands playing at Ballard's with their requisite flocks of teenagers hooting and calling in a desperate search for someone to hold on to.

When I got to Daddy's boat I climbed inside, inhaling the fish and damp of it, the scent of something long buried. I curled myself against the hull and opened the box of Justin's papers, knowing out here it wouldn't matter so much. The ghosts here were strong and horrible enough to smudge these pages to nothing more significant than a story. All that mattered was what happened in the end.

And so I read on through the night. And when I was

done I leaned back to look up at the stars. Happily ever after. Okay. It was okay.

Because love prevailed. Love always prevailed in life as in fairy tales. Eve had her strength and cunning, her deception, a body that spoke of sex, but I had Justin. Justin was strong enough to know his heart. And I had his heart.

I walked home and paced down the hallway squeezing the edges of things—the table, a lamp, a banister rail—as if they could hold me down. I climbed the stairs to the bedroom. The door was closed, the light on. What I'd do is tell her she had one last chance. *Look,* I'd say, *I know you want him and it's not fair of me to get mad at how you feel. But if you go to him again, I swear I'll never forgive you, Eve. Never.* I opened the door.

And they were there. Both on Eve's bed. His hand pressed to her cheek.

Something dark burrowed deep inside me as I watched, my eyes feeling huge and dry as sandpaper. A knowing, something quivering and trying to take hold as I saw him, saw Eve, saw Eve seeing me and her face shifting like something round going flat. She glanced at Justin, then stood.

"What?" I whispered.

Justin shook his head, slowly.

I stepped into the room. "Tell me."

He shook his head again.

I grabbed Eve's arm and she shrieked, then looked into my face, pleading. "It wasn't, it really wasn't. Oh God, you have to understand." She looked down at my hand where it gripped her arm, then bit her top lip and pulled away, her skin flushed nearly purple. "Listen, okay? Whatever he tells you, you can't believe him. He hates me, Kerry."

No, no. "What?"

She searched my face. "He'll tell you things that you know I wouldn't do. I wouldn't hurt you."

"Hurt me?" Something was rushing through me like a waterfall of slime, down my throat and over my skin, my thoughts coated with a glossy hard glaze. "What did you do?"

Eve whirled around to look at Justin. She mouthed the word *Please.*

Justin's eyes flicked to her, then back to me. Eve turned and raced down the hall. I started after her.

"Wait!" Justin called.

I spun to face him. His face was tight with panic. "Just let me tell you."

I shook my head, no, please no, don't talk, don't say it, I don't need to hear.

"I swear I wanted to say something in the beginning," he said, "but I didn't know how. And Eve convinced me it would only hurt you to tell the truth. Which I really thought maybe made sense."

In the beginning. Something hit me in the lungs. I dimly felt my body sink to the bed.

"But that was so stupid of me to think it would just go away by me wishing it. Maybe Eve's the kind of person who can just bury things and then forget them, but I know I'll hate myself until I tell you." He tilted his head to the ceiling. "Because everything I say feels like a lie, and I know we can't ever be close again unless I know you forgive me. I came here tonight because I knew I had to tell you all of it, because us, you and me, it means everything. All I ever wanted in my whole life was you."

"So tell me already." My body was shaking but my voice was steady and deep. I felt like I was swimming, scissor-kicking through lake water. "I can take it. Just tell me."

"Okay." Justin nodded. "Okay, what happened is Eve came to me." He spoke to the wall over my head, then shifted his eyes down quickly to my face. "She came to me after the night on the boat. She'd had a nightmare, she said. And she needed me, she said. And I needed something too, needed you there." His voice was high, his words fast, like a tape on fast-forward. "I know there's no explanation, I don't have any excuses. But once it started it just kept on going, and I wasn't thinking the whole time, just feeling this incredible hollowness."

What was he saying? I heard his voice but couldn't combine the syllables into words, the words into phrases, the phrases into sentences with meaning.

"I actually thought it was you at first, I swear I did. She opened the door and the light was behind her and I thought, she understands how I'm feeling. Everything in me she understands and she knows what I need to make it all go away. And I swear she wanted me to think it was you, she had her hair back behind her ears, she didn't talk, she felt the same, the sounds she made, and by the time I realized..." He shook his head quickly. "It was only that once, that one night. Eve tried to convince me not to tell, even said she'd sleep with me again if I didn't. But I don't want her, I never did."

I needed desperately for him to stop talking. Every

word from his mouth wrapped around my heart like a rubber band, squeezing. "Could you leave please? I can't listen to this right now." Strange how bright, how melodic my voice.

But the pause after his jumbled words was loud, almost as painful. He stepped forward, back, away with the other foot like the stilted steps of a line dance. "Okay, okay, Kerry, I'm sure you need to think about this alone. I'll be at home if you want to talk to me, if you want to yell at me, I'll understand. Or hit me, whatever you need. Oh Jesus, Kerry, I'm so sorry." He backed towards the door, backed into it so heavily the floor shook. "I'm sorry," he repeated in a whisper, and then he was gone.

I sat on the bed, trying to think, trying not to think. I knew I should be feeling something—anger, hurt, maybe even hilarity. What a cliché, my boyfriend sleeping with my twin sister. I tried to laugh, a high-pitched trembling gurgle. I pressed the heels of my hands against my eyes, but unspeakable images flashed behind them, sharpened by the darkness. Eve. Justin. His bed, Eve's bed, my bed, rhythms and sounds.

A rush of heat seared through my chest. So this was what a heart attack felt like. Not just the clawing pain but suffocation, like hands squeezing my heart and lungs.

I hugged my pillow and tried to breathe, in out, in, out, curled my fingers, feeling her throat between my hands. I imagined Eve behind glass, clambering among the frogs in science class, waiting to be dissected alive. She scuttered, terrified, against the bell jar walls, mouthing *I'm so sorry* as she slipped into an ether sleep. And I stood, watching, scalpel in hand, and I smiled.

31

SOMETHING WEIRD HAPPENS with intense anger. It's like your body can't handle it all at once and so it comes in waves, black and salty. The anger swirls around you, over you, and then it sucks back, pulling away till you know there's nothing left in you but skin and bones and rattling lungs that somehow draw in air.

I don't remember anything from those first few days, that's how complete the drowning was. I don't remember what I did or what I thought. Did I look at Eve or Justin? Talk to them? I doubt it because what the heck would I have said? The first thing I remember was a few days later when I came up with the plan.

Not a plan really, but a desperation, and when it first came to me it certainly wasn't something I intended to carry through. It kept me upright though, having something to center myself on, somewhere to dig my feet so the wave couldn't overwhelm and carry me away.

It was late afternoon and LoraLee was out front planting tomatoes. I'd offered to go inside for the rusted pipe she used as a shovel. And looking out the window at the matted hair at the crown of her head, I reached for the ancient book. The book that had maybe drawn him to me. The book that would maybe bring him back.

I flipped quickly through the pages, searching for the chapter I'd seen months before, the idea that took the waves of anger and pressed them into a dense salty marble that lodged cold as ocean ice in my chest. And I centered myself on that coldness because really it was all I had.

LoraLee rocked back on her heels and I froze. She wiped the sweat off her brow, squinting her eyes against the noon sun. "Kerry? 'Neath the table, you sees it?"

I grabbed for the pipe. "I got it. Be there in a sec, okay?"

In the section titled "Poisonous Herbs" were pages on pages of crosshatched sketches, calligraphic script describing berries and leaves and essences. I scanned through, my stomach knotting at the black-cauldron-sounding names: mugwort, wormwood, witch hazel, bloodroot. Bloodroot. I fingered the picture of the white-petaled flower. Bloodroot grew in LoraLee's garden, one of the first flowers to come up in spring. But the fragile petals got torn by rainstorms almost as soon as they arrived, and by April we had to weed the bare stems away.

I'd also seen them blooming at a marsh along Rodman's Hollow. I'd picked a flower once for my hair and the orange dye had stained my hands for days. I could go there, I could find it. If I wanted, I knew I could. Esmerelda tempts her sister with a deadly sleeping potion, but with a twist the tables turn. The potion goes to Eve.

I slid the book back on the shelf, then brought the pipe outside to LoraLee. She watched me carefully as if she could see through the blankness in my face, but I smiled and bent to dig my hands in the earth. I wasn't in my right mind, and yes, I knew this, but it didn't matter. The plan filled the empty spaces where my heart used to be. It was a roller coaster of pain on fear on desperation, too much speed, too much momentum. For now it was the only thing that made sense.

It's the wanting makes things happen, that's what LoraLee had said. And so I focused on the wanting and filled myself with red and bitter hatred.

It seemed every day I found new pictures of Justin, slipped into the slats of a mirror, hidden under my pillow, in my wallet. They were tucked in my school notebooks and framed on my dresser and night table. And as I pulled them out, buried them carefully into my shoebox like seeds waiting for spring, I remembered how I'd once gazed at them in the hours we were apart. Now I knew Eve must have done the same.

The signs had been there all along. From the beginning she'd given me pretenses and lies and I'd swallowed them like cod liver oil, never questioning, always believing it was for the best. The one person in the world I was supposed to be able to trust, like my father. Like my mother.

And I hated them all.

And I wanted Eve dead.

Was this what happened with serial killers? An accident, an anger goes too far and suddenly they're pushed into the realm of murder. I'd broken an invisible wall the night of Ryan Maclean's death, pushed through an uncrossable boundary now open and waiting for me to cross again.

The trail through Rodman's Hollow was stifling, no trees to shade it from the sun; just the impossibly vivid green of the hillside and the purple asters with their dusty sweet pollen splashed everywhere too bright. Round a bend and over the hill, and there was the pond, a fairy pond circled by smooth stones. The water was still, reflecting gray against the hazy sky, skirted by mosquitoes and water striders. And there was the bloodroot, headless, each with one leaf wrapped around its reddish stem, yellowing with heat and age.

I knelt and plucked a stem, opened the small aspirin bottle I'd brought and slipped the stem inside, then tore another stem and another from their roots. Four stems pressed into a bloody mash inside the bottle. When I'd finished I wrung my hands in the lukewarm pond, watching the water swirl with fading color. But still the evidence stained red on my palms, as if the job was already done.

Moonlight cast shadows over stone and grass, through curled fingers of tree branches. The first settlers were buried here, the Dodge family, the Roses, the Balls, some of whose descendents still lived on the island. How would it be to die knowing your children would live on this land you'd discovered? And your children's children, on and on forever, the most lasting of legacies? Look at Daddy's legacy. His legacy was death.

I knelt by his grave, the simply carved headstone,

name and date, beloved father. I rested my cheek against the chiseled edge, feeling an overwhelming emptiness. I'd lost him, lost Justin, so how could I live if I lost her too? And I almost turned back, ran home and forgot.

Almost.

But in the end there was really no choice. The decision was not my own. It was desperation. It was love and hate that ground together against my gut and made up their own mind.

And that night before I went to bed, in the airiness of waking sleep, I cooked. A cast-iron pot on the electric stove, a bubbling stew with a smell so rancid it bit inside my nose. Only cooking, a meal that may or may not be eaten, eaten by her, eaten by me, by him. It didn't matter now. All that mattered was the cooking and the possibility of an end.

I stared at the men in their dark suits, leather binders tucked against their chests. Nobody ever wore suits on the island, not to work, not to the fanciest restaurants. And even watching from the bottom of the dark well where I now lived, I knew something was happening.

They were walking from Town Hall, talking in low drones, three of them and then another two emerging with First Warden McCoy, hopping into gray sedans and driving up the road. I stood a minute, staring at the license plates. Washington, DC. I had to go home.

There was a line outside the Book Nook. Always this time of day there was a ritual trek of off-islanders who waited for papers delivered on the ten o'clock ferry. They'd come to the island to get away, but still felt obliged to search for the *Boston Globe* or *New York Times,* news from the cities they'd left. Today, though, the line stretched around the block, more islanders than mainlanders. And there was old Mrs. Scott, Mrs. Scott who never left her front porch, who had her groceries delivered by neighbor boys and thought newspapers were an infringement on her peace. But there she was, leaning crooked on her walker and talking to Mary Bates, her low-drooping eyes bright with the thrill of scandal.

I started quickly up the hill, legs weighted with trepidation, strode across the street towards home, then froze. Officer Carerra's Jeep. Parked in our drive. And I felt a sudden loosening around my diaphragm, like relief.

I opened the front door, glanced from Eve to Brad Carrera and back, suddenly longing to let myself melt and flow beneath them, to confess. *What do you think I am, both of you? I'm worse.*

Eve watched me, her eyes wide and wary, then folded her hands under her chin like a plea. "They found a body," she said. "All that time they thought Ryan Maclean ran away, he was actually dead."

A body. I saw him as he had been, mouth filled with water, arms floating and reaching for us. I licked my tongue against the insides of my teeth in rhythm, *one*-two-three-four, *one*-two-three-four.

"So why are you here, Brad?" Eve said. "Why're you telling me?"

Brad Carrera took off his wide-brimmed hat, held it at his chest. "This isn't official police business at all, but now there's a body I think I need to ask some questions just for my own peace of mind."

My eyes felt like they were coated with thin sheets of ice. I forced myself to look away, to smile, to start towards the stairs like the conversation had nothing to do with me. And then I saw it.

There on the shag runner to the stairway were three mahogany-colored spots, smudged into the fibers. And on the stairs a thin-dripped trail. How hadn't we noticed it before? I glanced to Brad and back to the floor. I held my breath and drifted to stand over the spots, blocking his view of the stairway.

"Peace of mind," Eve said. "Okay then, you just let me know how I can give you peace." Her voice was slightly strained, but not so much that you'd notice if you weren't looking.

"See, the two of us, we may be the only people know what-all went on between you and the congressman. And I'd rather not bring it out if there's no reason for it. Too many people might get hurt by it, we both know that. All I want for my own peace is that you tell me you had nothing to do with him drowning."

"Of course I had nothing to do with it! His wife told the cops he was drunk and I guess he went out to the beach, fell off the bluffs. Sounds straightforward to me. Unless, I don't know, maybe he felt so guilty over me and that girl he raped and what he did to his wife that he jumped off. I ended things between us a long while before he disappeared."

She was a good liar; her eyes flashed with anger, no hint of fear. God she was good, but of course I already knew that well enough.

"You know I had to ask, right? First thing I thought when he disappeared was how maybe you and him were planning some kind of secret rendezvous. And I wanted to talk to you but I didn't want to start a stir, what with things being in enough of a stir already." He twisted his hat in his hands, as if he was steering a car. "Or hurt you either, you know I still feel something for you. We had a good time while it lasted."

"Yeah we did, didn't we." Her voice was soft, like she was speaking to a child, or a lover.

"Guess I'll always feel a kind of something for you."

She smiled widely, too brightly. "Me too."

"Anyways, it's best for everybody involved if there's no more controversy. I'm sure there's people who'll think this is suicide and some people who think it was his wife offed him. But long as there's no proof, we all just got to assume it was some kind of dumb-ass accident."

"Guess he was kind of a dumb ass," Eve said.

Brad combed his fingers through his hair. "Guess what matters with the congressman is that the autopsy report shows it was definitely a drowning."

"Well sure it was."

"No foul play we can find, and there's ocean water in his lungs."

Eve's smile faded. She turned to me. We watched each other, unblinking. "What's that mean exactly?"

"Just means it's the water that killed him. His body was pretty beat up, contusions just about everywhere from him falling off the bluffs. Knocking him out, I'd guess, which must be why he drowned."

"He breathed in water?" Her voice was hoarse.

"Well that's what drowning is, right?"

Just then the front door swung open behind me. Justin stepped into the foyer, his eyes wild. "I saw the car.

What's going on?" He was going to confess; his voice was clenched too tight. *There was water in the lungs. We did it. Tell him we did it.* I backed away up the stairs. Justin looked up at me, his lips tight, then turned back to Eve.

Eve shook her head, her face pale. "Brad was just leaving, weren't you, Brad. You just came to relive the good old days."

"You sonofabitch." Justin's eyes seemed naked, unguarded.

Brad raised his eyebrows. "There a problem here?"

"I think there is. Sixteen years old is statutory rape, or didn't they teach you that in the academy?"

"She was the one went after me first, Justin. This was completely mutual."

Eve's eyes flicked from Brad to Justin and back, her lips pressed between her teeth.

"Yeah, I'm sure the cops'll buy that." Justin smiled. "Oh, wait, you are the cops."

"Look, stop your little jealous tiff here. I know what you tried when me and her were still together. She told me how you were after her even back then when you had no right, but it's your business now, I'm through with it. You can have her."

What he tried? I made a noise, a kind of muffled gasp. Eve glanced up at me, then sidled to the door and out onto the porch.

Brad watched her go, the screen door clanging shut behind her, then set the hat back on his head, the wide brim and odd tilt making him look slightly ludicrous. "What she's like, Justin, she's like a fireworks display. Thrill a minute and oohs and aahs, can't look away, but once it's over, all that's left is the smoke. Your ears are ringing, your neck hurts like hell, and all you want to do is just pack it all up and go home."

Justin glared at him, the hatred like a scar marring his face. I couldn't watch it, couldn't watch, so I walked down the hall to the bedroom. I gripped the edge of the dresser, my teeth clamped.

Ryan Maclean had been breathing. He'd breathed underwater, which made all the difference, meant it wasn't only Justin who'd killed him but all of us, heaving the body over the stern, watching him float, letting him sink. In this bedroom I'd stood over him and checked for a pulse, felt nothing except the warm sweat on his neck, and then I'd pronounced him dead.

"Kerry..."

I flattened my hand against the dresser.

"You're going to have to talk to me eventually, Kerry. This can't go on forever."

I wouldn't turn to him. I wouldn't. I shook my head, still facing the wall, feeling a shell all around me, hard as stone but precarious as dynamite. I couldn't let him touch it or I would explode. And if I exploded, I knew I'd have to take everyone with me.

"Mom and Dad are asking questions," he said. "Lots of questions and I don't know what to say. And Eve, you can see it in her face, it's like everything's fallen in on itself. I don't know why she came to me that night, I don't think she even knows. We were all in this awful frame of mind, we weren't ourselves, you know that. So we have to just talk this out, the three of us. You have to."

I steeled my shoulders. Talk it out? What the hell was wrong with him?

Justin stepped towards me and touched the back of

my head. I flinched away. But inside under everything I felt the burn of his touch, deep red like longing, bright red like anger, hot red like blood.

"It was only one time," he whispered. "That one time, twenty minutes, one mistake."

I was shivering, I was so chilled and sweaty and hot and cold at once, and his words were echoing, swelling inside my head. I knew what could happen in twenty minutes.

"I love you, Kerry, you're a part of me. One mistake can't take that away."

In twenty minutes a boy could make love to a girl, and a girl could mix a pot of poison on a stove.

"And maybe it was the world's worst-ever mistake because it was with Eve, God, I know. If I could do anything to take it back, I swear I would."

In twenty minutes, that girl could pronounce a live man dead, a pronouncement that would make that man die for real.

"But the fact is that I can't take it back. It happened but it's over. I hate myself for hurting you, but all I can do now is swear it won't ever happen again."

I whirled around in a sudden panic. "You son of a bitch!"

"Kerry—"

"With my sister! You goddamned liar, tell me the truth for once. How long were you after Eve? Did you go to her when she was still with Brad?"

"No, Kerry, of course not! I don't know what she told Brad or why, maybe to make him jealous or because she wanted it to be true. I have no idea whatever went on in that head of hers, but I swear it was all lies."

"You swear? You swear!" I screwed my face into a sneer. "I don't care anymore, Justin, can I tell you something? You know there was water in his lungs? Mr. Maclean had water in his lungs, which means I killed him. But the truth is I don't give a damn. I killed him and I could kill Eve, too. Kill you both without blinking!"

I swiped my arm at him, then ran, his hand grazing my back as I sped on burning legs, down and out and to the street. I was thinking, almost hoping, he'd run after me, grab me like he had that first day we'd kissed. And if he did grab me, I didn't know what I would do. I would let him, I would hit him, I would kill him.

But he let me go, a fact that mocked me. He let me go, of course he did because I wasn't Eve. I could never be Eve. Fireworks. It was true, that power Eve had even in childhood. Two twins, identical except that one had always known how to draw the smiles, the attention, while the other clung and watched and tried to absorb. Eve knew our roles, fostered them. There was no reason for Justin to choose me.

I stopped at LoraLee's, knowing I couldn't go inside, because what could I tell her? And what could she possibly say that would make anything any better? But still I stood for a long while watching her door.

What I could do, I could live here, sleep here on the porch beneath the clanking chimes, enfolded by the chokecherries and geraniums. And in time I'd be able to snip Justin and Eve out of the fabric of my thoughts, snip out my mother, the despair that must've been behind my father's death, the existence of a certain Tupperware container. All gone, all these holes and I'd be like something moth-eaten, fragile like lace, but bleached clean. I sat on the porch step and lay back to look up at the rotting rafters.

The door opened behind me. "Kerry, chile."

I startled forward, then jumped to my feet.

"I's jus' thinkin' 'bout you." She smiled so I could see the pink holes where two of her teeth used to be. "Lookit them tomato we done, the new flowers. We be havin tomato samwiches 'fore you know it."

"LoraLee …" I whispered.

She watched me for a minute, eyes probing, then nodded sharply. "Look like you needs some tea."

I followed her to the kitchen, sat at the table while she went outside for water. I had no idea what I wanted to say to her, what I could say. I watched her back as she lit the woodstove, wishing she could read my eyes, and also afraid that she would.

She sat across from me and leaned back in her chair, her hands folded over her stomach. Her whole posture seemed to say *Go on, then.*

"Can I try on your ring?" I asked.

LoraLee raised her eyebrows and handed it to me. It was wide enough to slide over my thumb. I twisted it, feeling its worn, wooden smoothness like a kiss against my skin. *How could you let him leave?* I wanted to ask. Instead I spoke the other question behind it all. "What do you do when you don't know what you're doing?"

If she was surprised by the question, she didn't show it. She tapped one finger on the table, pondering. Finally she nodded. "God give you everything you needs to make any decision," she said. "You jus' listen to what He tell you."

"He's not talking," I said, then handed back the ring, watching the spire of steam that rose from the teakettle.

LoraLee stood and pulled two mugs from the shelf. "You got His voice inside you, if you jus' listens hard enough."

"Remember back when you said you don't believe in heaven because you don't believe in hell?" My words were fast, desperate. "What about the devil then? If you believe in God, don't you have to believe in the devil?"

"The devil voice is man's voice," she said, setting a mug in front of me. "A distraction voice."

I waited for her to explain, but she just sat back in her chair and blew on her tea. I thought I knew what she was saying anyway. The devil had always been there in me, just waiting, a voice I'd only heard before in snatches on frigid, moody winter days.

"Like this. When I's around your age, I almos' lef' school and start to work like my momma done all her life, scrubbin' other mans' floors. But there a woman, Mabel, who work the kitchen, and when I tell her my plan she brew me a cup-a ginger tea."

I looked down at my tea, letting the mug burn my fingers, holding tight even when they screamed with pain.

"She say, 'Lookit your momma with her chap hand and redstain eye, and ask yourself if this what meant for you.' Then when I drunk her tea she read the leaf I lef' behin', tell me that's not my future. She say you's gonna finish your school and go north, live somewheres with ocean on all side." LoraLee nodded. "And mebbe she don't really know a thing 'bout tea leaf, mebbe she jus' tryin' to set me straight, but it felt right to me, so I done what she say. I finish school and set on my way up north. I follow where my feets lead me, and soon as I find this place I knowed I's home. Notion of workin' on hands and knees, that were my devil, and whether she knowed it or not, Mabel was my voice from God. She brung me here and also she make me want to study tea."

I looked down at my red-burned hands. *You don't know the devil's voice,* I wanted to tell her. *I killed a man, I'll kill my sister, I may kill myself. That's the devil.*

"So the moral is, you allus got His voice inside and outside too. You let it in and it learn you everything you needs to know." She smiled at me, then widened her eyes. "You burn your hand? My Lord, chile, what you done?"

"Nothing, it's nothing."

"I'll git you some aloe." She jumped up and strode to the windowsill, split off a leaf and smoothed the oil onto my fingers.

I pulled away. "How do you do it?"

"Do what?"

I shook my head. "Go on like this, live alone with no family, no one really close to you."

"I got my own self. That's enough for me." She nodded slowly. "You got peoples who give the worl' for you."

I stared down at my aloe-slicked hands. "I thought I had my father, but now I realize I never did, not the most important parts. And Eve..."

"You has Eve. You has Eve the most."

A barking laugh caught in my throat. "You don't know. You don't know her, and now I realize I never did either. I saw the mask of her, the part that looked like me, but it was such a lie."

"Not a lie. She love you, Kerry, you has to believe it. She jus' confused, she need somethin' and she don't know where to look."

"How could she? How could they?" My voice broke and I waited for her to ask, and if she did what would I say? So much was crammed inside me it no longer fit. I'd start talking and then wouldn't be able to stop.

But she didn't ask, just watched me with narrowed eyes. "Sometime it's the peoples you love the best that you hurt most. S'like a reflex, you hit out without meanin' to, but when the hit's done you 'spect it to be over. You don't mean nothin' by it."

"You don't know. They think they can twist me and kick me and it doesn't matter. They think I'm nothing, just a Kerry doll who wears a smile and waits for a chance to be kicked again but I'm not! I won't!"

She reached for me and I let her hold me, wanting to sob but there were no tears left, nothing left in me but the knowing. Drained empty of tears and them and me, nothing left inside but black.

That night I woke sometime near midnight, and even before I opened my eyes I could feel Eve beside me, watching. I peeked between my lashes.

She was kneeling by the bed, face slack, tears streaming down her cheeks. She cried silently, without trembling or pulling in breath; it might have been varnish glistening against her skin.

I suddenly remembered a day we'd made a pact with tears in our eyes, our pinkies locked in promise. If one of us died, we vowed the other would follow so we'd be together in heaven. Because we were nothing without each other. Because surviving would be a betrayal.

I opened my eyes and made myself screw my face into a mask of disgust. "What?"

She rocked back as if slapped. I glared at her and then turned away but Eve gripped at my sleeve. "I have to tell you."

"Don't even try."

"Oh God, I'm sorry, I'm so sorry. I've just been trying to think of some reason, some way it could mean something, some way to make it better. But there isn't, and now I don't know who to go to."

"Why don't you go to hell."

"No, Kerry, you have to let me tell you. There's something worse than this, worse than all of it."

I laughed, high-pitched and dry. "Worse than killing the man you stole away from his wife? Worse than pushing him off the side of Daddy's boat and watching him suck in water?"

Eve watched me, shook her head. "The thing is… the thing is, you got your period two weeks back."

The words punched terror through me. Because I understood immediately.

We'd first gotten our period five years ago, within the same week, and after that we'd been completely in sync, sometimes a day or two early or late in our cycle, but always early or late together. I watched the dull glow of fear on her face. And I knew.

"I'm pregnant," she said.

The word hung in the air like something palpable,

something round and fleshy I could press between my palms. "No," I said.

"I took all the tests, three kinds of tests, and they all came out. They came out."

Oh God. There was a heat building up inside me, raw and sore. And part of me wanted to curl up with her, maybe crawl with her under her bed until the whole world disappeared. The other part wanted to shake her, shake it out of her. Instead I spat back. "Well what the hell did you think would happen?"

Her face was swollen and pleading, and I wanted to be there, be her sister, but it was too much. I dug my nails into my palms. "What're you gonna do now, hunh, Eve? Now you tossed the baby's father into the ocean, what're you going to tell it when it grows up?"

Eve's face stiffened. She looked away and wiped at her tears with the palms of both hands. She stayed still for a moment before looking back at me. "Justin's the father."

Her voice was so smooth, so calm, but the words that she spoke made no sense at all. The room was swirling, air rushing past my ears. I smiled and imagined she'd said something else, maybe *Justin's no bother,* or *Justin is hotter.*

"It's his, Kerry. It couldn't be anyone else. Me and Ryan, we always used a condom."

"You're such a bitch," I said matter-of-factly, like I was complimenting her hair. "I get it, you know. I get what you're doing. Yeah, you think, I'll pretend I'm pregnant so it's the last straw in ending things once and for all between them, and then I'll have a nice fake miscarriage and go back to screwing every guy who wants me."

"Shut up!" She was crying, her words cut sharp by sobs. "I'm pregnant, Kerry, and Justin's the father. And I'm not telling him, not yet until I know for sure what I'm going to do. But I've felt it all this time inside me, I could tell from the beginning, from the minute after we made love—"

"You bitch!" I swiped my hand at her, and she cried out and jumped away.

"Maybe I *will* have this baby!" she said. "Maybe I'll have it and I'll marry Justin, and there's not a goddamned thing you'd ever be able to do about it!"

She ran into the hall and I listened to her footsteps raining down the stairs.

She'd been wearing an old flannel nightgown, ivory with faded roses, which now reached only mid-calf and had a tear at the hem. For some reason I went to the dresser and pulled out the matching nightgown I hadn't worn for years. I held it as I reached under my bed for the shoebox holding all my pictures, felt for the bloodroot-stained Tupperware hidden underneath. And for some reason it made me laugh. I laughed and laughed, a silent shaking, maybe because I was just plain tired of tears.

It wasn't me. It wasn't. It was something hot and boiling deep like lava.

I hated her. Not just hated, despised with a strength that squeezed my lungs. I wanted to yank at her hair, dig my nails under her skin. Instead I reached into her drawer. The smell of perfume, pink and red satin and lace, and a clanking plastic bag.

I opened a bottle of Eve's gin and swigged it. The liquid sizzled on my tongue. Also in the bag was a six-pack of beer and an assortment of miniature bottles. I lifted a small tan bottle of Kahlua and opened it, took a sip, sweet and hot. My hand was shaking as I swiped my finger through the Tupperware and plugged the acrid black sludge into the neck of the Kahlua bottle. I capped the bottle and shook it slowly, staring at the bottle, not sure what I expected to see. But it looked the same, so innocent, orange writing on the tan label.

I didn't think what I was doing, couldn't have even if I'd wanted to. And even though I wasn't thinking, somehow the bottle found its way into the plastic bag, the bag into Eve's drawer, me on my bed staring at the ceiling. A melody ran through my brain, a flute airy and hollow. I looked down at my hands, a murderer's hands, and I listened.

32

I WAITED. That's what the next two weeks were, not a passive waiting but a prickling, terrified and hungry wait.

Every once in a while I'd slip the Kahlua from Eve's drawer and press it between my palms, filled with a gnawing horror of the bottle and of myself. And then my mind would yelp, and I'd shove it back in the drawer like it was a spider or a hot potato, feeling nothing except *please, please.* Please stop this. Please save us. Please let it be over soon.

I spent as much time as possible in the bedroom, maybe trying to keep Eve away, tensing when she approached her dresser. If I'd actually seen her reach for the bottle, I don't know what I would have done. But for the most part she stayed away, coming home only late at night. I eyed her secretly, pretending to be asleep. In all that time we didn't speak.

And then came the day, the last day, when I walked into the bedroom and saw Eve on the floor with my shoebox. I froze.

She was staring meditatively at the pictures. She hadn't heard me enter the room. Under the pictures I could see it, the black-stained Tupperware I should have thrown away.

She lifted a picture, the two of us flipped upside down, panties showing in parallel cartwheels. She held it for a long while cradled between her palms, and watching this I ached for her, for those two girls in their summer dresses and matching day-of-the-week underwear.

Eve lifted another and then another, eyes fixed like she was memorizing. Then suddenly, without warning, her jaw tightened and she tore a picture in two.

I sucked in my breath and she turned to face me, her eyes red but her shoulders hunched with determination. She hesitated for only a second before reaching again into the box. Her eyes locked on mine as she slowly tore a picture, wearing a slim smile.

And then she tore another, and every cell in my body was crying out for her to stop, stop before it was too late. Because we'd lived through this before: Daddy on the couch with our photo albums, peeling the pages with tears in his eyes and clawing at our mother, tearing, tearing with shaking hands as Eve and I stood petrified, watching and somehow knowing what it meant. It was over. The past was gone, no more waiting for things to change. And we saw then that it was easier to be angry than to hold out hope.

And so instead of voicing the plea that echoed through me now in exactly the same way it had then, I grabbed the remaining pictures from the shoebox and threw the shoebox under the bed before she could see the Tupperware inside. I began to rip the photographs blindly, then tossed the scattered pieces to drift like confetti over our heads.

Eve didn't move, just stared at me as if I were crazy. She looked down at the torn pictures, and her eyes hardened. "I've decided," she said. "I'm keeping the baby."

"You idiot! You'd ruin your life just to get back at me?"

"You think this has anything to do with you?" Her voice hitched. She shook her head quickly. "What do you expect me to do?"

The thickness in her voice shocked me. And part of me actually wanted to stop this, to just turn away, but another part of me, a much bigger part, knew this was not an option. I forced a smile. "Poor little Eve, pregnant and alone, it breaks my heart. Screwing every guy in screwing range like it could make them love you, but who loves you now?"

"It's not me after him, Kerry, I told you already. Not—" Her voice broke. She looked up at me. Without makeup her face seemed unnaturally pale and bloated. "How it was, the truth is he started with me first that night. I was so scared and all I wanted was for him to just hold me. I was crying and he held me and then he kissed me, and *I* was the one who pulled away."

I felt everything inside me stop, paralyzed. I wanted to slap her, stop her from talking, but when I looked into her face I knew she was telling the truth. "You fucking liar."

"So I pulled away and he stared at me, and then he jumped up and ran. He ran into his office and I sat there feeling like I was this close to just making it be over, throwing myself into the water with both of them, Ryan and Daddy, that's what I wanted to do. But in the end I saw the light in the office and I followed him." She fisted a handful of torn pictures. "I don't know why, Kerry, but that's what I did. And things just happened."

"God," I said slowly. "I just realized. I know what's going on. You went to Justin because you knew you were pregnant. You slept with him so you could tell him the baby was his."

"Are you kidding? Who do you think I am? You really think I'd do that?"

"I know exactly who you are, and I *know* you'd do it. It all makes perfect sense. That's why you were puking that night, from morning sickness."

A sudden flash of panic scarred her face, but then it hardened into anger. "I wasn't pregnant! I told you we always used condoms, and besides the timing isn't right. Justin's the father, Kerry, and what do you think, that I forced him? He wanted me too."

"He used you because you happened to be there and you happened to be willing. Just exactly like Mr. Maclean and Brad Carrera used you, except it turned out you were both using each other."

"He said he was in love with me."

I bit my tongue hard until I knew I could speak without choking. "And so did Brad and so did Mr. Maclean. Are you really that gullible? It's just a way into your pants, Eve, the easiest way to get the slut to fuck them." We sat there for a moment, locking eyes, the girlhood game. Whoever looks away first.

"The money?" she said hoarsely. "The Caines' money? Yes, I took it from the shop, a little each month because we needed it, and I was planning to pay it back as soon as I could. But then Justin saw me take it, Kerry. Back when I was still with Brad he walked in on me. And he's wearing this little smile, he comes over and says he loves me and then he kissed me. On the lips. And I've got the money in one hand and him on my lips, so what am I supposed to do?"

I stared at her, and she lifted her chin. "So I kissed him back." Her words were rough and hollow. I could see the pain in her face and worse than that, a sort of sympathy. She was telling the truth.

"Then he started giving me money, hundreds of dollars. Maybe it was just to help us out or maybe to get me not to tell, I don't know, but what I think is it was always me. I think what it was, he wanted you because he could kiss you and imagine he was kissing me."

"You bitch!" I swung my arm, but Eve caught my wrist, narrowing her eyes.

"You know how he feels, don't you. Deep down part of you always knew it. Which I guess is why you're trying to poison me. Guess I'm a little less competition if I'm dead."

I froze, trepidation knuckling my stomach. "What?"

She dropped my wrist and sneered. "Come on, Kerry, I'm not stupid. I see the way you look at me every time I open my dresser drawer. Your face gets all white and you hold your breath, let go again when I close it. What did you do, poison the vodka? Alcohol kills, isn't that what they say?"

I shook my head slowly, opened my mouth but couldn't speak, my tongue searching for a word, a denial, but completely forgetting the syllables it might use to construct it.

"I knew there was something going on, and now look at this container in your shoebox. Two and two make a pretty easy four, Ker. So don't pretend you don't know Justin's in love with me."

I could feel each of my ribs pressing sharp and distinct against my lungs. "You're crazy."

"Am I?" Eve reached under my bed and pulled out the blackened Tupperware. She popped the lid and sniffed at it, made a face. "Would you really, seriously have let me drink it? What would you do if I'd started? Just watch?"

A strange redness swirled in front of my eyes.

"You wouldn't really, I'm pretty sure of that, you're not strong enough. You just felt better pretending you had the guts."

I stared at her, then punched my fist against the wall. "You're crazy! If I wanted Justin, all I'd have to do is tell him. All I'd have to do is tell him I forgive him."

"You think? Then why'd he make love to me?"

"That was sex, Eve, not love. You never got the difference, did you?"

Eve nodded slowly. "Well, maybe I'll give you a chance to prove it once and for all." She slid the Tupperware across the floor so that it hit my heels. "Let's try something."

I kicked the container away.

"C'mon, Ker, don't you want to know? See who he'd choose, all things being equal? We'll give him a choice and see." She watched me carefully. "Like another game. We can write letters, you can tell him how much you love him, how you forgive him and you want him back, whatever. And I'll tell him how I feel. Whoever he chooses wins."

I dug my nails hard into my thighs. "Wins what?"

"Wins Justin, obviously, isn't that only fair? If he chooses you, I'll leave. I'll get rid of the baby and then leave. And if he chooses me..." She slid a scrap of photograph, two sandaled feet, up and down against her leg. "If he chooses me, you admit I was right, it wasn't my fault. I keep the baby, and whatever happens with Justin happens."

I twisted my face in disgust, fear tingling down my arms into my palms. I knew the fear made no sense. It was me he loved, I knew it deep in my bones. But he'd slept with Eve. If he really loved me, real magic, destined, soul-mate love, then how could he have shared this part of himself, this absolute most important part with somebody else?

Because I wouldn't let him share it with me. The realization stung me. It was as simple and as trite as that. "Fine," I said.

Eve squared her shoulders and nodded sharply. She stared at the wall as she spoke. "Okay. So we can write notes and leave them taped to his office door. Maybe I'll tell him I'm waiting in Daddy's room and you tell him you're waiting here. Whoever he goes to first, whoever he chooses, that's who wins."

"You'll tell him about the baby."

She made a face. "That'd be cheating, Kerry. I'm not going to cheat. I'm as curious as you are what he'll do, and if I cheat we'll never know what he really wants."

I pressed my lips between my teeth and nodded sharply. She walked to the desk, rooted through a drawer.

Two pieces of white paper, two blue Bic pens, everything was the same. I sat on my bed watching out of the corner of my eye. This wasn't Eve I'd been talking to.

Not the Eve who'd crawled into my bed on stormy nights, huddling like the force of our joined hands could protect us. Eve had died months ago and been replaced by the very thing we'd been afraid of on those nights, that slippery, shadowy thing that clawed at doors and under skin, took over your body and turned you into itself.

I watched her scribbling the words she hoped would send me away, and I suddenly imagined I could see a new fullness in her breasts and a roundness in her belly. The image cemented the facts. We were no longer identical, no longer sisters. We were nothing.

Dear Justin,

I've been dreaming about you every night, imagining us together. And I think the thing is, maybe that's exactly what we need so we forget everything bad that happened, and get even closer than we've ever been before. I want to make love to you, tonight and every night from now on for the rest of our life. So I'll be waiting for you in my bedroom, and you should come there first thing when you get home, and I promise I'll make it a night to remember.

I love you with all my heart,
Kerry

I folded the note and printed Justin's name on the front, then turned to Eve. She'd been watching me, but when I looked up she pretended to be reading over her letter. I stood. "You finished?"

Eve nodded. "Let's go."

So out we went to tape the notes on his door. When we were done Eve turned to me, her eyes darting to the sky like she wanted to say something. But when I looked at her, she just pressed her lips together and nodded.

We went back upstairs, me to our bedroom and Eve to Daddy's, my legs feeling wobbly and boneless. The whole idea was totally ridiculous, I realized that. What would Justin think when he saw what we were doing? The most likely thing he'd do would be to run in the opposite direction. "Stupid kids," he'd say.

But part of me was thinking, whatever happens, this'll be the end. If he chose me, Eve would have an abortion, and then she'd go somewhere off-island like she'd always planned. And if he chose Eve…

He would choose me. Of course he would.

I went to her drawer and reached inside the plastic bag for the bottle of Kahlua. I squeezed it tight in my fist, feeling a wash of desperation. But it didn't matter. Soon none of it would matter. I slipped the bottle under my pillow and went back to the drawer, sifting through Eve's tangle of new underwear. A garter belt, how did that work? Panties so lacy they covered nothing at all; really, if you thought about it, defeating the purpose of wearing panties. A bustier to give you boobs so high you could use them like a shelf to balance books upright. I stripped and pulled them on, then eyed my body in the full-length mirror. A touch of Eve's dark lipstick, thick mascara, rouge to define the hollows in my face and I looked like someone else. I looked older. I looked like Eve.

Justin had once told me that my dancing was the sexiest thing he'd ever seen. So when he opened the door, I'd run to him with a move that was dancelike without looking like an obvious dance. I practiced a *pas de bourrée*, a light running step on my toes, followed by a *petit jeté*, landing at the door. But as soon as I landed the jump, a boob popped out of my bustier.

I grimaced and stuffed it back, then lay across my bed and pulled in my stomach, threw my gaze to the door. I arched my back, and my boob popped out again. I hunched my shoulders, tucked it back and whispered, "God, I need you," then winced. Too stupid, way too melodramatic. I swung my feet to the floor and made my eyes sharp. "Come here," I mouthed. I imagined his face, the shock and then the melting. I reached my arms towards him. "Come here."

I heard Eve's footsteps coming from Daddy's room and I jumped up, ran to the closet for my robe. The door opened, and Eve began to speak. "Listen, Kerry." She stopped short when she saw me, and let out a sharp, barking laugh. I pulled the robe to my chest and we eyed each other for a minute, and then Eve turned away and closed the door.

Wait! I wanted to cry. *Come back! What were you going to say?* Instead I stood there staring at the door, then finally slipped the robe over my shoulders and sat on the bed to wait.

When Justin's car finally pulled into the drive, I stood and let the robe drop to my feet. I was shivering as I watched him head towards the house. Partly because I was only wearing lingerie. And partly because I was terrified.

It seemed to take an eternity for him to walk past the potting shed, squint his eyes to peer at the door, step closer to see what might be there. All slow motion, moving frame by frame: raised eyebrows, lifted head, paper unfolding, slow frown.

He read my letter first, and when he'd finished he looked up at the window. I crouched down. So I didn't see his reaction when he opened the next letter, or if he even had. When I peeked over the window ledge, all I saw was the top of his head hurrying forward, hurrying to me.

I arranged myself again on the bed, tossed my hair over one shoulder and hooded my eyes into a seductive gaze. His footsteps raced up the stairs, coming to me, and I couldn't breathe. It was the last day of my virginity, the day I'd reunite with the person I loved most in the world, and I wanted to cry out with it but didn't have the air. And just when I thought I might explode, the footsteps disappeared.

They disappeared.

I stood and pressed my ear to the door, covering my arms over my bare chest. Dimly I heard the click-shuffle-snap as Daddy's door closed and locked.

33

I WAS SURE at first Justin had made a mistake. Of course he had. Feeling suddenly vulnerable, I pulled on a T-shirt and jeans. I sat on my bed, waiting for him to realize he was confused, believing it for far longer than I had a right to. And when the realization came of what he'd done, it was all at once, like I'd been hit with a massive sack of sand. I couldn't move, just sat there feeling weighted, pinned to the bed. My ears were ringing. My breasts, still inside the bustier, felt separate from me, like they'd been pasted on.

And then I felt my body moving, gliding along the floor and down the hall. My ear was against their door, calm voices. Calm. Not a mistake.

"...how hard this was, Justin. It was hard for me, too."

"But Kerry!"

"She said she'd accept it whatever you chose, you just have to tell her. Tell her how it's not my fault, not anyone's fault, but you just fell in love with me. She knows deep down how you feel."

"I never wanted to hurt her."

"She knows that too."

My body was floating away and down the hall, its knees buckling, stumbling, losing its balance.

Justin had chosen Eve. Eve knew he would.

... I thought it was you at first, I swear I did....

... It was only that one time, twenty minutes, one mistake....

... You're a part of me, one mistake can't take that away....

But he chose Eve.

And what did I have now? I had the hurt and hate of what I'd done. I had this body which meant nothing, even to itself. Things were moving through my brain, scuttling like spiders, too fast to be focused on. And underneath a clear picture was forming. The picture was black and sharp and it directed me.

In the bedroom, I reached under my pillow for the bottle. The liquid inside tasted sweet and bitter and gagged me after only one gulp. I took another and another and my head began to spin until I didn't know which was up and which was down. I crawled to my bed and waited.

Death took a long time coming. I felt it descend like a sodden blanket over my face. *Hello,* it said, *I know this doesn't feel good, but soon it will. Just wait, I'm on my way!* This is how they would find me. Eve would think at first I was asleep, but tomorrow morning when I didn't wake up she'd shake me and feel my cold hands and scream.

There was a tightness in my head that moved to my chest, and I could feel my heart slow and still. *I'm dead. I'm dead.* Justin would fall to his knees with anguish, hating himself and hating Eve and realizing what a mistake he'd made. Everyone I'd ever known would come for the funeral. They'd stand in the rain without umbrellas and cry for my lost life. And later passing tourists would read my headstone, subtract the dates and frown, wondering why I'd died so young.

The tightness spread from my heart down into my stomach, where it squeezed like a fist. Not so much nausea but a churning cramp that doubled me over. Oh God, oh God, I'm dying and how dying hurts! It curdles in your gut and presses your stomach up through your chest to your throat, oh God! and I barely made it to the trashcan.

When it was over I carried the can to the bathroom and cleaned it out, then brushed my teeth. Daddy's door was still closed, and I knew what they were saying, poor Kerry, ignorant desperate Kerry, we'll miss her when she's gone.

There were two slips of paper outside the door. He must have dropped them when he'd run to her. I lifted them, their edges crawling against my palms like something alive, and then in a fit of blind anger, I tore them in half, in quarters, in eighths, into hundreds of meaningless tatters which fluttered to the hall floor.

I pulled the bulb from a bathroom sconce, wrapped it in a towel and stomped it with my foot. I took the base with its jagged glass edge, curled up on my bed, cradled it between my palms and closed my eyes. My mind felt like wet cotton, my body felt like fresh, uncooked liver. I ran the broken bulb against my wrist and felt the cold tongue-lick of glass against my skin. I sliced harder, then stared down at the beaded blood. And then again, a widening red crevice of hurt; so hard that the glass fell from my shaking hand, my eyes blind from the pain.

I brought my wrist to my mouth and bit my teeth against it, but as my teeth dug deeper my heart seemed to beat even harder. I could kill, so why couldn't I die? There were so many people out there who wanted to live but were dying, so why couldn't God just make some kind of trade? It would be so easy to just let go, just slip into dreamless, painless, blameless sleep. But God didn't seem to care what people deserved. He was stubborn. He had His own set of rules.

I stared down at the torn pictures still on the floor: a severed leg and two clasped hands, an amputated head with a grape-purple face. And I suddenly got it. I suddenly understood God. Because to live would mean not only that I'd lost, but most of all that I'd look again and again at everything I'd lost. It would writhe and root inside my gut, would slash at my wrists day after day, reminding me of what I'd done. Of me.

I tore off the bedcovers, pressed them against the wound, felt my wrist throbbing and pulsing with streams of blood. I waited for the blackish red to seep and puddle warm, but when I pulled off the covers and inspected the stain, all I saw were dishearteningly insignificant spots and smears, already almost dry. I stared down at my wrist for a minute, then stood.

I didn't pack, only pulled the plastic bag out from under Eve's bed. I took a handful of bills, the money Justin had given to Eve, and then lifted the picture in Eve's bag, two girls at the beach in their new pink bathing suits. I pressed it between my palms, hands at my face like in prayer, then slipped it into my knapsack along with the bottle of Kahlua, reminders.

Daddy's door was still closed. All was silent behind it. I gathered the shredded notes I'd scattered and jammed them into my pocket. More reminders.

I turned down the hall and started for the stairs, and then Daddy's door opened. I froze.

Eve stood there, barefoot, her shirt rumpled. She watched me for a long while without speaking, then nodded slowly.

She knew.

She saw my face and saw the knapsack and knew. And I wanted to say something. I wanted to tell her something that would slap her, enfold her, slow things down enough to give myself a chance to change my mind. But as I opened my mouth to speak, my thoughts racing but my mind blank, she smiled, a slow, slim smile that didn't touch her eyes. She smiled at me and there was nothing more that could be said. I turned away and started down the stairs, imagining Eve standing there with her hands in fists, looking victorious and yet defeated, both.

It was several hours before the first morning ferry, and so I walked the streets. I walked on feet that felt numb, staring in muted shock at the red flame of morning on the horizon, its wide veins scarring the sky. I walked past the cemetery without stopping. I walked past the entrance to Rodman's Hollow, and I walked past the Macleans'. I walked along the bluffs, looking out over the jagged peaks, and when I was done saying good-bye to my past, I started up the hill to LoraLee's. She was the only one who'd give a damn that I was gone.

I opened her door without knocking. Her house was dark and warm, like a womb. She lay in bed, her chest rising heavily with each breath. I watched for a minute, then sat beside her on the thin mattress. "I'm leaving," I said.

LoraLee's head jolted forward. She rubbed at her eyes. "Kerry? That you?" Her voice was hoarse. She raised up on her elbows and watched me without speaking. After a moment I shook my head. "I've done things, things you don't know about, and I can't stand it here anymore."

She raised her eyebrows at me and I turned away. "Because I thought he was mine and I tried to keep him, but truth was, none of it was really mine at all." My voice broke. "And truth was, in the end it was all my fault, because I was the one who was stealing."

"Girl?" LoraLee sat up and pressed my hands between hers.

The warmth of her fingers made my eyes fill. "So I'm leaving."

She watched me carefully, then shook her head. "Who gonna take care of you?"

"I'll take care of myself, I can do it now. I don't know where I'm going but maybe Boston to start, and then I'll find a great job and a great place to live, and I'll forget about all of this."

"Forget?" She brought one of my hands to her pouchy cheek and held it there. "You leave now you won't forget, 'cos there still too much battlin' inside you. You leave and that's okay 'cos mebbe the feelin' here is too hard to face now, but 'fore long you come back 'cos you has to. You 'member that when the time come. You 'member why you's feelin' empty and strange and then you come back when you's ready to move on."

I sat for a long while, watching her, one hand still on her cheek, the other cradled in her palm. Finally I buried my head against her chest and let her hold me. We rocked. We rocked until there was nothing else.

SIX

Canopies on the Soul

June

2007

34

IT WAS AN HOUR after our mother had left, and Eve and I sat with LoraLee on Eve's bed. LoraLee handed back the letters I'd given her, and I shook my head. "Why?" I whispered. "How?"

"She come to me," LoraLee said. "When your daddy die she come to the island. She come to be certain in her own mind that you's cared for, and she see'd me with you, see'd how I's there for you and she say to me, you don't owe me nothin', don't know me from Adam, but I's gonna axe you the biggest favor I ever axed of anybody. She say every year I been gettin' a letter that show me I done right by leavin'. Now he gone and I don't get them letter no more."

"So she was using you to ease her conscience," I said.

LoraLee watched me with narrowed eyes. "You got that wrong, chile. She feel pain in her heart every day for what she done. She say to me, she say these chilluns is the only thing I done what is good in this worl' and I couldn't even do right by them."

"She didn't even try!"

"She try the bes' she knowed how, Kerry. What matter is you sees how your momma kep' on lovin', and how your daddy kep' on lovin' your momma even when she don't show him nothin' to deserve that love. And someday, chile, I think you see how you kep' on lovin' your momma too. That don't never stop."

"After what she's done—"

"Affer what she done, my foot. I tell you a lesson, Kerry, most important lesson life learn me. Onest you loves a person, that don't jus' die." She stared at me pointedly. Her voice was soft and deep. "Everyone you ever love, anyone who ever love you, lay a light like a canopy on your soul. Your soul, it fashion up of those canopy, one on another, and you can turn yourself away, you mebbe covers them with time or anger. You can close your eye to it, but when you opens them the light still there. The light still there and still you shine. That there's how it works to be a human. The love become a part of you."

Eve picked a piece of lint off her sheet, smiled at it. I watched her for a minute, then narrowed my eyes. "How could you not tell us, LoraLee? All those times I'd talk to you about my mother and you'd sigh and shake your head like you felt sorry."

"I did feel sorry. It mebbe soun' bad, but there ain't no good answer here. Jus' to wait and hope she grow enough to face you by the time you's old enough to unnerstan'. Till then it's better to think she be there if she could. Better to think she don't know where you is."

"She's right, you know." Eve reached for her water, drank it in three echoing gulps, then lay back down. "She knew Daddy was dead and still she couldn't bring herself to take us back in her life. If we'd realized it, we would've felt so worthless."

"We did feel worthless."

Eve watched me without speaking. After a minute LoraLee stood. "I leaves you two be."

"You can't leave, not until you explain it. Why would she come here now? What does she expect from us?"

"She don't 'spect nothin', chile. Sure, she want forgiveness, but that's your choice." LoraLee started toward the hallway, then stopped suddenly and turned back. "I wisht I coulda did more for you, coulda tole you sooner how you's in her mind. But what I can tell you again is she done the bes' she could by you, the bes' that she knowed how. You 'members the money come to your door? That money come from your momma."

"No," I said. "You gave us money, the brown envelopes. We saw you put them on the doormat."

LoraLee raised her eyebrows. "From your momma. She studyin' then, schoolin' to make herself a better life and she didn't have much to spare, but what she have, she send for you." LoraLee smiled and walked to the hallway. "The bes' that she knowed how, you 'member that. That's all anyone can do."

We watched after her. "You're okay, right?" Eve said finally.

"This is worse," I whispered. "Knowing she thought her only obligation was money, that's worse."

"I don't think that's it. She saved our teeth, Kerry."

I stared at her and she shook her head. "I mean, yeah, I still hate her for leaving, but this does help me understand her better." She shifted to face me. "I saw her eyes, Kerry. I thought they'd be the empty eyes you see on druggies, on serial killers, but they weren't at all." She smiled crookedly. "They were my eyes."

Eve was right, now when I pictured our mother's

eyes they were Eve's eyes, strong even against the glare of what she'd never have. Even her tears had seemed resolute. "I wanted her to look sorrier," I said, "like she understood what she'd done."

"She understands, I think, but she doesn't take responsibility. And I guess I don't need her to anymore. Guilt doesn't change anything, that's what Justin always says." She shrugged. "Anyway, it doesn't hurt me anymore. All of this, what she did or didn't do, I'm coming to terms. Months back, this probably would've made me so angry I could explode. But now..." She stared into her empty water glass, then set it back on her nightstand. "Now I'm starting to realize people do what they need to do. No one means to hurt you, they just don't know any better. They're just trying to help themselves."

I brushed at the water that had dribbled onto her collar, then lay beside her.

"I've been thinking about it," she said. "How we're twins, so biologically, genetically, we're the same. And when we were born we both had this same potential to do good, be honest and upright, all that crap. That's how I should've turned out, what I wanted. But somewhere down the line, without consciously making a decision, we came out different."

She glanced at me, then shook her head against the pillow. "So I was looking for a reason and what I think is maybe I felt guiltier. Mom left and from the beginning I thought it was my fault." Her voice shook and she cleared her throat. "That somehow she felt this... *heat* I had inside me, this wanting, I wanted everything."

"That's crazy, Eve," I said.

"I'm just telling you how I thought. What happened

is it became a self-fulfilling prophecy. You focus on the bad parts of you, the bad thoughts, and they grow." She reached for the button that would deliver her medicine. At the muted beep she exhaled a rattling sigh. "If you think of yourself as a bad person, you do what you can to confirm your inner expectations. It's okay to lie, to steal, to steal your sister's boyfriend away with lies because you can't help it. That's who you are."

I curled my legs up to my chest. Eve's eyes were glazed. "Mom left because she couldn't make herself stay. Daddy died because he was stupid, because he was sad, and there's nothing we could've done. Neither of them was happy about leaving us, and the things you did to me, the things I did to you, we never wanted to hurt each other, not really."

The tears stung behind my eyes. I blinked quickly and nodded.

"You know I asked Justin to help me die the other day."

I pulled her hand to my chest, rubbed a finger against her nail. "I know," I said. "He told me."

"And now I'm going to ask you."

My hand froze. "Eve—"

"I feel like I've reached this resolution inside myself now, like I'm ready to go. And I want to give you whatever it takes to reach that same resolution so you can help me. It'd have nothing to do with—"

"Stop!" I brushed her hand away.

"It's okay. Just take your time and think about it is all, how it could be about love, not anger."

I stared at the window. Since I'd gotten here, I still

hadn't ever told Eve that I loved her, like I'd forgotten how to say the words.

"And I need something else from you."

I shook my head.

"See, I need you to be there for Gillian. Be here."

I didn't understand, but then with a shock, I realized what she was saying. "I can't," I said.

"Yes you can." She lifted her head, then let it drop back onto the pillow. "You will because she needs you, she needs a mother just as much as we did, maybe more because she's never been without one. I couldn't forgive myself for leaving her just like we were left."

"This is so different, Eve."

"Is it? Not in the mind of a twelve-year-old girl it's not." She smiled a strange, flat smile. "And listen to me, Kerry, because also I need you to be there for Justin."

"No," I said quickly. The word felt like a gulp.

"Thing is, Justin was yours first. And hell, I'm not blind, Kerry, I know what's going on around me." She made a strange crow-like sound, somewhere between a caw of laughter and a choke. "Now he's yours again."

I jumped to my feet, an impulse, then slowly sank back to the bed. When I knew I could speak without my voice shaking, I turned to face her. "Tell me the truth, Eve. *Was* he mine first? Was he ever really?"

She turned her head away from me, then brought the back of her hand to her mouth and whispered, "I don't know."

I stared at her.

"I mean, yes, of course he loved you. Back when his stories were the most important thing to him, you guys shared that in a way we never did, which to him probably felt like you were sharing his soul. But the thing is, he was also drawn to me for those kinds of indefinable things that attract a person to someone else. He always loved you, maybe he was even happier with you, but he felt passion for me."

At the word *passion* I felt a sudden searing rage, more anger than I'd felt since I'd returned, maybe more than I'd felt for thirteen years. I dug my knuckles into the mattress and said, "And you fed on that, didn't you? You could've had any man you wanted, but you had to prove to yourself that you could seduce the one man who was supposed to be off-limits."

Eve turned back to me, looking vaguely stunned. "I didn't seduce him! Okay sure, maybe I was teasing him a little, but I flirted with everybody, you know that. Even though I couldn't control anything else in my life, I knew I could control men. But not Justin. Even if part of me was jealous, I wouldn't ever have intentionally taken him away. He knew I was a flirt too, Kerry. It wasn't like I was irresistible. Not if he was really trying to resist me."

"So what happened that last night?" I said hoarsely. "The night I left?"

She lay there, her body slack, then gave a sharp nod. "Okay." She glanced up at me. "Okay, I'll tell you. Here's the thing. I don't know if he loved me. But he thought he did. Or at least he told me he thought he did." She pulled the covers to her chin and closed her eyes. I could smell her breath, fruity and stale. "The night we wrote the letters, I was trying to prove something to you. He'd come to me, I was pretty sure he would, and when it was over you'd see how this was Justin's fault even more than mine."

"I couldn't believe you'd do that to me," I said hoarsely. "Do you understand how it was? With everything that was going on, when I needed both of you and neither of you was there."

"I know." She picked at the plasticine she now used to hold her wedding ring on her scrawny finger, then looked up at me, her eyes swimming with tears. "That's all I've thought about all this time, how it must've been for you. And the night Ryan died, I swear I didn't go to Justin planning to sleep with him. I kept seeing Ryan's face, how he looked at Jill Stanton's party, his eager boy face, and I had to find some way to get it out of my head."

"You slept with Justin so you could stop thinking about Mr. Maclean's face? Why didn't you just use alcohol? Or, I don't know, hit yourself over the head."

"He kissed me first, I swear to you; what I told you back then was the truth. I went into his room just needing somebody safe to hold me, and he had me pressed back on the bed and I was the one who pulled away. So he ran to his office and I'm lying there on his bed and all these images are throwing themselves at me." She squeezed her eyes shut. "Ryan's face, his voice, I had to stop thinking. Fuck, Kerry, a man had just died because of me!"

"Because of you?" And suddenly I realized what she'd said. "You saw Mr. Maclean at Jill's party."

She stiffened. "No."

"Tell me." I grabbed her under the chin, forced her to look at me. "Tell me!"

Her eyes reddened. "Kerry..."

"What did you do?" And suddenly I could see it all, Eve slinking up to him in her green silk dress, her hooded eyes and slim, seductive smile as she whispers in his ear. Then nibbles it. "You came on to him."

"No I didn't. I didn't! I mean, not really. I just was so pissed off at everything, remembering how Mrs. Maclean hung off him that afternoon at graduation, her face when she looked at him. He was so used to being adored, and I guess what was in my head, I wanted him to know I never adored him like that, to think I was using him the whole time even more than he was using me. So at the party I blackmailed him."

"You *what?*"

"It just got mixed up in my head, seeing the kids graduating, knowing how his sons would probably end up going to Brown or Harvard while we'd be stuck making six dollars an hour serving fried fish. So I told him I wanted twenty thousand dollars. I told him I'd call the papers." She laughed sharply and said, "I'd prove it by telling them about the mole on his ass. He had a mole shaped like North Carolina."

It was incredible, really, unbelievable. Eve had been seventeen, a child with a force invisible on the surface like a riptide, the guts to take down one of the most powerful men in the state. "How come you never told me this?"

"About the mole? I thought it was kind of private. A mole on the ass isn't the most attractive thing."

"You're not funny," I said.

"You wouldn't have understood, Kerry. You would've blamed me for everything, and I couldn't take that."

This, of course, was true. Even without knowing what she'd done I'd blamed her. I raised my chin. "So. What did he say?"

"I remember all of it, you know? Every single word. It's like that whole night's been branded on me. I keep it in this separate compartment of my brain, but it's all still there." She shook her head, as if in amazement. "So I threatened him and first he goes, 'You wouldn't dare,' and I said, 'You really want to test me on that?' So he pulls me into a back bedroom and he says, 'I know you don't want to hurt me because you love me.' And then he kisses me, and first I'm pushing him away. But then I don't know what happened. I guess I thought about you out with Justin and there I was all dressed up and all alone, so pathetic, and somehow I found myself kissing him back."

I watched her, unblinking.

"Just for a minute, I mean it stopped almost right after it started, but then he says, 'I have to be with you tonight,' how his wife doesn't touch him anymore, the kind of bullcrap he'd been giving me from the beginning. And I say, 'If you want to discuss the money, you can come by the house. But otherwise I never want to see you again.'"

I tensed and slid away from her, to the end of the bed. "You invited him in."

"No. I mean I would've, I guess, if he'd been acting sane, but he was banging on the door, totally drunk, first shouting how he loves me, and then how horny he is. I mean shouting it, 'I'm gonna explode!' And I was so freaked out I ran upstairs and kept screaming at him to go away, which is when he broke in."

"And tried to rape you."

She looked up at the ceiling. "I kissed him at the party, which I don't know, maybe it made him think the whole thing was a tease, that I'd pretended to blackmail him just to get him back into my life. Hell, maybe he thought the rape was a game, too."

I suddenly remembered the night I'd seen Eve with Ryan on Daddy's boat, her hands tied with a silk scarf, her fake-sounding moans. I felt a twisting nausea, like an uncoiling snake.

"It's all I could think about for weeks after, how he'd literally deflated when I first told him I never wanted to see him again, like I was sucking the air out of him." She wiped at her eyes, then stared at the dampness on her hands. "And when I found out I was pregnant I just kept thinking, How am I going to be able to look at this baby without wanting to kill myself?"

I felt the blood drain from my face, a cold numbness. "You said the baby was Justin's."

She glanced at me, then shook her head. "How could I have known whose she was?"

"You said Ryan always wore a condom!"

"He sometimes wore a condom." She hugged her chest. "Sometimes not. So when I found out I was pregnant I just assumed based on probability, one time with Justin versus umpteen times with Ryan."

"But you told me!"

"What else could I do? Part of me thought if I kept telling you the baby was his I could make it be true."

I slammed my fist on the bed. "The whole thing was a lie!"

"But it turned out not to be, right? I mean look at Gillian, she has his hair, his smile, his big front teeth. She's his daughter."

"You know that's not what matters." I shook my head

blindly. "You knew this would make him more yours than mine. You knew I loved him and you didn't even give a damn!"

"I wasn't thinking about you! If I let myself accept that the baby could be Ryan's, how could I live with the fact that I'd just killed him? I was alone too, and I was grasping for whatever I could." She swiped at her face. "But the night I told you I was pregnant, you know what I really thought? I thought you'd maybe yell at me, but then you'd understand how much the whole thing hurt and how messed up I was inside. And we'd cry together. We'd both feel so awful for what I was going through that it'd bring us back together."

I let out a grating laugh, a sound like a revved motor.

"And we'd figure out what to do together," she said. "I *needed* you to help me figure it out."

"That's so like you." My voice was cold. "You know if I was you it would've been completely the other way around. I would've said the baby was Ryan's, would've *hoped* it was his so I wouldn't have to live with this constant reminder that I'd ruined your life."

Eve's forehead creased, almost pleading. "So you're better than me, we've established that."

"How can you be sarcastic about this? You said you understood how it was for me, but you don't have any idea. I was destroyed! You didn't just take Justin away, you took away everything I believed in. You took my world away!"

"I know."

"You don't know!" I jumped up and raised my arm, muscles tensed to hit her, and then she made a weak choking sound and her face went pink. I dropped my arm and watched her, suddenly terrified she wouldn't be able to find her breath. And there she was, struggling for air, so thin her bones would rattle like dried spaghetti if I punched her. My rage disappeared with a jerk, like somebody had pulled it from me. She'd needed me and I hadn't been there, the thing you should always be able to count on regardless of circumstances, that the person who's been with you since the hour of your conception won't desert you when you're most in pain.

"Damn you," I said, but she was dying, she was dying and she'd suffered for this too. She was dying and this was one thing I could give her, the thing she needed most. I sat back on the bed and angled her head with the pillow to help her breathe, rubbed softly, helplessly, at the soft fringes on her scalp.

"I'm so sorry, Kerry," she whispered.

I watched her for a minute, then buried my head against her chest. "Me too," I said. "Me too, I'm sorry too."

"I thought we'd both leave him. I swear that's what I thought the night we wrote the letters, that you'd see how he was choosing me but I was choosing you. This dumb-ass romantic image, you and me walking off into the sunset and leaving him behind, not thinking how it'd look to you, how you'd feel. But then when you left..."

I clutched at her nightgown, spoke against her chest, half feeling what I was saying, half of me numb. "It's true, you know. Nothing's strong enough."

She set her hand lightly on my hair. After a minute she grasped it, as if willing me to stay in place. "And then what I thought," she said, "I thought you'd go away for a week and feel awful. And then you'd come back and we'd make up, like every fight we ever had. But you didn't come back, and I was pregnant and the truth is..." She pulled her hand away. "The truth is I loved him, Kerry. While you were here I could fight against it but deep down I was in love with him. I grew up with him too, he was my hero too. All our lives I had the same dreams of him you had."

"I know." I lifted my head, looked into her face. Her eyes seemed brighter even through the tears, brighter than I'd seen them since I'd come back. "And it's okay," I said. "All of it's okay now."

She pressed the heel of her hand against a tear on her upper lip. "Do you hate me?" she whispered.

"No. No, God, of course not." And there was more I needed to say. I wanted to tell her I loved her, words that had once come so easily. But what I felt was more than that; I felt the pointlessness of it all, how decisions made years ago when we were too young to make decisions had taken away everything that should have been ours. All this time I'd been blaming her and punishing myself, all because of a fight between children that should've been dusted off years ago and looked at for what it was.

"I never did," I said. But Eve didn't respond. Her hands were slack over the blanket; she scarcely seemed to be breathing. I put my hand on her chest for reassurance. "I do love you," I whispered. And I'd like to think she heard the words, but maybe the only thing that mattered was that I'd said them.

35

I SAT at the kitchen table and opened the catalogue I'd ordered just for fun. Overhead the fluorescent light flickered bright and dim, bright and dim. I scanned the pages feeling overwhelmed: Art History, Nineteenth-Century Lit, Music Appreciation—The Baroque Era. I knew even with a GED I'd have no chance of getting in. But God, wouldn't it be amazing? Wouldn't it be incredible to understand things I'd never even known existed, to understand, really understand, what it was that made things beautiful?

Justin strode in with a pad of paper, a huge smile on his face. "UMass?" he said.

I shrugged. "Just looking, just for the hell of it."

"You'd be the first grad in your family. Your name would go down in the Barnard book of history." He grinned and waved his pen at me. "So speaking of books, take a look. First good thing I've written in months. I was looking out the window and I just felt this tremendous urge to write, and it came out of me like magic, like it's been waiting there all along."

"They call that your muse, right? Your muse took a break but now it's come back. That's great, Justin."

He glanced at me. "It's a love story."

I looked up at the flickering light. "Oh?"

"Or not a love story per se, more a story of settling into destiny, my king and queen growing old together."

Canardia, I thought blankly, *named for his wife, Eve Barnard-Caine.*

"See, I was blaming you for my writer's block, but now I know it wasn't you at all. It really started after the chemo stopped, when the morphine wasn't enough and she was hurting so bad. And part of me was thinking maybe it would be for the best. And another little part of me was thinking maybe it would be best for me too, it was all so hard, and when she asked me to help her..." He stared at his pen, then threw it on the table, lowered himself into a chair. "It was eating at me and eating at me so there was nothing left."

"I know."

"But what I see now, what's helped me is realizing that I can't help her die. Of course I can't, I should've realized it so much sooner. And now it's such a relief to stop struggling with myself, to let destiny decide how she'll go."

I lifted his pen, reading the print on its side as if that could tell me something. All it told me was that he was no longer using the pen I'd given him.

"I got this card today from Gillian, Father's Day."

I smiled flatly. "Happy Father's Day."

"It is, you know, I'm happy today. You know what she wrote? The only thing inside, she said thanks for taking care of Mom." He smiled. "For taking care of Mom, and what I was thinking was what if I gave Eve what she wanted, even if it was out of love, and God forbid somehow Gillie found out what I'd done? She'd never forgive me."

I took his hand. "You shouldn't have been put in that position. It's an impossible decision."

"And it's more than that. Maybe there was a time when I was so angry at having my life taken away, at being controlled like she controlled me, that I thought no way will this ever feel right. But now this is my life, it feels like home, and I need Eve here for as long as I can have her."

"Having your life taken away?"

He watched me for a minute, his hand gripping mine, tight enough to hurt. "It should've been us, you know that."

I felt the bite of something dark and acidic in my stomach. I dropped his hand.

"I've accepted what happened, and I love Eve so much, I do. But this wasn't how I thought things would turn out."

"You went to her first, Justin."

He stared at me blankly, then went on as if he hadn't heard. "I know it's wrong of me to blame her, especially now. But she was so needy, and she must've known what that would do to me. I was nineteen and she was so vulnerable and scared about what had happened to her life." He stared at his notepad, then threw it on the table upside down. "I was trying to comfort her, to protect her and she took advantage. I don't blame her for it, but I'm trying to make you understand what it did to me, having her all over me at a time when we were all so confused. I didn't know what I needed, but I needed something. And she was there."

"You went to her first," I said again. "Even before the night Ryan died. Stop lying to yourself, Justin. It wasn't anything she did, it was you."

He stood suddenly and walked to the window. When he turned back his face was pale, flickering with the light, dim, bright, dim, bright. "It doesn't matter now anyway. What happened back then doesn't matter because now I need her. I love her so goddamned much."

I stared at the table, the words racing through me, faster, faster until I couldn't hold them back. "How could you, Justin?" I said. "Why didn't you just tell me the truth?"

Suddenly, without warning, Justin leaned forward and pressed his lips to mine.

I startled back and he reached for my arm. "Kerry—"

"What are you doing? You love Eve, you need her, and now you grab at me?"

Justin's face seemed to sink inward. "I don't know."

"You just want some kind of reward for telling yourself that you love your wife, figuring out you love her enough to watch her suffer for God knows how long? That's really honorable, Justin, you're a saint."

"I don't know! The whole thing, all of it's been such a mistake, I'm just trying to make the best of something so screwed up."

I remembered suddenly Eve's long-ago words. Justin had wanted me so he could kiss me and imagine he was kissing her. Eve was dying, and now he wanted me again. My hands were shaking. I squeezed them into fists and stood. "The best for who?" I said.

He watched me without speaking. His Adam's apple bobbed as he swallowed, bobbed again.

"I loved you," I said. "Maybe I'll always love you, but I'm not sixteen anymore. I know enough not to pretend things should be different from what they are." I held his eyes for a minute, then walked away.

In my room I pulled the envelope from under my bed, the letters that had sent me away. I turned them face up, began to work them against the line I'd already pieced together. I didn't feel the time sliding past, barely noticed the outside sounds of wind and tree branches or the arc of sunlight coasting from one window to another and then slipping behind the trees.

When I'd finally finished, I stared at Eve's letter.

Justin,

What I told you last night, it was a lie, you knew that didn't you? I'm just sick of playing around and second guessing. So this is the last game. I'm pregnant, Justin. With your child. And I'm going to keep it, whatever happens with us. There's a hole in me, and my whole life probably since Mom left was built around it. I used to think maybe you could fill that hole, but it turns out I didn't need you. I'm full up now for the first time. I'm in my Dad's room if you want to talk it out.

Love, Eve

I fingered the scraps, now soft with age. He'd read my letter first, the letter of a child, and then he read Eve's and chose adulthood. And who could blame him? Either of them.

I took the scraps into the bathroom, lifted the toilet

lid. They flushed in a lazy spiral and disappeared without a trace. She'd told him about her pregnancy. She'd told him, but she'd had every right to. Me, Eve, Justin, Gillian, not a love triangle but a love square. And wherever that square had started, it didn't matter now. All that mattered was that after Eve was gone we'd hold her space.

And so I couldn't stay.

Justin had chosen Eve and it wasn't my space to take.

36

YOU MEAN YOU *EAT* FLIES?" Gillian asked the eight-armed, black-leotarded girl.

"Certainly," the girl said. "Flies, bugs, grasshoppers, choice beetles, moths, butterflies, tasty cockroaches, gnats, midgets, daddy long legs, centipedes, mosquitoes, crickets. Anything careless enough to get caught in my web."

We watched, Justin to my left, Eve on his other side laughing wholeheartedly at everything, even lines the rest of the audience found only worthy of a chuckle. She'd taken off her catheter for the performance, but even though her face had reddened as Justin ushered her from her wheelchair across the row of seats, now I couldn't see even a trace of the pain she must be feeling.

Onstage, Gillian was glowing. An hour ago she'd grimaced at her pink self in the mirror. "I look like a hot dog."

"That's because I didn't draw in the whiskers yet," I'd said, and added a spray of black lines against the pink circles on her cheeks.

When I was done we'd stared at her reflection. "Do pigs even have whiskers?" Gillian said.

"I guess they don't."

"Do we have time to wash them off?"

Across the classroom, a teacher had clapped. "I need Fern, Avery, the Arables and all the pigs."

"Guess not," I said.

And Gillian had made a face at me. "I have never been so humiliated in all my life."

But once she'd reached the stage, her whole demeanor had changed. She was Wilbur the pig, modest, ingenuous, alive.

"Look," Eve whispered to Justin. "She has boobs."

It was true; in her pink leotard you could see Gillian's new breasts, the size of golf balls. I started to chuckle, but then saw Eve and Justin turn to grin at each other, with the pride parents might have discovering their child's first tooth.

I smiled widely so I wouldn't cry, not exactly sure what it was that made my eyes sting: the little kids so serious in their animal outfits, Gillian's new breasts, her happiness, the three of us. All of it together. Like Eve, I had the simultaneous urge both to laugh and to cry at every line; it felt beautiful, but also, somehow, like an ending.

At intermission we sat a minute without moving, staring at the drawn curtain. "Wow," Justin said finally.

"They're amazing," Eve said. "All the kids, they're so *here,* of this earth, you know?"

"They don't even know when they're funny," I said. "That's what makes it all so hysterical, they say their lines like what they have to say is the most solemn, important thing on earth."

Eve smiled softly. "It is the most important thing. I

wish I'd seen this a month ago, a year ago. Seen how life goes on."

"Year after year," Justin said, "it's all the same. You remember our school plays? In sixth grade I played Mark Antony in *Julius Caesar*. It was the crowning achievement of my life, probably still is."

"Were we like that?" Eve said. "I don't remember ever feeling like that even back then, like your existence matters, like the world cares what you do with your life."

"I was sure it did," Justin said. "I think I kind of still believe it." He gave a short, scoffing laugh. "God, that sounds conceited."

"Not conceited, it's the truth," I said. "But I guess I never felt like that either. Maybe it had to do with being a twin, feeling replaceable."

Eve glanced at me quickly, then back at the stage. "You weren't ever replaceable."

I smiled at her. "Neither were you," I said.

As soon as the curtains opened on Act 2, I was a goner. I let myself go, keeping a finger near my eyes to catch the tears before they fell, until I noticed Eve, her eyes distant, her cheeks wet. I kept my eyes on her face as Charlotte the spider prepared to die, knowing her tears, like mine, were more about life than about the dying.

"Why'd you do all this for me?" Gillian asked. "I don't deserve it. I've never done anything for you."

"You've been my friend," the spider girl said. "That in itself is a tremendous thing. I wove my webs for you because I liked you. After all, what's a life, anyway? We're born, we live a little while, we die. By helping you, I was maybe trying to lift up my life a trifle. Anyone's life can stand a little of that."

Justin took Eve's hand. After a minute, he took mine, too. We sat there watching the little girls who would be women, who weren't yet ready but were maybe more ready than we thought. "She looks like you," Justin whispered. And Eve and I turned to smile at him through our blurred eyes, as if he was talking to us both.

Eve had been struggling to breathe, her jaw stretched with effort, a blue tint beneath her nails. I knew everything now. I also understood that I'd never know for sure if Justin had ever really been mine, or even if he'd ever been completely hers. But I also realized that none of it mattered. All that mattered was that she would find the strength to pull in one more breath, that the pause after this next rasp would be no more than a pause, that we'd have the time to say everything that needed to be said.

Eve had hurt me, taken away my life, but she hadn't known enough about life to understand what she was doing. So it had happened, so there were lies. But there was also no going back.

I propped Eve on pillows but the angle hurt her neck, and so I tilted the head of the bed slightly and rubbed my palm over her chest, talking in what I hoped was a soothing tone about the murky summer heat, a heron migration and bumper boats in the harbor. Inside, though, my heart was ricocheting off my ribs, my own breath laboring as if to mirror hers.

I knew she wasn't listening, and after a while was sure she must've fallen asleep, but when I stood to cover her, she grabbed my wrist with more strength than I'd known she still had. "Please," she whispered.

I looked down at her scrawny fingers, the tiny sores that had started this week all up and down her arms. I knew what she wanted, of course. She'd been asking again and again, each time with more fervor. The problem was she knew that even though it all might be over in hours, it might take weeks or even months; months like this or worse. She might fall into a coma, might lose kidneys and liver and stomach but still live. It was horrific to think about, but even more horrific to imagine helping her die.

I kissed her fingers, then pried them from my wrist. "You should sleep."

"Fuck it," she said. "You think—" She couldn't finish, fought for breath.

I rubbed again helplessly at her chest. "I know" was all I could say. She swiped my hand away, her wrist loose, and I wanted to stay but I couldn't bear to just stand there. So I walked from the room, every muscle in my body knotted.

Justin was standing in the hall. He rocked heel to toe, heel to toe, a heartbreakingly childish posture. His eyes were red and I reached for his hand.

"You're good with her," he said. "Really you are, you know just what she needs and how to give it."

"She needs to die."

Justin ignored me. "Somehow you can get past it, let her say what she needs to say without showing how it hurts to watch her."

"She needs to die," I said again, then closed my eyes tight. "She needs—"

"I know." Justin slid his arm around me and I leaned

against him, buried my head against the soap-sweat smell of his shirt.

His other arm enfolded me, and my stomach churned with an aching homesickness, a loss and longing to do with Eve and Justin both. So when he cupped his hand at my chin, I tilted my face to him, let him kiss me, kissed him back, pulled his tongue to rasp warm and sweet against my tongue. My head was racing with senseless voices. I was shivering with them, unable to pull closer and unable to pull away. Until the voices swelled to anger, and with a sudden agonizing jolt I cried out and pushed him. I stumbled back, sucked air in and out through my mouth as if I could erase the taste of him.

He looked down at me. "Oh," he whispered.

I backed to the door, nearly fell.

"Kerry, I'm sorry, I just…I don't know. I don't know what I'm doing."

"Nothing. It's nothing."

"I don't want to hurt you, hurt anyone."

I shook my head, opened the door and stepped back onto the porch, feeling an almost physical tearing, like walking through taffy.

Justin followed me onto the porch and shut the door behind him. He stood there a moment watching my face before he spoke. "Okay." His voice was tight, his face flushed. "Okay, Kerry, you know it's out there between us. Ignore it or not, it'll always be there, and I've been trying to ignore it, but Jesus, it's driving me crazy. It's like I see you and you're everything I loved in Eve, and I realize that maybe the only things I loved in Eve were the things that reminded me of you."

"Don't!" I stumbled down the porch steps and raced down the drive, thinking, *No, no, God no*... I could hear his footsteps following, the crunch of gravel, so I ran to the shed that had been Justin's office. I ran inside and closed the door, leaning against it.

He banged his fist against the door, then thrust it open, propelling me back. His hand grasped the back of my head, his breath heavy as he pressed his mouth on mine, so hard my teeth bit against the inside of my lips. He slid his face to rest his cheek against my cheek. "It's right," he said hoarsely. "It's so right."

My legs were too weak to move. I shook my head, but even as I did he lifted me.

He lifted me and kicked the door shut and I didn't let myself think. Without seeing it happen, without knowing how it had come to be, I was on the dusty floor, Justin over me. And somehow there was suddenly no question in it, only need. All of it coming together, the dusty green of the shed walls, the shells and stones on the window ledges, this floor where I'd sat with him and entered the magic world in his mind, all slipping me back to a place I'd never left. The feel of him was so familiar, the red mole on his shoulder, his taste, smell, his lips on my lips, my neck, my breasts, the precise curve of his back, I knew it all so well. And somehow Eve was there, too, part of this joining, the Eve who'd joined us in tidal pools and fingerpaints, had listened to stories on rainy afternoons. This joining was not in spite of her but with her, a heavy aching sadness as I stroked him and finally, with a torturous bliss, guided him inside me. He moved against me slowly, rasped breath like Eve's labored rasp, like making love not as a person with a person but as wave on wave of warm water, melting and disappearing. Not feeling the floor against my back or the sweaty summer air, not skin or breath or heartbeat, only a shuddering that started in my chest and spread out through torso and arms and legs like life into something dead.

He stayed inside me for a long while after, running his fingers over my face like he was learning me again. I was sobbing, I couldn't help it. This had happened; it had happened, it was wonderful and it was wrong, and it was the last and only time.

Justin stroked back my hair, looking into my eyes. "You could stay," he said softly. "Eve wants you to stay."

"No she doesn't, Justin, not really. She just thinks it's the right thing to want."

"Maybe it *is* right."

I closed my eyes, absorbing the shiver of his hand against my cheek. "It's not," I said. "There's too much around it." Too much history, too much of Eve and something deeper, hidden, a fear that staying with Justin might make Eve's death a relief.

He didn't ask me to explain, only rolled off me. Finally he took my hand. "I know."

He stayed silent a minute and I laid my head on his chest, focused on the rise and fall of his breath and the softness of his skin against my cheek. Finally I spoke. "Then maybe we can do it, help Eve."

Justin stiffened.

"Because I guess what I was thinking, I kept thinking there was maybe something else I wanted from it. But now I know the only reason would be for Eve, to give her what she needs."

Justin pushed me away and lay back, staring at the ceiling. He shook his head against the floor.

"All this time she's been too strong to die before she was ready, before she'd said everything she needed to say. But now she's also too strong to live when she's ready to die. You know it's true."

He shook his head again, faintly.

"It's the only selfless thing we can do for her. Forcing her to live like this, it's like a punishment. She doesn't deserve that, Justin."

"Kerry please..." He squeezed his eyes shut. "I won't. I can't, especially not now, not after this."

"Can't because of her or because of yourself?"

He turned to look at me, then stood and pulled on his jeans. "You won't, Kerry. It's my decision to make."

"Technically, Justin, it's Eve's decision."

"That's bullshit. She's not thinking straight, and obviously neither are you."

"So you're going to put on blinders just because it's the easiest thing, and then when she dies they'll write you up in the *Times* as the long-suffering husband."

"Better than being written up as a murderer."

I shook my head blankly. "Is that what you think this is?"

Justin grabbed his shirt and glared down at me. "She's my wife," he said. "Don't you dare touch my wife." And then he kicked at my heaped clothes and spun away.

I pulled my sweater over my naked body and listened to the door slam shut. I should go to Eve and tell her the pain was over, it was time. I should go and absorb as much of her as I possibly could. But right now my legs were wet with Justin's sex, and I couldn't put the two things together. They weren't related. Weren't except in this one way. That Justin would never forgive me for what I was about to do and so, in the end, this would be my way of choosing Eve.

37

GILLIAN WAS CURLED against Eve's chest. I stood outside the den, a carton of ice cream in one hand, in my pocket a bottle of pills.

"You know what Mr. Allen told me?" Gillian said. "I went to him because I thought maybe you wouldn't feel strong enough to go to graduation, so he said he'd set up speakers and call you on the phone so you could hear it. I mean, if you can go for real that would be better, but if you can't at least you'll be able to hear."

I saw a muscle twitch in Eve's face. "That's really nice of him," she said. "I can't believe you're graduating sixth grade. How'd that happen so fast?"

"And Daddy can bring the movie camera. 'Member when you were in the hospital and he was filming the school chorus? And he forgot to take the lens cap off the camera and everything was black?"

Eve's strangled laugh sounded more like a bray. She gasped for breath and Gillian patted her chest. "And then all of a sudden you hear him whisper *Shit* and suddenly there we are. Maybe it would be better to do a webcam thing instead; Jason has one he uses to talk to his dad in Colorado, and that way if anything happens and you can't see everything, you could call Daddy's cell and tell him."

Eve squeezed her eyes shut. "You are so smart," she said.

"I'll ask Jason." She clapped her hands. "I'll call him now, okay? I'm sure he'll let us." She got up from the bed.

"Gillian, honey, hold on a minute. 'Cause I'm real tired now, and there's something I have to say to you before I go to sleep."

Immediately, Gillian stopped talking. Her breath was nearly as heavy as Eve's.

"Actually there's lots I want to say, but mostly that I'm sorry I've been such a lousy mom lately."

"It's okay, Mom, you're not lousy."

"Well, thanks for saying so anyway. But I want to make sure you know that through all of it I've loved you so much, more than anything. And I'm so proud of who you are. Sometimes I can hardly believe you came out of me."

Gillian sniffled and curled back on the bed, started fiddling with one of Eve's buttons. "I know that."

"Don't be embarrassed. I'm honestly proud of everything about you. There's so many times that you've just blown me away. Like back when you were five or six and you stepped on this anthill by mistake, and you were so upset about wrecking their home you built the hill back up again. And then you scattered bread crumbs around it every day for two weeks because you were scared you'd wrecked their kitchen."

Gillian made a face. "Now I'm embarrassed."

"Okay, maybe that was a bad example. But there's so many things I remember that make me feel proud." Eve brushed Gillian's hair off her face, then held her hands at Gillian's temples, spoke slowly. "So tell me something. When you grow up, when you're a big powerful lady in a big powerful job, what do you think you'll remember most about being a kid? Like say if your husband and your kids ask about your mom and how it was growing up with me, what do you think you'd say?"

Gillian didn't speak for a long while, still fiddling with Eve's button. Finally she said, "Remember last winter when you and me saw *Harry Potter*? And you found this tangle in my hair so you started combing at it, and then the movie was over and we kept sitting there and you kept combing even after everybody left. We were there for like an hour sitting without saying anything. I wish we could go back to that."

"Yeah," Eve whispered, and then she shook her head. "Your hair was a mess. You could've been hiding something important in there, and nobody would've known." She buried her hands under the covers and looked up at the ceiling. "*That's* what you remember most?"

"Also I remember that day a couple years ago when we were on the beach watching those spiral things, what's that called?"

"Sea smoke; sure, I remember that. It was freezing cold, and we started throwing rocks in to see if we could get a ringer. Anybody who saw us would've thought we were crazy."

Gillian shrugged. "Sure, but it was fun. And you said how those are spirits who watch over the island. And then you pointed and you said, 'See that biggest spiral there, that's your grandpa and he's been watching you and making sure you're safe, and cheering when you ace your spelling tests.'" She was quiet a moment, then lifted her head to look into Eve's face. "Do you really think that, or were you just saying?"

"I really think it, Gillian. I mean, I know it." She smiled weakly and said, "That's a good memory."

"There's lots of stuff I remember."

"Well, good," Eve said softly. "That's good." She cradled Gillian's head in both her hands and looked intently into her face. They stayed there for a long while watching each other, as if holding a silent conversation, and then finally Eve smiled and whispered, "Okay, then. Sweetheart, could you get your aunt Kerry for me please?"

"'Kay." Gillian jumped up. She startled when she saw me. "Mom probably can't eat that," she said, nodding at the ice cream.

"Actually she asked for it," I said. She'd called it her last wish.

Gillian grinned. "She's feeling better today."

"That's true, she's feeling better today." I bent to kiss the silky top of Gillian's head.

Gillian smiled up at me, then walked away, her gait springy. Eve followed with her eyes even after Gillian disappeared behind me, then turned her gaze to the ice cream. "Okay," she said. "It soft yet?"

"Probably," I said, then shook my head. "Not yet, okay?"

"Okay, we'll wait." Again this morning Eve had spent an hour writhing in impossible agony, laboring to pull breath through her failing lungs. But since I'd spoken to her, her breath had become even and calm, like her body knew there was no reason left to fight. "I can't believe I forgot her graduation," she said softly. "Or I guess I knew next week's her last week in sixth grade, but I didn't think she'd consider it such a big deal."

I cupped the ice cream container, watching her.

"Don't give me that look, Kerry. Please. I want to wait; hell I want to wait another year, but nothing's going to change, except that maybe you'll have second thoughts or I'll have second thoughts and then where'll we be? Would it really make it any easier for her?"

I nodded slowly. "No. I know."

"Make sure she goes, okay? To her graduation, make sure this doesn't stop her."

I nodded again, knowing she probably wouldn't go, that making her would be more of a cruelty than a diversion.

"And could you give her something from me? As a graduation gift? I wanted to give her my birthday bracelet, and Mom's locket."

"That'll be great, a great idea." I smiled. "And I'll tell her what they mean, that things continue."

"Yeah." Eve reached her hand towards me. I sat on the bed beside her. "So what happened, Ker? What made you change your mind about this?"

"I don't know. Lots of things. I guess because I remember how it feels when life is more of a punishment than death."

Eve watched me for a minute, then smoothed her palms over the sheets. "Look," she said, "I know how hard this all is for you. But you know it's the best thing you can do for me, the most absolutely selfless thing."

"Don't worry about me," I said hoarsely.

"But I do." Her voice trailed to a choke. She gasped

for breath, then closed her eyes and spoke in a hoarse whisper. "Of course I do. I know what's going through your head, Kerry, the things you're remembering."

The container was frosting under my fingers. I set it on the night table and pressed my hands between my knees.

"But the thing is, the thing you don't realize is even back then, after what I did, you wouldn't have been able to hurt me. I was thinking about it for a long while after you left, and the realization I had is you wouldn't have done it. When it came right down to it you wouldn't have been able to poison me."

"Eve, please. Please just stop."

"Look where you put that stuff, in my alcohol, right? I was pregnant, I was keeping the baby." She glanced at me and shrugged. "I stopped drinking."

I shook my head blankly.

"Maybe you didn't think it all through enough to realize what you were doing, but deep inside you knew exactly. Deep inside you knew I'd be safe."

She lifted her arms to me. When I didn't move, she pulled at my shoulders, pulled my head to her chest. "It's okay," she said. "It's over, and it has nothing to do with this."

I listened to the beat of her heart, her collarbone sharp against my cheek. I didn't feel my tears until they wet the cotton of her gown. I fiddled with her buttons as Gillian had done, and after a minute Eve stroked back my hair and began to plait it in a lopsided braid. "Stunning," she said when she was finished. "Had your hair done for the occasion?" She broke into grating laughter, harsh wheezing which made her start to choke.

I lifted her head and she angled it back, her neck facing the ceiling, her face reddish blue.

"You'll be okay," I said, my voice almost pleading.

Eve squeezed her eyes shut, struggling for air. "Okay but dead," she whispered.

"Eve—"

"I'll be okay and so will you." She lowered her head back to the pillow as her breathing slowed, then looked at me with glazed eyes. "It's funny, you know, because I thought…I don't know what I thought. I thought this would be different somehow, like it would feel different. This sounds dumb, but when I imagined it I pictured peace and warmth or this hand reaching out to guide me, some sense of destiny. I wanted it to feel like going home." Her voice trailed off and she smiled. "How stupid, right? But really I'm just so scared."

"Then we won't do this. Not today, okay? We can wait until you're ready."

"And then an hour from now I'd hate myself. I'm sick of hating myself." She gazed across the bed, her eyes distant. "The thing is, I thought I knew death. It's been standing around the corner for how long, but somehow it looks different when it's slapping you in the face. I should've realized that."

I took her hands. "Just tell me what to do."

"Well, first of all take that braid out of your hair. It'll be hard to swallow if I'm cracking up."

I sat a minute, not wanting to release her hands, then finally smiled. I pulled at the knots, wincing. "God, Eve, what did you do to it?"

"Remember how Daddy fixed our hair in the beginning, before he learned what he was doing? He gave us sailor knots instead of braids, so we spent hours untangling. It felt so damned lonely, realizing he didn't know how to take care of us."

I watched Eve carefully. "Listen," I said. "If there is a heaven? If there's some way to see people again, tell Daddy I love him."

"If he's up there, I'll give him hell for leaving. I've wanted to punch him out for years, so I can't wait to have the chance." She was quiet a minute, then nodded. "And then I'll tell him we love him and he did okay. With everything that was put on him to do, he did okay." She smiled crookedly and glanced at me. "It'd be amazing to see him, wouldn't it? I mean weird, but amazing."

"Totally," I said. "You think he still loves the Stooges? Or d'you think he's looking back and saying 'What was I thinking?' "

"I'd hope he still loves them. Can't imagine they'd let him play slapstick in heaven, though." She nodded at the ice cream. "It's turning into soup."

I reached for the carton, stirred at the brownish glop and somehow managed to laugh. "This is your last wish?"

"It was this or a Caribbean cruise, and I didn't think we'd get tickets on such short notice." She grinned, but when I didn't respond the grin faded. "So I guess I'm ready now."

How could she act so nonchalant? I shook my head. "I'm not."

She ignored me. "Take care of them, Kerry. I couldn't forgive myself if I thought they'd be alone with this."

"Okay," I said softly. "I'll do the best I can."

"You tell Justin I said good-bye, that I thought it was

better if he didn't know. Don't let him get so crazy that he can't take care of himself."

I nodded but I couldn't speak. This was all so very, horribly strange.

"Giving you lots of responsibilities, I know. Another thing, you have to keep telling Gillian about me, about how much I loved her. Don't let her forget."

"I won't, I promise."

"And if you ever talk to *her* again..." She smiled quickly. "To our mother, tell her I grew up to be a strong person. And tell her I had a husband who loved me and how I was a good mother. If she asks about me, you could tell her all that."

I nodded slowly. Eve smoothed her hands over her blanket. "Even if she doesn't ask, you could tell her. Just so she knows. And that's it, except you." She glanced at me and smiled. "You know how I feel."

"I know," I whispered.

"All of that, it never changed anything."

"I know. I know, but could you just..."

She nodded. "End of conversation. I was thinking this morning about a song, do you remember it? About the hearse, how did it go? Did you ever think when a hearse went by—"

"Eve!"

"That you might be the next to die." She grinned. "I don't mean it in a morose way, I just remember how we used to love that song, sing it over and over. And I just realized where we got it. Mom used to sing it to us, you remember? She'd sit on our beds and crawl her nails like spiders up our backs. What a heck of a song for five-year-old kids."

I smiled. "The worms crawl in, the worms crawl out."

"The worms play pinochle on your snout! God, I love that. I hope I get worms playing pinochle."

I stared at her, feeling a muted shock. But when she broke into sudden laughter I found myself laughing, too, remembering the two of us on the bedroom floor, playing Chutes and Ladders and singing in unison *a big red bug with big red toes crawls in your ears and out your nose...*

Eve struggled to regain her breath as the laughter overcame me. She reached forward and I held her and laughed, even as she reached into my shirt pocket and my laughter became hysterical, shook my body and filled my eyes with tears.

"Sing me another one," Eve said suddenly. "The one Daddy sang us about the desert."

The laughter froze on my tongue as she inspected the pill bottle. When she finally opened it I turned away, trying to focus on another life, the nights after our mother left. For months after, we'd fall asleep in the same bed, curled against each other as Daddy sat over us and sang in a hoarse, deep bass.

Desert silver blue beneath the pale moonlight,
Coyote yappin' lazy on the hi-i-ill

We'd hold hands, my cheek nestled in her neck. Our breath would come and go in unison, a halo of toothpasty air. I heard the rattle of pills and sang louder.

Sleep-y winks of light along the far skyline
Time for millin' cattle to be sti-i-ill...

In my head I'd see Eve's dreams. I'd imagine us on Daddy's boat with our mother, all of us floating on Daddy's voice, all four of us together.

So-o now the lightnin's far away,

The coyote's nothin' scary, just singin' to his deea-rie.

I lay beside her with my head on her shoulder. Her arms moved against me but I couldn't tell what she was doing, not really, as she reached for the melted ice cream, gulped at it, one arm up and then the other. I stiffened and sang on.

Ya-ay ho, tomorr's another day,

So settle down ye cattle till the mo-or-ning.

One arm and then the other and then the clunk of empty carton and empty bottle on the nightstand. And I was full up with something pressing outward against my skin, pushing up the hair on my arms, pushing out against my stomach and my chest, hollow but full like air in a taut balloon.

Eve sucked in a raspy breath and squinted at me. "It wasn't all bad, Ker, was it? More good than bad, or at least the good stuff was more important."

"Definitely," I said softly. "Yeah."

"I never thanked you. For being here, I never said that, did I? Even in the beginning when I hated you for coming now when I thought it was too late, the deepest parts of me felt so much better with you here, knowing you remembered how it used to be."

"Me too," I said. "That's part of why I came."

She smiled. "Don't miss me, Kerry, okay?"

I took Eve's hand and pressed it against my cheek, held it there with my eyes closed. Her hand was cold and moist and I tried for a minute to push my life into it. We watched each other silently until her need overcame my resistance and she closed her eyes, pulled her hand away.

Her body lay still, her skin unlined and lustrous, her chest as girlish-flat as the child we'd been. Sometimes on those nights after Daddy left we'd giggle and lift our tops. We'd press my chest flat against hers and we'd work to synchronize our hearts, *pa-dum, pa-dum.* Is that yours or is that mine? The stretching of my beat to hers, the pulling of her beat to mine, one of our best, most secret tricks, the beats that slowed and pulsed as one.

Now I lifted my blouse and pressed my chest against her chest. I felt my heart, *pa-dum, pa-dum,* I listened for hers and pushed to shape it. Is that yours or is it mine? The beat unyielding and pushing on as long as it would go. No longer. Our beat, my dance to that beat which was different but the same.

Epilogue

IT WAS AN IMMACULATELY CLEAR DAY when we said good-bye. I could see the contours of the mainland in the distance. We brought the urn up north, to the long sandbar at the island's tip. The Block Island Sound met the Atlantic there, and the two often squabbled over territory. But it was ultimately all the same ocean. Ultimately neither of them won.

It was particularly calm, only a thin drag over the sandbar as I waded into the sea. I reached into the urn, then brought my closed fist to my mouth. I kissed it and then opened it and let the breeze blow the ashes against me, breathed them in. I let her drift to the water, watched the waves billow and curl and claim her until finally, she was gone.

It was two weeks later that I got the call. "Just a few questions," they said and so I went to answer their questions. Through it all I imagined Eve, her laughter at the seriousness of the detective's face. *Just get off it,* she'd say, and so I acted with the same disdain. It didn't hurt to lie, because I knew the truth. Eve died of cancer and strength of will, that's all. And in the end they were satisfied with this. With only circumstantial evidence, they'd have to be. Of course I didn't think till later to ask the obvious question: why had they analyzed the blood of a woman who for months had been only steps away from death?

I think he'd hoped that by implicating me, he could absolve himself of responsibility. Responsibility for making love to me, for needing Eve's sickness to be over, for being grateful that I'd ended it for him. He felt guilty for all of it but couldn't let himself look at any of it. Like years before he'd convinced himself that he actually had been tricked by Eve. Like he'd thought he could free himself by confessing to that betrayal, Justin needed to be the hero in all his stories.

But it doesn't matter now. I don't believe in heroes or villains, only in mistakes. I know the false seduction of escape, hiding from the mistakes in an attempt to make them go away. What he'll see soon is they don't go away. They're relentless and they search for you until you stare them in the eye and see they're really not that ugly after all.

That's what I told my mother when I called after the funeral, how I understood the realization she'd faced when Daddy died. That regret changes nothing. That the time comes when you need to face your decisions, the life you chose, to make amends and reach some peace with how you lived it. Forgiveness of yourself is like forgiveness of others, it takes distance and growth and time. And I know that's what we both need now, distance and time. But I'll come back for her, I know I will. I need to learn who she is.

Really I think I should be grateful in a way for what I've lost, for what I have now and who I am—more, in a way, than I might have been. I have a high school degree;

I can write that on job applications. And next year I'll study nursing, which has started to feel to me like a calling.

And I have Gillian now, that's the most important thing. I write to her almost every day, hoping to give her some feeling of constancy, let her know that I didn't want to leave. I wonder what Justin thinks when he sees the letters. I guess in a way I'm writing to him as well.

I try to write messages between the lines, things I think will help him, but I'm pretty sure he won't get what I'm trying to say. He's not ready. There's so much I want to tell him, but I still haven't found the right way to say it. Mostly what I want him to know is that he needs to face his monsters. To realize that they don't change the person he really is, only his image of himself. An image is hard to deal with. Like photographs, which always seem to have so many more dimensions than two, swept into impossible significance by the knowledge of what came after.

There's a picture I keep in my bottom drawer beneath an empty bottle of Kahlua and an empty bottle of morphine pills, all the things I don't want or need but can't bring myself to throw away because they are my past. In the picture two girls stand at the beach, their arms around each other's shoulders. I think now if I dared to look at the picture, I'd see things that aren't really there. I think I'd imagine I could read their souls, see one clinging to the past, the other fighting to move on. I think I'd try to read love in the placement of their arms, read hate in the fact that they face the camera and not each other. I'd imagine I could tell that one would live and one would die, that one would steal and one would try to retrieve what was never really hers.

But I know that the truth is these two girls really are the same. They're just girls standing at the beach with wind blowing at their backs, cheeks stretched dry from sun and salt, and bathing suits that itch with sand. The truth is that both girls have dreams of love and laughter and tomorrow, and both girls wish that long summer would never end. I think now maybe it didn't, maybe it only faded and returned and faded again, in the way summers do.

It's a different thing altogether to lose a person in life and in death. I see her all the time now in new expressions I've adopted, a sideways glance in the mirror when I pass. And I see her on clear nights when I look into the emptiness to find her. She comes to me, a twin aura, through miles and worlds and lifetimes to let me know it's okay. That's what she'd tell me if she could, and what I'd tell them all if they'd let me. You can face what you've done, can sort through your past and tuck the bad parts with the good parts into a bottom drawer. You can remember that they're hidden without ever having to take them out again, and in time the edges will blur and you'll be left with the truth.

Acknowledgments

I AM INFINITELY GRATEFUL to Kim Lionetti, for believing, and to Caitlin Alexander for her enthusiasm and careful, insightful comments.

Thanks to my dad, one of the most generous people I know, for your encouragement, the example you set every day on faithfulness and commitment, as well as the quote on perseverance that hangs over my desk. Also to my mother, who will never understand this acknowledgment, will never even understand that this book is mine, but who taught me most of what I know about love.

Thanks to the friends and family who shrieked with excitement when I told you this was happening. You were the ones who made this all feel real.

Finally, and of course most importantly, thanks to Jerry. Without you I wouldn't have been able to even start this, let alone finish it. My name may be on the cover but this is as much your book as mine, from the Thomas Rathburn quote to the Boston scene and the nights we spent debating and laughing and refining the plot. I may be a writer, but I'll never be able to find the words to express how much I love you.

D0497941

A CHRISTIAN UNDERSTANDING OF EXISTENCE

Joseph Lange, O.S.F.S.

A CHRISTIAN UNDERSTANDING OF EXISTENCE

THE NEWMAN PRESS • WESTMINSTER, MARYLAND
1965

Imprimi potest: Very Reverend John J. Conmy, O.S.F.S.
Provincial

Imprimatur: Most Reverend Michael W. Hyle, D.D.
Bishop of Wilmington
October 15, 1965

 Library of Congress Catalog Card Number: 65-24592. Printed in the United States of America.

CONTENTS

INTRODUCTION

IN THE MIDDLE OF THE RENAISSANCE IN EUROPE, FIFTY years after Luther nailed his ninety-five theses to the church door at Wittenberg, eleven years after the death of Calvin in Geneva, and only four years after the close of the Council of Trent, St. Francis de Sales was born. The year was 1567. The counter-reformation was already in full swing. The Church was recovering the vitality, the vigor, and, above all, the spirituality redolent of a former age of controversy and conflict. It was an era of great courage, great deeds and great men. St. Theresa and St. John spear-headed the Carmelite reform. A Franciscan reform produced the Capuchins. St. Vincent de Paul founded the Sisters of Charity and the Congregation of the Missions. The Society of Jesus was established, and with it came a flood of Jesuit Saints: Ignatius Loyola, Francis Xavier, Francis Borgia, Peter Canisius, Aloysius Gonzaga and Robert Bellarmine.

From this teeming current of spiritual fervor and innovation, St. Francis de Sales emerges as the man who contributed most toward what we may call the modern Catholic mentality. Thomas P. Neill describes makers of the modern mind as "men who ride the intellectual tide of their time. They accept the age's fundamental assumptions, protest against what it condemns, promise what it most desires. They articulate the age's thoughts and desires. They are

nevertheless important figures in history. For the world is never the same after them as before. They act as foci for many ideas which without them would not be combined as strong forces for changes in history." [1]

St. Francis de Sales was for the Catholic mind what men like Newton, Kant and Freud were for the Western mentality in general. Borrowing heavily from the Fathers, the Scholastics, and particularly from the Spanish mystics and spiritual writers, St. Francis blended their ideas into an articulate Christian humanism, although his most widely publicized contribution to the life of the Church was the reawakening of the Catholic laity to their vocation to sanctity.

Unfortunately it was the prevailing opinion of his day that one could be a saint or aspire to sanctity only within the walled enclosures of a monastery. In opposition to this attitude, St. Francis wrote the *Introduction to the Devout Life,* in which he systematically develops a way of life for people in the world that is compatible both with their life in the world and their spiritual aspirations. That was three and a half centuries ago. Today the idea of a holy People of God has caught hold, but somehow the integrity of the Christian message has suffered. For that reason, Father Louis Bouyer of the Oratory could write the following:

> Modern authors praise the spirituality which derives from St. Francis de Sales for having at last given up wanting to model the Christian living in the world upon the monk. Such praise is somewhat ambiguous. If we admire the wisdom with which the saint succeeded in distinguishing between the essence of the monastic life which, once more, is to be identified with integral Chris-

[1] Thomas P. Neill, *Makers of the Modern Mind,* p. 397.

> tian life, and its accidentals—if we congratulate ourselves that he has discouraged Christians living in the world from imitating the externals of monasticism, while helping them to adopt and adapt its vital principles, nothing can be better. But if it is implied that such spirituality would allow some people to hope for a Christianity without austerity, without striving after an intimate communion with God, without penance and without interior life, no more serious accusation could be levelled against the so-called disciples of St. Francis de Sales.[2]

Father Bouyer makes an important point. Christianity is not Christianity without the cross, Christ's cross and ours. At the same time, Christianity is not all the cross and only the cross. It is the gift of salvation in the Word made flesh.

To make these words meaningful is the reason for this book. It is also the reason for the structure of the book. Part III is a description of a Plan for Christian living; but such a plan requires an understanding of Christianity itself, so Part II develops the biblical understanding of existence, the biblical content of faith. Christianity, however, cannot be fully understood except as redemption, reconciliation, expiation and justification. In other words, Christianity is the answer to the human condition, the condition of man without God, so we begin in Part I with an explanation of the human condition.

In Part I, I have used some of the terminology of Heidigger, gleaned mostly from John Macquarrie's *An Existentialist Theology,*[3] though I have not attempted or intended to limit myself to his ideas. My purpose has been to present

[2] Louis Bouyer, *The Meaning of the Monastic Life* (New York: Kenedy, 1955), p. ix.

[3] (London: SCM Press, 1955).

as fairly as possible a description of authentic human existence, the conditions which affect it and the anxieties which accompany it. I realize full well that the presentation is truncated; I understand the danger of misrepresentation; and I know it is only too easy to set up a paper argument which can just as easily be ripped apart. I do feel justified, though, in such a brief account and in the conclusions drawn, because I believe I have hit the highlights which are pertinent, and the conclusions drawn are those drawn by the existentialists themselves.

A word about terminology is also in order. The hyphenated terms such as being-in-the-world and being-in-Christ are used to convey a concept which indicates a relatedness between the terms joined by the hyphen. Being-in-the-world, for example, indicates a mode of existence of a human being. It means that the individual is tied up in his existence in the world, that he is involved in it, that he is affected by it. The same relatedness and involvement are indicated by the other hyphenated terms.

The conditions of human existence which are universal, called existentials, refer to conditions which do affect or can affect every man; that is, they are real or possible modes of human existence. In addition to these existentials are the conditions which affect the individual man. They are the opposite of universal because they are unique. If there are two children in a family, for instance, each one's existence is different because one is the older and the other, the younger. They are treated differently, so their environment is different. How well a man handles himself in his own unique existence will depend in a large measure on how he understands the universal conditions of his existence and their implications. It is particularly these universal conditions which are discussed in Parts I and II.

Throughout Parts II and III, I continually draw attention to the fact that the Christian believer's understanding of existence is different from the man who cannot believe. This is not an attempt to convince an unbeliever of the advantages of the faith. Rather, the principal reason is to make explicit step by step the understanding of reality that a man should have because he believes. He should understand himself and his world as a Christian, not as a pagan. Moreover, the faith to many is little more than regulations to be observed and dogmas to be accepted. These people have not understood the relevance of their faith except in terms of ultimate judgment, which means they have been deprived of the power as well as the peace of Jesus Christ. Part II is an attempt to show that revelation does indeed affect a man's understanding of existence, and Part III is a guide for translating this understanding into a way of life.

I am deeply indebted to the many people who have helped me in the preparation of this book. Many of my friends have given me more than they know by allowing me to share in their wisdom and experience, their love and their joy, their trials and their grief, their difficulties and their aspirations. Father Paul Francis, O.S.F.S., read the manuscript and offered a number of valuable suggestions. He is also mostly responsible for whatever good psychology is present in Part III. To him a special word of thanks is due. I also want to express my gratitude to *Sponsa Regis* for having allowed me to use material from articles I had written for them in 1962 and 1963.

JOSEPH LANGE, O.S.F.S.

Scripture quotations are taken from the new Confraternity of Christian Doctrine translation.

A CHRISTIAN UNDERSTANDING OF EXISTENCE

PART 1

THE HUMAN CONDITION

TO READ MEANS TO UNDERSTAND. IT IS ONE THING TO be able to pronounce all the words in a book, and quite another to be able to understand their use. In addition, understanding a book also depends upon the questions the reader asks of the book. What he reads he will judge according to his predispositions, and these are not always in accord with the intention of the author. To read the bible as history or as science, for example, with the expectation that its subject matter is historical or scientific, is to ask something of the book which the book is not designed to answer. This does not mean that such interest may not be present, but it does mean that the reader is going to miss the understanding which the author was attempting to communicate.

This book requires you to pose questions to yourself before you read it. What do you want from life? What would you like to be? What would you like to be spared? These are the questions, and they are significant. They are significant because the answers you formulate are a good index of your set of values. If you want wealth, status and security from life, evidently these are the things you think

are important and valuable. If you would like to have a nice home, two or three cars, a summer cottage and so on, then these, too, are valuable to you in various degrees. The answers to the other questions are just as revealing.

You do have a set of values; everyone does. Each man lives by what he values. He strives for the things he wants, and he wants what he values. Of course the things he values do not all attract him with the same intensity. Many of the things he would like to have, he could just as easily do without; but the very fact that he regards them as desirable indicates that he does attach some value to them. And if he could get them without too much trouble, then he thinks he would be happier for it.

But values, sets of values, are as individual as any person and every person. For that matter, by the time a person reaches middle age he has already had at least several sets of values. As a child he wanted toys and candy and fun. A few years later he wanted clothes and a job and a car. So from one stage of his life to the next he exchanged one set of values for another. But no matter in which period of his life he was, his set of values was his own and no one else had exactly the same set. No two people ever have the same set of values. We have all heard the story in which Daughter says to Mother: "We like the same things and we have fun together, so when he proposed, I said, 'Yes.'" But liking "the same things" in general, and having identical values down to both liking dill pickles, are two different things. We have different values, each of us, because we are different persons; but more about that later.

You should have a set of values, that is certain; but are you certain that your set of values is a good one? Are the things you want and work for, the things that will bring you

contentment and the joy of a good life? These questions, too, are serious because a good many people spend their whole lives running after the wrong things. That is why a good set of values is so important. Each man works and sweats and suffers for what he wants. And if what he wants is not capable of satisfying him, or if it is something that will hurt him, then he wastes his time, his tears, and his trouble.

Some people turn out to be preoccupied with sex, some become crooks. They know what they want, and it is pointless to hope to change them unless they can be convinced that what they want so badly is really not so valuable. In other words, they cannot be changed unless they change their set of values. Each person, in turn, is, to a large extent, what his values have enticed him to become.

How many of the things one values are worth as much as one thinks they are? How many things a man regards as distasteful are really so distasteful? It will take the rest of this book to suggest answers to those questions, and to do it adequately we will have to proceed step by step. The starting point must be a discussion of human existence, since it would hardly make sense to say that this or that is good for a man unless he first knows what he is and what he is for.

A BEING-IN-THE-WORLD

Perhaps the simplest thing a man knows about himself is that he exists, he is. There is neither a need to linger on the point nor a need to digress on the reasons for our conviction that we exist. It is obvious and certain. A man also knows that he can see and hear and touch and smell and

move around, or in other words, he knows that he is alive. He also knows that there are other things around him, some of which are alive and some of which are not, and all of this leads quite easily to the conclusion that he exists in a world of things, animals, plants, and other humans. He exists in the world—not just in a spatial sense, but in the sense that he is related to it.

For a man to exist means to live in the world. He is a part of it. He affects it and he is affected by it. Living in the world is one of the conditions of his existence, a condition that he cannot escape. Just as anything else in this world is subject to the forces of nature, so is he. He is warmed by the sun and wet by the rain. If he falls off a ladder, he falls to the ground the same way a paint can would. He is part of the world.

But somehow he seems to be different from the other things around him. He knows that. He may never have put it into words, but he knows it. He is a human being, while the other things are just "things." And there are good reasons for making that distinction between human beings and things. This is not one of those instances where a man feels something is right, only to find out that science has proven differently.

He is not a thing. No one would hesitate to say that human beings can think but things cannot. Undoubtedly, that is one of the major differences. A man can think. He can know, he can understand—and no thing can do that. It is true, of course, that animals can know and learn and remember, but no one has any difficulty in seeing the difference between animals and men. No animal ever wrote a book or fashioned a tool, so it would not be unjust to group them with plants and stones as "things."

There is another difference between things and men. Things of the same kind are all more or less alike. They suffer no loss of identity by being grouped. One golf ball of a particular trade name is just like any other. One oak tree is like the rest. But one man is not enough like another to say that they are alike. Each human being is unique, and it would be a great injustice to anyone to classify him as a member of a particular group and suppose that that takes care of that. To say a man is a White or a Negro or an American is about as informative as to say that he eats Wheaties for breakfast.

Another fairly obvious difference between men and things shows clearly enough from one's attitude towards them. Things are objects to be used. Heidigger spoke of them as *zuhanden,* to hand, there to be used. A man enjoys them or works with them or fashions them or plays with them—and the situation is never reversed. The distinction here is clear-cut. Things are *for* man, but men are not *for* other men. A man exists in the world, but though he is in it, he is not of it. It should become clearer as we go along that a man's authentic existence depends in a large measure on his maintaining this distinction between himself and things. It is he who confers meaning on things, turns them from mere objects to instruments and uses them. It is this separateness and superiority over things which confers on man what we call his natural dignity.

Finally, a man is different from things because a thing is what it is, but a man is always changing, or, at least, is always capable of change. Moment by moment a man can choose to do this or that or nothing at all. He can decide and act on his own initiative and by his own power, which is something no thing can do. If a thing changes, it must be

changed by someone or something else. A chair remains a chair until the forces of nature cause it to decay, or until it is broken up by someone or something. In other words, a thing is necessarily itself, but a man is always in the state of possibility.

In spite of all these differences, however, a man is, in a sense, a thing. As was mentioned earlier, he is as subject to the laws of nature as any thing. But there is this difference: a man is not simply and only a thing. Because he can think and because he has the capacity to initiate activity, he is more than a thing; he is immeasurably more. A philosopher might say that a man is both subject and object at the same time. As a subject he is a human being, the center of thought and choice and activity. As an object he is like any other thing.

This two-fold character of man leads to some important considerations. As an object, a thing, he belongs to the world of things. As a subject, he is able to think about himself, but when he does, he becomes an object to himself. He holds himself out at arms' length, as it were, and considers himself as he would anything other than himself. For that reason, he cannot help but recognize that he, as a man, belongs to this world as much as everything else does. As a matter of fact, it is quite necessary for a man to realize that as a man he is tied up in his existence with the world in which he lives. Any understanding of himself is incomplete, unless it considers that for him to exist means for him to be in the world, to affect it, to be concerned about it and to be affected by it. But, before we develop this point further, it would be convenient to discuss another condition of human existence—that a man lives with other human beings like himself.

A BEING-WITH-OTHERS

This, too, is obvious. A man exists, not only in a world of things, but in a world of people—people who affect him, who are concerned about him, about whom he is concerned; people who annoy him, people who please him, people who bring him joy, people who are people to him. There is no profit in belaboring a familiar fact. The point is clear: for a man to exist means to exist with others like himself, others who are human beings, not things.

As was mentioned before, people do not exist *for* men, but *with* them. One is not entitled to use them as he uses things, because to do that would be to fail to recognize their natural dignity as human beings and their right to self-determination, which stems from that fact. This is the first instance of a condition of human existence which is, at the same time, a challenge and a threat.

Others before us have written long and learnedly about the fundamental drives of human nature, the natural forces within us that come to us with our existence. Which forces are called fundamental depends on the level of the discussion and the particular approach of the author. Carl Rogers seems to have probed the deepest. He points to one fundamental drive, which he defines as the actualization, maintenance and enhancement of the experiencing organism.[4] What puts this drive into operation is the set of values held by the individual, and two concrete examples of this single vital force channeled into a positive direction would be self-assertion and the desire for pleasure. If these two particular manifestations of man's fundamental drive could dominate

[4] Carl R. Rogers, *Client-Centered Therapy* (Boston: Houghton Mifflin Co., 1951), p. 487.

a man completely, then self assertion would be personified in a purely proud man, and the desire for pleasure would find representation in the sensuous man. There never have existed pure types of either, but mixtures in various degrees are found in everyone. And that is why living with others, an inescapable condition of human existence, is both a challenge and a threat.

The pride in a man, the will to have his own way regardless, the will to dominate all of nature and men to suit himself, blinds him to the dignity of the "others" with whom he must live. The proud man is incapable of the primary attitude which must serve as the foundation of all human relations, the attitude of respect. He approaches all of nature as a tyrant. Other men are to him only so many "organization men" or factory "hands" or pawns. His sense of values is warped and he has become less than human, since he is not human enough to recognize the value of other human beings.

Each man, in turn, is faced with the same interpersonal relationship. Often, very often, he is tempted to use others or to force them to do his will. He would like to have others behave as he does. He forgets their right to be themselves. and whenever he does act this way with anyone, he is treating them as things instead of as human beings. It should be recognized that one's attitude towards others should be determined in the first place by the value each other person has, simply and only because he is a person. This is a question of value and it seems quite clear that the very nature of things demands that each human person be valued for what he is—a person, not a thing.

Incidentally, this value extends to every person, no matter how ugly or how repulsive or how small, and from the dig-

nity, worth, and value of the human being follows a code of human behavior towards other human beings, a code which is natural because it is human. One has no right to kill, injure, slander or abuse another human being. If a man appreciates and understands his own value, to do such things would never occur to him. This other man is a man like himself, a *man* with the right of self-determination, a *man* with the inalienable rights of life, liberty and the pursuit of happiness. And, as was just noted, this goes for all men regardless of size or capacity, which is why it is wrong to kill an unborn child or the aged. When the value of a human being is clearly understood, the enormity of such crimes stands out just as clearly.

There are times and situations in which men voluntarily surrender a share of their freedom to others, for example, when a man enters the army or agrees to work for another. Again, because men do live with others in an organized society, they submit to laws which have been enacted for the common good. And sometimes for the common good a man must submit to the authority of others or relinquish his freedom; for example, in dangerous times a man may be drafted into the armed forces against his will. But all of these are special circumstances in which either the common good demands such sacrifice or it is deliberately chosen. It should be noted, though, that these situations develop *because* one lives with others, because one is conditioned in his existence by them.

But what of parents and teachers who occasionally must force children to do something against their will? Obviously, children must not be allowed unlimited freedom. Children, because they are inexperienced and unaware of the dangers which surround them, must submit to the

authority of parents and teachers, who have the right to demand certain things of them. But (and this is the heart of the matter) no parent or teacher is entitled to force a child to do something because he lacks respect for the child. The concept of authority does not destroy the obligation of respect, it presupposes it. If one must force a child to do something, he must do it because he respects him, and he has no right to deprive a child (or any man) of his freedom because he dislikes him or because he is annoyed by him.

A man or a child is a human being, not a thing. One can kill an animal for food or study or recreation. He can restrict the movement of an animal in a zoo or by a leash. But a man is a man, and the very nature of things demands that he be treated as one.

Undoubtedly, the pride in a man is one power which blinds him to the unmistakable value of the "others" with whom he exists. The desire for pleasure is the second power, equally effective, no less universal. But the sensuous man does not confront nature and his existence as a tyrant. Instead, he sees the things of the world and others as the source of his pleasure. He may be brutal and vicious, he may be lazy and sluggish, he may be eager and refined; but he is blind. He cannot penetrate to the true value of anything because he can only see it from one point of view: will it please him?

If men are to live together peacefully, it is hardly necessary to say that they must live by the laws of an organized society. Each one must relinquish some of his freedom in order to safeguard it. But the sensuous man does not see things that way. He wants to do what he feels like doing. He wants no constraint, no limit to his unbridled lust to express himself. He wants no part of self-control. That

would be uncomfortable. He would not be getting his way. He wants thrills, possessions, "kicks," food. He wants to mix with the best. He wants, he wants—and he cannot stand being put off.

The sensuous man, dominated, driven, and captured by the desire for pleasure, is in no position to treat others as human beings. He treats them as he treats every "thing," only as something to give him pleasure. This means that, along with the proud man, he is incapable of the richest and deepest human experience—love for another.

Certainly, between human beings love stands out as the one experience which has no equal. Love ennobles and transforms a human being as nothing else can. Both the proud and the sensuous man, however, are excluded from any possibility of loving. The basic reason is easy to see. Neither one knows what he is worth, so neither can perceive any worth in anyone else. Only those who love themselves rightly, who know what they are and what they are worth, can see those values in another and love him for it.

The proud man, exaggerating his own importance at the expense of others, has blinded himself to his true worth and at the same time blunted his ability to appreciate anyone else. He can never love a woman, since he would not know how; but if he does marry, he will give his wife nothing of marital love. She will be to him the woman of his choice, a fixture of his household like a piece of dinnerware, something he can be proud of. Even the marital act will be brutalized. Instead of the sublime communion of man and wife in the total giving of one to the other, the proud man finds just another opportunity to dominate, to force, to tyrannize and to take.

The sensuous man is no better off. He, too, is so self-

centered that he finds it impossible to see anything lovable in another. Sexuality becomes for him just another thrill. He never thinks of giving pleasure or satisfaction. He does not know what it means to be thoughtful and considerate himself, although he wants others to be so to him. So he, too, is denied the joy of love.

In all of this, the key words are "self-centered" and "altruistic." The proud and the sensuous men are self-centered in different ways, but self-centered they are. They live in their own little worlds, cut off from fruitful and rewarding human contact. The walls of their little worlds are impervious to the value of a human being, so they pervert the natural order of human relations. For them, living with others has become a condition of their existence which they have not been able to meet as human beings. Instead of growing in stature day by day, by their contacts and service to others, instead of experiencing the joy of living love, they doom themselves day in and day out to an endless search for satisfaction along a road that leads nowhere.

A self-centered person is rightly judged by everyone to be a tragically mutilated specimen of humanity. His opposite is the altruist, one who goes out of himself to others, one who gives himself for others. He glows with an inner beauty that many may not understand, but all admire. His selflessness radiates a warmth and attractiveness which cut through suspicion and prejudice. There is something special about him. "He is a good man," we say, and he *is* good because he is perfectly human. The evident repulsiveness of the self-centered, proud, or sensuous man is a clear and decisive indication of the non-human values incarnated in such men. But the altruist is human in the real sense of the word. He

lives with others without trying to dominate them or use them. He is thoughtful and considerate, patient, mild and just. He meets the challenge and threat of living with others, because he is not seduced by the pseudo-values of momentary pleasure and self-indulgence at the expense of others. He knows the worth of others, and he knows that violating their rights and dignity would be a crime against nature which would inevitably reap his own ruination. He has found the joy and satisfaction that comes from living with others and for others; and he has seen too many selfish people unhappily groping aimlessly for what he has, to want to give up his way for theirs. In plain truth, he is human; they are not.

At this point it would be useful to summarize briefly what has been covered so far. We have spoken of human existence and we have seen already that when we say a man exists, we mean not only that he *is,* but that he is in the world and he is in the world with others like himself. He is subject to the forces of the world, as any thing is, and he is affected by others as well. We have also seen that although a man is a part of the world, he is, nevertheless, apart from the things of the world; he is different from them; he is superior to them. In addition, there is a basic drive in man which finds expression in many ways, of which two common forms are self-assertiveness and the desire for pleasure. We have also seen that living with others can be a threat and a danger to a man because of his tendency towards self-assertion and the desire for pleasure. In a word, it is natural for man (1) to exist in the world, (2) to exist with others, (3) to have a tendency to self-assertion and a tendency to sensuality.

A BEING-WITH-CHOICE

To these things we must add several others because the picture is not yet complete. Earlier we mentioned that a man is not simply a thing. He is a man because he can think; he is free and he is always in the state of possibility. Now we can enlarge on that. Man is always in the state of possibility because moment by moment he stands before the possible choices of acting humanly or inhumanly. This means that by his very nature man is different from the things of this world, and one way in which he is different is that he is not necessitated to be what by nature he should be. A cow is a cow and nothing can change that, but a man acts as a man by choice—he can also choose to act like a beast.

This is a tremendously important idea. There is such a thing as an objectively or authentically human man. From this, together with man's freedom, the idea of obligation or duty follows logically: a man ought to be authentically human even though he can decide not to be. It hardly makes sense to say that it is natural for a man to act as a beast. He should not; which is to say, he ought not; which is to say, he has a duty to himself to be human. If through the years he has acquired a true set of values, then he knows with each decision whether he has chosen to be human or not. The "voice" of conscience is nothing more than this. There is nothing mysterious about it. Before, during, or after a man does something, if he thinks about it in the light of the values he has acquired, he automatically judges it to be in harmony or in discord with those values. This judgment is his conscience. No man can completely set aside or ignore every natural human value, which is why

every man sometimes suffers "pangs" of conscience when he does not act humanly.

Freedom for man, then, is more than a condition of human existence. It is a responsibility. A man can choose to be what he ought to be, and so be human; or he can choose to do what is not human, and in the process destroy himself.

We have already seen one way in which the very conditions of our existence make it difficult for a man to live as a human being. Because of his human tendencies to self-assertion and sensuality he can choose to be less than human towards those with whom he must live. There is another way, too, by which living with others stands as a formidable obstacle to a truly human life. One lives with others and is affected by them as much as he affects them. Responsibility is not an easy thing to bear, but it is an easy thing to share. A man does not mind doing something if "they" do it—and "they" do much. In other words, because a man lives with others, he stands a good chance of being swallowed up by them. He easily relinquishes his individuality to lose himself in the crowd. This time it is not a matter of something he does to others. It is something he does to himself. He is not treating others as factory "hands" or "organization men." He treats himself that way. He does not wish to be himself, either because he is afraid or because it would be uncomfortable. He sacrifices his freedom and his values in order to be submerged in the morass of the mob.

It is not this or that person that stands in the way of his authentic existence. It is the indeterminate mass: "they," "the people," "society." For the most part, especially in our institutionalized society of today, a man is not so much an individual as he is a part of society. Subject to the pressures

of mass media such as television, radio, and the press, to the influence of mass employment, mass education, and all the things these mass systems imply, his identification with the group submerges most of a man's individuality. He mechanically follows the established way of doing things. He never asserts himself for fear he will lose his identification with the group and stand out as an individual. And he seeks to quiet all the uneasiness of his flight from responsibility by constantly reassuring himself that, after all, "they do it."

How often he holds back from doing something or saying something because to do so would set him at odds with the group, or so he thinks. The vicious circle of such thinking was perfectly expressed by Bruce Marshall in *The World, the Flesh and Father Smith*. He wrote: "We are afraid to be ourselves in crowds because we are afraid not to be like what we think our neighbors are; and our neighbors are afraid not to be like what they think we are." [5] And how unfortunate it all is.

By living mechanically day in and day out a man gives up his freedom, not by choice, but by default. By cowardly refusal to speak out or to act contrary to the group, a man relinquishes still more of his freedom. In actual fact, he becomes a slave. Far from living a human existence, he strays farther and farther from what he should be each time he seeks refuge in the group. So living with others is quite obviously a difficult challenge. A man does live with others. He must. It is certainly a condition of his existence. But precisely because he does live with others he is in danger of failing to be what he should be, either because he fails to grasp their true value or because he seeks to identify himself with them.

[5] (Boston: Houghton Mifflin Co., 1956), p. 86

A similar difficulty stems from the fact that he lives in the world. This has been put off until now because it was necessary to develop first the radical superiority of man over things of the world, and to emphasize the fact that a man not only is human, but that he ought to be human, even though he can choose not to be. He is, without doubt, a worldling, a part of the world; yet, although he is a thing, he is not only a thing. In a very real way he is distinct from the world of things, and it is only by maintaining that distinction that he can really live as an authentic human being.

Unfortunately, the daily existence of many men today is characterized by their preoccupation with things. They seek to find the meaning of their existence (or give meaning to their existence) in the accumulation of things, in personal comfort, in the "good life." They have become absorbed in the world. They are at home there, they seek their security there, they understand themselves and their possibilities exclusively in terms of the world's values. They are so concerned about the things of this world that they have resisted and obliterated the consciousness of their fundamental difference from the things of the world. And this, more than anything else, reveals the danger which the world holds for every man.

The man who does not grasp his superiority to the things of the world soon finds himself smothered and hopelessly trapped by it. Since the satisfaction he seeks from things is inevitably of short duration—this is the universal experience of men—he plunges on at a dizzier pace with ever increasing effort, only to find successive dissatisfaction and an oppressive sense of futility. "Why," he asks himself, "why am I in this rat race?"—a question which betrays the fact that the pursuit and possession of things cannot provide the

answer. Nor can he formulate a satisfying answer for himself. Having concentrated on the things and affairs of the world, he has no other values to work with. He is bewildered and he is lost, hopelessly lost in a web of his own making. Long ago he surrendered himself to the power of the world.

That power of the world is precisely the thing that makes it a very real threat to every one. The world is there. It is always there, attracting, inviting a man to lose himself in it. As an inescapable condition of his existence, he must contend with it day in and day out without relief. Because he is in the world, he must eat and sleep and find relaxation. A father must provide for his family. A wife must shop and cook and clean. The danger here does not lie in doing these things, but in becoming a slave to them. When a husband and wife feel they must have a home in the suburbs, for example, "must" in the sense that they feel they require it in order to be happy, then they have begun to slip (or just gone a little farther) into the swirling vortex which leads to nothing. Next will come the "need" for a better car, a better this and more of that. They have not understood that they are apart from the world and superior to the things of the world. They have not been convinced that "superior" to the things of the world means that things are not necessary for their happiness.

A BEING-IN-TIME

Time can only be recognized by the observation of change: something which was, is no longer the same. Since there was a before and there is a now, there has been and is duration, which we speak of as the passage of time. Time

does nothing, accomplishes nothing, only passes. It has the character of something given, not made, beyond control. It is a source of interest, because we are affected by it; it is a source of one of our limitations. It takes time to learn about people and things. It takes time to learn how to do things. It takes time to move from one place to another. It takes time to communicate. It takes time for wounds to heal, plans to work out, and love to grow deeper.

In the face of the indisputable requirements of time (though in this everyone often ignores even his own experience), it makes sense to adopt an attitude towards one's existence that is consistent with the limitations which come to him because he exists in a time-conditioned world. This attitude we call patience. If it does take time to know, to do, to mature—and all the rest, it follows that to take this into account and to be willing to submit to it, in other words, to be patient, is human. But to rebel against this condition of his existence with the concomitant disturbances that it produces, to attempt, always without success, to dominate his existence in a way calculated to circumvent the necessity of the passage of time, is very often described as being human.

Certainly, to be weak, to be prone to impatience, to desire the quick fruition of one's desires is common. But the weak and impatient man is not the authentically human man, just as the proud or sensuous man is not authentically human. The man who is patient is the one who understands and accepts the fact that his existence is time-conditioned. Proud and sensuous men, on the other hand, are also usually impatient. They resent this limitation of their existence which stands imperturbably beyond their control.

To be patient certainly does not mean obsequious acquiescence in the face of a force too powerful to overcome.

Patience is not laziness or lack of effort or procrastination or weakness. Rather, it is an abiding attitude of one who understands that his existence is conditioned by a force beyond his control. He is not disturbed because he must wait for plans to jell and friendships to mature. He expects it and he accepts it. To refuse to accept it is arrogance or stupidity. To wish that it were not so would be a vain attempt to live in a world of one's own, rather than in the real world which the authentically human man accepts with patience.

The fact of one's time-conditioned existence reaches a man and affects him not only in that he has to wait for things to work out, but also because his repeated experiences of things can lead either to greater appreciation or to insensibility. The ripening of a friendship takes time; it requires the experience of many moments shared. From each new experience of the other a new perspective, a new insight is gained—or can be. But, at the same time, continuous exposure can lead to familiarity, and familiarity to blindness. How many things one takes for granted!—the ones he loves and the ones who love him, his home, his surroundings, his health, and all the rest. The challenge in all this is in overcoming the tendency to bluntness by being human enough to think of what one has and of what one is doing. To succumb to the numbing force of repeated exposure to things of value would hardly be called human.

Time, then, is a real and relentless condition of human existence. As with the other conditions of existence, it also poses a threat to an authentically human way of life. Because one is limited by the conditions imposed upon him by his existence in a time-conditioned world, he is exposed to the dangers of impatience and bluntness. Only by courage-

ous and self-disciplined action, together with attentiveness to values, will he be able to meet such dangers and be human.

A BEING-OF-CHANGE

It would seem that to speak now of change would be redundant, having just spoken of time, inasmuch as change occurs only because time passes and change is the very reason that we are able to recognize the passage of time. But, though they are certainly intimately related, they are not the same thing; nor is their effect upon a man the same. Like time, change requires from a man submission to a force beyond his control, a condition imposed upon him from without by the circumstances of his existence. Any attempt to rebel or withstand the inevitability of change is tilting against windmills, and is foredoomed to failure. Things change, people change, and situations change.

Changes can occur suddenly or slowly, from bad to worse or from bad to better, or vice-versa. The question is: how does change affect our existence? or, to put that another way: how does one meet the problem of change as a human being?

The problem, it seems, is primarily the problem of adjustment. It is not the fact of change that affects a man, but the new condition that now confronts him and to which he must adjust, because the former condition has dissolved into the past. The essence of change is transition, and transition itself does not affect him. The end point of change (which is the beginning of another change) is what imposes itself upon him. Frequent changes in one's existence, that is, in

himself and in any of the things that affect him, call for frequent adjustments. Slower changes do not present him with so many new situations so rapidly, so they do not require so much of him.

The ability to adjust is the result of the complicated interaction of many things. Basic among them are the ability to understand the new condition that confronts him and the ability to work out for himself the proper attitude or the proper course of action that it requires. People who panic because of sudden change, or who are bewildered by frequent change, lack either the training or the ability to understand and think for themselves. They need someone else to do this for them, someone who will explain to them what is going on and tell them how to react.

Also at the root of the ability to adjust is a willingness to adjust, and this works all sorts of complications. Since this will be discussed more comprehensively later, suffice it to say here that the willingness depends reciprocally on understanding. Prejudices, predetermined attitudes, and action-controlling attitudes, can only be swept aside by understanding the real situation for what it is and by having the courage to accept it. Neurotics and psychotics and reactionaries [6] all refuse in one way or another to accept reality, specifically, the reality of one's constantly changing existence. They refuse to understand it, preferring instead to live in a world of their own, a world which does not require of them the responsibility or the difficulty of adjustment.

[6] Reactionaries are sometimes called traditionalists or conservatives. They want things to remain as they are. They *react* against change, so "reactionary" is a better name for them. A traditionalist or conservative may very well and very easily desire change and accept it, while still wishing to hold onto and maintain what is good from the past. The true conservative is one who is willing to change on the basis of principle.

Change, then, and all that it implies, is a genuine condition of human existence. It has, in common with the other conditions of human existence, universality, challenge and blessing. The authentic human being meets the challenge of change with the understanding of its inevitability and with the courage and understanding necessary for adjustment.

A SEXUAL-BEING

Because a man is human, not an animal, not a thing, his whole existence is conditioned by his basic humanness. He is in the world, but not of it. His attitude—and only he can have attitudes—towards any phase of his existence makes sense only if the human element is included. With sex and sexuality [7] it is the human element that introduces the mystery, the radiance, and the beauty.

We are, to be sure, male or female, physiologically and psychologically. This is fact, elemental and basic, simple, impossible to hide and impossible to ignore. In the light of scientific data, it is even harmful to attempt to ignore it. From the cradle on, children are conditioned by sex. Depending on their sex they are treated differently, clothed differently, and exposed to different things. They mature at different ages usually; they are taught to want different things. They are taught different skills and they develop different interests. Their attitude towards themselves and towards others is conditioned by their sex. Society, the milieu in which they exist, expects different behavior and different interests from them, a situation which has existed in every

[7] The word "sex" is used here to indicate maleness and femaleness; "sexuality" is used to indicate genital activity and those things related to it.

society that has ever been studied. A woman is expected to be feminine; a male is expected to be virile; and each of those qualities carries with it the connotation of many things which have been described at length, even in such unlikely places as magazines and newspapers. Because of the proliferation and availability of such information, it does not seem necessary to elaborate on it here. The point is that one is conditioned in his behavior and his outlook by sex.

Sex is also a source of limitation. Physiologically, and by the restrictions of society, each man is limited in all the ways mentioned earlier as well as in demeanor, conversation, the kind of work he can do or is permitted to do—and so on.

What is more, sex affects a man in a unique way. Sex is essentially deep.[8] When it speaks, what it utters is no mere passing word. Sexuality stems from the very core of the human personality and, except under extreme conditions, no other natural urge, no other natural tendency manifests such depth. Within the framework of everyday existence, even the will to survive is pushed far in the background by the intrinsic power of sexuality, a power which arises from the fact that it is of the very essence of man to be sexually determined and oriented. No other power within or without a man affects a mature human being so often or so effectively. When sexuality is stirred up, body and mind react in a way which indicates that they are fused at this essential point in a man's being. In sex one is human. One cannot be human except as female and male.

So deep, so closely and thoroughly bound up are body and mind at this point of union, that is, in the sexual deter-

[8] Cf. *In Defense of Purity* by Dietrich von Hildebrand, (New York: Sheed and Ward, 1933).

mination of the individual, that use and abuse of one has a marked effect on the other. A good example of this strong inter-relationship is that frigidity is most often a matter of attitude rather than a physical disorder. How often psychology has indicated that many neuroses and psychoses express themselves in sexual deviation. Human beings come as male and female in every cell of their bodies and in every fiber of their being. They are essentially so.

What precisely constitutes this maleness and femaleness is physically obvious, psychologically not so obvious. Metaphysically, that is, at the very root of one's being, it is quite obscure. Aristotle had a dictum: performance stems from being, which in this instance would mean that since male and female are different in their physical and psychological make-up, it follows that they are different in their being. A man is a man is a man. A woman is a woman is a woman.

Also in their physical and psychological make-up, man and woman are complementary. This, too, reaches down to the very depths of their being. There is an essential incompleteness, an essential loneliness of a solitary human being. All four concepts are important: complementary, essential, incompleteness and loneliness. It is no simple animal or brutish urge to mate that can account for the very deep loneliness of a man without a woman. Whatever it is, it must be specifically human, as we have already developed at length earlier. The fact of the profound loneliness of the solitary human being is attested to by case after case in clinical psychology and psychiatry. It must have its root in an essential incompleteness, a lack of wholeness which is of the very essence of man. And, further, this incompleteness cannot be filled up by anything other than a member of the opposite sex to whom the other is physically and psychologi-

cally oriented. Case histories of abnormal psychology are filled with the tales of those who have tried, always unsuccessfully, to find fulfillment and totality with a substitute. Man is for woman, woman is for man; and complementing each other, both find liberation from loneliness, which is partial fulfillment.[9]

The point of all this insistence on the essential nature of these characteristics is to indicate their depth, as well as to distinguish them from the surface characteristics which are sometimes mistaken for them. A man and a woman complement each other sexually, not only in their anatomies which are obviously designed for sexual union. A particular man and woman are not only complementary in their likes, dislikes, interests and abilities, etc.—a complementariness which also is a result of their sexual differentiation; they are also complementary at the most profound level of their being. The loneliness of a widow or single woman or bachelor is never successfully met by activity or friends. Again, this loneliness grows out of an essential incompleteness which can only be filled up by the union of two complementary beings, each of which is incomplete and oriented towards the other.

The way in which this union of man and woman actually results in a sharing of each other's being is mysterious. The

[9] Three points: (1) A discussion of a religiously motivated celibate life is not *ad rem* here. Cf. *In Defense of Purity* by Dietrich von Hildebrand.

(2) The loneliness experienced by the man or woman who is "alone" can, of course, vary in intensity. The fact that it affects so many so strongly argues for its depth and power.

(3) The fulfillment spoken of throughout this discussion refers only to this area of a man's existence, sexual fulfillment.

precise nature of the union is mysterious. The fulfillment is mysterious. Since we are here touching on matters which lie deeply hidden at the core of our being, we are unable to reach them by analysis or observation. We can only recognize their presence in the ways in which they manifest that presence, indicate their significance, and acknowledge the mystery which clothes them.

Sex, and everything connected with it, is mysterious because it is deep. In a very real sense, sex is at the core of the innermost personality of a human being. It is the most secret and most personal center of each person, and that is why the revelation of it to another amounts to sharing with the other the depths of one's being. As von Hildebrand has indicated, the disclosure to another of what is most personal, one's deepest emotions, for example, is accomplished by a sense of shame at such self-revelation; and this, he believes, is the reason for the shame which is associated with sex, whenever it is out of the only context which can render it beautiful. It makes sense. Revealing oneself to another and giving oneself to another in sexual union is much, much more than baring one's body to the gaze of another and experiencing a physical union. If this were not so, then the sense of defilement and the burden of shame that accompany it are far out of proportion and inexplicable. For the same reason, the sense of oneness and union, the beauty and splendor of such an experience when it is filled with love—this, too, would be impossible to explain.

Too often it has been said that the sense of guilt and shame which accompany extra-marital sexuality is the result of an outdated and outmoded code of morals, which is still being foisted upon a modern people who have no need for it. These ideas in all their various forms find expression

from blunted and coarse men who have rendered themselves incapable of recognizing the value which their very nature yearns for. They cannot be right. It is not a code of morals, but the inner nature, the inner dynamism of their own being that they are contradicting. Incomplete and empty they are, incomplete and empty they will ever be.

Everything that a man experiences adds to his being, everything he learns, everything he enjoys, everything he endures, every attempt at self mastery, every sorrow, every pain, every conquest, every act. And each man grows in being in proportion to the nobility, the value of the individual experiences which he exists. Certainly, acquiring a Ph.D. is greater than learning to hammer a nail. And much greater than either is learning to live in the world and with others as a human being. Now sometimes it happens that one discovers another who is to him another self. He is able to peer into the depths of her being and she into his. We say they are in love, for love is revelation. One sees in the beloved that which no one else can see. They know that they are for each other. They want each other exclusively and forever, and having each other is enough for them. This is marital love, which, when it is sealed by the inviolable determination to be forever the other's own, seeks to express itself in physical union. Two in one flesh they become, filling up the emptiness of each other's being, finding fulfillment in this communion of love and life.

No other natural experience is so enriching and so rewarding. If other experiences add to a man's being, this one does so in a measure beyond measure, or better, in the only way capable of erasing his essential loneliness by completing his being. In other words, it is in sexuality and by sexuality that man and woman find their deepest communion and ful-

fillment; but only when it is initiated and saturated in love, and that specific love which we call marital love. Certainly there are more noble expressions of love, as when one sacrifices everything for the one he loves; but in this there is lacking the actual revelation of oneself and the total self-donation which sexual union involves, giving oneself to one's beloved entirely, mind *and* body. Only in and by sexuality is this possible, which is why it stands as the final expression and most complete expression of love's desire: total self donation and total union.

Understanding sexuality this way, in its nobility, beauty and depth, makes it impossible to accept those discussions of sexuality which treat it as a pleasure similar to eating, drinking, and the rest. Precisely because of its different dimensions sexuality is not at all on the same superficial level. Those who attempt to find satisfaction only from the pleasure of sexuality, who isolate the pleasure from love, these are the ones who are doomed to miss the greatest thing that could happen to them. They are soon glutted with the pleasure and anxious to find new ways to excite themselves. Their being is impoverished and they do not know why.

In all this, what makes sexuality human is that it has meaning as well as function. To say that animals breed because of an instinct within them to relieve tension, that man is sexual inasmuch as he is animal, so, he, too, is driven by an irresistible urge, and then to claim that this is the obvious and only way to understand sexuality in man—such argument ignores completely the fact that man is not just and only an animal. It does, in fact, reduce him to an animal, which he is not. It is specious reasoning arising from the failure to acknowledge the completely different character of those things in man which man and animal have in

common. Nothing is the same in both. Whatever a man does or endures he can enrich with meaning, and no animal can do that.

What makes sexuality specifically human is its meaning, and it derives its meaning from the fact that it is in and by sexuality that one finds the final expression of his love and the completeness for which his being cries out.

Sexuality is without doubt a powerful force in anyone's life. It is a condition of one's existence, full of promise and fraught with danger. The challenge to remain chaste and inviolate until love unfolds the beauty of another being to him, to whom he can cleave, with whom he can share his being, is the challenge to be human. To submit to the siren call of pleasure, to unbridled lust, is to embrace disaster and the disintegration of all that is human. There is no master like sexuality and no slave worse off than one who has failed to meet the challenge of sexuality.

To live as an authentic human being, then, a man must live in the world and with others as a sexual being, in a time-conditioned world where he must endure change, and he must meet successfully the challenges posed by each of these conditions of his existence. But, even if he comes this far, his satisfaction and contentment are not assured. He still has one more hurdle to leap, one further difficulty to resolve: he must discover for himself the reason for his own existence.

ANXIETY

As a human being, a man knows and thinks and reflects. His knowledge comes to him from listening, reading and experience, but much of what he knows he never puts into

words. He just knows it. He knows, for example, that things change. The sun comes up in the morning and sets at night. Summer fades into Autumn. His mother grows old. He can no longer do what he used to do. He definitely knows change. And he knows emotions and tastes for which there are no names or words. The deepest human experiences transcend the power of language; and when a man exists before one of these, he is speechless.

Nor is the scope of his knowledge limited by the extent of his education. Every man is capable of deep knowledge of profound subjects; for every man can go beneath the surface of things and events, and search for unity and meaning. In fact, the very knowledge which accrues to him over the years forces such inquiry upon him. And that is why the possibility of anxiety is as much a condition of human existence as being in the world and being with others.

Anxiety, as a psychological state, is a possible state for every man because it is grounded in man's finitude, in the fact that he is in the world but not of it, responsible for his existence although he is not the complete master of it. Every man, as he acquires knowledge from his existence, also acquires values. These values beget desires and desires lead to frustration and conflict. When one is deprived of the object of his desire, he experiences frustration. When he is forced to choose between conflicting desires, he is deprived of that which he cannot choose. In either instance, the result is depression; and depression can lead to anxiety. In the mood of depression one becomes more negative in his thinking, more liable to be impressed by his finitude, more liable to have his value structure shattered by the awareness of fate and death, emptiness and meaninglessness, guilt and condemnation.

Every man who has arrived at maturity has found himself face to face with the knowledge that it is not at all necessary that he exist. There were no necessary causes that forced him upon the world. It could easily, very easily, have happened that events would have arranged themselves in such a way that he would never have been born. For that matter, it is just as clear, once his own existence shows itself as unnecessary, that nothing else is necessary in this world—his job, his family, his friends, his country. Any one of these things might have been different. And the conclusion, which his own experience has revealed to him, is that he is not his own master. We have a host of everyday expressions which arise from such knowledge: "It's in the cards." "It's fate." "That's the way it goes." "What can you do about it?"

This realization is unsettling for several reasons. For one, it elicits an unnamed fear about the unknown possibilities of the future that are beyond his control. In other words, it produces anxiety. Without knowing what he is afraid of, he is afraid—and that is anxiety. Perhaps he will attempt to fix his fear on something concrete, and in the process become unreasonably afraid of something in the future. The reason is that it is much more comfortable to be afraid of something than of nothing.

But whether or not a man finds an outlet for this anxiety is beside the point; the point is that the realization that he is not the complete master of his destiny can produce the anxiety. Further, the realization is unsettling because it leads inevitably to the consideration of his own extinction. He knows that death is inevitable. It may be that the thought of his own death led him to the awareness of the unnecessary character of his existence. The two topics are certainly related, but which way he comes to such knowledge is immaterial. That such knowledge reaches him is inevitable,

and the consequence is anxiety. Few things are more feared than death and few things are as mysterious. Death is a serious topic, too serious to be brushed aside by anyone for very long. Death is final, the end of existence as we know it. Is there a hereafter? Am I immortal? If there is a life beyond, what is it like?—these are desperate questions leading to the anxiety of death.

And other questions follow from these anxieties to produce anxieties of their own. When a man comes to realize that his life is, in many ways, governed by forces beyond his control, he may begin to question the possibility of his own future happiness. And when the spring of his youth has lost some of its resilience, when the horizons are no longer so bright nor the dreams so hopeful, when the sobering effect of trouble and sorrow and failure has taken its toll, then the power of the forces outside himself begin to appear even more oppressive, and he begins to wonder: where does it all lead and what am I doing here?

It leads to death, of course, and in the light of death, a light that shines more brightly as the years go by, the meaning of life becomes more and more obscure. The reasons for existence, which earlier had served the purpose of staving off disturbing doubts, begin to lose their substance in the light of death, for those reasons were only shadows which cannot stand the light. Thrills, pleasure, fame, fortune and power lose their power to satisfy as reasons for continuing an existence which is often difficult and hard. There are not and have not been many who have "everything," but there have been some, and some of these have chosen to end their lives rather than continue a meaningless existence. For most, the hope of something better keeps them going, or perhaps the fear of extinction outweighs the torment of life.

Then, too, there are those moments when the bottom falls

out of a man's world, when suddenly he feels empty. Perhaps something he believed in or hoped for abruptly fails. Things which used to give him comfort become insipid. Of a sudden, the world becomes cold and gray—and meaningless. In either case a man becomes anxious. He suffers from the anxiety of emptiness or the anxiety of meaninglessness or from both, because he exists, at least for the time being, in the darkness of a world without meaning.

To all of this must be added another pair of anxieties that are as human and as universal as the rest. They are the anxieties of guilt and condemnation. A man does not need to be more than a man to know that he has done wrong. We have already spoken of conscience. To some it speaks more frequently and more accurately than to others, but it is there. Each man knows he has not always done as he should, so each one knows guilt and self-condemnation. The reasons for guilt are as individual as a man's existence, but guilt need not always have to do with conscience and moral systems. A man may also feel guilty for not having made more of his opportunities, for not having made something of himself, for not having done this or that. And, likewise, neither does condemnation require belief in an eternal judge or an afterlife of torment, for guilt carries with it the verdict of condemnation. What actual effect that condemnation may lead to is covered by the mystery that causes a man to be anxious. It is not that he fears something. Rather, he does not know what to fear.[10]

These forms of anxiety (of fate and death, of emptiness and meaninglessness, of guilt and condemnation) are not to

[10] This division of anxiety into the forms mentioned is treated in some detail by Paul Tillich in *The Courage To Be* (New Haven: Yale University Press, 1952).

be relegated to the category of neurotic or psychotic experiences, though they may take those forms. To be sure, the experience can have an almost infinite variation in intensity, but the possibility of the experience is human and is a part of every man's existence.

These forms of anxiety spring from a common source, the very nature of man, because man is finite. In his own person, and in every phase of his existence he is limited. His personality, his background, his parents, his relations, his neighborhood and school, his build, his color, his culture, the age in which he lives, the opportunities open to him, his health and physical make-up, his capacity to think and speak and work and suffer and love—in all these things he is limited, so limited and in so many ways that sooner or later he realizes it.

One can be anxious because even his life is limited. He can be anxious because he realizes that he is responsible for an existence of which he is not the complete master. He can be anxious because he is limited in his capacity to sustain interest in life, so he is empty. He can be anxious because the chaos of life has failed to betray its meaning. Or he can be anxious because his limited determination has not been able to prevent him from doing things for which he now feels guilty.

The anxieties which come to a man because of his limitations, his finitude, are not pleasant experiences. For the most part he avoids them as best he can, and in the process he gives the world and others a greater measure of power than they should have. The abnormal escapes are into dream worlds, the unreal worlds of neurotics and psychotics. The common escapes are less spectacular, but just as crippling. It is true, of course, that escape is not the only

remedy for anxiety, but it appears to be the common and almost universal practice. If anxiety does not lead to the Ground of Being, that is, to God, it logically leads to despair.

To avoid thinking about the direction of his life or the finality of death, a man may lose himself in his work or in the pursuit of pleasure—and "lose" is the proper word, for such a one becomes ever less human by obliterating the distinction between himself and things. He adds to the already treacherous allurements of work and pleasure the value of escape. To avoid a nagging sense of guilt and personal responsibility, he may try the same escape or he may lose himself among others. The "they do it" tranquilizer is almost always an escape from anxiety.

Perhaps the most dangerous aspect of all this is that a certain measure of contentment is possible as long as the escapes continue to work; for as long as a man is content, he is almost impregnable against the ravages of anxiety. But the contented man finds that his contentment is elusive. So he works his way deeper and deeper into the world of things, or seeks an ever greater identification with his group in a never ending effort to prolong his contentment. He is lost, and he has no remedy for it because he does not even know that he is lost.

This, then, is the picture of the human condition, or perhaps better, the human predicament. Admittedly, it is more of a line sketch than a finished portrait, but I think our purpose here is served better by a brief outline than by copious detail.

The picture is of a man conditioned in his existence by forces within and without—strong forces, powerful forces, ever present forces. Pitting his own weakness against such

opposition, a man feels helpless—and how can he feel otherwise? It is so easy to compromise, so hard to fight; so easy to run after sweet enticements of the world, the flesh and others; so hard to resist, to remain true to one's own nature.

With every failure a man becomes more and more irrevocably ensnared in the anguish which comes from trading his freedom and self-respect for pseudo-values. His life is empty and meaningless, he toils without reward and suffers without relief. And the most unfortunate part of all this is that it all seems so inevitable, so universal. The existentialist philosophers (many of whom are atheists), who started publishing in Europe just after World War II, have addressed themselves to the prodigious problem of understanding man in all his complexity, in all his relatedness, and they have been described more than once as depressingly pessimistic. Their analysis of life, of human nature, and of all of human existence leaves no doubt that man, left to himself, has little chance of ever living up to his human potential or of ever being really happy. In the words of Jean Paul Sartre: "Life is nausea" and "Man is a useless passion."

PART 2
THE GOOD NEWS

THE BIBLE IS AN IMPORTANT SOURCE OF ADDITIONAL information about the human condition, that is, about the way in which a man understands his own existence. To the believer, the Bible is the word of God, God speaking to his people. To the unbeliever, the Bible is only an interesting book; to some it is nonsense. To the believer, the Bible is revelation, knowledge of himself, of his origins, of his destiny, and of his God. To the unbeliever it is unbelievable. The Bible does, in fact, corroborate the analysis of the human condition which we have just completed. In addition it supplies the answers to the problems of human existence and the hope of a better existence. The key to it all, the most fundamental idea, is where we must begin; that is, with the idea of Himself that God has revealed to us.

THE HOLY GOD

At some point in time God revealed Himself to man. Neither the date nor the place is known, nor the manner of revelation, nor its full content. But it must have happened somehow, somewhere, or there is no explanation for the Hebrew understanding of a God who is above and beyond all of nature, who is, in fact, its Creator. No other ancient

civilization, no other people, not a single individual ever arrived at the concept of creation—that a single being pre-existed the world and brought it into being out of nothingness. Not even Plato or Aristotle or Plotinus, the greatest minds of antiquity, were able to conceive of such a thing. Oh, it is certainly without doubt that every ancient culture had its gods. It is equally certain that some cultures had myths similar to the creation narrative of Genesis. But not one of these gods was ever liberated from the material world of those who worshipped them. And the myths which describe the formation of the world describe just that, its *formation* from formless matter, not its *creation* from nothingness by a being who pre-existed it. There were the gods of Fire, Wind, Sun, and Earth, and the all too human gods; but nowhere outside of Hebrew tradition was there a god above and beyond all creation, a Creator.

The editor of Genesis, who put together several oral traditions in his compilation, did not hesitate to contradict himself in several places when describing the origins of the world and all that is in it. It seems obvious that his intention was not to describe the time and sequence of creation at all. What is significant is that he places side by side two lists of things and attributes their origin (that is, the origin of everything) to God. That is the whole point. Everything that exists does so because God has created it. In several psalms and in other places throughout scripture this belief in creation is repeated and re-emphasized. For example, Psalm 99 (100)[11] reads: "Know that the Lord is God; he made us, his we are." And all of Psalm 103 (104) is a beautiful

[11] The two numbers are given because the numbering of the psalms depends upon the text from which the translation was made. The current Hebrew text forms two separate psalms, 9 and 10, from what in other texts are called 9A and 9B.

hymn describing poetically the wisdom and power of the Creator.

I think it is interesting to note here that neither science nor philosophy has ever proven or disproven creation. The reason is easy to find: it is impossible to do so. What is more, they have no business discussing it in the first place. Creation as described is a fact, a fact impossible to observe, and therefore beyond the discipline of science which demands observation by its very method. Philosophy can only prove truths, and no logic in the world can prove a fact. No one can prove that I am sitting in a chair right now. He can observe it, but he cannot prove it without observations. So it is with creation. The only way the ancient Semitic tribe, which later developed into the Hebrew people, could have come by the idea of creation, would have been either by insight or revelation. The most brilliant minds of antiquity never reached the conclusion that their world was created, so it seems more likely that the fact of creation was revealed by God to the people of His choice. This is what we believe.

What does all this mean in terms of human existence? Well, it does make a difference to a man if he knows that he is not just a man, but a creature of a Creator. A little orphan girl, who has never known a mother or a father, knows that she is a little girl but she has no idea of what it means to be a daughter, the daughter of her mother. Men and women who have never heard of God, who find that they cannot believe in God, know themselves only as men and women. They have no idea of what is means to be a creature, no idea of what it means to owe their very existence to a being outside of themselves, or to belong to one who sustains them in existence, whose will to create them is the ultimate reason of their existence.

When I was a boy, I had a lead casting set, which I used to make soldiers. After pouring the molten lead into the molds and waiting for them to harden, I would take them out and admire what I had done. I had made something. It was mine. To the believer, God is the one who made him, God is the one who made him as he is. So he understands that he *belongs* to God, as does everything else. Whatever he is, whatever he must endure, whatever comes to him in any way, does so because his God is also the Creator.

Before we go any further, we must pause to discuss at some length the most fundamental characteristic of God, what the ancients called the "Holiness" of God. As the discussion proceeds you may ask yourself: "But what has this to do with myself, with the way in which I understand myself?" As you proceed further, I hope you will find the answer. I might point out again that we not only are, but we are related; and because we are related, we can only understand ourselves if we understand the terms of those relationships. In the instance just discussed, we cannot know ourselves as creatures unless we know that there is a Creator, and we cannot fully understand what it means to be a creature unless we fully understand (at least as far as possible) what it means to be the Creator. We have not fully developed that idea yet because we cannot understand God as Creator until we understand that God is God, which is to say, that God is Holy.

God is God. He is frightening and fascinating, mysterious and majestic, terrible and terrifying. In short, He is Holy. This, I believe, is the most profound, the most important, and the most neglected revelation of the Bible. To describe it, let us begin with the words of Isaia:

> I saw the Lord seated on a high and lofty throne, with the train of his garments filling the temple. Seraphim were stationed above; each of them had six wings: with two they veiled their faces, with two they veiled their feet, and with two they hovered aloft. "Holy, holy, holy is the Lord of hosts!" they cried one to the other. "All the earth is filled with his glory!" At the sound of that cry, the frame of the door shook and the house was filled with smoke. Then I said, "Woe is me, I am doomed! For I am a man of unclean lips, living among a people of unclean lips; yet my eyes have seen the King, the Lord of hosts!" (Isa. 6:1-9).

The smoke or cloud that filled the temple had been a symbol of God's presence ever since the Exodus (the journey of the Hebrew people from slavery in Egypt to freedom in the Promised land). According to the description,

> The Lord preceded them, in the daytime by means of a column of cloud to show them the way, and at night by means of a column of fire to give them light. . . . Neither the column of cloud by day nor the column of fire by night ever left its place in front of the people (Ex. 13: 21-2).

And while still on this same journey to the Promised Land, one day the Hebrew people camped at the foot of Mount Sinai and Moses went up the mountain to pray. While he was there, God told him to tell the people to prepare themselves for three days, for on the third day He would descend upon the mountain in the sight of them all. The mountain was to be roped off at the base and no creature, human or animal, was to approach beyond the ropes

or he must be stoned to death. The description of that event goes like this:

> On the morning of the third day there were peals of thunder and lightning, and a heavy cloud over the mountain, and a very loud trumpet blast, so that all the people in the camp trembled. But Moses led the people out of the camp to meet God, and they stationed themselves at the foot of the mountain. Mount Sinai was all wrapped in smoke, for the Lord came down upon it in fire. The smoke rose from it as though from a furnace, and the whole mountain trembled violently. The trumpet blast grew louder and louder, while Moses was speaking and God answering him with thunder. When the Lord came down to the top of Mount Sinai, he summoned Moses to the top of the mountain, and Moses went up to him (Ex. 19:16-21).

It was at this time that Moses received the ten commandments. He came down from the mountain and the narrative continues:

> When the people witnessed the thunder and lightning, the trumpet blast and the mountain smoking, they all feared and trembled. So they took up a position much farther away and said to Moses, "You speak to us, and we will listen; but let not God speak to us, or we shall die" (Ex. 20:18-19).

So Moses took upon himself the task of meeting and speaking with the Lord and one day he said to Him: let me see your glory. God answered:

> "I will make all my beauty pass before you, and in your presence I will pronounce my name, 'Lord'; I who show

favors to whom I will, I who grant mercy to whom I will. But my face you cannot see, for no man sees me and still lives" (Ex. 33:19-20).

It was also at this time that Moses received the directions for making the Ark of the Covenant and the tent that would cover it. Once this was made, the cloud that had accompanied the Israelites settled over the tent of the Ark. When Solomon's temple was finally finished and the Ark placed in the inner sanctuary, the cloud once again appeared, this time for the last time, and it filled the whole temple. And Solomon said: "The Lord said that he would dwell in a cloud" (3 Kgs. 8:12).

I think that sums it up nicely. The cloud was a symbol of God's presence with His people; but at the same time it also symbolized the fact that God was unknowable, mysterious, hidden. Our vision cannot penetrate a cloud, and our minds cannot fathom the immensity or the mystery of God. The word "holy," which the Seraphim used in the vision of Isaia, originally had the same meaning: set apart, distinct from, above and beyond. This was the Hebrew notion of God from the very beginning, and the Holy God of Israel was unique throughout all the ancient cultures for this very reason, as we mentioned above. The Hebrew God was Holy. He was above and beyond the world, He existed before the world began—in fact, he created it.

The point of all this is that we do not know God as he really is, simply because we cannot. He is different from ourselves. He is not a man nor even a superman, which is why he has been aptly described as "The Entirely Other." There is no doubt that we never really know another as well as we know ourselves. We can guess at their secret thoughts

and motives because in many ways they are like us. Not so with God. He is the Entirely Other. Again in Isaia we read: "Thus saith the Lord: . . . 'Your thoughts are not my thoughts nor your ways my ways. For as high as are the heavens above the earth, so are my ways above your ways and my thoughts above your thoughts' " (Isa. 55:8-9).

This idea of God, which we find revealed in the pages of Sacred Scripture, is that of a God so far above and beyond all creation that no created thing, man included, could bear to see Him. The experience would be more than we could endure. "To see God is to die" is a phrase that occurs again and again in the Old Testament. In the vision of Isaia even the Seraphim covered their eyes so that they would not see him! This is the aspect of holiness which arises from the majesty and mystery of the Entirely Other.

We are all familiar with the feeling of uneasiness, of fear, which takes hold of us in the darkness of an unfamiliar deserted house. Ghost stories play upon those feelings, and they are often accompanied by "crawling of the flesh" or goose-pimples. We are afraid of the uncanny, of the mysterious. In an extreme situation it can be terrifying. It can also be fascinating and alluring. How many have felt almost irresistibly drawn to investigate a deserted house or a dark cavern, or just to walk through a cemetery at night alone? How many have been fascinated and drawn to flirtation with death? These too, are aspects of holiness; for that which is holy is mysterious, and because mysterious, it is terrifying and fascinating.

Add to that the impression one experiences when confronted by genuine greatness: in the presence of a tremendous physical upheaval, such as an earthquake or a hurricane; at the sight of something great and beautiful, such as

an entire forest ablaze in the glory of autumn colors; or at the foot of a great waterfall, or a breathtaking panorama of earth and sea and sky; one feels overwhelmed with a sense of awe. Reporting his impression of the first A-bomb detonation Brigadier General Farrell wrote:

> We were reaching into the unknown and we did not know what might come of it. . . . The whole country was lighted by a searing light with an intensity many times that of the midday sun. . . . Thirty seconds after the explosion came, first, the air blast pressing hard against the people and things, to be followed almost immediately by the strong, sustained, awesome roar which warned of doomsday and made us feel that we puny things were blasphemous to dare tamper with the forces heretofore reserved to the Almighty. Words are inadequate tools for the job of acquainting those not present with the physical, mental and psychological effects. It had to be witnessed to be realized. . . . The feeling of the entire assembly, even the uninitiated, was one of profound awe.[12]

This, too, is an effect of holiness, the awe which one feels when faced with the overwhelming.

That God, our God, should be so described is not easily accepted by many of us. The holiness of God, this holiness, is not familiar or popular. To many of us God is a kindly, benevolent gentleman who patiently puts up with us and who is always anxious to forgive. He is kind and gentle and there is nothing fearful about him—let alone something terrible and terrifying. And yet, I speak the truth to you, nothing could be further from the truth. To use Bouyer's phrase, our God is not a "doting grandfather"; He is the

[12] As quoted by Robert Jungk in *Brighter Than a Thousand Suns,* tr. by James Cleugh (New York: Harcourt, Brace and World, Inc., 1958), p. 201.

Entirely Other, the Holy, the awe-inspiring God of overwhelming majesty.

This is the idea of himself that he has revealed to us in the Bible, if we will only open our eyes to see it. At the risk of overstressing a point, because it is so important and because without it there is neither understanding nor mystery, I want to offer at least a token sampling of texts in support of this point.

Everywhere that God's great power is mentioned, His holiness is implicitly affirmed. He is the Creator, who simply by willing it can call into existence whatever He wishes. He arranges the affairs of men and of nations. He controls the elements and the forces of the world. Throughout and before the Exodus He displayed his fearful might, as we have already seen. From the founding of the Kingdom to its spread and affluence, to its destruction and restoration and, finally, to the sending of the Christ, God made it clear to the Hebrew people that He was their God. From time to time he raised up prophets, often against their will, men who would speak out to remind the people, His chosen people, that He indeed was their God.

There was Isaia: "Get behind the rocks, hide in the dust, from the terror of the Lord and the splendor of his majesty! The haughty eyes of man will be lowered, the arrogance of men will be abased, and the Lord alone will be exalted" (Isa. 2:10-11).

And there was Jeremia: "The Lord is true God, he is the living God, the eternal king, before whose anger the earth quakes, whose wrath the nations cannot endure; he who made the earth by his power, established the world by his wisdom, and stretched out the heavens by his skill" (Jer. 10:10-12).

Ezechiel wrote of visions of wheels and strange figures beyond human imagination, his way of attesting to the mystery and transcendence of God. Investigating the question of the origin of evil, the book of Job ends, too, with descriptions of weird and unusual things; that is, with the conclusion that God's reasons are beyond our comprehension, simply because God is beyond and above all of creation.

The psalms, too, are a constant witness to awesomeness, the terrifying mystery and majesty of the Holy God who is our Creator.

> Serve the Lord with fear, and rejoice before him; with trembling pay homage to him, lest he be angry and you perish in the way, when his anger blazes suddenly (Ps. 2:11-12).

> For great is the Lord and highly to be praised; awesome is he beyond all gods. For all the gods of the nations are things of nought, but the Lord made the heavens. Splendor and majesty go before him; praise and grandeur are in his sanctuary. Give to the Lord, you families of nations, give to the Lord glory and praise; give to the Lord the glory due his name! Bring gifts and enter his courts; worship the Lord in holy attire. Tremble before him all the earth . . . (Ps. 95(96):4-10).

> The Lord is king; the peoples tremble; he is throned upon the cherubim; the earth quakes. The Lord in Sion is great, he is high above all the peoples. Let them praise your great and awesome name; holy is he! (Ps. 98 (99):1-3).

> Great is the Lord and highly to be praised; his greatness is unsearchable. Generation after generation praises your works and proclaims your might. They speak of the

splendor of your glorious majesty and tell of your wondrous works. They discourse of the power of your terrible deeds and declare your greatness (Ps. 144(145):3-6).

I think by now the point is made: God is God. To the believer, the Creator is the Holy One, mysterious, fascinating and terrifying. He is the Entirely Other. Such an understanding of God can produce a profound effect on the way we understand ourselves; but before we attempt to work that out, it must be emphasized that this idea of God was not something that was destined to be altered or discarded with the coming of Christ. God is every bit as much God now as he was before; and the New Testament, too, is eloquent witness of God's holiness.

The human response to God's holiness is a mixture of those elements we have already discussed: fear, awe, and fascination. To these must be added reverence, and others which we will come to later. Throughout ancient times and in the Christian era, too, places have been set aside for special worship. They are called shrines or sanctuaries, holy places, for "sanctuary" comes from the Latin word meaning "holy." The shrines are places which are holy, that is, set aside, set apart for the worship of God who somehow manifested some special sign in that place. Notice that reverence for God extended itself to include things in some way connected with Him. Any display of divine power or visitation from a divine messenger carried with it to the Hebrew believer the implication of God's presence. So it is no wonder that we find Mary, in the New Testament, afraid in the presence of the angel who announced to her that she was to be the mother of the Messiah.

When the birth of Christ was announced by the angels to the shepherds, they threw themselves to the ground and covered their eyes, because they were afraid. Many of the accounts of miracles recorded in the New Testament end with the phrase (or its equivalent): and the people were afraid. Perhaps most striking is the account of the Transfiguration in Matthew (17:1–8). Christ took Peter, James, and John up Mount Tabor and was transfigured before them. His countenance was radiant, His garments glowing. Moses and Elias appeared and carried on a conversation with Him. Evidently by this time the Apostles had grown accustomed to seeing Jesus work wonders. They may have been amazed once again, but they were no longer afraid.[13] Peter even made the suggestion that it was good to be there and why not pitch three tents, one for Jesus, one for Moses, and one for Elias. Then, a cloud appeared, the symbol of God's presence ever since the Exodus; and a voice thundered from the cloud: "This is my beloved son in whom I am well pleased." At that moment, and not before, Peter, James and John threw themselves to the ground and covered their eyes, because they were afraid.

"Fear of the Lord is the beginning of wisdom," says the Old Testament. The author of the Epistle to the Hebrews wrote: ". . . we have grace, through which we may offer pleasing service to God with fear and reverence. For our God is a consuming fire" (Heb. 12:29). Jesus himself in many ways and in many parables insisted on the primacy of God, of the need to be concerned about Him above all else. "Seek first the kingdom of heaven and all the rest will

[13] At this time they could not possibly have known that Jesus was himself God. This did not come until Pentecost.

be added to you besides." The first commandment is to love the Lord your God with your *whole* heart and your *whole* soul and your *whole* mind. And when he taught us to pray, he said to say: "Our Father, who art in heaven, hallowed [that is, holy] be thy name . . ." (Matt. 6:9).

The Christian saints, too, have always recognized God's holiness. St. John Chrysostom, one of the four great Doctors of the Eastern Church, wrote: "We call him the inexpressible, the unthinkable God, the invisible, the inapprehensible; who quells the power of human speech and transcends the grasp of mortal thought; inaccessible to the angels, unbeheld of the seraphim, unimagined of the cherubim, invisible to the principalities and authorities and powers, and, in a word, to all creation. . . ." [14]

St. Theresa of Avila advised the sisters of her reformed Carmelites that it takes courage to draw near to God. She wrote:

> The brilliance of the vision is like that of infused light or of a sun covered with material of the transparency of a diamond, if such a thing could be woven. . . . Almost invariably the soul on which God bestows this favor remains in rapture, because its unworthiness cannot endure so terrible a sight. I say 'terrible,' because though the sight is the loveliest and most delightful imaginable, even by a person who lived and strove to imagine it for a thousand years, because it so far exceeds all that our imagination and understanding can compass, its presence is of such exceeding majesty that it fills the soul with a great terror. It is unnecessary to ask here how, without being

[14] Migne, *Patrol Graecae* p. 721, as quoted by Rudolph Otto, *The Idea of the Holy,* tr. by J. W. Harvey (New York: Oxford Univ. Press, 1958), p. 180.

told, the soul knows who it is, for He reveals Himself quite clearly as the Lord of Heaven and earth.[15]

The Church, too, perpetuates her awareness of God's holiness in her central act of worship, the renewal of the Sacrifice of Christ, the Sacrifice of the Mass. The solemn moment of consecration is approached slowly and reverently by way of many prayers of preparation and ritual purification; and afterwards there is a gradual, reverent withdrawal. Just before the Canon of the Mass, there is a hymn of thanksgiving and praise, the Preface, which often ends with the formula: "Through whom the angels praise thy majesty, the dominions worship it, the powers tremble. . . ." This is followed by the prayer of the seraphim in the vision of Isaia: "Holy, holy, holy, Lord God of hosts. Heaven and earth are full of thy glory."

There it is. The Holy God of Israel is the Holy God of Christianity, and it is only this understanding of God that reveals the mystery of the Hebrew-Christian religion. Why has the Holy God created us? Why does He suffer us? Why has He redeemed us? How could He become a man? Why is He concerned about us? These questions will always remain unanswered, for therein lies the mystery, the mystery of Creation, Incarnation, Redemption and divine love.

With such an understanding of God, we begin to assume the attitudes of a man of faith. When we finally become aware of the supreme majesty and overwhelming splendor of the God who dwells in unapproachable light, we cannot help but feel unworthy and sinful and insignificant. We begin to understand how the saints could say of themselves:

[15] *Interior Castle,* c.9, "Sixth Mansion," from *The Complete Works of Saint Teresa of Avila,* 3 vols., trans. and edited by E. Allison Peers (New York: Sheed and Ward, Inc., 1946).

"I am unworthy. I am nothing. I am a sinner." We begin to realize that this evaluation of themselves sprang, not from a morbid self-depreciation, but from a vivid awareness of the reality of God.

When a man stands at the shore of a great sea, contemplating its vastness, he cannot help but feel small and insignificant. And when he extends his vision to the wide reaches of space and the huge galaxies which expand throughout it, he may very well come to the conclusion, as others have, that he is but a speck of cosmic dust. Now let his vision go beyond even that to the Holy God who is its creator, whose splendor and majesty are but dimly reflected in all of this, His creation—what are his feelings then? In a word, he feels humble, for humility is the awareness and acceptance of one's own nothingness, sinfulness and unworthiness before God.

When illumined by the Light of the world and confronted by Him who created heaven and earth, we begin to understand ourselves for what we really are. We can no longer accept the illusion that we have made ourselves into something quite worthwhile. There comes a moment, a brief instant at least, when, exposed to the sudden realization of what God is and finally secured in the grip of that experience, we become transparent to ourselves. We understand our utter insignificance and our defilement.

And, as we become more and more penetrated by the idea of His divinity, as we begin to understand more clearly and appreciate more fully the content of the words, "My God," at the same time we gain an insight and a perspective which lights up our whole existence. All of reality becomes transformed before our eyes. We see with the clear vision of a man who has been elevated to the vantage point of

God. All ordinary standards of judgment fall like scales from our eyes and we see. We see ourselves and our world and everything in it for what they undoubtedly are. We know with unshakeable certitude that this is God's world and that it is nothing.

The realization of the holiness of God is elevating and liberating. Our day to day humdrum dullness and bluntness are shattered by the intrusion of a reality that cannot be ignored or silenced. For once, for the moment, we understand—and it seems as though we understand everything. All of a sudden everything in existence falls into place. We know what we are, what the world is, what everything in the world is for. The multiplicity of our experience, which has always served to confuse and distract us, has been reduced to unity. At once we see all things in God.

What a difference between this understanding of ourselves and our existence, and that of a man who does not or cannot believe in God!

CREATURELINESS

Now we are in a position to attempt an understanding of ourselves as creatures of the Creator, for now we can understand that we are creatures of the Holy God. *God* is our Creator; our Creator is our *God*.

We have already indicated that understanding ourselves as creatures of a Creator means that we accept as fact that we are not simply and only men and women existing alone and autonomously. We belong to our Creator. He made us. We owe Him our very existence. Now, because we know our Creator is God, we know that even though we exist, we are nothing before Him.

We say that we belong to God, because creation was not a once-and-for-all divine act. He did not say: "Let the world be created," and that was that; and here we are, who knows how many billions of years later. God's creative activity endures at this moment in everything that exists. He is present in everything at every moment sustaining it in existence. The psalmist puts it this way: "If you hide your face, they are dismayed; if you take away their breath, they perish and return to their dust. When you send forth your spirit, they are created, and you renew the face of the earth" (Ps. 103[104]:29-30).

This means that God is present *in* everything, and everything is utterly dependent upon Him. We are in God, He is in us, and this is the reason we exist. His knowledge of us is complete down to our innermost desires and most secret thoughts. His power over us is absolute or, from another point of view, our dependence on Him is absolute. We cannot blink an eye or move a finger or think a thought without Him, without His creative power sustaining our activity. Literally, He is our life and our vitality. This is not pantheism, for we are not God . . . but we are literally nothing without Him.

Obviously, it follows from all this that God has a claim on us. If He asks anything of us, it seems equally obvious that we should give Him what he asks. Who is the creature of the Holy God who would dare to refuse? Everything in the universe follows the strict physical laws which express the will and the design of the Creator. Even on the atomic and nuclear level, where statistical analysis obscures cause and effect, even there there must be a causal relationship that remains to be discovered. Everything, in other words,

is limited in its behaviour by the design of the Creator who made it—everything, that is, but man.

The author of the creation narrative describes man as a creature of this world. As this narrative explains it, God made man out of the dust of the earth and His own spirit. Notice the parallel here between our analysis of the first part of this book and this description of man's being by a primitive Hebrew. By ascribing man's origin to two sources, earth and the spirit of God, he describes, in his own way, the dual nature of man. Man is of the earth, definitely part of the world, by God's own design. He is also part spirit, for the spirit of God is the source of his life. At the same time, it is the source of his difference from all the rest of creation.

The writer goes on to say that God places man in a garden, where there is a copious supply of water and food, and that the only thing man had to do was to tend the garden and guard it. These things, too, indicate further insights of the author. To a desert nomad, as these ancient Hebrews were, such a situation would represent a "paradise," a land of plenty. A man could be happy there, very happy; but he was to find his happiness, not just in repose, but in working, in living in harmony with the existence determined for him by his Creator. This, too, correlates with the analysis of Part I. God made man to live on earth, to be a part of the world, to affect it and be affected by it. The believer understands that he is here and that his existence is conditioned by the world, because that is the way God intended it to be. In these few lines from Genesis he discovers the reason for his existence-in-the-world: God wills it. He has already learned that he cannot discover why

God wills it, but for him it is enough to know that it is the result of an act of God.

In the garden there were many trees, pleasant to see and good for food. It was the author's way of saying that man was in very comfortable surroundings, free from want and anxiety. There were two trees in particular, though, that the author mentions and names. The first was the "tree of life;" the second, the "tree of the knowledge of good and evil." It seems that the point of drawing attention to the presence of the tree of life and its accessibility to man was to indicate that in the beginning, man could continually avail himself of the source of life; or, more simply, man would never die—yet another reason for the happy condition of man in the beginning.

The tree of the knowledge of good and evil presents a different set of circumstances. This tree was the object of a divine injunction and warning. The narrator writes: "And the Lord God commanded man thus: 'From every tree of the garden you may eat; but from the tree of the knowledge of good and evil you must not eat; for the day you eat of it, you must die' " (Gen. 2:16-17). The meaning seems clear enough. Man is free, but not entirely free. Certainly, the command and the penalty make no sense unless man already knows the difference between good and evil; so to partake of the knowledge of good and evil, to appropriate it to himself, must mean for man to decide for himself what is good and evil, which only God has the right to do. Very cleverly, the author has described a fundamental condition of man's existence, which is, at the same time, a source of antagonism between him and his Creator. Man is finite, limited in many ways, in this instance, in his choice. He is

free, but not entirely free. There are many, many things he can do, but he cannot do everything. His choice in many ways is unrestricted, but there are some things he is forbidden to do. To be sure, he can choose to do them anyhow, but then he clashes against the divine warning: If you do, you shall die.

Here, too, is confirmation of another condition of human existence as we saw it in Part I. Man is always in the state of possibility. He can choose life or death. He can choose to do what he ought and so achieve peace and inner harmony, or he can choose to do what he should not, and destroy himself in the process. The Bible reveals the choice from a different aspect. Here it becomes a choice between autonomy and subordination to God's will. From this point of view we have a divinely revealed condition of human existence, and like every condition of existence, it is universal and inescapable.

Man always stands poised before the possibility of freely determining what he shall do. He can submit to the will of his Creator, or he can arrogate to himself the right to decide for himself what he may do. The tension is experienced by every man, and the creation narrative makes it clear that this has been the condition of man from the beginning. Many are the men who bitterly resent this restriction in their freedom. Many more are they who ignore it. They decide for autonomy. They decide that they, and not their Creator, shall set the limits of their freedom.

In this lies the meaning of sin, the meaning of moral guilt, and the cause of estrangement. From all that has been said previously of the majesty of God, a man's decision to defy God can only be described as enormous arrogance. It could

be ludicrous or pitiful to watch a man pit his weakness against the violence of a raging flood, but even the awesome power of nature is nothing compared with the Holy God; so when this same man stands before his God and says: "I will not submit," the grossness of his arrogance precludes any thought of humor or pity. This situation is serious, as serious and as grave as any could be, and the possible consequences are so overwhelming as to be unthinkable.

Sin is defiance of the *Creator*. A sinner is the man who chooses to disobey the God who created him and who, at this moment, sustains him in existence; who, for that matter, actually gives him the power to make such a choice!

This was the choice made by man in the beginning, so the Bible tells us. At that instant God could have annihilated man or the entire universe, but for reasons known only to him, he did not do it. Instead he declared that his friendship with man was over, and he imposed penalties, among which was death. The author of the Fall narrative says all this by describing a series of events. He says that man and Creator were on friendly terms before the fall; the Lord used to walk with man in the garden. But once man chose to make himself like God by arrogating to himself the right to decide for himself what was right or wrong, he knew immediately that he had done wrong, and he no longer felt comfortable in God's presence. He knew the meaning of guilt and estrangement. God had been his friend, but he chose to defy Him. Now he was afraid of God. He tried to hide, but God found him and confronted him with his deed. He tried to excuse himself and it did not work. God found him guilty and imposed the sentence he had foretold. He barred man from the garden and from His presence, which

means from access to the tree of life. Lacking that, he woud die.

To the believer, all of this can be taken in two ways, both of them valid. It can be understood as the revelation of an original condition of man which was forfeited by this original sin. The author makes no attempt at describing either the nature of the sin or the immediate cause. What he does say is that man was destined by God to live happily with Him, as long as he chose to accept the limitations placed on his freedom. The possibility of transgression is apparent when it is realized that man could choose either his destiny or complete freedom, that is, freedom without any limitation. And, finally, the author says that man chose total freedom rather than this destiny his Creator had prepared for him. This defiance of God led to estrangement, which has been the condition of unredeemed man ever since.

In addition to this interpretation, we can also find a description of the human predicament, valid for any man, any time, anywhere. It is this. Man is born in the image of God, essentially innocent, the state of "original innocence," as it were. He finds himself free to choose either submission or autonomy. If he accepts the limitations of his freedom, he will continue to live at peace with God and himself. If he chooses autonomy, he begets sin, guilt and estrangement.

At this point, then, the believer understands his creatureliness as existing before the Holy One—not just as creature, but as fallen-creature; not only as nothing before His majesty, and not simply defiled as anything is in the presence of His splendor, but as sinfully defiled. To grasp the full reality of his creatureliness, he knows he must accept as fact that he exists before his God as guilty and estranged. This is a reality that the non-believer cannot accept.

SEX

The creation narrative also sheds light on the meaning of sex and sexuality. Unlike the pseudo-Christian (or, perhaps more realistically, the misinformed Christian), the narrator is not afraid of sex or sexuality. He neither condemns it nor ignores it. In this he foreshadows the treatment of the subject as it is further discussed by poets, prophets and other writers of the Bible; which is to say, he treats it as a condition of human existence, a matter of fact, too important to be ignored.

As usual, he makes his point by letting action be the conveyance of his insights. The dramatic episode offers an understanding of sex by describing the formation of woman together with its causes and effects.

The sequence of events begins with the observation by God: "It is not good for man to be alone. I will make him a helper like himself." To be alone does not mean only to be isolated from another. It means to have *no* other, or more precisely, to have no *other* with whom one may commune. To be alone is to be capable of love and union with another, although there is no possibility of fulfilling that capability because there is no other. A man who is alone, in this sense, is hopelessly frustrated, and the evaluation given is precise: "It is not good."

To remedy the situation, a decision is made to make man a "helper like himself," a phrasing which is more meaningful if we go back to the original. Today we think of a helper as a fellow worker, as one who assists us in performing a particular task. The qualification here, "like himself," in the Hebrew is literally: "as in front of him," which forcefully indicates that this type of helper for man is not to be

the kind that will work along side of him at a common task, one who will help him do something. "To be in front of him" graphically represents a polarity, an I-Thou relationship, a complementariness on the level of being, not of doing. This being that God will create for man will remedy his loneliness and fill up his emptiness by loving him and by giving him someone to love. Each will be ordered to the other, to give and receive from the other. Face to face, each will penetrate the inner depths of the other's being and find there the complement of his own.

To illustrate this further, the author then describes a great animal parade. God forms the beasts of the earth and has them pass by Adam, who gives a name to each. God listens to the names to discover whether or not Adam will find any of the animals to be suitable companions, inasmuch as a name in primitive societies represented the way in which the object affects the observer. Since Adam did not find his "helper" among the animals, God decides to act again.

This time God puts Adam to sleep. While he is unconscious, God removes one of his ribs and from it fashions Woman. When Adam awakens, he sees the woman and says: "She now is bone of my bone and flesh of my flesh; she shall be called Woman . . ." (Gen. 2:23).

Dramatically, the narrative has built to a climax, and here the point is made quite clearly. Woman was formed from man while man was unconscious. His relationship to her is below the level of consciousness, that is, without knowing why, he knows he is incomplete without her and he yearns to be united to her; for he knows that in this union he will find himself fulfilled. From her side, she, too, seeks to be united to man, because from the first moment

of her existence she has been a part of man. Together they will make a whole, which individually they could never achieve, and for which they would always yearn. Each would see in the other a self that was not self, a likeness that was different. They will be two in one flesh, separate as individuals, yet one in that new life which they will have together.

Notice that biblical thought, far from hiding or, even worse, condemning sexuality, attributes its origin to God himself. Sexual differentiation and orientation, the desire for sexual fulfillment and the experience of oneness it affords is prior to any decision of either man or woman. It is of their very being to be so, and their being is from God. The believer not only need not be ashamed of his sexual urges, he *should* not be. They derive from his being, which came to him that way from God.

From another point of view, the truth of this narrative is confirmed each time a man and a woman fall in love. They want each other, exclusively and forever. Each recognizes the other as a gift from God (though sometimes they speak of God as Fate or the Stars or Good Luck). And both know that they belong to the other and are mutually fulfilled in their oneness. The believer can see the hand of God in all this, and on that account recognize its sacredness, goodness and beauty in a way that a non-believer could not conceive. The believer can grasp a purpose and meaning to love and sex, which adds to his understanding of himself and his beloved. The unbeliever is deprived of all this.

As the narrative and the rest of the Bible indicate, sex after the Fall becomes a powerful source of tension. Sexual union was originally intended to be the experience by which oneness is recaptured and fulfillment achieved. By divorcing

it from its original purpose and meaning in any one of the many forms of sexual deviation, man was not only destroying himself, but acting contrary to God's intention. This became crystallized when directives were formulated concerning sexual behavior. Every bit of it confirms the original insight of the creation narrative: man was made for woman and only woman; when a man and a woman join in marital union, they become two in one flesh; they are then a whole; each has become the other's by becoming one with the other. From this it follows that neither is any longer entitled to enter into further unions, for each has given up that right when the first union is consummated. The Ten Commandments include: "Thou shalt not commit adultery" and "Thou shalt not covet they neighbor's wife." Moses permitted divorce, Christ said, because of the obstinacy of the people, but from Christ's time onward, it would no longer be permitted. His words are clear and final, an affirmation of the original divine intention and the law of being which God implanted in human nature itself: "What God has joined together, let no man put asunder. . . . And I say to you, that whoever puts away his wife, except for immorality, and marries another, commits adultery; and he who marries a woman who has been put away commits adultery" (Matt. 19:3-9).

There are some believers, as well as non-believers, who have a horror of sex and sexuality—and wrongly so, as should be obvious from the previous pages. Wrongly informed, they are victims of an impossible internal conflict that should never be. God made them as they are and they struggle vainly against their very nature, an inescapable condition of their existence. Some have erroneously blamed St. Paul for this because he wrote: "It is better to marry

than to burn," an answer to a specific question and hardly the expression of his total view on marriage and sex. St. Paul also extolled virginity, as did our Lord, but, again, in a specific context in which virginity is recommended for those who can take it, or better, for those who receive this as a gift from the Lord.

As a matter of fact, it is St. Paul who uses marriage as the symbol of Christ's union with the Church: "Husbands, love your wives, just as Christ also loved the church. . . ."—and St. Paul knew what marital love was. He writes: "He who loves his own wife, loves himself." and he continues: "For no one ever hated his own flesh; on the contrary, he nourishes and cherishes it, as Christ also does the church. . . . 'For this cause a man shall leave his father and mother, and cleave to his wife; and the two shall become one flesh.' This is a great mystery—I mean in reference to Christ and to the Church" (Eph. 5:25-32). No other natural human good has been so exalted and so blessed.

Marriage, in which sexual union permeated by love is the divinely ordained expression of fullest love, is the image of Christ's union with the Church. In marriage here on earth, the ultimate expression of love is the total giving, body and soul, of one to the other in sexual union. Christ's love for the Church is compared to such love by St. Paul—and still some say that Paul did not appreciate marital love or marriage!

What all this means to the believer is simply that God intends that a man should find his fulfillment and wholeness with one woman—and vice-versa. By their very nature, their being as He created it, this is so. The value of sexuality and, ultimately, its enduring pleasure is to be found in this communion of one man with one woman for life. It will never

be found in casual affairs or in the pursuit of sexuality for pleasure alone, a pleasure divorced from meaning and true value.

To the believer, everything that was said of sexuality in Part I holds true. In addition, though, he knows the God-given meaning and purpose of sexual union, and he knows the defilement of sexual deviation because he knows it to be sinful as well as self-destructive.

THE JUST GOD

Before we can elaborate further on a Christian's understanding of existence, we must pause to consider another aspect of the Face of God. Again the reason is that we not only are, but we are related. To understand ourselves as destined to a final judgment, a judgment which will search out every detail of our life, it is necessary to know something of the Judge. It will certainly make a difference whether the Judge overlooks many things or whether He demands that all things be right. The seriousness with which we take this business of living before God will depend, in some measure at least, on our understanding of the value which our God and Judge places on righteous living.

The term "just" in reference to God can mean several things. It can mean that He is Himself just, upright, beyond reproach, good in every way; or it can mean His will to have things right. The latter is evidenced both by His activity as judge and by His will to justify men (which we will consider in some detail later). At no time should we forget that God's justice is not man's justice. God is God, the Holy God, and his decisions are absolutely free. Whatever

comes to us comes as gift, and to ask why God chooses to justify one man and not another is the extreme of impertinence, as though God has to answer to us!

The first indication of God's justice comes to us in the creation narrative, where, as we saw earlier, God judged and punished Adam and Eve. Notice that when things were just, that is, when they were right, when man accepted his subordination to God and the limitations it imposed, there was no need for God to act as judge. Today it is the same. It is only when we decide for autonomy, when we destroy the order of justice, that God appears as judge. To the point here, though, biblical faith from the beginning knew God's justice— that God was just, that He would judge, condemn, and punish the evil in men.

Without attempting to indicate every instance of God's judgment and justice, a recounting of some will help to reenforce the point. Cain was found guilty of murdering his brother and for this he was punished. The story of the Great Flood and the Tower of Babel are further instances of justice insisted upon as only the Holy God could insist. Sodom and Gomorra knew the judgment and power of God. Pharoa repeatedly felt the punishment of God for failing to comply with the directives given him by Moses. Throughout the Exodus the Hebrew people often learned the lesson of their God's judgment and justice. For doubting him they were kept wandering in the desert for forty years; those involved in rebellion were quickly destroyed by earthquake and fire.

It was also during the exodus that God spelled out for the Hebrew people just what He expected from them. His justice was codified and the people were informed of his commands. In the highest place were the commandments,

the ten commandments given to Moses at Horeb in the desert. There God sealed a covenant with the Hebrew people, an agreement that He would be their God and they, His people. The first three commandments indicate the right relationship between man and his God:

> "I, the Lord, am your God, who brought you out of the land of Egypt, that place of slavery. You shall not have other gods besides me. You shall not carve idols for yourselves in the shape of anything in the sky above or on the earth below or in the waters beneath the earth; you shall not bow down before them or worship them. For I, the Lord, your God, am a jealous God, inflicting punishments for their fathers' wickedness on the children of those who hate me, down to the third and fourth generation but bestowing mercy, down to the thousandth generation, on the children of those who love me and keep my commandments.
>
> "You shall not take the name of the Lord, your God, in vain. For the Lord will not leave unpunished him who takes his name in vain.
>
> "Take care to keep holy the Sabbath day as the Lord, your God, commanded you. Six days you may labor and do all your work; but the seventh day is the Sabbath of the Lord, your God. No work may be done then, whether by you, or your son or daughter, or your male or female slave, or your ox or ass or any of your beasts, or the alien who lives with you. Your male and female slaves should rest as you do. For remember that you too were once slaves in Egypt, and the Lord, your God, brought you from there with his strong hand and outstretched arm. That is why the Lord, your God, has commanded you to observe the Sabbath day" (Deut. 5:6-15).

And the last seven clarify the right relationship between one man and another:

> "Honor your father and your mother, as the Lord, your God, has commanded you, that you may have a long life and prosperity in the land which the Lord, your God, is giving you.
> "You shall not kill.
> "You shall not commit adultery.
> "You shall not steal.
> "You shall not bear dishonest witness against your neighbor.
> "You shall not covet your neighbor's wife.
> "You shall not desire your neighbor's house or field, nor his male or female slave, nor his ox or ass, nor anything that belongs to him" (Deut. 5:16-21).

In effect, the covenant established a new intimacy between God and man. The Hebrew people became a chosen people, upon whom God would bestow His blessing and concern. In return, they would be expected to follow His commandments, or, as Moses put it: "Hear, O Israel! The Lord is our God, the Lord alone! Therefore, you shall love the Lord, your God, with all your heart, and with all your soul, and with all your strength" (Deut. 6:4-5). This love for God, or concern for His commandments, was to be their expression of faith and gratitude for all that He had first done for them in choosing them to be His people and in promising them His concern and protection. The history of succeeding generations shows clearly that the Hebrew people were strong on remembering the promise of God, but weak in recalling their own part of the bargain.

One after another, prophets appeared in the midst of the

people, raised up by God to advise, warn, condemn, and edify. Before Solomon there were, among others, Nathan, Samuel, Gad, Elias and Ahias, Miryam, and Debora, as well as many who are unnamed. Their message, if we recognize the oversimplification, might be described as a recall to covenant obligations; a condemnation of every violation of the commandments and a warning that Israel would know God's protection when she was faithful, His wrath when she was sinful.

With the division of the kingdom after Solomon and the further expansion of Israel, the first of the "great" prophets arose in the northern kingdom, Israel, to shed a new light on the justice of God. The prophet was Amos; the date, the middle of the eighth century; the times, prosperous and untroubled. The Israelites considered themselves the favored of God with reason, for the northern kingdom had reached the apogee of its power and good fortune. The future loomed bright. To this hope, Amos introduced a disturbing and unpopular modification:

> Hear this word, O men of Israel, that the Lord pronounces over you over the whole family that I brought up from the land of Egypt: You alone have I favored, more than all the families of the earth; therefore I will punish you for all your crimes (Am. 3:1-2).

And the reason for this punishment:

> Because you have trampled upon the weak and exacted of them levies of grain, though you have built houses of hewn stone, you shall not live in them! . . . Yes, I know how many are your crimes, how grievous your sins: oppressing the just, accepting bribes, repelling the needy at the gate! (Am. 5:11-12)

And he continues:

> Seek good and not evil, that you may live; then truly will the Lord, the God of hosts be with you as you claim! Hate evil and love good, and let justice prevail at the gate . . . (Am. 5:14-15).

God is angry with Israel because His chosen people do not love one another. They cheat, rob, and murder. They oppress the poor and ignore the helpless. And this is the sin that brings down on them the vengeance of the Lord. The lesson is clear, and though it certainly is not new to Israel, its emphasis here is significant. God, through Amos, is reaffirming in an unmistakable way that concern for one's neighbor is a necessary part of the covenant. Without it God will not recognize the Israelites as His people. He will not even accept their worship:

> I hate, I spurn your feasts, I take no pleasure in your solemnities; your cereal offerings I will not accept, nor consider your stall-fed peace offerings. Away with your noisy songs! (Am. 5:21-23)

God Himself is just, and He demands that His creatures be just.

Following closely upon Amos was the prophet Osee, and Osee takes a similar view of the future of Israel. He is horrified and alarmed by the flagrant infidelity of the Israelites to their God. Idolatry was rampant, defiling even the rulers of the people. Temples to foreign gods were built; child sacrifice, Baal worship, worship of God under the image of a bull, temple prostitution, and even processions and feasts to foreign gods were commonplace; only a remnant were faithful. "There is no fidelity, no mercy, no knowledge

of God in the land. False swearing, lying, murder, stealing and adultery! in their lawlessness, bloodshed follows bloodshed," is Osee's complaint (Os. 4:1-2).

And in a later passage he prophesies (that is, he speaks the mind of the Lord):

> I am the Lord, your God, since the land of Egypt: you know no God besides me, and there is no savior but me. I fed you in the desert, in the torrid land. They ate their fill; when filled, they became proud of heart and forgot me. Therefore, I will be like a lion to them, like a panther by the road I will keep watch. I will attack them like a bear robbed of its young, and tear their hearts from their breasts; I will devour them on the spot like a lion, as though a wild beast were to rend them. Your destruction, O Israel! who is there to help you? (Os. 13:4-9).

What Osee told the people of the Northern Kingdom (Israel), Isaia preached to the Southern Kingdom (Juda):

> Though you pray the more, I will not listen. Your hands are full of blood! Wash yourselves clean! Put away your misdeeds from before my eyes; cease doing evil; learn to do good. Make justice your aim; redress the wronged, hear the orphan's plea, defend the widow (Isa. 1:15-17).

After Isaia came Jeremia, who had to live through the siege, fall and destruction of Jerusalem. Much against his will he was selected by the Lord to deliver the first warning to his people and the final prophecies on their chastisement. If you wish to know the sins of Israel and Juda, the cause of their downfall and the terrible punishment meted out by God on His faithless people, read Jeremia.

Continuing the theme of Amos, he delivers an oft-repeated message from the Lord:

> Only if you thoroughly reform your ways and your deeds; if each of you deals justly with his neighbor; if you no longer oppress the resident alien, the orphan, and the widow; if you no longer shed innocent blood in this place, or follow strange gods to your own harm, will I remain with you in this place, in the land which I gave your fathers long ago and forever (Jer. 7:5-7).

And for those whose image of God is that of a kindly old gentleman, these words of Jeremia are a profitable lesson:

> I will dash them against each other, fathers and sons together, says the Lord; I will show no compassion, I will not spare or pity, but will destroy them (Jer. 13:14).
>
> The Lord said to me: Even if Moses and Samuel stood before me, my heart would not turn toward this people. Send them away from me. If they ask you where they should go, tell them, Thus says the Lord: whoever is marked for death, to death; whoever is marked for the sword, to the sword; whoever is marked for famine, to famine; whoever is marked for captivity, to captivity. Four kinds of scourge I have decreed against them, says the Lord: the sword to slay them; dogs to drag them about; the birds of the sky and the beasts of the earth to devour and destroy them (Jer. 15:1-3).

The justice of God, this justice which judges, condemns, and punishes injustice, so evident in the Old Dispensation, is no less evident in Christianity. The message of John the Baptist was simple, as simple as that of the prophets of old: Repent. Repent because you have sinned. "For even now

the axe is laid at the root of the trees; every tree, therefore, that is not bringing forth fruit is to be cut down and thrown into the fire" (Luke 3:9).

When Christ was asked what one must do to be just, he invariably answered by insisting on the observance of the commandments. And, although we sometimes do not hear his warnings because we find it more comfortable to concentrate on his mercy, the warnings are there—and unmistakably clear.

> Enter by the narrow gate. For wide is the gate and broad is the way that leads to destruction, and many there are who enter that way. How narrow the gate and close the way that leads to life! And few there are who find it (Matt. 7:13-14).

> Every tree that does not bear good fruit is cut down and thrown into the fire (7:19).
> Not everyone who says to me, "Lord, Lord", shall enter the kingdom of heaven; but he who does the will of my Father in heaven shall enter the kingdom of heaven (Matt. 7:21).

> Therefore, just as the weeds are gathered up and burnt with fire, so will it be at the end of the world. The Son of Man will send forth his angels, and they will gather out of his kingdom all scandals and those who work iniquity, and cast them into the furnace of fire, where there will be the weeping and gnashing of teeth. Then the just will shine forth like the sun in the kindom of their Father. He who has ears to hear, let him hear (Matt. 13:40-43).

Words such as these can strike terror in the heart of

a believer. They crystallize and concretize the anguish, the anxieties of judgment and condemnation. To be sure, they are not the whole message of salvation, since there is also mercy; but they are a part of that message. They are real and there is no escaping them or their consequences. God is merciful, yes, but He is also just. His mercy we will discuss later. At this point, it is His justice that concerns us. His justice is something we cannot overlook if we are to accept the whole of revelation, and so face the whole of reality.

All of this is important to the believer for many reasons. For one, he cannot fully understand his relation to others unless he sees it at least partially illuminated by God's justice. Furthermore, he cannot appreciate God's mercy in his behalf unless he really understands his radical unworthiness of that mercy. This he cannot grasp unless he knows the God of justice, before whose face he is a sinner.

A CHRISTIAN-IN-THE-WORLD

As we have already seen, the creation narrative indicates that man was created for this world—not for some "next" world, but for this one. He is neither angel nor animal. He is human. To attempt to exist as something other than a human being would be a mutilation of his being and at least an implicit rejection of God's will for him. Since it is by God's will that he is what he is, a human being, living a human existence, then it seems obvious that this is what God wants him to be—human. St. Paul said that we would all have to be changed somehow before we would be ready for heaven. In the meantime, we are human, and

it is as human beings that we are to work out our Christian existence in the world.

All of this is very much to the point because it helps the believer to a clear understanding of what is real. There are some strange notions about Christian existence that have popped up from time to time through the centuries, changing names and disguises. They try to make Christian existence inhuman. There are those who have condemned pleasure, as if it is inhuman and unchristian to enjoy oneself. There are those who have condemned some foods and beverages, as if Christ had never said: "There is nothing outside a man that, entering into him, can defile him; but the things that come out of a man, these are what defile a man" (Mark 7:15). There are those who have been in favor of polygamy, celibacy, divorce, retirement from society, rigorous fasts and penances, hours of prayer each day . . . and so many other things, all of which is supposed to be Christian. To be sure, some of these things for some people under special circumstances are not only compatible with Christian existence, but conducive to it; but this is not true for the vast majority of Christians, nor is it required by Christianity.

To be a Christian-in-the-world is to be a being-in-the-world. A Christian affects the world, is affected by it, and must be concerned about it. The Christian believes that he is subject to this condition of his existence because this is the situation for which God created him. In other words, the Christian believes that his Creator wants him to eat and sleep, work and love, and want to be loved in return. He knows that in doing these things he is pleasing his God who made him the way he is and gave him these things to do. There is no autonomy here. By being human and con-

cerned with things authentically human, he is being Christian. St. Paul said: "Whether you eat or drink or do anything else, do all for the glory of God" (I Cor. 10:31).

There is a problem here, though, just as there was a problem when discussing existence-in-the-world in Part I. The problem is that the world is also a threat to Christian existence. This time it is not only that authentic human existence is threatened, but that our relationship with God is also in jeopardy. We have already seen that the world outside of us is dangerous because it is there, always there, demanding our attention and concern. Christ said: "The first commandment is Thou shalt love the Lord thy God with thy whole heart, and with thy whole soul and with thy whole mind" (Matt. 22:37), which may be paraphrased: God and God's will must be the most important concern we have. Here it is not a question of becoming submerged in a world of things. Worldliness, for that is what this is called, consists in being so concerned about the things of this life that we lose sight of the fact that God and His will must be our most important concern. Once again, what is best for us as human beings is precisely what God expects of us—with this difference: it is not to achieve an authentic human existence that we must avoid identification with the world; that will come as a by-product when we give to God and our Creator the first place in our concern.

This business of living as a Christian-in-the-world without being absorbed into it is a constant theme in the New Testament. Christ comes back to it again and again. In the Sermon on the Mount he began with: "Blessed are the poor in spirit, for theirs is the kingdom of heaven," which means that those who are not attached to the things of the

world are those who will be blessed. This is not an indictment against possessions nor a blanket approval of poverty and squalor. Christ here is declaring that real values lie beyond appearances. It seems that having much should be desirable and rewarding, but Christ says that blessedness will not come from that. Instead, blessedness will be given to those who face the reality of the nothingness of things, in spite of appearances to the contrary, and who adjust their attitude towards things accordingly.

In the same sermon he says:

> Do not lay up for yourselves treasures on earth, where rust and moth consume, and where thieves break in and steal; but lay up for yourselves treasures in heaven, where neither rust nor moth consumes, nor thieves break in and steal. For where thy treasure is, there also will thy heart be (Matt. 6:19-21).

> No man can serve two masters; for either he will hate the one and love the other, or else he will stand by the one and despise the other. You cannot serve God and Mammon.

> Therefore I say to you, do not be anxious for your life, what you shall eat; nor yet for your body, what you shall put on. Is not the life a greater thing than the food, and the body than the clothing? Look at the birds of the air: they do not sow, or reap, or gather into barns; yet your heavenly Father feeds them. Are not you of much more value than they? But which of you by being anxious about it can add to his stature a single cubit?
>
> And as for clothing, why are you anxious? Consider how the lilies of the field grow; they neither toil nor spin, yet I say to you that not even Solomon in all his glory was

> arrayed like one of these. But if God so clothes the grass of the field, which flourishes today but tomorrow is thrown into the oven, how much more you, O you of little faith!
>
> Therefore do not be anxious, saying,"What shall we eat?" or, "What shall we drink? or, "What are we to put on?" (for after all these things the Gentiles seek); for your Father knows that you need all these things. But seek first the kingdom of God and his justice, and all these things shall be given you besides (Matt. 6: 24-33).

Well could the people have said: "Master, this is a hard saying." There is no question about that, but this is what a Christian believes. You cannot serve two masters. Absorption in the world is slavery to the power of things, and one aspect of Christian freedom lies precisely in this liberation from the oppressive power of the world. When a man understands this reality, when he accepts the Christian belief that the accumulation of things will never bring him lasting contentment or fulfillment, a heavy burden drops from his shoulders. The chains of attachment to and absorption in things fall away. Because he believes, he can understand what is real and what is worthwhile, and this truth sets him free.

Once again, there is nothing wrong and certainly nothing unchristian in working, and working hard, to have nice things, to live comfortably, to be secure. Christ's teaching has nothing to say about that, not even the parable of Lazarus, the wealthy man who worked hard to set things up so he could retire with plenty, only to die on the night of its completion. What Christ condemns is absorption in the

world to the point where God and God's will are ignored or forgotten. What Christ blesses is a spirit of detachment from things so that attention to God and concern for His will may be cultivated and given its proper place.

In another parable Christ makes the same point: do not let yourself get so busy that you are not able to hear the invitation of God who calls you; do not become so absorbed in things that you distort your sense of values and fail to recognize what is real: that God is the Holy God, the Creator, that we are *His* creatures and that this is His world not ours, that He has a claim on us that we cannot, or at least must not ignore. He said:

> The kingdom of heaven is like a king who made a marriage feast for his son. And he sent his servants to call in those invited to the marriage feast, but they would not come. Again he sent out other servants, saying, "Tell those who are invited, Behold, I have prepared my dinner; my oxen and fatlings are killed, and everything is ready; come to the marriage feast." But they made light of it, and went off, one to his farm, and another to his business; and the rest laid hold of his servants, treated them shamefully, and killed them.
>
> But when the king heard of it, he was angry; and he sent his armies, destroyed those murderers, and burnt their city. Then he said to his servants, "The marriage feast indeed is ready, but those who were invited were not worthy; go therefore to the crossroads, and invite to the marriage feast whomever you shall find." And his servants went out into the roads, and gathered all whom they found, both good and bad; and the marriage feast was filled with guests (Matt. 22:2-10).

Elsewhere in the New Testament are the metaphors of life after the flesh and life in the spirit, living in darkness and living in the light, a life in sin, or a life in Christ. In no case do they mean that the things which involve the body and its cares are evil, or that we must live as separated souls in the world. Life after the flesh is a life absorbed in the world, where the pressures of day to day existence blot out our concern for God and His will. It implies a forgetfulness or ignorance of the meaning of all that we do and of our dependence on God as well as our position as creatures. It means becoming so absorbed in what we do that we do not see what stands behind and above it all. Life after the flesh, a life of sin, and life in darkness are all the same thing; because to be absorbed in the world to the point where concern for God is ignored, is certainly a life in sin (estrangement from God) and a life in darkness where we cannot distinguish between what is real and what appears to be real.

St. Paul characterized a life after the flesh when he wrote:

> Now the works of the flesh are manifest, which are immorality, uncleanness, licentiousness, idolatry, witchcrafts, enmities, contentions, jealousies, anger, quarrels, factions, parties, envies, murders, drunkenness, carousings, and suchlike. And concerning these I warn you, as I have warned you, that they who do such things will not attain the kingdom of God (Gal. 5:19-21).

These are the things a man does who has lost himself in the world. This is the unrest and inner torment he suffers because he is attempting to identify himself with the world, instead of living in it, always careful to preserve his dis-

tinction from it and always careful to keep himself awake to the reality that his faith discloses to him.

This point is made nicely by Etienne Gilson when describing the philosophy of St. Bonaventure:

> The world has been created as an image of, and a witness to, the glory of its creator; but the material world itself does not know it; man alone has been created with a knowing mind and a loving heart, in order that, by knowing and loving all things in God, he might refer them to their origin, which is, at the same time, their end. When man is thus conceived as a high priest in the lofty temple of nature, his essential function is to lend his own voice to an otherwise speechless creation, to help each thing in publicly confessing its deepest and most secret meaning, or rather its essence, for each of them *is* a word, while man alone can *say* it.[16]

Dietrich von Hildebrand calls attention to the same problem in *Liturgy and Personality* when he discusses the "awakeness" which should characterize a Christian:

> This awakeness forbids us to be so absorbed by certain goods as to forget God the "first truth"; it prevents us from living so intensely in the visible world which surrounds us as to forget what stands behind and above that world and in whose light alone all that which belongs to the visible world acquires its genuine visage. It is the awakeness whereby we do not allow ourselves to be absorbed by what is at hand, by urgent business and the day's work; it keeps us centered on God, His kingdom,

[16] E. Gilson, *The Unity of Philosophical Experience* (New York: C. Scribner's Sons, 1937), pp. 49-50.

our vocation, and the supernatural meaning of our lives. In one word, it is the awakeness which is a dwelling in the presence of God, an abiding in His light. Both dimensions are interlinked. The more we live with our gaze fixed on God, abide in the consciousness of this only true world and our own fundamental situation and see everything in that light, the more are we open and receptive, the more does the deep content of all that falls under our spiritual eyes speak to us and the more acute is our ear for hearing the voice of God. From this awakeness organically flows also the knowledge of the dangers threatening our ultimate vocation and the need to watch over temptations. Where do we feel more deeply the consequences of original sin than in our bluntness and thoughtlessness? . . . When a ray of God's glory touches our soul and our heart is overfilled, how long does this condition last before we drop back into the periphery and are absorbed by trifles? God may grant us a great gift, He may let us discover a human being whom we understand ultimately and who likewise understands us, a human being whom we may love with Jesus and in Jesus, in whom we may grasp the unduplicable design of God which he represents, towards whom we have an ultimate mission, and who has an ultimate mission towards us. Yet how soon do we grow accustomed to this gift, how soon does God's kindness become something habitual in our eyes, how soon, in our inertia, do we grow deaf to the call of God implied in the gift, and let it be carried away in the whirlpool of the commonplace? What bluntness in marriage, in friendship, in our relations with children! What bluntness towards all the goods which God's bounteousness bestows on us, towards the beauty of nature, the

splendor of truth, health, freedom! For how much of all this do we thank God? How soon does that for which we longed as for something rare and precious, grow commonplace in our eyes! [17]

The conclusion of all this is the conclusion that existence-in-the-world is as much a condition of existence for the Christian as for the nonbeliever. Everything in Part I that concerns it applies in full to the Christian, though for him it does not end there. Fortunately, as a believer he can see the meaning of such an existence and he knows how to go about it. The reality of God and of his relationship with God colors his vision to the extent that this world is for him entirely different from the world of the unbeliever. The Christian knows that this world is where the Lord wants him to be. He knows that his Creator *wants* him to work and laugh and love, so his day is not just more of the rat race, but service for the Lord. In all of the concerns and activities which take up his time and effort in providing for a family and leading a full life, he knows he is pleasing his God, and he experiences the inner peace which comes with such knowledge. He knows, too, that at the end of it all he must admit that he is an "unprofitable servant," as Christ put it, but there is satisfaction in that, because that is all that is expected of him.

A CHRISTIAN-WITH-OTHERS

The revealed word of God also adds richness and depth to the believer's understanding of his relation with others.

[17] D. von Hildebrand, *Liturgy and Personality* (London: Longmans, Green and Co., 1943), pp. 122-3. Used by permission of David McKay Company, Inc.

He knows that one of the conditions of his existence is that he lives with others like himself. The pages of Scripture tell him that his God intended it to be that way. When woman was created and the power to bring a child into existence was linked to the mystery of love's fullest expression, all by God's design, the conditions were established to populate the world, to insure that others like himself would surround him and be affected by him.

Again, a Christian's understanding and appreciation of God as the Holy Creator is fundamental to his appreciation of everything else Christian. Believing that his *God* created the world and everything in it, that He is present to it and governs it, the Christian knows that whatever happens in this world only happens because his God wants or permits it. This means that everyone he has ever had contact with, has come to him from the hand of God. Believing, too, that God is good (we will develop this later), the Christian also believes that all these encounters with others are intended by God so that some good will come from it. Either he is to affect others or they are to affect him, or they are to affect each other so that somehow some good will result. This means that the believer understands that not only his being-with-others is intended by God, but even his being-with-this-other and -that-other individually is similarly intended by God; and from both of these insights his understanding of this condition of his existence, this being-with-others, is basically different from the man who does not believe.

This business of living with others is not to be taken lightly. The word of God has demonstrated clearly that our Creator takes it seriously. Christ himself summed up all of Old Testament teaching in the two commandments: love God *and* love your neighbor. Of the ten commandments,

the last seven concern the others with whom we exist before God. So learning to meet this condition of existence as a Christian, as one who knows he is the creature of his Creator, must be one of the fundamental concerns of his life.

Earlier, in our discussion of God's justice, we mentioned the prophet Amos and his message: the people of Israel had incurred the wrath of God by failing to live up to their part of the covenant. Specifically, Amos lashed out at the chosen people because they had no concern for their neighbors:

> Because you have trampled upon the weak and exacted of them levies of grain, though you have built houses of hewn stone, you shall not live in them!. . . Yes, I know how many are your crimes, how grievous your sins: oppressing the just, accepting bribes, repelling the needy at the gate! (Am. 5:11-12)

So seriously does God consider concern for one's neighbor that He made it a condition for establishing contact with himself. Through Amos He said to the sinful Israelites:

> I hate, I spurn your feasts, I take no pleasure in your solemnities, your cereal offerings I will not accept, nor consider your stall-fed peace offerings. Away with your noisy songs! (Am. 5:21-23)

In other words, the law of brotherly love is singularly important to God. For a man to be just before God, he must first be just to his fellow man. To the believer, to the man who has accepted this understanding of existence, the real value of just interpersonal relations clearly distinguishes itself from the pseudo-values of grandiose self-interest. The believer knows that nothing is more important to him per-

sonally than his own relationship to God, and since God Himself has insisted on just relations with others as an indispensable condition of His friendship, he knows, too, the real value of human justice and concern for others. It is not simply and only the human thing to do, it is God's will, the will of the Creator, the will of the Holy God who alone makes things real. There are no exceptions to this in all of revealed truth, Old Testament or New. God expects this from all whom He has touched with his saving mercy by granting the gift of faith, the power to see the real world and to understand what is of real value. The justice of God on this point is inflexible: a serious lack of concern for one's neighbor will result infallibly in estrangement from God. This is the teaching of the Law and the Prophets and of Christ himself.

Osee wrote:

> Hear the word of the Lord, O people of Israel, for the Lord has a grievance against the inhabitants of the land: there is no fidelity, no mercy, no knowledge of God in the land. False swearing, lying, murder, stealing and adultery! in their lawlessness, bloodshed follows bloodshed! (Os. 4:1-2)

And Isaia wrote:

> What care I for the number of your sacrifices? says the Lord. I have had enough of whole-burnt rams and fat of fatlings; in the blood of calves, lambs and goats I find no pleasure. When you come in to visit me, who asks these things of you? Trample my courts no more! Bring no more worthless offerings; your incense is loathsome to me. New moon and sabbath, calling of assemblies,

octaves with wickedness: these I cannot bear. Your new moons and festivals I detest; they weigh me down, I tire of the load. When you spread out your hands, I close my eyes to you; though you pray the more I will not listen. Your hands are full of blood! Wash yourselves clean! Put away your misdeeds from before my eyes; cease doing evil; learn to do good. Make justice your aim: redress the wronged, hear the orphan's plea, defend the widow (Isa. 1:11-17).

Jeremia, too, was just as insistent and forceful:

Only if you thoroughly reform your ways and your deeds; if each of you deals justly with his neighbor; if you no longer oppress the resident alien, the orphan, and the widow; if you no longer shed innocent blood in this place, or follow strange gods to your own harm, will I remain with you in this place, in the land which I gave your fathers long ago and forever (Jer. 7:5-7).

And so it goes through all of the prophets. God has created the world and man. Establishing the conditions of human existence is part of that creation, and one of those conditions is that man should live with others like himself. The norm of his relations with others is inherent in the very structure and dynamism of man's nature as well as in the principles revealed by the Creator himself. So important are justice and concern for one's neighbor that the Creator has made them the necessary condition of His mercy.

When God revealed Himself in the Christ, there was no change in this demand, though there was a significant change in understanding existence-with-others. The latter point we will reach in a moment. For the present it is important to recall Christ's own words: "Do not think I have

come to destroy the Law or the Prophets. I have not come to destroy, but to fulfill" (Matt. 5:17). It is significant, I believe, that Christ described his mission this way. It is just as significant that the Apostles recalled it and selected it to be handed down (tradition means "that which is handed down") to us. Not everything Christ said and did was recorded—St. John tells us so. In their preaching, which preceded the writing of the Gospels, the Apostles, under the influence of the Holy Spirit, selected the teachings and miracles that were necessary to present the Christian message. That this particular saying of Jesus was included indicates the continuity between Hebrew and Christian teaching, as we have already noted in our discussion of God's holiness and justice, and in this case makes even more forceful Christ's teaching in the Sermon on the Mount: "If thou art offering thy gift at the altar, and there remember that thy brother has anything against thee, leave thy gift before the altar and go first to be reconciled to thy brother, and then come and offer thy gift" (Matt. 5:23-24).

This is the teaching of the prophets, or as we believe, the teaching of God through the prophets. Christ himself insists upon it in many places. When he taught us to pray, he said: "Forgive us our debts as we forgive our debtors." And afterwards he said: "If you do not forgive men, neither will God forgive you your offenses" (Matt. 6:12 and 15). Over and over again we read the same thing:

> Then Peter came up to him and said, "Lord, how often shall my brother sin against me, and I forgive him? Up to seven times?" Jesus said to him, "I do not say to thee seven times, but seventy times seven.
>
> "This is why the kingdom of heaven is likened to a king who desired to settle accounts with his servants. And

when he had begun the settlements, one was brought to him who owed him ten thousand talents. And as he had no means of paying, his master ordered him to be sold, with his wife and children and all that he had, and payment to be made. But the servant fell down and besought him, saying, 'Have patience with me and I will pay thee all!' And moved with compassion, the master of that servant released him, and forgave him the debt.

"But as that servant went out, he met one of his fellow-servants who owed him a hundred denarii, and he laid hold of him and throttled him, saying, 'Pay what thou owest.' His fellow-servant therefore fell down and began to entreat him saying, 'Have patience with me and I will pay thee all.' But he would not; but went away and cast him into prison until he should pay what was due.

"His fellow-servants therefore, seeing what had happened, were very much saddened, and they went and informed their master of what had taken place. Then his master called him, and said to him, 'Wicked servant! I forgave thee all the debt, because thou didst entreat me. Shouldst not thou also have had any pity on thy fellow-servant, even as I had pity on thee?' And his master, being angry, handed him over to the torturers until he should pay all that was due to him. So also my heavenly Father will do to you, if you do not each forgive your brothers from your hearts" (Matt. 18:21-35).

"Be merciful, therefore, even as your Father is merciful. Do not judge, and you shall not be judged; do not condemn and you shall not be condemned. Forgive and you shall be forgiven; give, and it shall be given to you, good measure, pressed down, shaken together, running over,

shall they pour into your lap. For with what measure you measure, it shall be measured to you" (Luke 6:37-38).

If all this sounds like a command coupled to a threat, a do-this-or-else sort of thing, in a way it is. But that does not make it the primary motivation of Christian concern for others, nor is it the complete Christian attitude towards interpersonal relations. It is a part of it, though, just as the consequences of anything we do constitute a part of that reality. Christianity is freedom, not constraint by threat, yet the Christian message itself includes a threat. If you do not choose freedom, you choose the justice of God who will judge you as you have judged, who will forgive you as you have forgiven. This is an aspect of the real human condition which the non-believer does not see, but which is real nonetheless. It very rarely happened that Christ ended his teaching on any point with a threat. On this matter of concern for others, he did, which means that it is important to pay attention. To the believer it is an indication of the value, the real value of concern for others. To him it must be one of the major preoccupations of his life. It is that important.

Christian teaching on existence-with-others, though, goes beyond the bare command and the revelation of the eternal consequences. Christian concern for others and Christian freedom in dealing with others rests on a different motivation, a specifically Christian attitude arising from a specifically Christian revelation. Old Testament revelation establishes the dignity of each individual man by pointing to man's origin from God, his lordship over the rest of creation, his intimacy with God before the Fall, and his rights to just treatment from others. The Old Testament describes

man as a special creature of God, on a higher plane than all the rest of creation, made in the image and likeness of God, and an object of God's special concern (this, too, we shall return to later.). This means that each person with whom we share our existence, however remotely, is something special. Every one of them is important to God. In addition to their intrinsic worth as men among men, which we worked out in Part I, each of them is God's creature, each of them is important to God. In a word, God loves them, each one of them, as He loves you and me. The final proof of that love was the Incarnation of God Himself. By becoming man, by taking up human sinful flesh and offering Himself to the Father in the totality of death for our sins, Jesus showed us once and for all the depth of that love which God has for man. "Greater love than this no man has than he lay down his life for his friends." Or, in the words of St. Paul: "It is in this that God has shown his love for us, that he died for us while we were still sinners." Each man's dignity and real value ultimately derive from these facts: that each is a creature of God, each is made in His image and likeness, and each is loved by God. This is a reality appreciated only by the believer, which means that still another aspect of the real world is hidden from the non-believer.

The Old Testament revealed God's love for man and God's desire for men to love one another—that is, to be concerned about them, to care about them, to respect them, to see to their needs, to be just. Christ went further, and those who believe in Christ, those who live from a Christian interpretation of existence, will be marked by a willingness to show concern even for those who hate them. They know that this is what Christ wants them to do:

> "You have heard that it was said, 'Thou shalt love thy neighbor, and shall hate thy enemy.' But I say to you, love your enemies, do good to those who hate you, and pray for those who calumniate you, so that you may be children of your Father in heaven, who makes his sun rise on the good and the evil, and sends rain on the just and unjust. For if you love those that love you, what reward shall you have? Do not even the publicans do that? And if you salute your brethren only, what are you doing more than the others? Do not even the Gentiles do that?" (Matt. 5:43-47)

A Christian will also be marked by a willingness to accept more than his neighbor can do to hurt him. Christ said:

> "You have heard it said, 'An eye for an eye,' and a 'tooth for a tooth.' But I say to you not to resist the evil doer; on the contrary, if someone strike thee on the right cheek, turn to him the other also; and if anyone would go to law with thee and take thy tunic, let him take thy cloak as well; and whoever forces thee to go for one mile, go with him two. To him who asks of thee, give; and from him who would borrow of thee, do not turn away" (Matt. 5:38-42).

This is sometimes misunderstood, so a word of explanation is in order. Christ is describing the spirit of generosity that should animate those who follow him. Generosity has two sides, accepting and giving; both are important. He begins by reminding us of the laws of justice and the principle of retaliation. Then He says: do not resist. This does not mean that He advocates the abolishment of justice or the seeking of retribution when one is wronged. There is

no justification for that conclusion. Instead, He offers a principle of conduct which He wishes His followers to accept: do not resist. In other words, his followers, though they have the right of retribution when they are wronged, should not ordinarily avail themselves of that right. Christ wants his followers to be patient and forbearing and forgiving. Our Lord does not command, He offers a principle of conduct; and there is a difference. A command binds whenever the circumstances apply—in this case, the attitude of non-resistance. If Christ's words here actually were a command, then we would never be entitled to seek restitution or resist evildoers, and to do so would be sinful. But, Christ Himself rebuked the servant who slapped him and St. Paul had recourse to legal means to avoid being killed by the Jews. In other words, this teaching of Christ should be understood as a principle which He feels should be characteristic of His followers. He indicates that those who wish to be His disciples should not be anxious to seek revenge or restitution if they suffer wrong, always insisting on their rights. They should learn to rise above this pettiness and accept the wrongs they suffer from their neighbor.

After stating the principle, Christ gives some examples to clarify his point. They were only examples and we should not try to make any more out of them than that. In short, they are not rules of conduct for concrete situations. The first example is meant to show that one who suffers injury, instead of seeking justice, should show his readiness to suffer the same injury again. The second example is a bit more elaborate. Not only should one give his tunic if sought, but his cloak as well. This indicates not only non-resistance, but a readiness to suffer even greater loss. The third ex-

ample indicates the same thing: one should be willing to volunteer for more than is asked or required.

There is a transition here from non-resistance to outright giving. As regards our neighbor, our Lord does not want us to be seeking justice all the time. He wants us to be ready to accept injustice, and then He goes further; He wants us to be ready to do more, to suffer more than we are required to. This requires an attitude of genuine Christian generosity. It is no longer just a question of non-resistance. Be willing to suffer more than your neighbor can do to hurt you—this is the attitude that is second nature to one who generously attempts to love his neighbor; be willing to give what you have or to do what you can for him—this is Christian.

A Christian should also be marked by a willingness to help those in need. It is true that Old Testament teaching also made a point of this, but it is important here for two reasons: first, because it is the point Christ made when asked to clarify what was meant by "neighbor" when He said, "Thou shalt love thy neighbor as thyself." Instead of answering that question, Christ described what a neighbor does when he finds someone in need. In effect He is saying: Your neighbor is the one who needs you. Show him love by helping him.

Secondly, this willingness to help those in need is remarkable in Christian teaching because Christ said that He would understand as done to Himself whatever we do to others:

> "Then the king will say to those on his right hand, 'Come blessed of my Father, take possession of the kingdom prepared for you from the foundation of the world; for I was hungry and you gave me to eat; I was thirsty and

> you gave me to drink; I was a stranger and you took me in; naked and you covered me; sick and you visited me; I was in prison and you came to me.' Then the just will answer him, saying, 'Lord, when did we see thee hungry, and feed thee; or thirsty, and give thee drink? And when did we see thee a stranger, and take thee in; or naked and clothe thee? Or when did we see thee sick, or in prison, and come to thee? And answering the king will say to them, 'Amen, I say to you, as long as you did it for one of these, the least of my brethren, you did it for me.'
>
> "Then he will say to those on his left hand, 'Depart from me, accursed ones, into the everlasting fire which was prepared for the devil and his angels. For I was hungry, and you did not give me to eat; I was thirsty and you gave me no drink; I was a stranger and you did not take me in; naked, and you did not clothe me; sick, and in prison, and you did not visit me.' Then they also will answer and say, 'Lord when did we see thee hungry, or thirsty, or a stranger, or naked, or sick, or in prison, and did not minister to thee?' Then he will answer them, saying, 'Amen I say to you, as long as you did not do it for one of these least ones, you did not do it for me' " (Matt. 25:34-45).

This is why St. John could write: "If anyone says, 'I love God,' and hates his brother, he is a liar. For how can he who does not love his brother, whom he sees, love God, whom he does not see?" (I John 4:20). Christ accepts us done to himself whatever we do to others! What a difference this makes to the man who can believe it, to the Christian who has received the gift of faith. Every encounter with those in need becomes an encounter with Christ. Every act of generosity towards others becomes an act of generosity

to Christ. Certainly there is a reality here that can bring richness and meaning to a man's life.

A Christian should also be marked by a concern for the salvation of others. This will show itself in three ways: (1) recognizing the seriousness of scandal and avoiding it, (2) giving good example, and (3) attempting to correct those who need it, when the situation calls for it. On scandal Christ said: "But whoever causes one of these little ones who believe in me to sin, it were better for him to have a great millstone hung around his neck, and to be drowned in the depths of the sea" (Matt. 18:6-7). To speak or act in such a way as to lead others to sin is scandal. It follows from the fact of our existence with others that what we do affects them. This is particularly true of parents and educators, who are mostly responsible for the values one receives as a child, when most of one's deeply rooted values are learned. Someone once said: "What we say is often drowned out by what we are." There is truth in that—and responsibility, a Christian responsibility.

The responsibility extends itself to living the faith as the best way of helping others to salvation. I do not hesitate to agree with Kierkegaard that Christian apologetics (*arguments* for the existence of God, etc.) is a kind of scandal to the Christian world. If men lived before God as true believers, no arguments would be necessary. Christ said: "Let your light shine before men, in order that they may see your good works and give glory to your Father in heaven" (Matt. 5:16); but first you must have the light! It is the real Christian who brings faith and inspiration to others, not those who can manufacture arguments.

Correcting others is a more complicated situation, and Christ had something to say about it:

> But why dost thou see the speck in thy brother's eye, and yet dost not consider the beam in thy own eye? Or how canst thou say to thy brother: "Let me cast out the speck from thy eye"; and behold, there is a beam in thy own eye? Thou hypocrite, first cast out the beam from thy own eye, and then thou wilt see clearly to cast out the speck from thy brother's eye (Matt. 7:3-5).

Through an example Christ indicates how absurd it is for us to attempt to reform others before we are, ourselves, thoroughly reformed. Reforming others is a delicate operation, as delicate as removing a speck from the eye. The eye is extremely sensitive and can be painfully affected even by the smallest objects. It takes a keen eye to detect the object and a steady hand to remove it. A similar situation holds in the moral sphere. The human personality is extremely sensitive to adverse criticism, no matter how trivial. What is more, human shortcomings are hardly ever what they appear to be. More often than not they come from causes deeply embedded in a man's make-up, which means that it takes a keen mind to diagnose their true nature and a steady hand to apply the remedy that will cure them. A person who is himself affected by many imperfections is in no position to help. Actually, one who turns his zeal towards uprooting his own defects will never feel entitled to busy himself with those of others, because he will never be entirely successful with himself.

There are occasions, however, when it is a Christian responsibility to correct others. This may be because we are in a position of authority or because the situation itself is serious enough to warrant it. A speck in the eye is a small thing and should be ignored. Something serious requires attention, and on this, too, Christ had something to say:

> But if thy brother sin against thee, go and show him his fault, between thee and him alone. If he listen to thee, thou hast won thy brother. But if he do not listen to thee, take with thee one or two more so that on the word of two or three witnesses every word may be confirmed. And if he refuse to hear them, appeal to the Church, but if he refuses to hear even the Church, let him be to thee as the heathen and the publican (Matt. 18:15-18).

The salvation of others is important to a Christian, important enough to draw on his energy and ingenuity to do something about it; but when it comes to correction, there is a limit to what Christ expects of him.

Much of the Christian attitude towards others can be summed up in the word "love." Those things we have just discussed represent the Christian understanding of that word translated into action. For Christ, to love is to be concerned, to be gentle, long-suffering, forgiving, merciful, tender and generous. For Christ, living with others means loving them. One who believes in Christ lives in the consciousness of Christ's words at the Last Supper: "A new commandment I give you, that you love one another: that as I have loved you, you also love one another. By this will all men know that you are my disciples, if you have love for one another" (John 13:34-35).

The record of apostolic teaching, that is, what the apostles preached—which was eventually written down as the gospels—is clear proof that they learned the lesson well themselves. In their epistles, too, they came back to it again and again: love one another. St. Paul, whose theology of justification has sometimes drawn attention away from the rest of what he had to say, was no less emphatic:

Love one another with fraternal charity, anticipating one another with honor. Be not slothful in zeal, be fervent in spirit, serving the Lord, rejoicing in hope. Be patient in tribulation, persevering in prayer. Share the needs of the saints, practising hospitality. Bless those who persecute you; bless and do not curse. Rejoice with those who rejoice; weep with those who weep. Be of one mind towards one another. Do not set your mind on high things but condescend to the lowly. Be not wise in your own conceits. To no man render evil for evil, but provide good things not only in the sight of God, but also in the sight of all men. If it be possible, as far as in you lies, be at peace with all men. Do not avenge yourselves, beloved, but give place to wrath, for it is written, "Vengeance is mine; I will repay, says the Lord." But "If thy enemy is hungry, give him food; if he is thirsty, give him drink; for by so doing thou wilt heap coals of fire upon his head." Be not overcome by evil, but overcome evil with good (Rom. 12:10-21).

From yet another angle, Christian love for others is a fundamental source of Christian freedom, the inner freedom which comes to a heart that is not locked up in its own misery. In Part I we described the dehumanizing, the crippling and enslaving dehumanizing, which comes to a man who gives way to self-assertion and the desire for pleasure, to pride and sensuality. Christian love for others is the remedy for all that.

To understand this better, a digression is necessary. From a believer's point of view, every created thing and every creature is good, good because God made them. Every one of them serves the function of elevating our hearts and reminding us of their Creator. But things are good in various

degrees: some because they satisfy our needs, some because they are sources of genuine happiness. The latter are far superior to the others. The inferior goods bring us momentary pleasures and satisfactions. The superior goods elevate the heart, recollect it, draw it out of itself, make it forget itself. A life in a good and elevating environment is a superior good to which no inferior good could compare. A child brought up in a good home could not buy that good with all the money in the world. There he acquires a true sense of values. There he learns self-discipline. And there he learns to love his God. A noble profession is a superior good. A doctor or a nurse or a teacher or a scholar has a life open to him that can be enriching and fruitful. As a matter of fact, such a profession can be so good that one can lose himself in it, so completely can it absorb his interest and heart. Another great good is the economic and social situation which allows a man the freedom to develop himself intellectually or artistically. Such freedom from want is a special good in itself because it liberates a man from the cares and worries involved in providing for himself.

In general, the higher the value of some good, the more surely it elevates the heart, the more surely it draws us out of ourselves, the more surely it draws us to God. Superior goods call us to lift up our hearts. The more deeply we understand them, the more readily we recognize them as gifts, as things which have not been earned but given, the more we are moved to give thanks to the giver, our God and Father. The higher goods, then, are powerful solvents of pride and sensuality.[18]

At one time or another every one of us has experienced

[18] The theoretical development of all this can be found in *Christian Ethics* by Dietrich von Hildebrand (New York: David McKay Company, Inc., 1953).

some of these higher goods and the effects which they can bring. There are days when we feel perfectly healthy, brimming over with life and energy. The whole world looks good at a time like that. We feel warm and friendly, we overlook all sorts of things that on another day would annoy us terribly. The point is that this good health, this feeling of well-being, brings out the best in us. We become expansive, less self-centered, liberated from pettiness, less attached to the lesser goods. This is the mission of the higher goods. They bring us out of ourselves.

Love is the altruistic response to the understanding of a unique personality. It is the act of reaching out to the other and for the other in response to the recognition in depth of the other's being, not as an *it,* but as a *thou.* The love of others with whom we share our existence, inexorably, is certainly one of the higher goods of this life. The joy of deep friendship, of sharing one's existence with another, is a human good which is rich and warm and satisfying; and a friendship which rests on a Christian basis is that much more so because it is that much more noble. When both persons live out of this same Christian interpretation of existence and have before them a clear understanding of what is real and of what is of value, when both work for the same Christian goals, and when both have already been liberated from pettiness by their love for God and the awareness of their own and each other's exalted vocation as Christians, there is more than just this or that experience shared; there is a common faith, a common understanding. If any higher good is ennobling and rewarding and liberating, it is love for others.

The highest of all human goods is love, and the highest form of love for another human being is marital love. We

all know, at least from poetry, song and story, what effect real, true marital love can have on a person. He thinks of nothing else, wants nothing else, hopes for nothing else, but love. He takes no notice of anything else. He has been liberated from trifles and the whole world is beautiful. In marriage the effect deepens and the good becomes better. Man and wife seal their love with a vow of fidelity till death, setting their mutual self-donation above all temporary moods and disappointments. Marriage provides this unique opportunity for man and woman to give themselves to each other totally. There is no other human experience like it and no other reaches the depths of human nature as this one does. There is no greater opportunity or situation which can so effectively draw them out of themselves and so liberate them, emancipate them from slavery to themselves. How often we hear a husband or wife thank God for the other! How easily they recognize what a great good their marriage is, that they have not deserved it, that they understand it as a gift from God. What is more, in loving each other in Christ they are fulfilling his commandment from the depth of their hearts.

Christian love for others, far from being an escape or weakness or unnatural or restricting or legalistic, is the very opposite of these things. Christian love is service, concern, care, patience and all the rest—and in *this* is fulfillment, meaning and liberty.

There is not and cannot be any limit to a Christian's love for his neighbor or family or wife; that is, a Christian cannot love others too much. There is, though, a danger in loving without understanding, a very real danger that only faith reveals. A sadly familiar experience, which is in evidence all around us, shows that a love which is not guided by an

understanding of what is real can, and often does, result in disaster. A mother who loves her children and mistakenly gives them everything fails to understand that she is preventing them from appreciating the value of things or of developing a sense of responsibility and achievement. Her love is sincere enough and real enough, and she is not loving too much, but she does not understand how to express it. It hurts to punish, it hurts to deprive; but sometimes that is real love, whereas indulgence would not be.

In Christianity there is no limit on love of our neighbor, but that love must be guided by what is real. Christ's insistence on loving God with our whole heart, soul, mind and strength, and our neighbor as ourselves, means that God is to be loved as God and our neighbor as our neighbor. His insistence on this was clarified when He said: "He who loves father or mother more than me is not worthy of me; and he who loves son or daughter more than me is not worthy of me." (Matt. 10:37) Unregulated love is so great a good that it is capable of absorbing us completely unless we are on guard against it. If a man has a friend who comes to him burdened with trouble and says: "Let's go out and get drunk so I can forget my trouble," there is nothing of real love in joining him on a drinking bout. If a wife commits adultery with her husband's boss so that her husband will get a raise, there is nothing of real love in that. A man who will cheat or lie or steal for his family or friends is destroying himself because, though his love is real, it is misguided.

Putting God second or ignoring him completely is sin, a life after the flesh, a life in darkness. It is easy enough because of the power of love itself, because of strong emotional demands, or because of conscious or unconscious

distortion of reality. More often than not, a man shapes his understanding of reality by what he does, and no reasons to the contrary can reach him. His emotions respond to this distorted picture of reality and his love drives him to sin. Again, the fault is not in loving, but in understanding.

To carry this a little further, it becomes apparent that when a man acts out of love for his friend in a way which he knows is contrary to God's will, he sometimes does it because he is guessing at the possible consequences of standing up for what is right. Many times he guesses wrong, and every time he would be better off deciding for God rather than his friend. How often does it happen that a woman gives in to a man because she wants to please him, when not giving in would please him more, though she does not suspect this. Both would have been better off if she had chosen for God, but she guessed wrong. And, even if he would have nothing more to do with her, would not both of them have been better off in the long run? Examples like this are easy to multiply.

The lesson in all this is that God and God's will must come first; love for our neighbor must come second. Any reversal will inevitably result in disaster.

In Part I we discussed another way in which living with others can be a danger to authentic human existence. There we saw the danger of surrendering our individuality to the "others" by allowing ourselves to be absorbed in the group. A believer understands this to be a violation of God's will for him in addition to being self-destructive. He comes forth from God as a unique personality and his vocation is to fulfill in his lifetime the divine idea of himself. All that we said in Part I about this danger is true for the Christian, but from a different point of view. The Christian understands his being-with-others as a-creature-of-God-in-Christ-with-

others-who-are-also-creatures. In other words, his understanding of existence-with-others is governed by his faith, which unfolds before him a reality and a set of values hidden from the non-believer.

This brings up the final consideration on this point, that others constitute another danger for the Christian, precisely because he is a Christian. This is a danger which the non-believer does not even suspect. When a man believes in Christ, he does, by that very fact, set himself in opposition to the values of the world. Christ Himself warned us of this:

> "Behold I am sending you forth like sheep in the midst of wolves. Be therefore wise as serpents, and guileless as doves. But beware of men; for they will deliver you up to councils, and scourge you in their synagogues, and you will be brought before governors and kings for my sake, for a witness to them and to the Gentiles. But when they deliver you up, do not be anxious how or what you are to speak; for what you are to speak will be given you in that hour. For it is not you who are speaking, but the Spirit of your Father who speaks through you. And brother will hand over brother to death, and the father his child; children will rise up against parents and put them to death. And you will be hated by all for my name's sake; but he who has persevered to the end will be saved" (Matt. 10:16-22).

And He continued:

> "No disciple is above his teacher, nor is the servant above his master. It is enough for the disciple to be like his teacher, and for the servant to be like his master. If they have called the master of the house Beelzebub, how much more those of his household! Therefore, do not be

afraid of them . . . and do not be afraid of those who kill the body, but cannot kill the soul. But rather be afraid of him who is able to destroy both soul and body in hell. Are not two sparrows sold for a farthing? And yet not one of them will fall to the ground without your Father's leave. But as for you, the very hairs of your head are all numbered. Therefore do not be afraid; you are of more value than many sparrows. Therefore, everyone who acknowledges me before men, I also will acknowledge before my Father in heaven. But whoever disowns me before men, I in turn will disown him before my Father in heaven" (Matt. 10:24-33).

All of this is reminiscent of the last beatitude from the Sermon on the Mount:

> "Blessed are they who suffer persecution for justice' sake, for theirs is the kingdom of heaven. Blessed are you when men reproach you, and persecute you, and speaking falsely, say all manner of evil against you, for my sake. Rejoice and exult, because your reward is great in heaven" (Matt. 5:10-12).

In these passages there are (1) prophecy of opposition, (2) encouragement in the face of it, and (3) a revelation of Christian value. Christ understood of what spirit He was, and He knew that that spirit was foreign and antagonistic to the spirit of the world. Those who cannot believe cannot understand the value of loving those who hate them, of doing good to those who harm them. The spirit of the world is "an eye for an eye and a tooth for a tooth." Get what you can get for yourself, and don't worry about those you trample on the way. Beat out the other guy before he makes a sucker of you. Get ahead at any cost. Anything which does not fit

this creed, this dogma, the world will ridicule and argue against and oppose. Whenever a Christian tries to be a Christian in the midst of all this, people will try to talk him out of it on the insidious grounds of moderation, common sense, the good of others, and so on. In other instances opposition may be in the form of physical violence or glaring hatred. Whatever form it takes, there will be opposition, simply because there is a difference in values, a different understanding of existence. Christ foretold it and He promised assistance at the same time, so, He says, there is nothing to fear. Then He goes on to indicate what is worthwhile fearing and what is not. Do not be afraid of bodily harm, He says. Rather, be afraid of those who can take away your faith and make you like themselves. The opposition endured will bring an eternal reward, but giving in will only bring self-destruction.

Once again, and I hope this repetition is not too tiresome, it is the Christian faith which makes this interpretation of existence possible. The non-believer cannot understand his existence this way. For the believer, Faith uncovers the reality behind appearances, reveals the depth of meaning, and discovers the beauty of value. Living with others, for a Christian, is certainly all of what was described in Part I, but for different reasons. And living with others, for a Christian, is more than loving others. It includes the understanding of the meaning of that condition of our existence, of its source, of its value, of the direction it should take, and of the real dangers it affords.

THE GOD OF MERCIFUL-LOVE

In the previous pages we have occasionally, but sparingly, mentioned God's love for us. We have saved the de-

velopment of this topic until now because all the rest was necessary as a preparation for it. To understand the meaning of that phrase, "God's love for us," so that it becomes real and living, so that it becomes more than just another meaningless group of words so easily rattled off in conversation and sermon, it was necessary first of all to probe the helplessness and futility and meaninglessness of human existence without God. It was also and especially necessary to understand the otherness of God, His holiness, so that we might appreciate our nothingness before Him. Then we had to grasp the essentially hopeless condition of every man because of sin, the condition of estrangement from God, before which man is powerless precisely because he has offended the Holy God. We have no right to forgiveness, because there is no such right. Right and duty are categories of justice, and it was necessary to establish God's justice, not only for the sake of reality, but also to fix our attention on the unhappy condition of fallen man who must stand condemned before God.

All the contents of this chapter, and of most of the rest of the book, hinge on the understanding of our fallen-creaturely-condition. The title of this chapter is meant to convey the same thought. God's love for us is not simply love, it is mercy. Everything that God does for us is mercy. Because God is God and we are His creatures, because God is God and we have sinned, we have no claim on justice, no right to anything but condemnation and punishment. According to every concept of justice, every man should be condemned and punished. That the God of Justice does not do this is uncomprehensible and thoroughly unreasonable—which is to say, it is merciful. Few things are more inhuman than mercy because few things are so irrational. The ability

to reason has long been a source of pride among men, and the thousands of books written by men about justice point both to man's rationality and the reasonableness of justice. But mercy is not logical. It upsets all the neat categories and distinctions of justice. It violates all the intrinsic necessities of justice, and, to make things worse, it cannot be regulated, which is a horror to the lawmakers.

To be merciful is to hold another in debt and gratuitously to forgive him that debt. How do you make rules about that? You cannot say it is all right to forgive so much, but no more than that. It is not logical (and, in terms of justice, right) to forgive at all. You cannot say it is all right to forgive under one set of circumstances but not another, if the debt is a true debt. Again, it simply is not logical to forgive at all. Yet, consider what God does. In order to overcome the estrangement which had existed between man and Himself, of His own initiative and freely, He forgives every man everything and re-establishes contact! This is mercy, something we have learned from God, because we could never reason to it.

But, and I must repeat this, this is the condescension of God, of the Entirely Other. This is the Holy God who forgives. It is the awe-inspiring God of overwhelming majesty who freely reconciles us to Himself. At one time I thought of having "GOD IS GOD" in huge letters superimposed on every page of this book, so important is an understanding of this reality for a true understanding of Christianity, of God's merciful-love. When we speak of the God of *love* throughout the rest of the book, then, let us remember that it is the *God* of love of whom we speak.

Inasmuch as it is the love of God, then, that concerns us, it is merciful-love. But before we can continue, we must

pause to make one more clarification. We must indicate what we mean by love. It is certainly no great mystery that words are used in many different ways, and if our discussion is to make sense, the words we use must be able to be understood by all of us in the same way. This is especially true here of the word "love."

To begin with, we should not expect the love of God to be romantic. We cannot throw our arms about Him and embrace Him, and we cannot expect that from Him. A man does not love his wife the same way he loves his children, his parents, his brothers or sisters or friends. Right there, there are six different forms of love, each of which expresses itself differently. Why should we expect the love of God to be like any one of them, when they are all different from each other? The love of God for us is not to be equated with anything human, though it does express itself in a divine way according to the characteristics which every love has in common—which is why they are all given the same name.

Love is knowledge and concern. It is heart speaking to heart. It is joy in possession of each other and emptiness when the other is gone. Love is tenderness and the desire to make the other happy. Love is providing for another. It stirs up the desire to be one with the other, the desire for each other's presence and nearness. It awakens the desire to be recognized for what it is. It is satisfaction just in giving. Love is all of this and more—and these are the things we should look for when we search the pages of Scripture to learn about God. In actual fact, there is no need to search. The testimony of God's love fairly leaps at us from those pages, if we read them with faith. If anything at all is apparent in Scripture, it is that God has been con-

tinually concerned about mankind. From the time of the Fall itself, the Bible is the account of God's efforts and God's plan to end the estrangement between man and Himself. Since the restoration of friendship and love with God is the meaning of the word salvation, the Bible has sometimes been called salvation-history. In this sense, it is a love story, the narrative of what God has done for man, what God has done for us. Let us begin at the beginning.

The very fact of creation is testimony of love, of the love of the transcendent God who made it possible for man to love and be loved. Initially God was man's intimate friend. The description in Genesis of God walking and talking with man was designed to make this point. God provided for man, spoke to him, and shared his thoughts. With the Fall all this was changed, but God promised the possibility of reconciliation at the same time as he declared the friendship at an end. The divine promise was couched in the Lord's words to the tempting serpent: "I will put enmity between you and the woman, between your seed and her seed; she shall crush your head, and you shall lie in wait for her heel" (Gn. 3:15).

God put His plan in motion when he called Abraham from his family and nation to make him the father of a chosen people. To Abraham God made a promise:

> "This is my covenant with you: You shall be the father of a multitude of nations . . . I will establish my covenant between you and me and your descendants after you throughout their generations, as a perpetual covenant, that I may be a God to you and to your descendants after you. . . . I will be their God. . . . You shall keep my covenant, you and your descendants after you throughout their generations" (Gen. 17:4-9).

This was the beginning of a new era, a beginning of friendship renewed. God took the initiative. He gave Abraham the faith to believe in Him and promised to care for him and his decendants. They would be "His people." Here is love, for here is concern and desire for reunion.

The narratives covering the years between Abraham and Moses describe the beginnings of God's active part in the history of His people. To the prophetic eye of the narrator, everything was specially arranged by God, from the choosing of Isaac's wife to the conception of children, Joseph's betrayal by his brothers, and finally the migration of the people to Egypt. In these narratives, too, there is love; for throughout there is tenderness and God's giving, His constant giving to His people.

After the people had become enslaved under Pharoa, a series of remarkable events occurred, beginning with the incident of the burning bush on Mount Horeb in the desert of Midian. The people were unhappy with their lot, and the sacred writer says: "As their cry for release went up to God, he heard their groaning and was mindful of his covenant with Abraham, Isaac and Jacob" (Ex. 2:24). So God spoke to Moses out of the burning bush and commissioned him to go to Pharoah to demand the release of the Israelites. Out of love for His people, God was about to act. When Moses asked God for His name so that he might tell the people who it was who sent him, God answered: "I am who am."

To our age and mentality this hardly seems significant, but to the ancient Hebrew it was unbelievable condescension. This deserves a little explanation. To be able to name something meant that one had grasped the meaning, the essence of that thing. It meant, too, that one had a certain

power over the thing he was able to name. For God to have given His name to Moses that Moses might give it to the people, was for God to give Himself to them. He could do no more for them in order that He should be theirs—and they knew it. They understood the intimacy revealed by such a gesture, and so great was their reverence for the name that the time came when they would no longer allow themselves to pronounce it.

In addition, this event, the calling and commission of Moses, also marks the actual beginning of the chosen people. The covenant, which really had been more of a promise to Abraham, now found fulfillment. For it was in the Exodus that the chosen people became a people, led out of slavery and ushered into the promised land by the power of the God who loved them. The Exodus, too, was the positive proof to the Hebrew people that their God was the living God who acted, really acted, out of concern for them. Over and over again during those years of wandering God demonstrated His protection and nearness. Could they ever forget the Angel of Death that passed over their homes? or the Red Sea closing in on the warriors of Pharao? or all the battles won? Would the memory dim of the column of fire that preceded them by night and the cloud by day? And the Sinai experience! God coming down in fire and lightning, terrifying all who saw it . . . and His ordering a tent like theirs for Himself, where He dwelled above the ark . . . could they ever forget these things? Moses was determined that they should not forget, so he ordered a feast to be celebrated each year to commemorate their liberation. The feast is called Pasch or Passover. The people dress in traveling clothes to remind them of their passage from slavery to freedom by the power of their God.

After the Exodus, through succeeding generations, the people multiplied. By the power of arms they cut out a nation for themselves and settled down to live in it peacefully. To the biblical historian, who was interested in telling what God had done for His people, every battle won and every improvement of their condition was the result of their God intervening in the world, shaping their destiny because they were His people and He loved them. After a time they formed the confederation of the twelve tribes under the judges, a confederacy which was held together by their common allegience to their covenant God. All was well. God was with them and He was their Lord.

As time passed, they became dissatisfied with their political situation. They wanted a king. They wanted to be like their neighbors. To many this was a major crisis in their history because they were the people of God and He was their only king. Eventually, God himself gave them a king, so the prophet tells us. It was a prophet, Samuel, who selected Saul to be this first king. He was followed by David, the beloved of God, to whom God renewed His promise. David attempted to reconcile the monarchy with the rights of His God. He had the ark brought to Jerusalem, the capital of the United Kingdom, and he made the priesthood a part of the ruling class. At the same time, through a series of highly successful military campaigns (successful because God was with him), David extended the boundaries of the kingdom. In the process a strong secularizing influence was introduced into the chosen people. The Empire, for that is what it became, embraced all sorts of non-Hebrews, and with Solomon's success as merchant, trader, builder, and emperor, the secularization proceeded quickly and without interruption.

As we mentioned earlier, this was Israel's Golden Age, the height of her power. It was also the beginning of a great prophetic activity, not in the sense of future events being foretold, but rather in the word of God being preached and written by men selected by God to be His messengers. The prophets were primarily men sent by God to interpret Israel's past and present from God's point of view. Their mission was to reveal God's activity and concern for His chosen people, to remind them of the covenant and its obligations. And yet throughout there is also promise, promise of a future glory for God's people, a promise which never seemed to be fulfilled.

We have already spoken of Amos and how he came upon the scene after Solomon's death and the division of the kingdom. He spoke of justice and he spoke of doom. Somehow a belief had arisen among the people of a day of reckoning; "The Day of the Lord" they called it. On that day, as they thought, God would judge the idolatrous nations of the world and destroy them. The Kingdom of Israel would be extended to the whole world. God's victory would be complete. But Amos said:

> Woe to those who yearn for the day of the Lord! What will this day of the Lord mean for you? Darkness and not light! As if a man were to flee from a lion and a bear should meet him; or as if on entering his house he were to rest his hand against the wall, and a snake should bite him (Am. 5:18-20).

All through the book of Amos the message is repeated and elaborated—until the very end. There he strikes a note of hope:

> But I will not destroy the house of Jacob completely, says

> the Lord. For see, I have given the command to sift the house of Israel among all the nations, as one sifts with a sieve, letting no pebble fall to the ground. By the sword shall all sinners among my people die, those who say, "Evil will not reach or overtake us." . . . I will bring about the restoration of my people Israel . . . say I, the Lord, your God (Am. 9:8-14).

Notice how Amos (and it will be the same with the rest of the prophets) interprets everything from a religious point of view. It was God who was judging His faithless people. It was God who would bring about their downfall. It was God who would save a remnant and from it rebuild His people. In all of this Amos is quite positive. This is the way it is going to be. There is no doubt. Everything that has happened did so precisely for the reasons Amos gives. He is sure of it. We are not so sure of things because we are not prophets. We can interpret events religiously, but we can never be sure we are right. But Amos was a prophet, and as with all of the prophets, he was not so by his own choice. It is understandable that his message from the Lord was not too well received, and we gain an insight into what makes a prophet when we hear his answer to Amasia, a priest sent to get rid of him by Jeroboam, the king of Israel:

> To Amos, Amasia said, "Off with you, visionary, flee to the land of Juda! There earn your bread by prophesying, but never again prophesy in Bethel, for it is the king's sanctuary and a royal temple." Amos answered Amasia, "I was no prophet, nor have I belonged to a company of prophets. I was a shepherd and a dresser of sycamores. The Lord took me from following the flock, and said to

me, Go, prophesy to my people Israel. Now hear the word of the Lord" (Am. 7:12-16).

Almost contemporary with Amos was Osee, who condemned Israel and prophesied her doom as roundly and clearly as Amos, but his own attitude toward God was tempered by a personal tragedy. From the rather obscure passages relating to Osee's personal life, it seems that he was directed by God to marry a temple prostitute, who continued to ply her trade—at least she seems to have been consistently unfaithful. The tragedy of the situation lay in his continuous unsuccessful efforts to turn her into a respectable woman. It seems he was in love with her and that he hoped by his own great love somehow to make her worthy; but heartbreak followed heartbreak. Certainly, an experience such as this has a profound effect upon a man. It gave to Osee an insight into what might be God's attitude towards His people, that God, without forgetting each man's sins, might nevertheless continue to love him. Justice is not forgotten. Judgment is still made and the verdict is still guilty. At God's direction Osee named his children "She-who-is-not-pitied" and "Not-my-people" to indicate that judgment.

The Israelites had made themselves radically unworthy of God's love. But to them and to every man Osee brought hope by revealing the possibility of God's mercy, by revealing the possibility of God's accepting His people as they are, and even more, by revealing the possibilty of God's *making* a man worthy in spite of sin by the unspeakable power of His own love. To Osee, sin was not merely a breaking of the covenant, an infraction of justice, a disobedience; it was infidelity to love. He introduced into bib-

lical literature an image of the relationship between God and His people that was destined to a remarkable future. It was Osee who first spoke of the nuptial union between God and His people:

> I will betroth you to myself forever; I will betroth you to myself in righteousness and justice, and in kindness and mercy. I will betroth myself to you in faithfulness; and you shall know the Lord. . . . I will pity 'Her-who-is-unpitied'; and I will say to 'Not-my-people.' "You are my people"; and he shall say, "My God" (Os. 2:21-25).

It was Osee who first made God's love articulate. Certainly, all that God had done for His people was evidence of His love. Now, though, through His prophet He put it into words. The prophecy of doom was counterbalanced by a prophecy of restoration in terms of a love that would be so strong that only marriage could serve as its image.

In the Southern Kingdom, just before its destruction, Isaia preached the same prophecy of doom and restoration. Because God so loved His people He sent His prophets to them to tell them of His love and of the supreme importance of their love for Him and one another, but His words fell on deaf ears. Like so many others before and since, they became so absorbed with the earthly kingdom they had established, they could no longer see God's love. To them, as to so many before and since, God was a remote historical figure who had done some marvelous things, but certainly nothing to get involved in, nothing to get worked up about. Isaia, like Amos and Osee before him, tried again to call the people to faith and trust in their God, and seeing their lack of repentance, went on to tell them of their impending destruction. They would not listen, so stronger measures must be used. The Lord will destroy them:

> The Light of Israel will become a fire, Israel's Holy One a flame, that burns and consumes his briars and his thorns in a single day. . . . On that day the remnant of Israel, the survivors of the house of Jacob, will no more lean upon him who struck them; but they will lean upon the Lord, the Holy One of Israel, in truth. A remnant will return, the remnant of Jacob, to the mighty God (Isa. 10:17-21).

Here it is again, God's plan of salvation, the Day of the Lord, the Day of Judgment which only a remnant will survive. In Isaia, too, we find the prophecies about Emmanuel, "God with us." Scripture scholars today assure us that these messages from God, these prophecies, were meaningful to the people to whom they were addressed. They described a contemporary event which the people knew; yet God intended more by them, for they would also apply to the Christ centuries later. God, who knows and shapes all of history, could do that. At any rate, Isaia wrote of the child born of the virgin who shall be called Emmanuel:

> For a child is born to us, a son is given us; upon his shoulder dominion rests. They name him Wonder-Counselor, God-Hero, Father-Forever, Prince of Peace. His dominion is vast and forever peaceful, from David's throne, and over his kingdom, which he confirms and sustains by judgment and justice, both now and forever (Isa. 9:5-6).

And in Chapter eleven he writes:

> But a shoot shall sprout from the stump of Jesse, and from his roots a bud shall blossom. The spirit of the Lord shall rest upon him: a spirit of wisdom and of

> understanding, a spirit of counsel and of strength, a spirit of knowledge and of fear of the Lord, and his delight shall be the fear of the Lord. . . . On that day the root of Jesse, set up as a signal for the nations, the Gentiles shall seek out, for his dwelling shall be glorious. On that day, the Lord shall again take it in hand to reclaim the remnant of his people. . . . On that day, you will say: I give you thanks, O Lord; though you have been angry with me, your anger has abated, and you have consoled me. God indeed is my savior; I am confident and unafraid. My strength and my courage is the Lord, and he has been my savior (Isa. 11:1-3, 10-11; 12:1-2).

After Isaia came Jeremia, whose mission was to give a final warning to the unrepentant people of God. Developing the nuptial image of Osee, he condemned Israel for its infidelity:

> The word of the Lord came to me saying, Go and proclaim in the hearing of Jerusalem. Thus says the Lord: I recall your youthful devotion, your bridal love, how you followed me through the desert, through a land unsown. . . . I brought you to a garden land, to eat its fruits and its good things; but you came and defiled my land, and made my heritage an abomination. . . . If a man divorce his wife, and she leave him, and become the wife of another man, can she return to him again? Is not that woman wholly polluted? But you have played the harlot with many lovers, and would fain return to me! the oracle of the Lord (Jer. 2:1-2, 7; 3:1).

Jeremia, also, had another message. God's anger would strike, there would be no further delay; but God would not abandon His people nor His plan for their salvation. He

was chastising them because He loved them, because only in punishment could they see their guilt and His love. Through Jeremia God promised a new covenant:

> The days are coming, says the Lord, when I will make a new covenant with the house of Israel and the house of Juda. . . . I will place my law within them, and write it upon their hearts; I will be their God, and they shall be my people. No longer will they have need to teach their friends and kinsmen how to know the Lord. All, from least to greatest, shall know me, says the Lord, for I will forgive their evil doing and remember their sin no more (Jer. 31:31ff).

The old covenant was to be replaced by a new one. The remnant would know God's love on that day, for He would engrave it on their hearts. The promise of old was taking a new shape. The plan of salvation was being filled in piece by piece. God was carrying it through.

About the same time as Jeremia was working in Jerusalem, Ezechiel was preaching among the exiles from Israel, which had already fallen. In one vision Ezechiel saw the glory of the Lord leave His dwelling among His people. He would no longer live in the temple among them. He was deserting them because they had deserted Him; and now, left to themselves, they would die by famine and sword. They did; and when it was over, the survivors were deported in large numbers, according to the custom of their Babylonian conquerors.

Even in exile the people were unrepentant for a time. False prophets were continually telling the people that the exile would end very soon, and the people believed them. Against the popular trend, Ezechiel's mission was to guide

the people to repentance, to awaken in them the faith which would tell them of the relevance and importance of God's love for them. And like the other prophets of this age, Ezechiel, too, added to the promise and reaffirmed it:

> Thus the nations shall know that I am the Lord, says the Lord God, when in their sight I prove my holiness through you. For I will take you away from among the nations, gather you from all the foreign lands, and bring you back to your own land. I will sprinkle clean water upon you to cleanse you from all your impurities, and from all your idols I will cleanse you. I will give you a new heart and place a new spirit within you, taking from your bodies your stony hearts and giving you natural hearts. I will put my spirit within you and make you live by my statues, careful to observe my decrees. You shall live in the land I gave your fathers; and shall be my people, and I will be your God (Ezech. 36:24-28).

God, who had through the centuries demonstrated His love and concern for His people by dwelling with them, in the cloud and column of fire, in the tent over the ark and then in the inner sanctuary of the temple, now was promising to dwell *in* them. The Entirely Other was to become at the same time the Intimately Close. Love would bring not only presence and nearness, but oneness!

Also during the exile a disciple of Isaia (whose writings appear in the book of Isaia from chapter 40 to 55) wrote the words usually applied to John the Baptist:

> A voice cries out: In the desert prepare the way of the Lord! Make straight in the wasteland a highway for our God! Every valley shall be filled in, every mountain and

> hill shall be made a plain, the rough country, a broad valley (Isa. 40:3-4).

It was probably another disciple of Isaia who told of the signs which would accompany the day of the Lord, the same description that Christ used when He identified Himself to John: "Then will the eyes of the blind be opened, the ears of the deaf be cleared; then will the lame leap like a stag, then the tongue of the dumb will sing" (Isa. 35:5-6).

The former disciple also wrote of the Suffering Servant, how he is whipped and mocked and spit upon, despised, like a sheep led to slaughter, silent when oppressed, numbered among the wicked, crushed with pain, stricken to death.

> Yet it was our infirmities that he bore, our sufferings that he endured while we thought of him as stricken, as one smitten by God and afflicted. But he was pierced for our offenses, crushed for our sins; upon him was the chastisement that makes us whole; by his stripes we were healed (Isa. 53:4-5).

The chosen people would be reduced to one man who would represent them all. He is innocent and obedient, and though he is to suffer, he will be exalted. His mission is to be universal because he is to bear reproach not only for Israel, but for all people. Here is God's plan for salvation revealed through His prophets. The height of Old Testament prophecy had been reached. There remained now only to fill in a few details and set the scene.

The eventual conversion of the exiles produced the Lamentations and several psalms, eloquent and moving testi-

mony of a change of heart. A thoroughly chastened and repentant people were brought back to their own country under Cyrus the Persian, who had defeated their Babylonian captors. And one of the best indications of this recovered sincerity is the fact that instead of attempting to reestablish the Davidic monarchy and a new empire, they chose to devote their efforts to rebuilding the temple according to the instructions given them by Ezechiel.

Under the Persian officials, Nehemiah and Ezra, the formless conglomeration of repatriated Judeans was molded into a community, whose cohesion developed from submission to and reverence for "the law of the God of Heaven." In other words, the restored community became such only because the people accepted not only the God of their Fathers, but the law of God as well. The law of God given through Moses assumed an importance without parallel. It was the core of their communal existence and the personal responsibility of each. The Scribes of post-exilic Judaism were a product of this law-conscious nation. The general principles of the Mosaic law needed to be reduced to practical, particular situations; and for this, legal experts were required. The Scribes became the interpreters, teachers, and, in many cases, judges. Their development of a body of laws to cover any and every conceivable situation placed a burden on the people that was almost impossible to bear.

The Judean community was growing all the while and enjoying moderate prosperity. Then, at the beginning of the second century, Palestine was overrun by the Greek Seleucid kingdom, which had no intention of being so tolerant. Judaism was henceforth forbidden, its cult suspended, its Sabbath observance banned; and copies of the law were

ordered to be burned. The only possible answer to such an ultimatum was revolt, and revolt it was.

The Maccabean brothers led the Jewish forces through a protracted war which won for them religious freedom and political freedom as well, though this state of affairs was to last only a short time. Less than a century later, the mighty Roman empire engulfed the tiny nation; and this is the way we find it "in the fullness of time," at the beginning of the Day of the Lord.

According to the now-familiar prophecies of Isaia and others, Christ was born during the reign of the Roman Emperor Caesar Augustus. The holy God disguised his glory beneath the veil of human nature. "The Word was made flesh." The living God became the incarnate God. He lived in the form of a man. He spoke as a man, grew as a man, died as a man.

Before his birth, Zachary, the father of John the Baptist, announced the coming of the Saviour and the role his son would play:

> "Blessed be the Lord, the God of Israel, because he has visited and wrought redemption for his people, and has raised up a horn of salvation for us, in the house of David his servant, as he promised through the mouth of his holy ones, the prophets from of old; salvation from our enemies, and from the hand of all who hate us, to show mercy to our forefathers and to be mindful of his holy covenant, of the oath that he swore to Abraham our father, that he would grant us, that, delivered from the hand of our enemies, we should serve him without fear, in holiness and justice before him all our days. And thou, child, shall be called the prophet of the Most High,

> for thou shall go before the face of the Lord to prepare his ways, to give people knowledge of salvation through forgiveness of their sins" (Luke 1:68-77).

The Baptist, when he was grown, took up his role as forerunner of the Christ, preaching and baptizing in the region around the Jordan. His message was simple, as we mentioned when treating of God's justice. He said: Repent, prepare yourselves for judgment, get ready to meet your saviour.

A short time later in the synagogue of Nazareth, Jesus read to the people of his home town a passage from Isaia. Luke describes it this way:

> And after he opened the volume, he found the place where it was written, "The Spirit of the Lord is upon me, because he has anointed me; to bring good news to the poor has he sent me, to proclaim to the captives release, and sight to the blind; to set at liberty the oppressed, to proclaim the acceptable year of the Lord, and the day of recompense." And closing the volume, he gave it back to the attendant and sat down. And the eyes of all in the synagogue were gazing on him. But he began to say to them, "Today this Scripture has been fulfilled in your hearing" (Luke 4:17-20).

So began the work of the Christ.

We know He was rejected by His own people, in spite of miracles, in spite of His personal magnetism, in spite of everything. Sometimes this is quite puzzling, and perhaps it calls for a word of explanation. Up till now we have only hinted at the prophecies about the Messiah, the Son of David, the king; but these are the very prophecies that were uppermost in the minds of most Jews. Many of the psalms

and all the prophets who had spoken of the restoration of the kingdom seemed to imply the coming of a king such as Israel had known before. The people saw no reason to suspect anything else.

Daniel had written of the "Son of Man" who came on the clouds of heaven and "received dominion, glory, and kingship; nations and peoples of every language serve him. His dominion is an everlasting dominion that shall not be taken away, his kingship shall not be destroyed" (Dan. 7:13-14).

This prophecy, among others, was responsible for the development of the ideas of the full restoration of the kingdom; and except for a small group, most of the people seemed to have felt that the prophecies of judgment and punishment had already been fulfilled in the destruction of Jerusalem and the redemption from captivity. The common hope was for the restoration of the kingdom and the subjugation of all the nations of the world.

Aside from the descriptions of this attitude in the Gospels, perhaps the best indications of it are in the apocryphal works written in the century or so before Christ. These writings are often inconsistent and always worldly. The Messiah-King is represented as a victorious general who rebuilds the kingdom, brings peace and prosperity, and restores all the scattered tribes to the land of their fathers. No one, it seems, had ever connected the Suffering Servant, spoken of in Isaia and the psalms, with the Christ. It is little wonder, then, that the people failed to recognize their Saviour and King, who preached but did not rally to battle. Even after the Resurrection the apostles themselves questioned Christ about the time of the restoration of the kingdom!

The people were mostly mistaken in their evaluation of

Jesus and His mission, it is true, but they were certainly right in calling Him a prophet. We have already seen a number of instances which show the harmony of Christ's teaching with that of the prophets before Him. It would be useful here to repeat a bit of it.

In one place he said: "Do not think I have come to destroy the law or the prophets. I have not come to destroy, but to fulfill" (Matt. 5:17). And in an allegory which deserves retelling, He recounts the earlier rejections of God's efforts to reform His people, and ends by declaring that this is the last act of the salvation drama. Now salvation will go to the Gentiles:

> "There was a man, a householder, who planted a vineyard, and put a hedge about it, and dug a wine vat in it, and built a tower; then he let it out to vine-dressers, and went abroad. But when the fruit season drew near, he sent his servants to the vine-dressers to receive his fruits. And the vine-dressers seized his servants, and beat one, killed another and stoned another. Again he sent another party of servants more numerous than the first; and they did the same to these. Finally he sent his son to them saying, 'They will respect my son.' But the vine-dressers, on seeing the son, said among themselves, 'This is the heir; come; let us kill him, and we shall have his inheritance.' So they seized him, cast him out of the vineyard, and killed him. . . ."
>
> Jesus said to them, "Did you never read in the Scriptures, 'The Stone which the builders rejected has become the corner stone; by the Lord this has been done, and it is wonderful in our eyes'? Therefore I say to you, that the kingdom of God will be taken away from you and

will be given to a people yielding its fruits" (Matt. 21: 33-44).

By His insistence on the first commandment and in a hundred other ways, Christ emphasized the primary importance of recognizing our God as God, as the Holy One, as our Creator and our Lord.

His emphasis on brotherly love is without equal, but strongly reminiscent of the prophets of old: "Blessed are the meek . . . blessed are the merciful . . . blessed are the peacemakers" (Matt. 5:4-9). ". . . If thou art offering thy gift at the altar, and there remember that thy brother has anything against thee, leave thy gift before the altar and go first to be reconciled to thy brother, and then come and offer thy gift" (Matt. 5:23-24).

He calls Himself a good shepherd and judge, merciful and just. He announced and described the kingdom of heaven over and over again, finally contradicting all the popular notions by declaring: ". . . the kingdom of God is within you" (Luke 17:20).

Just before His passion, at the Last Supper, He declared the old covenant to be at an end by establishing the new one to be sealed in His own blood: "This cup is the new covenant in my blood, which shall be shed for you" (Luke 22:20).

Before Pilate, Jesus acknowledged His kingship. In His passion and on the cross He showed Himself to be the Suffering Servant. He was the Remnant of Israel. At His Resurrection He achieved the victory over sin and death.

When the apostles and disciples received the Holy Spirit, Ezechiel's vision of the dry bones was turned into reality: the new Israel was animated by the Spirit of God Himself.

Under the influence of this Spirit on Pentecost morning Saint Peter announced the unfavorable judgment of God on His people, the rejection of all but the "remnant"; and by quoting the prophecy of Joel about the day of the Lord, Saint Peter was, in effect, identifying himself and the disciples as that remnant, since they were the followers of the Christ:

> "Men of Judea and all you who dwell in Jerusalem, let this be known to you, and give ear to my words. . . . This is what was spoken through the prophet Joel: 'And it shall come to pass in the last days, says the Lord, that I will pour forth of my Spirit upon all flesh; and your sons and your daughters shall prophesy, and your young men shall see visions, and your old men shall dream dreams. And moreover upon my servants and upon my handmaids in those days will I pour forth of my Spirit, and they shall prophesy' " (Acts 2:14-18).

These times are called the "last times" because in Christ is established the new and *eternal* covenant. There will be no other. This has been the final and decisive act of the living God in the long history of God's plan to reconcile man to Himself. Saint Paul wrote to the Romans:

> But now the justice of God has been made manifest independently of the law, being attested by the law and the prophets; the justice of God through faith in Jesus Christ upon all who believe. For there is no distinction, as all have sinned and have need of the glory of God. They are justified freely by his grace through the redemption which is in Christ Jesus, whom God has set forth as a propitiation by his blood through faith, to manifest his

> justice, God in his patience remitting former sins; to manifest his justice at the present time, so that he himself is just, and makes just him who has faith in Jesus (Rom. 3:21-26).

What Osee was unable to do for his unfaithful wife, God does for those who accept His Christ. For, while Osee could forgive, he could not remake his wife. But God forgives and "*makes* just him who has faith in Jesus." Through Christ has come hope in spite of sin, salvation in spite of guilt, and love in spite of unworthiness.

The new life given to Jesus at His resurrection is a life that He can share, in fact a life that He does share the moment a man believes and is baptized. Elevated by this new life, a man becomes the "new creature" envisioned by Isaia. He is reconciled to God because he shares in this new life of Christ Himself. He has become an adopted son, coheir with Christ.

This is the mystery of God's love for man, not only in word, but especially in deed. The one theme running through all of Scripture is this salvation history, the words and events in Hebrew history interpreted and presented as the acts of God, the unfolding of His plan to overcome the estrangement between Himself and man, which man had chosen at the Fall. Recalling our insistence at the beginning of all the things we should look for in order to discover that particular type of love we call divine, we cannot help but know that God has really loved mankind and men from the beginning. History is a witness of it, if we can read that history with faith. And in reviewing all of this, as we have done, we are only being true to what is so clear in apostolic tradition. The preaching recorded in the Acts of

the Apostles is full of references to what God has done for us, culminating as it did in the sending of the Christ. From all of this we have abundant evidence of God's concern for us, Our God is, without doubt, the God of love.

St. Paul, too, marvelled at the immensity and mystery of God's love for man. In one place he points to an important factor that we must always keep in mind, that God's love for us is all the more mysterious and all the more divine "For scarcely in behalf of a just man does one die; yet perhaps one might bring himself to die for a good man. But God commends his charity towards us, because when as yet we were sinners, Christ died for us" (Rom. 5:7-9).

This is the idea of God that the Bible in its unity places before the believer. The Holy God is the God of Justice and the God of Love. Once again, it is only the believer, the man of faith, who can see his God this way, and by reflection see himself as a creature who is loved by his Creator. It makes a difference.

THE CHRIST EVENT

Christ's origin, birth, life, death, resurrection, enthronement in power and sending of the Spirit, with the added dimension of their significance, add up to a totality embraced by the term "the Christ Event." This is to say that the Christian believer holds that more than just the person of Christ and his historical reality are significant. Christ is for the believer both revelation and salvation: revelation of the Trinity, of God's will to save, and of the divine way of being human as well as the human way of being God; salvation because he is the Way and because he is our

justification, redemption, reconciliation and expiation. First we will discuss the Christ event as revelation and then as salvation.

Christ as Revelation

As Schillebeeckx [19] has worked out so beautifully, the Christ event is itself the revelation of the Trinity, that there are three persons in the one God. Jesus, co-eternal with the Father as the Divine word, was sent by the Father into the world. As such, the Son is represented as coming from the Father and living His divine Sonship in a human way by obedience and submission even unto death. He repeatedly speaks of Himself as the Son of His Father as well as making it clear that He and the Father are one. He is, then, eternally begotten of the Father, which means that they are distinct as persons but one God. Jesus' submission unto death, as the human expression of divine Sonship, is immediately accepted by the Father, whose acceptance takes the form of raising Jesus from the dead and enthroning Him as Lord—a title reserved in the Old Testament to God alone. In other words, the man Jesus is raised by the Father to the glory of the Christ, Christ the King. This is the representation of the Father's return of love to the Son who has demonstrated His love by giving Himself up to death. The Father, then, through the Son, sends the Holy Spirit to finish the work of salvation. The Father begets the Son and Their reciprocal love becomes personified in the Spirit of Love; so there are Father, Son, and Holy Spirit, three persons in one God, and the Christ Event is the revelation of this mystery.

This is more than just an interesting bit of theology. It

[19] *Christ the Sacrament of the Encounter with God* by E. Schillebeeckx, © Sheed & Ward Ltd. 1963, published by Sheed & Ward, Inc., New York, 1963.

is the revelation of the trinitarian nature of salvation. We are not saved simply and only because Jesus suffered and died for us, but rather because the Father sent the Son who became a man like us, who died for us, who was raised to glory by the Father, and who sent the Spirit to continue and finish this divine work of mercy.

Jesus was also the incarnate revelation of God's mercy and love. True, He had sent the prophets who spoke His word and worked miracles for the people, and this was palpable evidence of His love; but in becoming man Himself, and particularly in taking upon Himself the sinful flesh of all fallen humanity, He demonstrates His love for us with an impact which could have been achieved in no other way. The culmination of it all came in the supreme sacrifice, when as man He lay down His life. What else could have been so deeply stirring, so genuinely human or so profoundly symbolic? Death is total. A man can give no more.

This was not the death of a man among others for a cause. It was the sacrificial death of the God-made-man for the salvation of all men. The disciple of Isaia said it: ". . . he was pierced for our offenses, crushed for our sins; upon him was the chastisement that makes us whole; by his stripes we were healed." Herein is the human expression of God's will to save us, of the fact that God not only knows us, but that He cares.

As Jesus, the Son of God was also the living revelation of the divine way of being human. He was the perfect religious man. Both His teaching and His life are witness to it. To be religious is to believe, and to believe is to understand existence from what has been revealed, from what is real. To believe is to live out one's existence from a set of real values which turn around the total picture of reality ex-

posed by revelation. This in the most perfect sense was Jesus. In Him there was never a shadow of outright sin or even of compromise. Of course, He was tempted—He was human—but temptation is not sin. In living a life of submission to His Father's will so that at the end He could say: "It is finished," Jesus gave us an ideal for imitation and an example to follow. He made visible and living what it means to be a human creature of the Holy God.

Undoubtedly, as an ideal, Jesus is an impossible ideal, since He cannot be perfectly imitated. But this is certainly not a valid reason for rejection. Every ideal is by its very nature impossible of fulfillment. An ideal is an idea, a mental image of that which is perfect. Because it is ideal, and not real, it does not suffer from the limitations of the real; but these ideals do form the basis for thought-induced activity. If a man wants to learn to swing a golf club well, he will first attempt to find out what makes a perfect swing, then he will attempt to imitate it. He may always fall short of the ideal, but it is the ideal which serves as his guide. In attempting to live human existence, an ideal is no less necessary; and for all of humanity Jesus stands before us as that "ideal." Aside from his miraculaus power, there were human qualities in Jesus, qualities that we like to see in a man because they make him the kind of man we would like to be, or would like to know. These are the qualities we would like the children to have when they grow up, the qualities that make a man good and fine and honorable.

It makes little difference which human quality of Jesus you wish to call the most outstanding, but certainly one of the most striking was His mastery of Himself and, therefore, His mastery of every situation in which He found Himself. In other words, as no other man before or since, Jesus

was free, free to determine what He would do and how He would do it. His life, as described by witnesses, is the portrait of a man who was on top of things because He was in command of Himself. Even during the passion, it was he who was in command. During the trial Pilate became unnerved and fell apart, but not Jesus. When Jesus chose to speak, His words were as clear and as forceful as ever. When he was silent, it was because He chose to be. And on the cross He maintained a control and a dignity almost impossible to imagine. One by one He took care of unfinished business. He appointed John to take care of His mother. He forgave His executioners. He pardoned one of those assigned to die with Him. He fulfilled the last of the prophecies of His death. And then, after declaring that everything was accomplished, He gave himself up to death.

His death was tragic because the death of any good man is a tragedy, but Jesus was not a tragic figure like a Hamlet. There was no flaw in His character that ultimately resulted in His undoing. Jesus suffered and was crucified because He chose to be, because this was his mission, this is what the Father wanted of Him. Neither was His the life and death of a fanatic or of one driven by compulsion. There is not a single shred of evidence to indicate either of these things. But there is evidence of His courage and wisdom and self-mastery. Jesus had a mission. He knew what was right and what was wrong. He lived by it and He cared what no man thought. He was a man's man. He stood up before the rulers of His people and to their face called them a brood of vipers, whited sepulchers, clean on the outside but rotten and full of filth within. He walked into their camp and threw out those who were buying and selling. He did not even hesitate to hit them in their pocket-

books. At the beginning of the last week of His life He went to Jerusalem, knowing that He would die; and on the night they came for Him, he waited for them to come, He made Himself available. There is a courage that is inspiring.

But a man is not a man just because he is courageous and strong. A man is also tender and compassionate and wise and prudent. There are enough episodes recounted in the gospels to indicate that Jesus was all of these. He knew that He had lost Jerusalem, and He cried—there is nothing unmanly about that. He knew that Lazarus, His friend, had died, that Martha and Mary were struck with grief, and He was deeply affected. Out of compassion He cured the sick, the blind, the deaf, and the maimed. Above all, He forgave sins. Time after time He confounded the learned with His grasp of reality as revealed by Scripture. His was not the wisdom of the learned men, the knowledge acquired from philosophy and experience. His was the wisdom of truth, which can only be grasped by those who are ready to accept it. His kind of wisdom is the kind available to everyone who is willing to accept reality, God's reality, without reservations and selfish interests. His is the wisdom one acquires, not from school and study, but from believing, believing in what lies behind appearances, believing in what is real, not what seems to be real. And from such wisdom came his prudence—not the selfishly motivated cunning or cowardice that often goes by the name of prudence, but the straight thinking of a man who knows what is really worthwhile doing and what he must do to accomplish it. Not to speak out when wrongs must be challenged is not prudence; it is cowardice. Not to do what must be done, because someone's toes may be stepped on, perhaps some-

one in authority, is not prudence; it is cowardice. How much pusillanimity, how much obsequiousness is hidden under the pretence of prudence! Jesus was not like this, and His prudence, as with all of His qualities, His human qualities, grew out of His vision of faith.

Above all, and as the foundation and source of all, Jesus was a man of faith. If it is permissible to use the phrase, Jesus was driven by one fundamental conviction: His commitment to the Father. He came, He said, because He was sent by the Father; and while He was with us, He would not do His own will, but His Father's will. To Jesus, to the man of faith, life was reduced to two basic responses: love of the Father and love of neighbor. Everything else is caught up in these. Everything else is the expression of these. Everything else is the fruit of these. For Jesus, to believe, to love, and to obey were all synonyms. With all of reality laid bare before Him, the beauty and goodness of it all, the beginning and end of it all in the Father, all drew from Him the response of love which only the man of faith can have. And by revealing to us the divine way of being human, He showed us that such love and faith amounts to the fullest acceptance of the Father's will.

Believing as He did in all the reality exposed by His faith, He showed us what a man is like who approaches his existence with the understanding of faith. The things which Jesus held to be of value, worthwhile having and worthwhile seeking, were the things so understood by the God-made-man, whose clarity of vision and depth of perception never could be equaled by any other man. If we go to learned and well-balanced men for advice, how much more should we look at and listen to Jesus to learn about existence and true values. In other places we have already dis-

cussed His teaching on many things; later we shall touch on others. At this point we are only attempting to indicate that Jesus is the revelation of the divine way of being human, of the ideal incarnation of all that is best in human existence, and, therefore, that He is the one who deserves to be consulted and listened to. Jesus is the Truth, the perfect expression of the Father's concept of the perfect human existence.

Christ as Salvation

The Christ of the Gospels, the son of Mary and the Son of God, once described Himself as "the Way, the Truth, and the Life." He was not a religious leader who pointed out the way. He is the Way. Not only with Him are we saved, but by Him and through Him and in Him. His life becomes our life, so that elevated to this life of a new-creature-in-Christ, it is by our identification with Him, our solidarity with Him, that we are saved. St. Paul describes the same thing by saying that Christ is our justification, redemption, expiation and reconciliation—four metaphors to express four different aspects of the Christ event.

Not for himself alone did Jesus suffer and die, but for all men. "I came that they may have life and have it more abundantly," He said. "The Good Shepherd lays down his life for his sheep." And the Nicene Creed says: "who for us men and for our salvation came down from heaven." This was His express intention and this is how the Father accepted it, which He signified by raising Jesus from the dead and establishing Him as Lord. We have been washed in the blood of the lamb, prefigured by the Paschal lamb of the ancient Passover in Egypt. His blood was the price

paid as expiation or satisfaction for our sins, the sins of every man. No other sacrifice would ever be required. The agony of crucifixion and death endured by the God-in-sinful-flesh was the full payment of all humanity to the Father, the once and for all expiation for sin. To make it our own we must believe and be baptized into the passion and death of Christ.

It is also in Christ that we are redeemed. Redemption is an image St. Paul borrowed from a Roman custom of a slave purchasing his freedom by paying a stipulated sum of money to a temple priest, who would then turn it over to the slave's master. Our redemption is redemption from the slavery of sin, and the cost was the blood of Jesus. The power of sin is the alienation from God which it produces. Slavery to sin is the expression used to indicate a man's total inability to overcome the effects of sin by his own power. Because the Father accepted Christ's death as the price of our redemption, sin was defeated once and for all in Christ; and we are no longer slaves, but free-men-in-Christ, free of guilt and free of death.

The justification metaphor emphasizes the radical change that occurs in the man who accepts the faith and is baptized. "God makes just him who has faith in Jesus," which means that the believer becomes a new-creature-in-Christ, no longer subject to the guilt of sin or the sting of death, elevated to a new life—a life in Christ, a life which he shares with the risen Christ, which is to say, a new life in which he partakes of the divine life itself.

> Do you know that all we who have been baptized into Christ Jesus have been baptized into his death? For we were buried with him by means of baptism into death, in order that, just as Christ has arisen from the dead

> through the glory of the Father, so we also may walk in newness of life. For if we have been united with him in the likeness of his death, we shall be so in the likeness of his resurrection also. For we know that our self has been crucified with him, in order that the body of sin may be destroyed, that we may no longer be slaves to sin; for he who is dead is acquitted of sin. But if we have died with Christ, we believe that we shall also live together with Christ, for we know that Christ, having risen from the dead, dies now no more, death shall no longer have dominion over him. For the death that he died, he died to sin once for all, but the life that he lives, he lives unto God. Thus do you consider yourselves also dead to sin, but alive to God in Christ Jesus (Rom. 6:3-11).

This is a theme which we shall continue to explore because it is certainly a central and determining factor in a Christian's understanding of his own existence. For the moment we shall simply make the point. The Christ event is salvific because through Chirst we are justified, made just through the generous, gratuitous, merciful love of God, given a new life in Christ through which we are alone in him, and as such, adopted sons of God. St. Paul said it in his Epistle to the Galatians:

> But when the fullness of time came, God sent his Son, born of a woman, born under the law, that he might redeem those under the Law, that we might receive the adoption of sons. And because you are sons, God has sent the Spirit of his Son into our hearts, crying, 'Abba, Father,' So that he is no longer a slave, but a son, and if a son, an heir also through God (Gal. 4:4-7).

Closely associated with the other three metaphors, since all four are aspects of the same Christ event, is the notion of reconciliation with the Father.

> If any man is in Christ, he is a new creature: the former things have passed away; behold, they are made new! But all things are from God, who has reconciled us to himself through Christ and has given to us the ministry of reconciliation. For God was truly in Christ reconciling the world to himself by not reckoning against men their sins . . . (2 Cor. 5:17-19).

Because expiation was made for our sins through the blood of Jesus, our sins have been forgiven, our guilt removed, and we have been created anew in Christ, sharing not only in His death, but also in His resurrection, having become new-creatures-in-Christ, pleasing to God and, therefore, reconciled to Him. We have been redeemed from sin and the power of sin, re-established in the friendship of God and made just.

The reality described by these few words is so immense as to be staggering. St. Paul said that it was foolishness to the learned and a scandal to the Jews. It is, nevertheless, the good news of salvation, the answer to the human condition, comfort and hope in exchange for anxiety, meaning and purpose in exchange for aimlessness, peace in exchange for inner conflict—all of which are available only to the man who can believe, who has been given the power to believe. That a man can be, and indeed is transformed from a being-in-the-world to a being-in-Christ by the power of God, is basic, unshakeable truth to the believer and the source of his redemption from the human condition.

The Christ event means and has brought about redemp-

tion, reconciliation, justification, and expiation. Redemption and expiation are release from the anxieties of guilt and condemnation, since sin has been atoned for once and for all. Emptiness and meaninglessness are defeated by the understanding through faith that what I do concerns God, who cares for me; that what I am, I am because my God, out of love for me, has made me so; that my God calls for me to return His love by living up to what I have now become. And, at the same time, the anxieties of fate and death succumb to the knowledge of my life being in the hands of my God who has not spared His Son to give me life, a new life in the Spirit, a life conceived and born in love, a life in which death is only a passing moment.

Christ Jesus is our salvation. He is the Way and the Life. He does not point to the way and give the life. He *is* the Way and the Life. It is in Him that we are carried to the Father, and it is in Him that we have our life and our being as new creatures who can say to God, "My Father." And it is most important to understand that all of this comes to us as a gift, totally undeserved and unmerited. Salvation is not our work but God's, the Father sending the Son and through the Son the Spirit. Ours is not salvation by achievement, but by grace, which means gift. St. Paul took great pains to make this clear and he went to some lengths to insure that there would be no mistake about it. He includes in the concept of redemption liberation from the Law, which he sees as the occasion of sin. The new-creature-in-Christ is redeemed from the power of sin because he can no longer glory in his observance of a law. He can no longer convince himself that he has earned his salvation. He can no longer use the law as a tool of self-assertion. Salvation is from faith in Jesus Christ—given, not earned.

The legalism, the twisted caricature of religion as observance of law, was forever supplanted by the gift of God in Christ.

This, too, is a point that deserves elaboration and understanding. As we described earlier, the restored Jewish community established itself under the Law of Moses. The motivation was certainly religious and the object was to render to God the honor and service that was His due; but the Law, not faith, was dominant. Legal experts grew out of the system; they were the Scribes. Systematically they spelled out the obligations of the Law to meet any conceivable situation. The Pharisees were the men who took it upon themselves to live up to this considerable and oppressive burden. The point again, however, is that faith was lacking. Fulfillment of directives concerned with external behavior is much easier than wholehearted commitment, and yet both have gone by the name of religion. Jesus openly denounced the Pharisees, not for the observance of the Law, but for their lack of faith, lack of commitment. It is possible to observe a whole code of laws in its entirety, all for the wrong reason. And it is for this reason that Paul claimed that the Law had failed as the means of salvation it was intended to be. Instead of fulfilling the Law as the expression of their love for the God who had first loved them, instead of understanding that salvation came to them as a pure gift and that their response would always be insufficient for all they had received, the Jews are condemned by St. Paul on the grounds that they had turned the Law into the occasion of sinful selfishness. They had convinced themselves that they were able to earn their salvation by observance of the Law.

Notice the parallel here with many a man's understanding of Christianity. To not a few believers salvation lies in the bare acceptance of dogmas and the observance of religious laws and precepts. The word for it is legalism, the same legalism which Jesus condemned in the Pharisees. It is this attitude, empty of commitment, which replaces faith with observance, humble gratitude with pride, and love with emptiness. Our modern scribes, the legalizers, might well heed the words of Jesus: "Woe to you lawyers also! because you load men with oppressive burdens and you yourselves do not touch the burdens" (Lk. 11:46).

Christianity is freedom, redemption not only from sin, but from the slavery of law. Jesus said: "Come to me all you who labor and are burdened and I will give you rest. Take my yoke upon you, and learn from me, for I am meek and humble of heart; and you will find rest for your souls. For my yoke is easy, and my burden light" (Matt. 11: 28-30). The lesson seems clear enough: sterile and burdensome fulfillment of duty, which Jesus preached against but which often goes by the name of Christianity, is not Christianity at all. For Jesus, religion is of the heart. Above all it rests on the recognition that God has done something for us independently of our own efforts. Consequently, it strikes at the roots of our pride of accomplishment and, at the same time, impels us to offer some return for so great a love. It is in this that the Christian finds rest. It is this that makes the yoke of Jesus easy and His burden light. Salvation comes to us as a gift. The very love with which we love the good God comes to us from God; and it is love which brings rest and ease and joy. To offer worship to God, to live as becomes one who has been given the

Spirit, is not a burden and a heavy responsibility. Instead, it is the eager response of a man whose heart has been captivated by love.

It would certainly be a mistake at this point to jump to the conclusion that a condemnation of legalism is also a condemnation of law. The two are not the same thing, and there is no justification for extending the judgment of legalism to law itself. Of course, the existence of law fosters the tendency towards legalism, because it is always a temptation to attempt to satisfy oneself with outward observance in place of inward commitment. But this does not make law or religious precept unChristian or irreligious. In addition to many other advantages, the ten commandments (and even their elaboration into moral precepts) help to spell out and make explicit the pattern of existence expected of a Christian, a being-in-Christ. Jesus did not condemn law. Rather, He shifted the attitude towards law from one of dead submission to authority to one of vitality and intense expression of love. For a being-in-Christ observance of law is not felt or understood as a duty; it is an opportunity, however small, to demonstrate love.

St. Paul understood this very clearly. He himself had been a Pharisee. He knew too well the burden which Christ lifted from his shoulders and he also knew what it meant to be free in Christ. For St. Paul the Christ event meant expiation, reconciliation, redemption, and justification. For him, to be a Christian meant to believe, to be totally committed to the interpretation of existence revealed through Christ, and to be baptized into the death and resurrection of Christ; and then receiving the Spirit, to be one with the risen Christ in glory. It is by this above all—living out of the consciousness that one is a new-creature-in-Christ, that

St. Paul explains what is meant by freedom in Christ. This part of the Christian message is so important that it deserves to be treated at length, and St. Paul speaks of it so forcefully that he deserves to be heard at length. Read carefully what he has to say.

In Romans he wrote:

> But now the justice of God has been made manifest independently of the Law, being attested by the Law and the Prophets; the justice of God through faith in Jesus Christ upon all who believe. For there is no distinction, as all have sinned and have need of the glory of God. They are justified freely by his grace through the redemption which is in Christ Jesus, whom God has set forth as a propitiation by his blood through faith, to manifest his justice at the present time, so that he himself is just, and makes just him who has faith in Jesus (Rom. 3:21-26).

And shortly afterwards:

> Therefore, my brethren, you also, through the body of Christ, have been made to die to the Law, so as to belong to another who has risen from the dead, in order that we may bring forth fruit unto God. For when we were in the flesh, the sinful passions, which were aroused by the Law, were at work in our members so that they brought forth fruit unto death. But now we have been set free from the Law, having died to that by which we were held down, so that we may serve in a new spirit and not according to the outworn letter (Rom. 7:4-6).

In Galatians he wrote:

> For if a law had been given that could give life, justice

would truly be from the Law. But the Scripture shut up all things under sin, that by the faith of Jesus Christ the promise might be given to those who believe. But before the faith came we were kept imprisoned under the Law, shut up for the faith that was to be revealed. Therefore the Law has been our tutor unto Christ, that we might be justified by faith. But now that faith has come, we are no longer under a tutor. For you are all the children of God through faith in Christ Jesus. For all you who have been baptized into Christ, have put on Christ. There is neither Jew nor Greek; there is neither slave nor freeman; there is neither male nor female. For you are all one in Christ Jesus. And if you are Christ's, then you are the offspring of Abraham, heirs according to promise. . . . Stand fast, and do not be caught again under the yoke of slavery. You who would be justified in the Law are estranged from Christ; you have fallen away from grace. For we in the Spirit wait for the hope of justice in virtue of faith (Gal. 3-5).

For the believer, then, the Christ event is both salvation and revelation. Through it he comes to know the peace which only Christ can give, for through it he gains not only hope and love and freedom, but the awareness of his tremendous dignity as a new-creature-in-Christ, a new-being-in-the-Spirit. In addition, he sees in Jesus-the-man the visible expression of God's will to save, and the tangible demonstration of what it means to live a truly religious life.

THE LIVING GOD

In the book of Deuteronomy it is written:

Later on, when your son one day asks you, what these

ordinances, statutes and decrees mean which the Lord, our God, has enjoined on you, you shall say to your son, 'We were once slaves of Pharao in Egypt, but the Lord brought us out of Egypt with his strong hand and wrought before our eyes signs and wonders, great and dire, against Egypt and against Pharao and his whole house. He brought us out from there to lead us into the land he promised on oath to our fathers and to give it to us' (Deut. 6:20-23).

The God of the Bible, the Holy God, the Just and Merciful God, the Loving God, is the Living God, the God who acts, the God who has done something for us, and the God who is now doing something for us. One of the reasons for quoting so liberally from Scripture in the previous chapters has been to prepare for this explicit treatment of what is already there implicitly, that our God is a Living God.

Our God, who has revealed Himself to us through Scripture, indicates in the passage from Deuteronomy above that this is the way He wants to be known, as the God who has done something for His people. All through the pages of the Bible, Old Testament and New, the prophetic interpreters of history make it quite clear that the Holy God is also the Living God, the God of history as well as the Entirely Other. Not only has God created the world, but he governs it as well. Nothing, absolutely nothing ever happens unless He wills it. In Hebrew history it was God who called Abraham and made to him a promise. It was God who gave him a son, and to him a wife and then a child. It was God who arranged for Joseph to be taken to Egypt, and for the Hebrew people to follow him there. It was God who brought His people out of slavery in Egypt and sealed the covenant with them at Sinai. And so it goes all through what we have

already discussed as salvation history—the account of how God expressed His love for His people by doing something for them.

Intervening in the affairs of men and nations throughout all of biblical history, God was understood by the people of biblical times, Old Testament and New, as the Living God. Certainly, down through the centuries since Christ, Christians, too, have thought of God this way. They have prayed to Him for favors and offered thanks for gifts received, which presupposes the belief that He both listens to our prayers and will do something about them, if it please Him. It is also true that even in recent times God has sent messages to us through Mary, as He did through the prophets long before, to warn us of the necessity of repentance and reparation. With striking resemblance to these same prophetic messages of the Old Testament, the revelations at Lourdes and Fatima warned that nation would rise against nation, and that great world wars would follow if the message were not heeded. In each case, war followed. The Living God is not dead and the fate of nations as well as individuals is still under His control. No amount of scientific sophistication or pseudo-wisdom will ever succeed in making men autonomous. This is God's world, not ours, and the greatest achievements of men or nations will always be insignificant dust before the Holy Majesty of the Living God.

There is a woman who is a diabetic. Her husband is also diabetic. One day he fell into a coma, and some time passed before he was taken to the hospital where he was given emergency treatment. The wife, of course, rushed to the hospital and waited outside the emergency room. When the doctor came to tell her of her husband's condition, his

duty was not an easy one. He told her that her husband had been under so long that there would be severe brain damage and that, if he should live, he would be reduced to the condition of an infant. He recommended that she resign herself to having him committed to an institution, which could care for him better than she could. Her husband did not die, but he was exactly as the doctor predicted. He did not know who he was or where, he could not dress or feed himself—he was like an infant. His wife did not commit him, though. Instead, she took him home and prayed for a miracle. She begged her God to cure her husband. For six months this went on without a single sign of improvement. Still she prayed. Still she believed. One morning, after about six months of being unable to speak or do anything for himself, he woke her up to *tell* her that she had better get downstairs and get his breakfast ready, or he would be late for work. As far as I know, at this time he is still well and working. Our God is a living God, who listens to us, who knows and cares.

The testimony and experience of divine activity, however, is not limited to occasional apparitions or to the response to personal prayers. Much more significantly, God manifests his interest and activity in our behalf through the Church, which Schillebeeckx describes as the "historical manifestation of God's own love for men in Christ and, at the same time, of its own love and adoration of God in the same Lord".[20]

Our redemption, our salvation is in Jesus Christ. The

[20] *Op. cit.*, p. 51. Father Schillebeeckx deserves to be read. It is difficult reading, but he works out in detail, much more detail than serves our purpose here, the visibility of God in the world through the Church and sacraments. Here and throughout the rest of this chapter, we are quoting from the work already cited.

Son of God suffered and died as a man for our salvation. His sacrifice for us was acceptable to the Father who raised Him up to glory and made Him Lord. But salvation history does not end there. The redemptive act of Christ was the act of the Son of God who was at the same time the historical Jesus; and while Jesus' sacrifice in history is irrevocably past and impossible to revive, because Jesus was the Son of God, His actions also had a divine character, which makes them eternally actual. From this it follows that Jesus' blood, shed on the cross for us, is eternally present to the Father, who eternally accepts it as the expiation for sin and the source of our salvation. We make this saving reality our own through faith in Jesus Christ and our baptism into His passion, death and resurrection. This means that, having been justified in Christ, we are now "one body in the Lord," as St. Paul said it. We, the New People of God, are the visible realization or the earthly extension of the body of the risen Christ, and this "body of Christ" is the Church.

This is what St. Paul meant when he wrote to the Ephesians:

> Wherefore I on my part, hearing of your faith in the Lord Jesus, and of your love for all the saints, do not cease to give thanks for you, making mention of you in my prayers, that the God of our Lord Jesus Christ, the Father of glory, may grant you the spirit of wisdom and revelation in deep knowledge of him: the eyes of your mind being enlightened, so that you may know what is the hope of his calling, what the riches of the glory of his inheritance in the saints, and what the exceeding greatness of his power towards us who believe. Its measure is the working of his mighty power, which he has

> wrought in Christ in raising him from the dead, and setting him at his right hand in heaven above every Principality and Power and Virtue and Domination—in short, above every name that is named, not only in this world, but also in that which is to come. And all things he made subject under his feet, and him he gave as head over all the Church, which indeed is his body, the completion of him who fills all with all. . . . But God, who is rich in mercy, by reason of his very great love wherewith he has loved us even when we were dead by reason of our sins, brought us to life together with Christ (by grace you have been saved), and raised us up together, and seated us together in heaven in Christ Jesus, that he might show in the ages to come the overflowing riches of his grace in Christ Jesus (Eph. 1:15-23, 2:4-7).

It is in us, the living members of the body of the Lord, that God now makes visible and tangible the saving power which is in Christ Jesus. Together we are the body of Christ, which is to say, we are the Church. This means that the Church is not merely a means of salvation, but salvation itself as realized in this world. Earlier we spoke of Jesus as the visible revelation of the divine way of being human, as well as the visible manifestation of God's will to save. In the same way we speak of the Church as the earthly counterpart of the risen Christ, who intercedes for us continually before the Father, through His passion and death which are eternally actual. The prayer of the Church is the prayer of Christ, head and members. Our love and adoration go to the Father through the Son, whose body we are, and are infallibly accepted by the Father, whose love returns to us through the Son, our salvation.

The activity of the Church, the body of the risen Lord, is salvation, and contact with the Church is encounter with Christ. This encounter takes the form of the Sacraments,

> the ritual making real of the saving mystery of Christ, and therefore . . . the embodiment—thus the concrete offering—of the gratuitous saving will of God in Christ.[21] . . . Each sacrament is the personal saving act of the risen Christ himself, but realized in the visible form of an official act of the Church.[22] . . . To receive the sacraments of the Church in faith is therefore the same thing as to encounter Christ himself.[23] . . . As the personal redemptive act of Christ in his Church, a sacrament is therefore the personal approach of Christ to a particular man. In the fullest sense of the word, a sacrament is the pledge of Christ's availability to a particular individual; the tangible pledge of his willing readiness to enter upon an encounter.[24] . . . The sacraments are signs of Christ's redemptive act in its actual grasp of a particular individual.[25]

In this life and at this moment the Living God reaches out to us, making Himself available to us in visible form through His Church and Sacraments. Although the glorified Christ is not visible, encounter with Him is no less possible than it was to the people of Palestine who lived with Jesus. We meet Him in the ritual of the Church's sacramental activity. At baptism we visibly demonstrate our willingness to believe and our desire to be justified by entering into the ritual of initiation. Christ comes to this encounter through the ritual itself, which is the act of His Church, His earthly

[21] Schillebeeckx, *op. cit.*, p. 70.
[22] *Ibid.*, p. 54.
[23] *Loc. cit.*
[24] *Ibid.*, p. 80.
[25] *Ibid.*, p. 81.

Body. And so it is with each Sacrament. The encounter is between two: Christ and ourselves, and the ritual makes visible both our coming and Christ's. The effect in us is a re-creation, the building up of the "new man" within us, a fuller experience of life in Christ, a deepening and growth of the life which we have in the Spirit.

Schillebeeckx has also written profoundly of the effects of the sacraments.

> A person receiving baptism is incorporated into the Easter mystery of the visible Church and thus into the eternal passover of Christ. On the other hand, when a person is confirmed he begins to participate in that fullness of the Holy Spirit which the visible Church possesses, and in her activity of sending the Spirit; thus he is incorporated into the eternal Pentecost mystery of the glorified Lord. Consequently baptism makes us members of the ecclesial People of God, the 'child of the Father.' [26] . . . Then in confirmation, as members of the Church and so as children of God, we are 'established in power'; within the visible Church, we receive a share in her fullness and bestowal of the Spirit, and thus in the Pentecost mystery of Christ himself.[27]

And from another point of view:

> Now Christ by his sanctifying service, his worship of the Father, is the High Priest. Therefore the Church, as the earthly representation of this sanctifying mystery of worship, is of its nature a priestly People of God. Thus initiation into the Church through the sacrament of baptism and confirmation is an initiation into the ecclesial priesthood of the faithful. Baptism invests us with the priest-

[26] *Ibid.,* p. 161.
[27] *Loc. cit.*

hood of the Church, and confirmation establishes this in power. . . . Baptism gives the priestly commission visibly to live in the Church as children of the Father, participating in the worship and apostolate of Christ's service. . . . The commission given by confirmation is the priestly one visibly to live as children of God established in power.[28]

For the other sacraments:

The ecclesial effect of the sacrament of penance is reconciliation with the Church as the sacrament of our reconciliation with God in Christ. The Church is the earthly manifestation of God's redeeming mercy, and confession is visible contact with the Church precisely under this aspect.[29]

The Eucharist too brings about, in the first place, a deepening of the inner belonging to the eucharistic People of God: it is the sacrament of the unity of the Church, the bond of which is love. Now Christ is present in the Church's Eucharist precisely as the bond of her unity, for it is his real presence under the covenant of the consecration. The individual becomes personally united with Christ in his sacrifice of the cross to the extent that, by taking part in the Eucharist and especially in receiving Communion, he enters into the sacrificial community of the Church. For the Church, the People of God, is the community of the eucharistic covenant, entry into which is the sacrament of personal communion with the Christ who sacrifices, of communion in that sacrifice with which the Father is well pleased.

Again in the anointing of the sick, it is clear that the

[28] *Ibid.*, p. 166.
[29] *Ibid.*, p. 175.

sacrament bestows the gift of grace by making visible connections with the Church. For the Church is the earthly representation of Christ's redemption which, overcoming sin, overcomes death. Now in the sacrament of anointing, the Church, precisely as conqueror of death, is acting for the Christian who is grievously ill. And her act is filled with the reality which it shows forth.[30]

Matrimony has an ecclesial effect which is also the sacrament of the bestowal of grace. In her visible life and activity the Church manifests herself as the bride of Christ. Matrimony thus unites the marriage bond of man and woman with the bridal relationship of the Church to Christ. And because the visibility of the Church is filled with the reality which it signifies, the union of two people in matrimony becomes through its objective ecclesial character a sign of corresponding inner grace.[31]

And, finally, the sacrament of Holy Orders confers a commission and a power to perform visible ecclesial acts, to minister to the People of God in the place of Christ.

The point of all this is to point out the depth of reality which lies open to the man of faith. Beyond the appearances of ritual, and acting within it, is the Living God. Through the Church and its sacramental activity we encounter Christ, Christ in His saving and redeeming activity, Christ in His offer of worship to the Father, Christ in His presence among us, Christ in tender compassion, Christ in the fullness of His life.

Perhaps if one day your son asks you: "What are these commandments, the laws, these precepts that God has pre-

[30] *Loc. cit.*
[31] *Ibid.,* p. 176.

scribed for us" you may answer: "We were once alienated from God and slaves of sin and death. God sent His Son to suffer and die to atone for our sins, to redeem us from the slavery of sin, and to bring us eternal life. Now we are His people. He meets us in the sacraments and He lives within us. May He be blessed forever."

A CHRISTIAN UNDERSTANDING OF EXISTENCE

In an appendix to *The Sickness Unto Death,* Kierkegaard points to a rather common but strange human trait: the confusion, embarrassment, and even offense which one experiences when offered too much. He gives the example of a laborer and the mightiest emperor who ever lived, claiming that the laborer would be as proud as proud can be to have once been noticed by the emperor, but if that emperor would send for him and invite him to become his son-in-law, that would be too much. The laborer would think it quite strange. He would be terribly embarrassed by it and think he was being made fun of. He would say to himself, "Such a thing is too high for me. I cannot get it into my head; it seems to me, if I blurt it straight out, foolishness." With that Kierkegaard continues:

> And now for Christianity! Christianity teaches that this particular individual, and so every individual, whatever in other respects this individual may be, man, woman, serving-maid, minister of state, merchant, barber, student, etc.—this individual exists *before* God—this individual who perhaps would be vain for having once in his life talked with the King, this man who is not a little

> proud of living on intimate terms with that person or the other, this man exists before God, can talk with God any moment he will, sure to be heard by him; in short, this man is invited to live on the most intimate terms with God! Furthermore, for this man's sake God came to the world, let himself be born, suffers and dies; and this suffering God almost begs and entreats this man to accept the help which is offered him! Verily, if there is anything that would make a man lose his understanding, it is surely this! Whosoever has not the humble courage to dare to believe it, must be offended at it. But why is he offended? Because it is too high for him, because he cannot get it into his head.[32]

This is a basic problem faced by anyone who is touched by the Good News of salvation, the Christian message. He must give up his understanding and believe. He must, with humble courage, dare to believe what he cannot understand, dare to relinquish a human understanding of existence and accept the Christian, exchange the solid world of his experience for the world of faith.

The truth is that the world of the Christian is entirely different from the world of the non-believer. It is this above all which sets the Christian apart and makes him different, even in outward appearance many times. He is to some a puzzle, to others a contradiction, and to still others an inspiration. Those who do not believe cannot understand him, which is something St. Paul observed in his own time. He wrote to the Corinthians:

> We, for our part, preach Christ crucified—to the Jews indeed a stumbling-block and to the Gentiles foolishness,

[32] S. Kierkegaard, *The Sickness unto Death* (New York: Doubleday, Anchor Books), p. 216. Reprinted from *The Sickness unto Death* by S. Kierkegaard by permission of Princeton University Press.

> but to those who are called, both Jews and Greeks, Christ, the power of God and the wisdom of God.

And a little further on he makes it clearer still:

> Wisdom, however, we speak among those who are mature, yet not a wisdom of this world nor of the rulers of this world, who are passing away. But we speak the wisdom of God, mysterious, hidden, which God foreordained before the world unto our glory, a wisdom which none of the rulers of this world has known; for had they known it, they would never have crucified the Lord of glory. But, as it is written, "Eye has not seen nor ear heard, nor has it entered into the heart of man, what things God has prepared for those who love him." But to us God has revealed them through his Spirit. For the Spirit searches all things, even the deep things of God. For who among men knows the things of a man save the spirit of the man which is in him? Even so, the things of God no one knows but the Spirit of God. Now we have received not the spirit of the world, but the spirit that is from God, that we may know the things that have been given us by God. These things we also speak, not in words taught by human wisdom, but in the learning of the Spirit, combining spiritual with spiritual. But the sensual man does not perceive the things that are of the Spirit of God, for it is foolishness to him and he cannot understand, because it is examined spiritually (I Cor. 2:6-15).

The Christian does live in a world apart. His understanding of existence goes beyond appearances to the reality which lies above and beyond them—and this reality is be-

yond the grasp of the man who does not have the gift of sight, the gift of faith. The non-believer lives in the world of immediacy, cut off by blindness from the depth and the ultimate ground which, supporting it, extends into the eternal profundity of the Trinity. Scripture calls the life of the non-believer a life in "darkness," compared to the life of the Christian, a life in the "light." There is no middle ground here. It is either/or. Christ said: "He who is not with me is against me. He who does not gather with me scatters." If one does not choose Christ, he is by that fact in darkness. In other things perhaps it is good to suspend judgment, but not in this. The message of salvation is presented as something of infinite concern to which one listens and says "Yes" or "No," and anything other than "Yes" is "No."

In Part I we discussed the human condition, the understanding of human existence without God, the authentic human being and the more important universal conditions of his existence. The description ended on a note of pessimism, but how could it be otherwise? The experience of thousands of generations of men has continually exposed the helplessness of man before the power of the world and the flesh. Men from all time, lost and absorbed in the masses and the things of the world, slaves to their passions, knowing nothing else, perpetuate and preach the very things that have brought them to destruction. It is this world of darkness, a world of emptiness, meaninglessness, and doom, that the vision of Christian faith lights up, bringing fulfillment, meaning, and hope. Throughout the whole of Part II we have attempted to point out the differences in understanding of existence which are held by the Christian and the non-believer. On many points besides, faith reveals

a side of reality about which the non-believer has no knowledge at all. Rather than review all of the contrasts which exist, we will attempt only to draw together the basic vision which serves as the framework for the Christian understanding of existence.

A man of faith knows that his life and whole existence are in the hands of the Holy God, who is at the same time his Father, his greatest benefactor, and his judge. He knows that he comes forth from God, exists in God, and one day will return to Him. He knows that the shortest portion of his immortal existence is spent in this terrestrial life, which passes quickly and opens into a life of eternal bliss or eternal doom. Before the Holy God he knows his nothingness and defilement, and before his judge he knows his sin. But he also knows this Holy God as Father, and he knows the warmth which that name evokes within him. His Father sent the Son, and through the Son the Holy Spirit, to offer him a new life, a life in the Christ, a life in the Spirit. So he knows his Father as his greatest benefactor; and he knows, too, that nothing in this life can compare with that gift of faith and life which he has in Christ. His heart is filled with gratitude and love. He is at peace with himself and he knows the joy which only Christ can give.

Because his vision is clear and penetrating, he can recognize the absurdities which pass for worldly wisdom, and the traps of the world, the flesh, and the devil. He knows his own weakness and he knows the strength he has in Christ; and the only thing he fears is sin, which alone can destroy that life which has been given to him. This same clear and penetrating vision reveals to him a depth of beauty in life, in people, in things that constantly renews and refreshes him, leading him in his thoughts and love to his Father, the creator of it all. He sees in the Church

the visible counterpart of the risen Lord and in the Sacraments the means of encounter with this same Lord and Savior, as well as the sustenance and source of growth in this life which he has in Christ.

He knows that he is never alone, because he is always with God. He knows that the eternally actual redemption he has in Christ, has come to him because his Father has freely given it to him—and to others as well. He sees himself as part of this great "body of Christ" which extends beyond the barriers of space and time to unite all the faithful in one communion in the Lord. He knows that his own efforts produce nothing before the Holy God, but he is consoled by the knowledge that he can, through, with, and in Christ, offer the worship that is pleasing to his Father. He is aware that no act of worship is only from himself, only his own. Instead he understands that he is of the People of God, one body in Christ, going to the Father through the Eternal High Priest and Mediator, Jesus Christ, the Son of God and Man. And because he knows the Father, he also understands the brotherhood of man; because he knows Christ, he knows of the People of God. The vision of faith reveals the face of Christ in everyone and everyone in Christ. He is not fooled by appearances. He finds something to love in everyone.

Since he knows that Christ has conquered sin and death once and for all, he does not fear, nor is he troubled by, guilt or condemnation or death. Since he knows his origin, himself, and his destiny are all in the hands of the Father, whose hand he clings to, he does not believe in fate; and he experiences fulfillment and purpose instead of emptiness and meaninglessness.

The Christian faith, the Christian vision, the Christian reality is the answer to the human condition.

PART 3

LIVING IN CHRIST

IT IS A MATTER OF COMMON OBSERVATION THAT MEN DO not always act in a way which is consistent with their professed understanding of existence. Perhaps what they claimed to understand they did not understand at all; or perhaps to understand and to understand are two different things. Kierkegaard thought so; in a powerful passage he described the irony of it:

> It is with this contradiction irony is properly employed. To perceive the comic in the fact that a person is actually ignorant of something means a very low sort of comic, beneath the dignity of irony. There is properly no profound comic in the fact that people once lived who assumed that the earth stands still—when nobody knew any better. The same thing will presumably befall our age in contrast with an age which knows more of physical law. The contradiction is one between two different ages, there is lacking a deeper point of coincidence; such a contradiction is not essential, and hence neither is it essentially comic. No, but that a man stands up and

says the right thing . . . and so has understood it, and then when he has to act does the wrong thing . . . and so shows that he has not understood it—yes, that is comic. It is infinitely comic that a man, moved unto tears, so much moved that not only tears but sweat trickle from him, can sit and read, or hear, representations of self-denial, of the nobility of sacrificing one's life for the truth—and then the next instant—one, two, three, slap-dash, almost with the tears still in his eyes—is in full swing, in the sweat of his brow, with all his might and main, helping falsehood to conquer. It is infinitely comic that an orator, with truth in his voice and in the expression of his features, profoundly touched and profoundly touching, can present the truth in a heart-rending way, can tread all evil and all the powers of hell under his feet, with an aplomb in his attitude, an assurance in his glance, a resoluteness in his step which is altogether admirable—it is infinitely comic that almost at the same moment, almost 'with his dressing gown still on,' he can run cowardly and timidly out of the way of the least inconvenience. It is infinitely comic that a man can understand the whole truth about how wretched and petty this world is, etc.—that he can understand this, and then cannot recognize again what he understood; for almost in the same moment he himself goes off and takes part in the same pettiness and wretchedness, takes glory in it and receives glory from it, that is, accepts it. O when one beholds a man who protests that he has entirely understood how Christ went about in the form of a lowly servant, poor, despised, and, as the Scripture says, spat upon—when I see the same man so careful to betake himself thither where in a wordly

> sense it is good to be, and accommodate himself there in the utmost security, when I see him apprehensive of every puff of wind from right or left, as though his life depended upon it, and so blissful, so utterly blissful, so awfully glad—yes, to make the thing complete, so awfully glad that he is able to thank God for it—glad that he is held in honor by all men—then I have often said to myself and by myself ". . . can it be possible that this man has understood what he says he has understood?" [33]

This is the problem that makes a Christian's existence a continuous struggle. It is the problem of becoming what he is, the problem of making his gift of Christian understanding a second nature, the problem of converting his original Christian commitment into a Christian frame of mind. When a man gives up his human understanding of existence, exchanging it for the Christian vision, the Christian faith, he does, by that very act, commit himself to a way of life consistent with his belief; but that does not mean that this initial decision is forever irrevocable or even that it will be the predominant factor in every subsequent choice. The man is still free and he is still human. He *is* a Christian, incorporated into the body of Christ, capable of working with and in Christ toward the working out of his salvation. The problem he now faces is no longer one of being, but of doing, and there is the rub. Every man who believes and is baptized exists in Christ—he is already saved. But precisely because he is human, because the sensible affects him, tempts him, lures him, distracts him, he is continually exposed to the power of the world and the flesh. Because he

[33] *The Sickness unto Death,* pp. 221-222, Appendix.

is free, he continually experiences the tension produced by the possibility of choosing autonomy or submission, of accepting the limitations of his freedom or rejecting them. The problem of Christian existence is the problem of learning to think like a Christian, the problem of learning to look at one's existence in the light of faith, the problem of building up a perduring and pervading Christian approach to all of life's situations. It is to this problem that we now address ourselves.

At the very beginning of the discussion it must be clearly understood that this work of becoming-in-Christ, as with being-in-Christ, is primarily the work of God. It is God who freely gives the faith and it is God who gives the increase. No man has ever deserved salvation and no man has ever earned sanctification. It is God's own love which is the cause of our faith and our love. As with everything else, the very faith with which we believe in Him comes to us from Him, and the very love with which we love Him is His gift working within us. Our being-in-Christ is the source of our becoming-in-Christ, and both are from the Spirit, who has been given to us from the Father through the Son. As we emphasized earlier, our salvation is by gift, not by achievement.

Another point, too, which must be understood right here at the beginning is that it is not our own idea of sanctity that is important; rather, it is God's idea of sanctity that matters. We are speaking of sanctity here because sanctity is the state of a man who lives out of a Christian understanding of existence. This understanding, the faith, is given, which means that it exists prior to and independent of one's appreciation of it. It is from God, not from oneself, and it is in a man's conformity to it, his giving himself up to it

that constitutes his movement towards sanctity. When a man has acquired a Christian frame of mind as a second nature, he is a saint; for it is this and this alone which makes a man a true son of God in the full sense of that title. It is essential to understand this because, in spite of the fact that centuries ago St. Francis de Sales exposed the error which seduced so many into thinking that sanctity was only for the priest or monk or nun, the idea is still prevelant that to be a saint is the business of "someone else," a nun or a monk or a priest. Too many still believe that the full Christian life, which is sanctity, belongs to those who have time for it (whatever that means), or to the special few who enter the convent or monastery or priesthood. On the contrary, the ranks of the canonized saints are filled with men and women of all ages, from all walks of life, from school children to housewives and businessmen, to workers and employers, to kings and queens. The truth, and the only truth, in this matter is that the faith, with baptism and confirmation, are commissions to live in the spirit—not halfway, but all the way.

The word "sanctity" today is an unfortunate word. It denotes a concept which is essential, but it also conjures up all sorts of forbidding and frightening misrepresentations. Because some saints have been extraordinary, too many have been led to believe that sanctity itself consists in this. It has not been understood that men and women who have been led by the Spirit to do extraordinary things have not been given to us as examples, but as witnesses to the power of God. St. Francis de Sales said that these saints are rather to be admired than imitated. In other words, sanctity does not consist in long devotions or hour upon hour of prayer, in long fasts or extreme mortifications,

in great suffering—or for that matter, in anything extraordinary. Again, sanctity consists in living the faith—and in nothing else. This should become clearer as we go along.

Saints are also often described as virtuous people, which is usually taken to mean that they are stronger than most of us, able to overcome temptations and lead a good life. There are half truths here, too, and misconceptions which must be straightened out before we can continue. To begin with, there is no such thing as will power, in the sense that there can be a stronger or a weaker will. Certainly a person can choose and a person can initiate activity, and this is willing; but it is the person willing, the living individual, not some force which a man may or may not have, somehow added onto the man. It seems necessary to say this since some of those who have written of virtue and the Christian life seem to make the will into a separate entity from the person. It is the person who chooses and the person who initiates activity, and this ability of the person is called his will. The person either wills or he does not will. He chooses or he does not choose. He initiates activity or he does not. These operations are analogous to the opening or closing of an electric switch. Either it is on or it is off. It may be operated with a bang or it may be operated very gently; the results will be the same. It will be either off or on, and the intensity of the operation will not affect the results. Whether someone decides to do something in a fit of rage or after calm deliberation, the effect is the same; a decision is made. And what this means is that any discussion of "building will power" is pointless and useless. A person is "strong" or virtuous because, at the moment when he needs to be, he is conscious of his Christian vocation and Christian values. The real question is not "How does

one build will power?" but "Why does one decide, choose, or initiate activity?" The answer to that question must always be the starting point of any meaningful analysis of virtue and life-in-Christ.

A person decides to do something because it has some value for him. In concrete circumstances he does not always choose between alternatives. Many of his decisions are motivated by a single value which he reaches out to obtain. It is not enough, though, that he knows something to be good; he must also grasp its value. Everyone will agree to the goodness of many things in theory without deciding for them, because their value has never been understood. In one case it is a sterile intellectual concept; in the other it is knowledge as value, knowledge qualified as desirable. I think that every believing Catholic will agree that daily participation in the Mass and daily Communion are good, yet few of them will make any effort in that direction. If you will pause for a moment and think of just a few things which you will agree are good, but have never attempted to do anything about, you will know the difference between sterile knowledge of good and fruitful knowledge of value. This is all very much to the point, because virtue is an attitude towards value, and an act of virtue is a response to value.

In the course of a man's life, from the moment he is born, he learns to evaluate things. In time he acquires a set of values, an understanding of his existence which serves as the framework out of which he builds his life. The goals he sets for himself will depend on what he considers to be worth doing, worth working for—or in one phrase, in what he considers to be of value. A virtuous man is the man who has understood what is real, grasped it in its desirability

and responds to its call. Quite simply, an act of virtue is a response to value, not a ficititious will power, and the building up of virtue is really a matter of building up a Christian frame of mind.

It is the *person* who decides for or against something, the person in all of his complexity, in the midst of his existence. He is affected in his evaluation of things much more by those things which reach him in his entire personality, rather than by those which appeal only to his intellect. A nice, tight, logical argument produces intellectual conviction, but not a value. A man considers something to be of value if he is not only convinced of it, but involved in it; that is, when he has experienced it. And his experience of it reinforces his evaluation. A man will quite readily approve of what he does and disapprove of, or at least be hesitant about, changing. And in the learning of moral values it is never enough to be exposed to principles or ideas. These must always be reduced to practice, to experience, to involvement. It is one thing to hear of the value of devoting one's time and energy to the service of others, and quite another thing to actually experience it. In other words, a value is a good which appeals to the whole person, whereas the concept of goodness and the logical conclusions appeal only to the mind. Once again, it is the value which draws the person to act.

For values to be effective in leading a man to do the right thing, that is, to be virtuous, they must be present in his consciousness at the time he needs them, and they must be sufficiently compelling to be able to compete successfully against lesser values. This means that the acquisition of virtue is not the same thing as the acquisition of values. To develop virtuous attitudes it is necessary to link up the

experience of value with concrete circumstances so that mental associations develop to produce a thought complex which will be set in motion by any circumstance which involves it. The repetition of virtuous action serves no other purpose than this, to intensify the experience of the value and to link it up with concrete circumstances. The more often one performs a virtuous act, the more readily he will do it again when the circumstances call for it, because its value will more readily come to his consciousness and his experience of it will be broader and deeper.

This is why we can speak of a saint as one who lives out of a Christian frame of mind. To a saint, the Christian understanding of existence is not something once accepted and embraced, but a deeply ingrained system of values, a second nature. The saint develops his Christian values over the years by experiencing them through prayer, reading, observation, and activity. One by one these values become interlinked, and ever more strongly so, by love for his God, who makes all of it possible and meaningful. We might think of this Christian frame of mind, perhaps, in terms of a screen in which each Christian value is represented by a single strand. The screen is not a single wire, but a complex of wires interwoven and interdependent. Together they make up one screen. Together, a man's Christian values make up a Christian understanding of existence, a Christian frame of mind.

Memory plays a large part in a man's life, and it plays an indispensable role in the life of a Christian. The thought complexes built up by the association mechanism of the memory help to insure the appearance in consciousness of the right motive at the right time. The more extensive the thought complex, the greater the probability of its effective-

ness. The association mechanism works because one thought is tied to another, and that to another and so on. A particular situation may remind a person of something, which in turn reminds him of something else, etc.; and all the while these thoughts are occupying the focus of consciousness, opposing motives will not be receiving any consideration. All of this implies two things: (1) there must be something to be remembered, so the mind must be fed with the true Christian values; and (2) thoughtless and hasty action must be avoided, since such activity does not give a person a chance to mobilize and organize his motives.

A virtue, then, is an attitude towards a particular value, an attitude which readily and regularly colors a man's understanding of a situation in which this value plays a part. An act of virtue is a response to the call of a value. In the early stages of acquiring a virtue, the repeated acts of response help to broaden the experience of the value and establish association of one's thought complex to the value. When the virtue has been acquired, the value responses, while constantly being enhanced by repeated experience, will arise primarily from the abiding attitude already acquired.

It should be clear from what has been said that a virtue is not a habit in the sense that smoking cigarettes is a habit, and it is not a skill in the sense that playing the piano is a skill. In both cases, ease of performance is gained by repetition and practice, but the facility is due to organic causes resulting in reflex action, and there is nothing virtuous in that. An act of virtue is a conscious response to a value, not an unthinking mechanical reflex. It should also be clear that a virtue is not the mean between two extremes, as if

a positive attitude could possibly be found between two negative ones. It is one thing to be prodigal and another to be stingy, and both types of behavior are born of negative attitudes towards the goods of this world. If one could imagine that a stingy man could become less and less stingy until he became prodigal, he would become not generous somewhere in between. His understanding and appreciation of the role of material things would have to become positive; he would have to become sensitive to moral values, instead of indifferent or antagonistic to them.[34]

A virtue is an attitude towards a value. In order to live a full Christian life, three basic Christian attitudes must be developed to serve as foundation for the rest. The first of these is faith; from faith comes Christian wisdom; and wisdom is implemented by prudence. An act of Christian virtue is a response to the real content of a situation. Faith reveals the reality which lies behind the appearances; wisdom discovers the Christian principles involved; and prudence applies the principles to the correct set of facts. Although in a sense it is true that an act of virtue is a spontaneous response to a value, that value may be tied up in a complex situation so that wisdom and prudence are required to grasp the real situation and indicate the proper response. Many values which confront us do not come by themselves, so other things must be taken into consideration. For example, it is a good thing to go to Mass and Communion every day, but that does not necessarily mean that everyone should do it. A mother with small children should not leave her children alone while she attends Mass.

[34] For a much more comprehensive treatment of the relationship between virtue and habit, temperamental quality, adaptation and custom, see *Christian Ethics* by D. von Hildebrand, pp. 357-378.

Finally, it should be noted that any progress in the deepening of the Christian life will always come as a by-product of living that life simply. Progress is not something which can be aimed at directly. It is not from us, it is from God. We do not earn it; He gives it. It is up to us to live up to our new being-in-Christ, our new vision in Christ, offering worship to the Father by responding eagerly, promptly, and wholeheartedly to His love which reaches out to embrace us each moment. With our eye fixed on Him and the content of each moment, He will reward us, not because we aim at reward, but because we are trying to please Him.

PRAYER

1. *A Morning Exercise*

A housewife plans her housework, a businessman plans his contacts and his day, a traveler plans his trip because, without planning, the probability of success is greatly reduced. In any area of a man's existence, failure is commonly caused by shortsightedness, neglect, lack of perseverance, laziness, or unforseen and unforseeable complications. Many of our problems we create for ourselves. We become so involved in the business of doing things that we ignore or forget our Christian vocation to living. Many problems arise because of surprise or because we are unprepared for them. The least number of problems occur because of conditions beyond our control or modification. Our life-in-Christ is no exception. If we do nothing to cultivate our faith, if we seldom talk to Christ or approach him in the Sacraments, or if we leave our Christian life to chance, we can hardly expect remarkable results.

A simple remedy for many of our problems and, at the same time, a valuable practice for anyone is planning. Plan your day. Each morning when you get up, sometime when you have a few minutes to yourself, plan your day. If you are a man, it may be while you are shaving or on your way to work. If you are a woman, it may be while you are washing your face or cooking breakfast or after you have packed everyone off to school or work. You ought to be able to work in a few minutes to yourself sometime early in the morning; it only takes a few minutes, especially after a little practice.

Begin by reminding yourself that you are with God and He is with you. Then ask his help to see clearly the trouble spots and opportunities that lie before you that day. Next, quickly run through the day, attempting to foresee what problems may arise and what you want to do. Knowing, then, what might happen, work out a way of handling your problems and plan your activities. Finally, make whatever resolutions you must, and ask God's help to keep them.

A housewife, for example, might work out her Plan this way. She might say to herself: "Good Lord, here we go for another day. Thanks for helping me yesterday. Please help me again now." She looks out the window on the way downstairs and she sees that it is raining, so her first thought is: "O boy! The children will be in all day. I'd better find something to keep them busy, or I'll go out of my mind or lose my temper, and I don't want to do that, Lord. Let me see, this morning I can get them playing that new game and when they get tired of that, I can. . . ." So she works out a way to eliminate a possible trying situation. She continues: "Now, they may be a problem still, but I don't want to lose my temper; so if they start getting to me, I'll call my

girl friend, just to get my mind off them for a while. Whatever happens, though, Lord, I'm going to try to remember that there is a little of me and a little of my husband and a lot of You in each of them, and I'll try to keep calm.

"The girls will probably be over for coffee this morning, too, and there is a chance we might start gossiping. If it should start, I'll change the subject to the dress sale at Sears'. This afternoon I ought to be able to work in a few minutes to read the Bible as soon as I'm finished the ironing. And tonight I'll get all dressed up for my husband and fix something special for dinner. He'll like that. Well, that's it. Help me out, Lord, and if anything else comes up, help me to keep calm and get through it without offending you. . . . Help me to make this a good day, for you and for those around me."

The example given may not be pertinent to your own particular situation, but I think it illustrates the application of the principles to the real situation. If you are a construction worker or a corporation president, a nurse or a student, a salesman or a secretary, you can do the same thing for yourself. It does not take very long, but it can do much towards making your day a Christian day. Putting first things first, you put the day in the hands of the Lord, and then you simplify your problems by planning practical solutions for them one at a time, which makes your chances of success much better. The solutions to any problem should always be a concrete pattern of thought and behavior. It does little or no good to say, "I won't lose my temper today," and leave it at that. But you can effectively attack your temper problem by working out a practical solution to the problem which might cause you to lose your temper, or by planning a concrete escape route. In either case, you

decide both on what should be done and how to do it. When the situation does arise, you will know just what to do because you have already planned it.

2. *Prayerful Reading*

Because you cannot hope to develop a Christian frame of mind unless it is filled with Christian thoughts, what you put into your mind is much more important than what you put out of it. Christianity is too often thought of as a religion of don'ts, a confining and fun-killing religion, a religion which requires those who follow it to become insipid or annoying pious prudes. And yet, anyone who reads the New Testament carefully must be impressed by the insistence on freedom, freedom in the Spirit. Christian freedom comes from a Christian understanding of existence, an understanding which is quite alien to the constant and persuasive voice of the world. A secular [35] world of secular values (pseudo-values) reaches you from every direction. Unless you are careful to keep your mind filled with true Christian values, you can all too easily be caught up in the huge sink of materialism and be trapped in the real slavery of those who run endlessly after a satisfaction which does not exist.

To keep in touch with God and Christian values means to read and meditate. I dislike using the word "meditate" because of its sometimes frightening overtones, but because some who read this book might think I have overlooked what is called meditation, I have included it. I also dislike the phrase "read and meditate" because the impression given is that they are two different things. Let me explain.

[35] The word "secular" here means "the world-without-God." Secular values, then, are those which do not take into account the place which such things should have in a divinely oriented world.

Meditation is usually described as a form of mental prayer. Methods are worked out which run something like this: (1) Place yourself in the presence of God and ask his help. (2) Decide on your subject and imagine yourself to be in the situation. (3) Consider one aspect after another. (4) Allow your affections free rein. (5) Make a resolution. (6) Try to summarize the main point in one short sentence which you can come back to again and again during the day.

That is mechanical and sometimes self-defeating. A much more fruitful method of learning and reviving Christian values, of establishing contact with God and of fostering good resolutions is prayerful reading. When you read a book you get ideas from a printed page. When you "meditate" according to the methods you must dig the ideas out of your memory; and I, for the life of me, cannot understand why it makes any difference where you get your ideas, except that it is easier to get them from a book. The confusion arose centuries ago when someone decided to put some order into religious practices. If you read a religious book, it is called spiritual reading. If you attempt to pray without a book, it is called mental prayer or meditation. It is a fact that the early Christians and hermits were satisfied to read prayerfully from Scripture. The sophistication came later. If some profit from the distinction, then by all means let them continue, but I think it makes much more sense to concentrate on our objective and use whatever will most easily and best help us. St. Theresa of Avila was one of the greatest mystics who ever lived. She started every period of prayer, she tells us, with a book. Sometimes she would just get started on a sentence and be carried into ecstasy, but sometimes she would read for the whole time

allotted. There is nothing heretical in saying that prayerful reading is as good as or better than the so-called "mental prayer." We have the example of a great saint as positive support.

By prayerful reading I mean reading a good religious book, with a mind to learning or deepening your Christian values. Since prayer is establishing contact with God, you begin by concentrating on his nearness and his life within you. Then you read. Read until something strikes you and sets you thinking. Compare it to other things you have learned or heard about the same subject. Contrast it with a materialist's or an atheist's ideas. Apply it to yourself and your behavior. Work out some way that you can put it into practice that very day. And, finally, ask God to help you carry out your resolution.

The best prayerful reading material is the Bible. There is no question of that. The Bible is the word of God—God speaking to us, God acting for us through His word. There is a sacramental effectiveness in Scripture—a power to reach us, a power to grip us, a power from God. The Eucharist is sacramental food, a sign which contains the power which it signifies. The word of God is sacramental food, too, food for the mind, where Christian values are ultimately rooted. If you take up Scripture every day and drink it in deeply, you will feel its power, you will know its effectiveness.

To make Scripture more meaningful, you might also read some of the newer commentaries or books which develop biblical themes. There are also a number of magazines devoted to explaining Scripture, such as *The Bible Today* and *Worship,* from the Liturgical Press. At times you may find the lives of the saints inspiring, especially recent biographies

which have at long last shaken off the saccharin and the inaccuracy of most vintage products. The important thing is to find something which will be both informative and inspiring, something which will help you to build up your Christian frame of mind.

The material of Part II of this book is basic Christianity. It is material which you must return to again and again, particularly the idea of God's holiness and the idea of the Living God. These ideas help to keep you grounded in humility and reverence and gratitude—and in reality. I feel that no other prayerful reading can do as much for you or should be repeated more often than one on God's holiness. As I pointed out earlier, no other idea is so liberating or rewarding.

It is also important to apply this prayerful reading to yourself. Isolated learning is useless. It is not just ideas that you are looking for, but values, and values grow out of ideas which involve *you*. Every Christian idea is a message to you from God, your Father. It demands, not a sterile intellectual acceptance, but involvement. The message is there. It is up to you to bring it to concrete realization. This is also the reason for making a resolution which you can carry out that very day. It is too easy to convince yourself that you *would* do great things if only or if ever the opportunity presents itself; but in dreaming of things that will never come, you not only run the risk of pride in your imagined virtue, you may also overlook a hundred opportunities to do some little things, Christian things, day after day. Reducing a Christian lesson to immediate practice, reminding yourself of your motives as you do it, reinforces your evaluation and gives you the experience of it. At the same time, the actual performance of some Christian-motivated action

will destroy any false fears and imagined difficulties. Without applying the Christian message to yourself in a practical way, the prayerful reading will be robbed of any real force for you, so do not neglect it.

You should spend at least fifteen minutes a day at prayerful reading, which is not a great deal of time. To the man who believes, nothing is more important or more meaningful than his life before God and with God. If he spends fifteen minutes a day reading the newspaper or watching television, he can certainly see the gross confusion of values if he begrudges fifteen minutes a day for strengthening his life in God. One thing here is certain: if he does not feed his Christian life with the word of God, he will never grow to Christian maturity. He will attempt to meet adult problems with a childhood faith, and find that his faith is not strong enough to carry him through. Think of all the books and magazines you have read, the how-to-do-it books, the novels and all the rest; then ask yourself why there has not been time for God. If you find that fifteen minutes a day is too much to devote to your life-in-Christ, then I say that this is the clearest symptom that you, above all, *need* fifteen minutes a day at prayerful reading.

3. *Moments*

As we pointed out before, one of the greatest dangers a man faces is the power of the world. It is there, always there, inviting him to lose himself in it, to forget who he is and why he is here. To offset this power and your own weakness in the face of it, you must take a moment here and a moment there to collect your forces, re-establish contact with God, and get yourself going again in the right direction. Over and over again all day long you must do this if

you are to keep from being absorbed in the world of things. It is a simple thing and it does not take anything away from what you are doing. Since it is only a moment, you can do it almost anywhere, anytime—even when you are surrounded by people at a party. The object is to collect yourself for a moment, withdraw within yourself—into your own private sanctuary, shut out everything else, and remind yourself of God's presence near you and in you. It is also a good time to renew your resolution from your last prayerful reading. Offer it again to your Father in heaven and ask Him to help you be faithful. This only takes a moment, but it is a moment of refreshment and renewal which is indispensable and very profitable. It helps to keep you situated in reality. It keeps you alert to the world opened up to you by your faith, and it helps to keep alive the values you acquired from your prayerful reading.

These moments are so vital that you should feel justified in working out any sort of device, no matter how bizarre, to help you remember to take them. You might, for example, put a large medal in your pocket or purse with your change so that when you reach for a coin, you will be reminded of God's presence and take a "moment." You might have some statues and crucifixes and religious art around the house to remind you; and it is a good idea to move these things around from time to time so that they will not just blend into the background. You might make it a habit of using some ordinary action to trigger your memory. For example, you might associate lighting a match or washing your hands with the "moments" that you want to have. Then, every time you do one of these things it will remind you of God's presence. On this you should use your imag-

ination freely. It is not only something worth doing, it is something which you cannot afford to do without.

4. *Formulated Prayers*

For many years now, most treatises on prayer have made a distinction between vocal prayer and mental prayer, an unhappy distinction which directs attention away from the primary consideration, that prayer is speaking to God. The poll-parrot recitation of formulas hardly fulfills this requirement; in fact, it is all too often an irreverence and effrontery to God, thoughtless and inattentive mouthing of words. As far as I can see, it makes no difference whether a man prays out loud or within himself, as long as he makes it a prayer, as long as he is really speaking to God.[36] The whole point is that a man's prayer should be the sincere expression of a man's thoughts to God, not just words rolling from his lips.

A much more meaningful distinction would be between formulated and unformulated prayers. Unformulated prayers are entirely one's own, the spontaneous outpouring of oneself to the Father, our Lord, Mary, or the saints. The formulated prayers that we find in the prayerbooks are someone else's thoughts and words. To make them into prayers it is not necessary to say them aloud, but it is necessary to make them one's own, to use them to express what one wants to say. Again and again it is essential to remember that Christianity is a religion of quality, not quantity. One Our Father said with attention and feeling is worth more than many said quickly and in haste. I am not saying

[36] The one exception to this is Liturgical prayer, which by its very nature should be vocal, the prayer of the People of God together.

that the speed of recitation is a deterring factor in the quality of a prayer, because some pray well quickly and some pray well slowly; but the important factor is that a formulated prayer should be used with attention to the meaning of the words, and the meaning should be the meaning you intend.

In the early days of your attempt to live a full life-in-Christ, you will find that formulated prayers can be very useful. As you continue you will find less and less need for them, except for the Our Father, the Hail Mary, and Psalms or other short prayers taken from Scripture, such as "Lord, I believe. Help me in my unbelief." These prayers have a special efficacy of their own. They say what we *should* say, and by using them thoughtfully, we can learn from them the values of true Christianity.

As you become more thoroughly steeped in Christian values, you become more alert to the real world, your own being-in-Christ, and your own destiny in Christ. You will find yourself spontaneously speaking to God a hundred times a day, and you will experience his nearness. These little rushes of the spirit are sometimes called ejaculations or aspirations. Again, it is not at all necessary that they be your own words, as long as they say what you want to say. For example, as you walk up a flight of stairs you might say: "My Lord, please help me to rise above my pettiness" or "My God, you climbed the hill of Calvary. Help me to carry my crosses well." Thoughts like these should come to you very often. They help you to keep in contact with the source of your life, the source of your strength, the ground of your being.

In addition to the formulated prayers already mentioned, there is one other type of prayer which is especially valua-

ble and fruitful, the offering or dedication of one's life and actions to God. In the *Introduction to the Devout Life* St. Francis de Sales offers such a prayer.[37] He suggests that you prepare yourself to make this formal renewal of your faith and baptismal vows by prayer and penance. Then, write it out and sign it. It is something very special which deserves special treatment. *Each month* and *each year* you should renew it, to remind yourself as forcefully as possible of what you have done and of what you are attempting to do, with His help. This is the prayer he composed:

> I, the undersigned, standing in the presence of the eternal God and of the whole court of heaven, having considered the infinite mercy of His divine goodness toward me, a most unworthy and wretched creature, whom He has created out of nothing, preserved, supported, and delivered from so many dangers, and loaded with so many benefits; but considering, above all, the incomprehensible sweetness and mercy with which this most good God has so graciously borne my iniquities; so frequently and so lovingly inspired and urged me to amendment, and so patiently waited for my repentence and conversion until this _th year of my life, notwithstanding all my ingratitude, disloyalty, and infidelity, by which I have so shamelessly offended Him, delaying my conversion and despising His grace; having, moreover, reflected that upon the day of my holy baptism I was so fortunately and holily vowed and dedicated to God to be His child; and that, contrary to the profession then made in my name, I have greatly and so often, so execrably and so detestably, profaned and

[37] This and succeeding quotations from the *Introduction* are taken from the translation by John K. Ryan, Doubleday Image Books. The prayer is from chapter xx, Part I.

violated my soul, applying and employing it against the Divine Majesty; at length, returning to myself, prostrate in heart and in spirit before the throne of divine justice, I acknowledge, avow, and confess myself lawfully attainted and convicted of treason against the Divine Majesty, and guilty of the death and Passion of Jesus Christ, on account of the sins I have committed, for which He died and suffered the torment of the Cross; so that consequently I deserve to be cast away and condemned forever.

Turning myself toward the throne of the infinite mercy of the same eternal God, and having detested with my whole heart and with my whole strength the many iniquities of my past life, I ask and humbly beg grace, and pardon, and mercy, with an entire absolution from my crime by virtue of the death and Passion of the same Lord and Redeemer of my soul. Relying on this as on the only foundation of my hope, I confirm again and renew the sacred profession of allegiance to my God, made in my behalf at my baptism; renouncing the devil, the world, and the flesh; detesting their base suggestions, vanities, and concupiscences for all the time of my present life and for all eternity. Turning myself toward my most gracious and merciful God, I desire, purpose, determine, and am irrevocably resolved to serve and love Him now and forever. To this end, I give and consecrate to Him my spirit with all its faculties, my soul with all its powers, my heart with all its affections, and my body with all its senses, protesting that I will never more abuse any part of my being against His divine will and sovereign Majesty, to whom I offer up and sacrifice myself in spirit, to be forever His loyal, obedient, and faithful creature, without ever revoking this act and deed. But if,

alas, I should chance, through the suggestion of the enemy, or through human frailty, to transgress in any point, or fail in adhering to this my resolution and dedication, I protest from this moment, and am determined, with the assistance of the Holy Spirit, to rise as soon as I shall perceive my fall, and return again to the Divine Mercy, without any sloth or delay whatsoever.

This is my will, my intention, and my unbreakable and irrevocable resolution, which I declare and confirm without reservation or exception, in the same presence of God, in the sight of the Church triumphant, and in the presence of the Church militant, my mother, which hears this my declaration in the person of him who, as her officer, hears me in this action. May it please Thee, O my God, eternal, almighty, and all-good, Father, Son, and Holy Spirit, to confirm in me this resolution, and to accept in the odor of sweetness this inward sacrifice of my heart. And as it has pleased Thee to grant me the inspiration and the will to do this, so grant me the strength and the grace needed to perform it. "O my God! Thou art my God," "the God of my heart," the God of my soul, and the God of my spirit. As such I acknowledge Thee, and as such I adore Thee now and forever. Live, O Jesus.

A dedication and offering of one's life to God is really no more than an explicit act of faith, the formal acknowledgement and acceptance of a Christian understanding of existence. Every time you consciously and deliberately renew your fidelity, your faithfulness, you reinforce and build up your Christian frame of mind. It follows, then, that this is something that you should do very frequently. In the morning offer to God your day and ask Him to help you live it as a Christian. There is no need here of any formal

declaration. A short, simple prayer of your own will do nicely. You might say, for example, "My God, I offer you everything that I will do today. I'll try to do it well for you, and I offer it to you through my Lord, Jesus Christ, your Son. Please help me." Then you might ask our Blessed Lady, the angels and saints for their help.

During the day, as you pass from one thing to the next, renew your offering and your prayer for help. The more you accustom yourself to doing this, the better chance you have of doing what you have to do in a Christian way, and the better are your chances of avoiding sin.

SACRAMENTS

Along with prayer and as its support are the Sacraments. The very foundation and source of your life-in-Christ is the gift of faith together with your initiation into the life of Christ's visible body, his Church, through the sacraments of Baptism and Confirmation. Your contact with Christ takes place in visible form through the ritual of the Sacraments. No more than that need be said. The eternally actual redemptive act of Christ comes to you in its saving power each time you receive a sacrament worthily. Your prayer life prepares you for that moment. Nothing is more efficacious in building your life-in-Christ than this reverent, humble, attentive encounter with Christ. When that is said, everything has been said.

Receive the sacraments as frequently as you can reasonably do so, always with an eye to what you are doing, never with the intention of gaining something. Give yourself up purely and simply to this meeting with Christ and

his saving power. The reward will be yours because you have sought Christ, not something good for yourself.

Receiving the sacraments is something you hear all the time, so it does not seem necessary to say more about it here. Do not be misled by the brevity of the treatment here. Think instead of what it means to encounter Christ, and that will make up for all that has not been said.

A DIRECTOR

St. Francis de Sales was one of the greatest minds that Christendom has known. His popularity as a guide to the Christian life for laity and religious earned for him the title of Doctor of the Church. In his *Introduction to the Devout Life* he wrote: "Would you like to walk in earnest toward devotion (a life-in-Christ)? Seek some good man who will guide and conduct you. This is the greatest of all words of advice." [38]

What St. Francis said about the director is the same advice given by St. Theresa of Avila, not too many years before. It is the advice given by everyone who has ever written on the Christian life, and it is the example of almost every saint who ever lived. We are all blind in our own concerns, we all get confused, and we can all profit from obedience to someone else. But he must be a good man. St. Francis de Sales said: "He must be full of charity, knowledge and prudence. If any one of these three qualities is wanting in him, there is danger. But I say to you again: Ask him of God. Having found him, bless his Divine Majesty, remain constant, and seek no other, but proceed on with

[38] *Op. cit.,* ch. iv, Part I.

sincerity, humility and confidence, for you will make a most happy journey." [39]

Sometimes it is not easy to find a good director and many times it is hard to find the time to consult with him. If he is good, it will be hard for him to find the time to work with you. In the beginning it would be wise and considerate to make an appointment with him at the rectory or religious house. Perhaps after that it would be enough to meet with him in the confessional at the regular times for confession; but if you expect to take much time, then do not trouble him in the middle of a busy Saturday afternoon or evening. Try to catch him when there is a lull. He will be able to guide you on this.

In your meetings with him, be completely open to him, trust him, and you will be safe. "Seek some good man who will guide and conduct you. This is the greatest of all words of advice."

INSPIRATIONS

As we have already seen time and again, your life-in-Christ is entirely dependent upon God. It is He who comes to you, who offers you the gift of faith, the gift of salvation, and every other gift. You are in His hands. You are under His Fatherly care and protection. All through your life and many times a day He prompts you, spurs you on, leads you, suggests things to you, and stirs you up to avoid what is evil, to accomplish what is good. These stirrings within yourself, if they lead you to do good, are called inspirations. They are from God and they become more frequent the more clearly you see with the Christian vision. It may occur to you to say a Rosary for a friend who is in the

[39] *Ibid.*

midst of a trial. You might be moved to visit someone in the hospital or to go out of your way to do something special for a member of your family—whatever it is, consider it to be a message from God. Receive it with joy in the awareness that your Living God is taking an interest in you, suggesting something to you to help you to the fullness of your life-in-Christ. Receive it with joy and resolve to do it at your first opportunity. When the time comes, do it. Then you will be a doer intsead of a dreamer. You will know the joy which accompanies the accomplishment of real Christian living. If the inspiration is to do something out of the ordinary, you should always first consult your director. He will be able to advise you prudently.

Inspirations deserve a special mention because you will undoubtedly experience them, and you can profit from them immensely. Think of them always as messages from God, and be grateful for them.

EXAMINATION OF CONSCIENCE

Each evening of your life you should examine your conscience. It is a good idea to make it a part of your night prayers so that you will never forget it. If you want to know how things are going and in which direction you are headed, you must pause from time to time to take stock. It is in this examination of conscience that you learn what faults to work on, so that you may attack them instead of just living with them.

As with any prayer, begin by reminding yourself of God's presence. Thank Him for caring for you during the day; then look back over the day. Recall where you had gone, the company you kept and the work you did. If you find that you have done anything good, thank God for it. If

you have failed, ask God's forgiveness and determine to confess it and make amends for it.

It will very likely happen that you will find yourself failing in the same things week in and week out. There is nothing to be discouraged about in that, as long as they are not serious sins, because everyone has some particular weaknesses and your weakness will always be with you. With time, patience, and planned effort, you can do something about them, but very likely you will still fail from time to time. With these little things it is always good to remember that if you humble yourself when you discover you have fallen, tell God you are sorry and resolve to make amends, you gain more than you lose. Sometimes, I think, God allows us to fall in these little things to remind us of our weakness and of our need to depend on Him.

Your examination of conscience can be an effective tool if you are faithful to it and use it well. Never neglect it. It is too important.

ACTIVITIES

Since your objective is to turn your Christian understanding of existence into a Christian frame of mind, anything which contributes to that purpose is worth doing. It is only in the experience of it, though, that its value will really disclose itself to you. Moreover, as you grow more deeply rooted in Christian values, you will undoubtedly want to do something. In almost every parish in America today there are parish activities of one kind or another. Discussion groups help you to gain new ideas and fresh approaches. They bring you into contact with good people who are intent, as you are, on living before God and with

Him. These associations are always good. The CCD catechetical program needs teachers and workers in other areas. Perhaps your parish priest could use your help in making contacts, in doing apostolic work. Perhaps, too, he could use a typist or a mechanic or an electrician. Men can also work as ushers and help to count the collection sometimes, or work with the boys. Women can help to clean the church. The service you give is a service to God—so it is worthwhile doing—if you can fit it into your schedule without upsetting your home.

Then, too, there are parish devotions, novenas, missions, October and May devotions—all of which are made available to you at the parish. Again, if you have time, you should try to do what you can.

RETREATS

Once a year you should make a retreat. If you cannot get away for a week-end, you should at least make a day of recollection. I believe that almost every diocese in the country has some place where a day of recollection or a retreat can be made. The retreat gives you a chance to disengage yourself from everything that you ordinarily do. The peace and quiet of the retreat house offers you a chance to unwind, to slow down and think calmly of your Christian life. You can assess the year past, make a general confession for that year, examine your relations to God and your neighbor, rekindle your zeal, renew your dedication, and reset your sights. The value of a week-end retreat is attested to by millions of men and women, who, having once made one, return year after year. You owe it to yourself and to your God to make it a yearly habit.

Finally, to try to tie all of this together, I include below an outline which I call The Plan. Since a life-in-Christ does not consist in many prayers, but in faith and a life lived out of a Christian frame of mind, you should never associate sanctity with long hours spent on your knees. In fact, you will find that day by day you can be in contact with God very often without interrupting your usual activities. The longest exercise listed is the prayerful reading. Other than that, it takes only a few minutes for each of the other exercises, not including attendance at Mass and parish activities.

THE PLAN

Each Day

(1) Morning Exercise—Plan it
- (a) Ask God's help to do it well.
- (b) Try to forsee what trials and temptations will come that day.
- (c) Devise some way to handle them.
- (d) Make whatever practical resolutions you need to make—but make them specific.
- (e) Ask God's help.

(2) Get to Mass and Communion—if possible.

(3) Prayerful Reading—Spend at least 15 minutes a day reading from a good book, especially the Bible.
- (a) Remind yourself of God's presence.
- (b) Read until a particular thought sets you thinking.
- (c) Apply it to yourself.
- (d) Make a practical concrete resolution to be carried out sometime during the day.

(e) Ask the help of God, the angels, and the saints to keep you going.

(4) Keep in touch.

(a) Take a Moment here and a Moment there to refocus your attention on God. Recall your resolutions. Acknowledge God's presence and concern. Pledge your fidelity.

(b) Make aspirations from time to time.

(5) Inspirations—Receive them with joy and resolve in a concrete way to carry them out.

(6) Examination of Conscience.

Each Week

(1) Confession, every week if possible.

(2) Sunday Mass and Communion.

(3) Parish activities.

Each Year

A week-end retreat, or at least a day of recollection.

The Director

Find a good man to direct you, one who is charitable, wise and prudent.

PROBLEM SOLVING

Unfortunately, what we have indicated above is usually not enough, because we are beings-in-the-world and beings-with-others as well as beings-in-Christ; because the sensible affects us so strongly, we are often tempted and we often fail. For that reason it is necessary to discuss problem-solving, overcoming temptations and suffering.

It is commonly accepted that tension is caused either by circumstances or by heredity. This situation or that, this circumstance or that, this person or that—these are the causes of tension. Or it may be that an individual has a "nervous disposition." In either instance, the scapegoat is always something beyond the individual's control and, therefore, beyond personal responsibility. The real difficulty with such an approach is that it cannot explain the facts. Circumstances which produce tension for one person are easily brushed off by another. A person who annoys one individual is loved by another. The "nervous disposition" excuse can always be traced to unregulated desires—and there is the cause of tension.

Every human being operates out of a value system, as we have already indicated. Values beget desires; desires can engender frustration or conflict; either of these do produce tension, and aggravated tension is called anxiety. The well-adjusted individual is certainly not without desires or conflicts or frustrations—no such human being exists. Adjustment refers to the manner of handling conflicts or frustrations, not to their absence. The well-adjusted individual knows how to live with these things and how to resolve them when possible.

The tension which is transformed into depressions or anxiety usually manifests itself by distorting all of the individual's faculties, preventing their normal function. It is a kind of psychic paralysis which shows up in self-centeredness, negative thinking, gloom, and immobility. The last of these is particularly crippling because the individual so afflicted does not want to do anything or listen to anyone, which means he deprives himself of the only avenue of escape from his condition. Anxiety has been called by St.

Francis de Sales the greatest evil next to sin. A depressed man is prone to take any means of escape offered, moral or immoral. Through his anxiety he sustains a loss of strength to maintain the virtues he has already acquired and a loss of the means to resist temptations. He can no longer think clearly or act prudently. He is in a sorry state.

Because such a condition is so serious, you must do everything you can to avoid it or to remedy it. As remedies, the following should be considered:

1. COMPOSURE. Keep calm. Never permit yourself the luxury of letting yourself go to the point of losing control. If things start to go wrong, quietly and calmly take charge, at least of yourself. Since all of your faculties operate best when you are calm, you will be able to solve your problem in a reasonable way if you make that effort to keep a grip on yourself.

Father Paul Francis, O.S.F.S., in a privately published paper, "Desire, Anxiety and the Devout Life," brought up a point which is particularly pertinent here.

> In view of widespread current practices of indulgent medication and chemical comforts, perhaps "tranquility" is a word better suppressed. In America, one out of six people uses the pill bottle to change perceptions and moods. Tranquilizers, barbiturates, energizers, amphetamines, narcotics and hallucinogens key up or grind down feelings to such an extent that mood medicine is relied upon to insure instant happiness. Millions walk through a blurred life with a chemically produced filmy veil protecting them from reality. Popular writers have given a slick label to this mentality, by calling it the something-for-nothing syndrome. This attitude is dedicated to the point of view that the world not only owes individ-

uals a living, but fun and happiness as well. Here there is a little room for self-discipline and control. Consequently, those of this persuasion never are able to solve problems.

2. Distraction. Busy yourself with a variety of external activities. The activity can distract. A variety of activities can maintain distraction, perhaps long enough for you to regain your composure. Distraction will never bring permanent relief, but it can temporarily free you from the tension which can be crippling.

3. Communication. Whether you feel like it or not, if you are tense and depressed, talk it out. Your problem is not insoluble, but it may very well be if you will not do something about it. Unburdening yourself to God, your spiritual director, your doctor or good friends may help to bring about a release from your pent-up emotions. An outsider can also offer an objective point of view. This is undoubtedly one of the most effective remedies open to you.

4. Ordered Action. If you find that you are frustrated in your legitimate desires, it certainly does no good to give up and then sit around feeling sorry for yourself. Do something about it, but not haphazardly. If you want something, think it through, and then follow through.

5. Do Something For Someone Else. As we already mentioned, tension and depression lead to self-centeredness and immobility. If you can lose yourself for a time in service for another, you can accomplish several things. First, you shift the center of focus from your own pain to the needs of someone else. Secondly, you are distracted from your own condition. And thirdly, you gain the opportunity

of re-evaluating your own problem in relation to the problems of others. You begin by giving and end up by receiving more than you give.

6. RE-EVALUATION. In the final analysis, the only remedy for depression and anxiety is re-evaluation. Since values lie at the beginning of the chain leading through desire to anxiety, a man's frustration and conflict can be effectively erased only by re-evaluation, which in turn will result in the re-ordering of desires on a realistic basis. Nuisances cannot be eliminated, but a person can keep them on the level of incidental irritation instead of paying them the costly compliment of elevation to intolerable tension. Severe deprivations can be made bearable circumstances. The key is proper and realistic evaluation. Everything listed above helps in some way to lead to or to make possible such evaluation.

If you find yourself depressed and tense, you can be sure that somehow, sometime, you lost your sense of direction. Your values became mixed up; your desires became inordinate. Perhaps you became too enthusiastic about something to the point where you lost your perspective. Perhaps you have never accepted the impossibility of some things or the hardship involved in others. Whatever the circumstances, it is certain to stem from unregulated desire, which, in turn, depends upon evaluation.

It is not at all surprising that a Christian can suffer from tension and depression. The Christian is as subject to inconsistency as anyone, simply because he has desires. St. Philip Neri said, "People are often the carpenters of their own crosses." How true it is. The very fact that one has desires makes possible unregulated desire, and this possibility

is increased by the immediacy and pressure of the world in which he lives. At the moment of frustration, however, the difference between the Christian and the non-believer should be quite clear. The believer holds the key to reality, has the penetrating vision of faith. The non-believer does not. The Christian can bring his faith to bear on his problem, see in it the hand of God, set it in the context of his life-in-Christ, find comfort and consolation in the knowledge that his Father has trusted him with this trial, find encouragement and inspiration from the sufferings of Christ and the saints, and, above all, resign himself to the will of God who permits this so that some good will come from it. The non-believer sees none of this.

This does not mean that the Christian should not make use of the other techniques listed above to alleviate his tension. It does mean that the Christian has the ultimate and permanent solution to tension: the Christian vision of all of reality, the total reality. With that vision, that faith, he can finally and eventually learn to regulate his desires.

Finally, it should be noted that the Plan outlined earlier provides the basic techniques for avoiding frustration and conflict. Introspection, or examination of conscience, serves to check on the nature and extent of one's desires, the possibility or impossibility of fulfillment—whether or not they fit into the Christian understanding of reality. Prayerful reading and all the other things help to form and fix values, Christian values, realistic values to serve as a framework for realistic and regulated desires. Resolutions provide for regulated, reasonable activity, which is the opposite of impulsive behavior, a common source of frustration.

OVERCOMING TEMPTATION

A temptation is anything which provokes desire for something sinful. Several things about temptation should be clearly understood. Something tempting is tempting precisely because it is desirable, because the individual understands it as such. Some people are amazed when they discover the attractiveness of forbidden pleasure. Some feel that it is unfair to be denied the satisfaction which they desire. All of them have failed to realize that the object of temptation would not be tempting at all unless it were desirable.

There are also too many who feel tainted or sinful just because they are tempted, and this is a mistake which needs to be erased. Perhaps an example will serve the purpose. On an ordinary day a young woman dipped into the mailbox and, to her delight, found a letter. The return address told her immediately that it was from an old friend. He was writing, he said, because he loved her, and he wanted her to come with him to his cottage for the week-end. She understood quite clearly what he wanted, and somehow the thought appealed to her at first. After all, it would be rather exciting. Just as suddenly, she came to her senses, realized that it was all wrong, and even became annoyed. She answered his letter with an unmistakeable "No."

In that story is the history of a temptation: (1) the person becomes conscious of the object; (2) he takes pleasure in it or is annoyed by it; (3) he decides for or against. Steps one and two are usually beyond control, which means they are involuntary, which means there is no possibility of sin. Sin is choice, decision. One must know that something is wrong and decide for it. Without the knowledge or the

decision, there is no sin. The young woman of our example did not choose to receive the letter. It just came. Many external temptations arise suddenly like that, and because a man's memory retains everything he experiences, it happens frequently enough that some ideas and images bubble out of that vast source into consciousness spontaneously and without choice. Again, there is no possibility of sin just in the fact of temptation.

The pleasure or annoyance which accompanies or follows from a tempting object is similarly involuntary. The emotions react to stimulus as regularly as the salivary glands to the smell of food. A physical reaction may even follow quite involuntarily from the temptation. So even if there is delight, there is no sin.

Sin lies in the choice of evil, not in temptations or feelings. Jesus was tempted and he never sinned. To find evil in the bare fact of temptation is to convict Jesus of sin.

Now, what is tempting to one is not necessarily tempting to another, which means that temptation, like virtue, is a matter of attitude. What might provoke one to anger, another may take in stride. What might be a temptation against chastity for one, another may find innocent. This is why the cultivation of Christian attitudes is the first step in fighting temptations. By concentrating on the gifts of God and the world revealed by your vision of faith, you can eliminate many of the common sources of temptation. Your Christian values will prepare you to recognize beauty where before you saw sin, and they will provide the solid basis for recognizing dis-values when they appear. To him who is pure, all things are pure.

Small temptations are much more common than great ones. Day in and day out, both saint and sinner are subject

to temptations to anger, envy, jealousy, vanity, insincerity, affectation, rash judgment, etc.; and since great temptations present themselves only rarely, it is these small ones which you must continually live with and conquer. Some men become rich by selling a large number of inexpensive articles. Some men become saints by remaining faithful through a large number of small temptations.

These small temptations are best handled by paying them no attention. Turn your mind from them quietly and quickly; quietly because they are not worth being disturbed about; quickly, because dwelling on them can give them a footing which can begin a chain of associations that you may not be able to stop. Do not even say to yourself: "I am not going to think about that." Simply and quietly turn your attention to something else. The best thing you can do is to use each of these little temptations as a reminder to turn to God. If you find yourself provoked to anger, quietly tell God that you are grateful for all that He has done for you. Then quietly go on about your business. Using each of these little temptations as occasions for renewing your fidelity to God turns each of them into profit, not because you seek such profit, but because you choose to please God.

Stronger temptations should lead you to God immediately. Think of His presence near you and in you. If the temptations persist, imagine yourself at the foot of the cross looking up at Jesus who hangs there suffering for you. Look at Him. Do not look at the temptation. Ask His help, renew your fidelity and then turn your thoughts to something, anything else. You might, for example, try to figure out what you are going to get your family for Christmas. The point is that you cannot banish a thought and let it go at that. The mind does not stay empty for very long. To suc-

cessfully rid yourself of one thought, you must replace it with another. The more strongly you feel about the second subject, the more forcefully it engages your attention, the greater are your chances of ridding yourself of the temptation. Finally, talk out your temptations with your director. Exposing them to another can be a great help in seeing them for what they are. By examining them in the light you destroy their aura of mystery and much of their appeal.

Temptations are not sin. They offer you the concrete opportunity of proving to yourself and to your God that you mean what you say when you tell Him, "I love you."

SUFFERING

We have already drawn attention to suffering a number of times. There is suffering in frustration and conflict, in self-discipline, in the little efforts one makes to keep calm, in turning from temptation, in patience and generosity, in holding back the word that might hurt, in saying what must be said. Suffering, to be sure, is a condition of human existence, and it never will be erased.

Self-inflicted suffering or deprivation has been a part of Christian life since our Lord said: "Unless you do penance, you will all likewise perish." There is a lot of foolishness in Christian penance, though, a lot of imprudence, and much wasted effort. A Christian is not a masochist or a morbid pain-lover. He deprives himself of things or inflicts pain on himself as the price of freedom, or to offer his suffering as atonement. There is nothing like the experience of deprivation, properly understood and rightly motivated, to bring a man to the realistic evaluation of the joy of liberty from the tyranny of possessions and, at the same time, a living grasp of the pettiness of material things. Mortifi-

cation, or self-inflicted punishment, provides the experience which is essential to a full and vivid evaluation. There is no Christian value in mortification which is unreasonable. A man who fasts until he loses his strength is weakened, not only physically, but morally. He lays himself wide open to temptation—and there is nothing very good in that.

There can be a joy in Christian suffering, the joy which comes from knowing that God will accept it in atonement for sins, as a proof of love, or for some good intention. Much of the world's suffering is lost and useless, but there is no reason for you to lose it. You have the vision of faith. You know that you are of the body of Christ, that there is a cosmic purpose even to your own little crosses. Time and again through the history of the Church, God has selected individuals to be victims, men and women who would spend their lives in suffering for God's purpose. There are people all over the world who can profit from *your* suffering borne in a Christian spirit of patience and generosity.

But mortification does not come easily to anyone. In addition, there is always some danger. One who chooses his own penances and sacrifices can easily go to excess, or even more easily ruin it all by taking great pride in it, by being quite pleased with himself for this fine thing he is doing. If you do choose to mortify yourself in one way or another, always obtain the approval of your director first. He will serve as a safeguard against both imprudence and pride.

A much more common source of suffering is God Himself. For that reason it is that much better. Your good Father in heaven knows what you need and what is best for you. He will hit you at the time and in the places that you need it most—and never be mistaken about it, it does come

from Him. He wants to purify you, to lead you ever more deeply into the strong solace of His love. Behind every pain, every hurt, is the hand of God. Look for it. You can find it because you have the faith. Think of the man who cannot believe. He cannot understand it, and that alone makes it infinitely worse. In a way it is almost a misrepresentation to call sufferings the little things that He asks you to endure, but they do hurt or annoy. We are little people, you and I, so He does not ask great things of us; or if He does, it is only rarely. But just as with little temptations, so with little sufferings, their great number makes them important. They could hardly be called crosses. Fr. Brisson, O.S.F.S., called them splinters. Every day you are offered a splinter here and a splinter there. Do not ignore them just because they are small. You have much to suffer for, great things and small. You can offer your sufferings for the missionaries in a foreign land, for the peace of the world and the peace of souls, for the conversion of someone you love. so that your children may turn out the way you and God want them to turn out. There is much to suffer for. Do not waste it. Gather your splinters. Together they are your cross.

It is Christian realism which makes possible this understanding of suffering, but make sure that you get things right. It does no good to say: "I wouldn't mind being sick, but it inconveniences the family." or, "I welcome the humiliation, but what of my wife?" or, "I willingly accept the pain, *but*. . . ." When God sends you a trial, accept all of it, not just the part you like. Let there be no "buts" about it. This is the hardest part of all: accept all of it, every last implication and complication. That is your splinter, nothing less.

SOME FINAL REMARKS

Any description of planned effort or any explanation of the psychology of religious activity almost invariably leaves the reader with the question, "But, where does God come in?" or the observation, "It is all so mechanical." At the beginning of Part III, I attempted to emphasize that it is, after all, God who does everything. It is He who gives the faith and the will. It is He who always goes before us, showing us the way, acting for us and within us. Still, He does leave us something to do, if only to prepare the soil so that He might work with it. St. Paul said: "So run as to obtain the crown." Our Lord said, "Do this, do that." Without doubt, there is much for us to do, and it can best be accomplished by planned effort. The planning, however, does not insure the outcome; it only prepares the ground. The metaphor of farmer and field is quite apt. The farmer does his work so that God will have something to work with. If the farmer never plants the seed, he can hardly expect a crop. If we do not read prayerfully and do all the rest, we can hardly expect God's love to fill our hearts.

It should be apparent, too, that the Christian life outlined in Part III is a far cry from the forbidding and frightening images of penitent saints. This is not at all the same thing as to say that the Christian life is easy. It is far from easy and it is far from painless. But it is far less painful and tense and anxious than a life without Christ or a life given halfway to Christ. Extraordinary saints are just that, out of the ordinary. We should never expect anything like that. If it should come, God will certainly provide the strength as well as the trial.

The point here is that your life-in-Christ will not change

dramatically the things you do, if you follow The Plan. You will still do the same work, recreate in the same way, probably keep the same company. The Plan intrudes on your time only very little. What will change and eventually even reach the surface is the Christian peace which comes to him who gives all to his Savior. What will make you different and set you apart is the serenity which only Christ can give, and the intensity which will shine from your eyes and affect the timbre of your voice. This, I think, is worth working for; but, it only comes to those who work for it. You can philosophize and speculate about the advantages and disadvantages of this or that, but unless you set your mind to it and get to work, you will be like the man who fell into a pit. While he was there he endlessly examined and recorded everything he saw. After five years he knew all there was to know about the pit, but he was still there, right at the bottom.

At the beginning of this book you were asked several questions: What do you want from life? What would you like to be? What would you like to be spared?

Are you sure now that you gave the Christian answers to those questions?

Give yourself to God who has first given Himself to you. May he be blessed forever!

About the Author

ELIZABETH JOY ARNOLD was raised in New York, and has degrees from Vassar College and Princeton University. She lives with her husband in Hopewell, New Jersey, where she is at work on her next novel. Visit her website at www.ElizabethJoyArnold.com.